DRESSED TO KILL

BOOK 2

DRESSED TO KILL

BOOK 2

Crown Fall

Podium

Published in 2025 by Podium Publishing
www.podiumentertainment.com

DRESSED TO KILL

BOOK 2

ACT 1

CHAPTER 1

Yesterday, I was arrested.

Today I camped in the Wild, sitting next to a crackling fire. On one side of me were my two best friends. On the other was the man who had attempted to destroy my life for the better part of the last decade. And now he was on my side, trying to hand me the keys to my own city. Maybe even the keys to change our nation.

One percent of all humans were Nobles; most were born into power, every level they clawed out from every monster they killed building up into an ever-flowing font of strength used to, ostensibly, defend humanity.

They cleared the dungeons, expanding the barriers that allow human settlements to persist against the constant degradation of the Wild.

Every time a Noble died, a random crafter would, instead of inheriting their parents' class, be elevated into the Nobility. Most of them died.

The other ninety-nine percent of humanity kept the rest of society running. For every Noble, there were a hundred crafters. Their armor, weapons, food, and housing were all created by the rest of us. Without crafters, the Nobility had no chance at maintaining as many dungeons as they do today.

My father was a Noble. I had never met him. He was probably still out there, somewhere. I didn't inherit his class, his power, or any of his wealth.

But I was starting to believe I didn't need them. Anyone could kill monsters. They just needed the right tools for the job.

For me, that was a giant sewing needle and a few supportive friends.

Sandy snored, leaning against Cinnamon's fluffy body. It was becoming increasingly obvious that Cinnamon was not a normal dog. There were very few normal animals at all in the Wild. Ironically, you were more likely to find those in the dungeons. Gerald was asleep atop one of the wagons, and I was wrapped in a blanket.

The flickering fire light illuminated Valjean's face. He frowned as he stared out into the brush around the circle of wagons.

"I'm jealous of your class," Valjean said.

Ever since we accepted his offer, he'd made no effort to talk to us. There was a gulf between us as wide as an ocean; a gulf in power, and in status. A mix of excitement and dread warred inside of me.

"Seamstress?" I asked.

It was a good class. I liked the class. It was mine, and it was something I shared with my mom.

Valjean chuckled.

"I wish I wasn't Chosen. Every day," he said.

There was a long silence. I didn't know how to reply to that. I had wanted to be a Noble with everything I had. But my father's legacy wasn't meant for me.

"Is it dangerous?" I asked.

"Dangerous? No. Nobles are a precious resource. The Academies train you well. Even the dangers there are overstated . . ." Valjean paused. "Hard, though? Very. There are no easy decisions. No easy answers."

"Can we really become recognized as Nobles?" I asked. "Even without the ability to check our status, they won't just . . . find out if we're Nobles?"

Valjean paused. He looked over at me, searching my eyes. Then, using his polearm, he poked the fire. A log fell. Sparks rose into the air. Valjean took his time formulating a reply. His horse—named Truffles, I had learned— grazed the ground behind him. Valjean's party didn't tie the horses up. Their horses were possessed of an uncanny intellect; the sparkle in their eyes when they looked at me unnerved me.

"The human Nobility isn't unified," Valjean said slowly. He took on the tone of a teacher beginning a lecture. "They're very . . . fractured. Factions of rivals war even inside of the supposedly unified bodies. Factions inside of factions. You'll likely need help on the inside."

I groaned, putting my head into my hands. Valjean paused. He waited for me.

"There's going to be politics involved with this, isn't there?"

"There are always politics involved." Valjean chuckled again. "That's part of what makes everything so difficult."

"But someone from your faction is inside the school and is going to cheat for us," I said.

"Yes. When you convince her."

"What?" I asked. "This isn't even guaranteed?!"

"I believe in you. You cleared the fourth floor of your dungeon with just the three of you and a tiny surplus of help from the people around you. I'll send a missive ahead strongly advocating for you." Valjean paused. His eyes scanned over to the wagon where Gerald slept before he looked back to me. "The thing is . . . the three of you are more powerful than three people should be. Three Nobles wouldn't make each other stronger. They might help each other complete their individual roles in fights—but the three of you amplify each other's force. And you don't just make a single one of you stronger—you're all stronger.

"You three have made one plus one equal three. Your strength is more than the sum of your parts. Our faction has been long looking for a way to improve the lives of the commoners. And to decrease the power the Nobility holds over the government. You'll find in time that simply being handed power does not make proper leaders. My faction—we are mostly Chosen. But there are other factions, too. The crafting guilds . . . I've never read anything to indicate they are aware of what you are doing, or of how possible it is exactly. But I don't believe they are unaware."

"The crafting guilds? From what I've heard of them, it wouldn't surprise me if they hid any knowledge of advancing on purpose," I said. Mom had talked about them before, the large organizations that oversaw the different elements of many crafting professions. The heads of the guilds would be among the highest-leveled individuals in the country.

Of course they would have known that the crafting class could fight.

When Sandy leveled Butchering to tier ten, she began to accumulate skill points every time she exercised her class. Just simply progressing, even via crafting, people would eventually become strong enough to fight. Under the crafting guilds, most crafters worked to produce the goods necessary for a city. The lack of variety provided diminishing returns to their total leveling, holding the entire population back.

I never even questioned why other seamstresses or crafters didn't take up weapons and try to kill monsters. The answer was obvious.

"It's too dangerous. And stupid. How many seamstresses would be willing to risk their lives when they could live comfortably in a workshop?" I said. It was Valjean's own argument, after all; that life in the city was so much more comfortable and capable of taking care of everyone, there wasn't a point in bothering to maintain the lives of the nation's far-flung villages.

I felt myself doubt that narrative even as I rationalized it. After all, every time I crafted a recipe, I saw flashes of the moments seamstresses solidified patterns, embedding them into the system for future crafters. I felt what they felt in those moments, of the lives they were living. I rarely ever saw simple workshops.

In one of the last patterns I crafted, the Houndsmaster set, I saw an entire camp full of crafters, seemingly deep within the dungeon.

There weren't any Nobles in that vision.

Valjean's horse leaned over his shoulder, pressing its head down and snorting loudly.

"Truffles?" Valjean asked, reaching up and patting the side of the horse's head. Truffles shook his head and snorted. The stallion's massive head was nearly the size of Valjean's torso; he must have had to jump to get atop the thing. I wondered how high Truffles's stats were.

Higher than mine.

Valjean reached for the polearm next to him.

I flinched at a sudden rush of displaced air. Valjean's arm had blurred as he flicked the polearm, throwing it with supernatural ease. There was a crash. I heard the sound of creaking wood and an eruption of splinters. Sandy stopped snoring and shot up.

Olivier's head popped over the side of one of the wagons.

"Fight!?" he shouted.

"No. It's dead. Back to sleep," Valjean replied.

Olivier rolled back over without another word.

"What the hell?" Sandy asked, rubbing her eyes.

Valjean sparked a lantern to life before walking a few steps out of the circle. A gigantic bird covered in oily black feathers hung limp, pinned to a tree. Valjean pressed a foot to the bird's chest, pulling his polearm free and flicking it. Blood splattered in an arc. He dragged the bird back to the camp with the same almost-bored expression he'd had sitting beside the fire.

"Good breakfast for tomorrow," he said, sitting back down as if nothing had happened.

Truffles went back to grazing.

I stared at him.

"Was that a skill?" I asked.

"Just a throw," he said. "But the clothes I wear are imbued with attributes. The meals I eat. The weapon I wield." Valjean shook his head.

All the levels I had gained, all the power I had accumulated; it was still nothing compared to proper Nobles. I stared at the monster, trying to guess how hard it would have been to kill. The bird was as large as I was; it looked like a monster belonging to a third floor or one of the more dangerous second-ring dungeons.

He had killed it with a flick of his wrist.

I needed to get stronger. Faster. The discontent at the disparity in our power grew into desire.

Valjean was right. Sandy, Gerald, and I together were stronger than the sum of our parts alone. How many crafters would I have to work with before each individual was stronger than a Noble?

One day, I would find out.

I was dead tired for the entire journey. The pervasive influence of the Wild constantly picked away at us. The world *hated* humans. Beyond the boundary of our towns, reality itself ablated everything we were and everything we created, wearing it away. A field of magical erosion covered the entire world. It itched at me when I was awake, and it itched at me when I slept. When I dreamed, it was there. When I ate, it was there.

Every few hours, Valjean or another Noble woke us by killing another monster in a spray of gore. The Nobles seemed almost comfortable with this. They traveled the Wild so often it had become mundane. Routine.

"Are we almost there?" Sandy asked.

"Yes," Gerald said. "You can smell it."

We sat on top of Valjean's wagon. The seating consisted of wooden crates strapped to a wooden roof; it was an open bucket. I had almost always seen it loaded with goods.

Gerald leaned off the side, staring into the woods. They were growing thinner.

Sandy leaned forward intently.

"Why does it smell so off?" she asked.

The road had gotten better as we neared the city, the forest regularly patrolled at the edge of the Wild. The path of carved mud gave way to a road paved with gigantic blocks of stone, worn by the weather and the Wild.

Olivier stretched and yawned, then perked up. He seemed relieved to have returned to the town.

"That's coal," I said.

Gerald looked at me with surprise.

"I thought you haven't been to Foundry."

"I haven't," I said. The center of Valjean's territory was Foundry, a second-tier city. Several border towns like Stitch surrounded it. My hometown was a first-tier city—considerably smaller. Its border had collapsed over the last few years, taking homes with it. The city would have collapsed entirely in a few more years as its border retracted into the dungeon.

Beyond the border towns, Wild dungeons dotted the landscape, scattered over the world. They disgorged monsters into it.

The pillars of smoke rising over Foundry became visible first. Then the forest thinned until it was clear-cut, the Wild pushed back, giving a clear view of the city's rising wall. Its metaphysical border extended beyond that, giving the air a thin shimmer.

When we crossed through the intangible threshold into the city's protection from the Wild, I felt my muscles relax.

"How many people live here?" I asked.

"A few thousand now," Valjean said.

The city could support more. The dungeons reset each night, time passing at an accelerated rate within the closed dungeons. Every city used the expanded space contained within, harvesting the land for crops, the lakes and oceans for fish, the land for metal, and of course, the monsters for levels and magical resources.

I wondered how many of the resources this city wasted.

The metal portcullis opened ahead of us. The wall itself was a feature of the dungeon as well; too-clean white marble expanded in a perfect circle around us. There were remnants of a city wall in Stitch, but I had never seen one.

Clearing the first four floors was the minimum to elevate a town to the first tier. Only then would the wall rise around the city. But without the dungeon being regularly cleared, the wall and border would retreat, leaving the town to decay.

The number of monsters that had to be killed rose steadily, with each tier requiring a massive leap. To raise the town to the first tier, we had to clear five dungeons in a single night. I shuddered at the thought of how many dungeons it would take to maintain Foundry. There must have been dozens of Nobles living here, all subordinate to Valjean.

I stared over at him where he drove the wagon. The other two went ahead into the city, crossing a cobblestone road. That wasn't part of the system; it had been laid by hand.

The wagon bumped as we rode over it. Stone chimneys rose from factories at the edge of the city, coughing pillars of black smoke into the sky.

"Oh, you guys should come tour this factory!" Gerald said, pointing. "They work with a magical alloy. It's incredible!"

"What do they make?" Sandy asked.

"Ingots!" Gerald said, still excited.

"And they do what with them?"

"They have to be purified to be shipped to other towns!" Gerald said. "They're very . . . resistant." He gestured with his hands.

"It smells even worse here," Sandy said.

"That's the smell of industry!" Gerald said. He pointed at a different building. "Dad helped manufacture casts for them. They produce gears and axles."

Valjean nodded at the head of the wagon.

"Bob does great work. He's a bit higher-level than many of the people living here." Valjean threw a look back over the wagon. "Many of the people in Stitch are. They would all have been incredible assets here in Foundry."

"They wouldn't be as high-level if they lived in Foundry," I replied.

I was more than a little bitter about the callous treatment of our town. I didn't know if that feeling would ever leave, regardless of Valjean's intentions.

Valjean paused, seriously considering my reply. Then he nodded.

"That may be true. The lack of easy solutions often means you're forced to use more ingenious methods to solve your issues." Valjean faced the road again. "But I'm not sure that value created from adversity can outweigh what the value of the crafting guilds can provide."

I snorted. I heard the things Mom said about the crafting guilds; it wasn't anything good. She had worked as a seamstress in them for some time long before she moved to Stitch.

Valjean turned back, raising an eyebrow at me.

"I doubt that they're really good for their crafters. The crafting guilds."

"Then come take a tour of my atelier and help me make it better," Valjean said. "I haven't interfered at all in the plan laid out by the crafting guild for its running. But that's for tomorrow. Today, we rest."

Valjean drove the wagon all the way to his own estate. I knew it was his estate without asking. A garden sprawled outward around a proper mansion resting on a hill near the center of the town. So near it, in fact, that the central dungeon of the city rested at the edge of his property. And across from that, there was a train station.

"You have a train?" I said, shocked.

"Hmmm?" Valjean asked. "Ah, no. I don't own the train. I don't even own the rails. They need a very expensive enchantment to resist the Wild outside of the city. It will be another twenty years before the loan on them is paid off, and that's not counting the maintenance fees . . ."

We crossed through an open gate in a metal fence that surrounded the entire estate, riding directly up to the property itself.

"We're going to be staying here?" Gerald asked. He was staring up at the building towering above him with a gleam in his eye.

"Yes. You'll be staying in the guest rooms for new or visiting Nobility. I've ten missives to pen and days of work, so I'm afraid I'll have to ask attendants to show you around." Valjean slid from the wagon to the ground. One of the attendants he mentioned ran up, dressed in formal wear, and grabbed the reins.

The attendant shot curious looks our way but asked no questions.

I climbed down the wagon and followed after Valjean.

I didn't know what I expected before he pushed the door open, but what I found was a reception desk. People in suits gathered at the edges of the room, discussing in politely hushed tones and stealing glances at Valjean. The walls were covered by shelves, and the shelves were choked with books.

This place wasn't just his home; it was the center of governance for his entire territory.

CHAPTER 2

Lizzie sat nervously across from the official. She had never been in the mayor's manor. The sound of hushed conversations and rustling pages was made disquieting by the soft clinks of armor and weapons. She kept glancing across to where a Noble had removed the belt holding her sword and laid it across the table. As the Noble dashed a quill across the page, she bumped an elbow into the sword repeatedly, moving it closer and closer to falling onto the floor.

Lizzie couldn't take her eyes off the dried blood on the Noble's armor.

"Miss Elizabeth?" the official said.

"Sorry, what?" Lizzie asked, turning to look at him.

He offered a reassuring smile, but his eyes carried worry.

"We have temporary housing available until a new domicile can be built. Unfortunately, you're going to have a few roommates. Did many of your things survive the fire? I can connect you with a storage facility if you can meet the fees."

"No, not much," Lizzie said. She wrung her hands. "Thank you."

"I'm just glad to be able to offer what help I can. And, of course, we'll mark you down for a reduction in taxes for two years. Though we can't do anything about guild dues. Again, my condolences. I'm glad that no one was injured, at least."

Lizzie sighed. Only a few nights ago, her rented apartment had burned down with a swathe of buildings. Most of them were industrial, and no one was injured in the fire, but the volunteer fire force struggled to contain the fire until a mage with water spells could arrive.

The official lifted a pen. His arm became a blur as he marked down an address and information about the residence, printing dozens of words across the page in moments.

"Your residence is conditional on your continued good standing in the eyes of the law. So don't go getting into any trouble." The official smiled and pushed the paper over.

Lizzie stared at it, sighed, and stood.

"Thank you," she said.

The new apartment was located near one of the more industrial areas of Foundry. She lugged a heavy wooden suitcase—all that remained of her possessions—and headed that way.

The building was in ill repair, with flaking paint and dirty, yellow-stained windows. They were likely unwilling to invest further in a complex buried away in the edge of the city. Lizzie walked to the apartment building's office, exhausted from the trek across the city. Her commute to work would involve crossing half the city now.

The property manager gave her two keys—one to enter the building, and a second for her own bedroom. It was tiny; the space featured only a minimalist bed frame with a tiny mattress on top of it. With the door shut, sitting sideways on the bed, she could reach out and touch the wall with her foot. She sighed and fell back into the bed.

She had lost almost everything in the fire. After buying the bare minimum of new clothes and the guild-mandated uniform, she would be back to basically nothing. No extra payment to send home to her family in the border town at the end of the year.

She had half a dozen younger siblings who all needed to eat. They couldn't depend on their town's generosity forever. Especially not with more people moving out each year.

But it wasn't like there was a lot she could do. After all, she was just a seamstress.

And there was only one place for seamstresses to work in the entire city.

CHAPTER 3

I had expected much harsher treatment after being arrested. The sense of pervasive defeat that hung over me since Valjean captured all of us was softened by the most luxurious penthouse I had ever occupied.

This prison had no bars. The guards here kept visitors out; they didn't keep me in.

The single room I occupied was larger than my entire house in Stitch. The floor was covered in a soft, rich carpet, completely different from the hard-pressed earth or tile floors I was used to. Windows stretched from floor to ceiling, offering me a view of Valjean's expansive estate.

And his estate wasn't just luxurious; it was a beating heart of business and governance. Guests moved in and out of the grounds throughout the entire day. Nobles practiced in outdoor ranges built into the garden. It took dozens of Nobles to maintain this city, purging the extensive network of dungeons every night.

When the teams of Nobles returned from the dungeon, they would sit in the foyer, completing reams of paperwork, their armor often still covered in flaking monster blood. The sight of men and women in plate and chain armor filling out accounting logs was almost comical.

Attendants brought me breakfast, cleaned my room, and offered to wash my laundry.

I brought my breakfast to Sandy's room. One of the attendants showed me the way. I felt nervous carrying the porcelain dishes, but I'd already picked them up and didn't want to hand them back.

Sandy had her own massive room. Each of the rooms featured tables with seating for multiple people. Sandy's was almost completely covered in food. I sat down in the one open space near the edge.

Even Cinnamon was gnawing on a massive bone in the corner of the room. There were several hastily laid rugs beneath him. His tail slapped into the floor repeatedly, but he hadn't even looked up as I entered.

"Why did they bring you so much food?" I asked. There were a dozen different dishes on the table.

"I asked for extra. It's free, right? Might as well take all of it."

I paused. Then shrugged. She was right enough.

"Should we go get Gerald?" I asked.

"Sir Gerald left the estate this morning," the attendant behind me answered.

"Oh. Thanks?" I said.

"My pleasure. Is there anything else you two will be needing?"

"No, thanks!" Sandy said. She continued eating. I sat down, paralyzed by the number of choices on display, before eventually grabbing and digging into the richest French toast I had ever eaten.

I sampled a half dozen plates. But none of them gave me any kind of buff.

Sandy leaned back in her chair and folded her hands.

"Valjean asked me to look over his butcheries today and see if I can improve them," Sandy said. She sounded nervous. "You know, he didn't even come in person to ask! He just told an attendant to instruct me to do it."

"Sorry," I said. "I think that's my fault. I told him I could probably improve his atelier." I offered a weak smile.

"I'm definitely figuring out how much I can steal from the leftover parts," Sandy said.

"That's a good idea. Maybe you can find something we can use," I said.

After breakfast, another attendant knocked on the door. She showed us to Valjean's foyer, where a man waited for us.

"Hello, Lady Gwen. And Lady Sandy, I presume. I'm Finn, I am Valjean's right hand man and a [Scribe] by class." he said. "Carriage ride? Or would you rather walk?"

Even as he spoke, he didn't stop moving. He had shocking orange hair and a face covered in freckles. He smiled under wire-thin glasses, and he exuded a sense of genuine sincerity that I thought was far too dangerous for any politician to have.

"Let's walk," I said.

I hadn't left the estate in almost a day and a half. The hot bath had been incredible, but I was anxious to stretch my legs. I let my eyes linger on each building and store as we crossed the city, sticking close to Finn. People stayed busy on the street. The entire city's layout revolved around the dungeon; carriages brought materials away from it even as it approached evening.

But as we traveled, we moved farther and farther away from the city's center of economic power, and the buildings became less and less well maintained. When we eventually reached the atelier, I almost couldn't believe its state. The hedges of grass between the road were ill maintained here, weeds popping up at the side of the atelier.

It was far smaller than I expected, slumped and pressed into the bottom floor of a building. Paint flaked from the dirty walls.

"Everything in the city is produced here?" I asked.

"This atelier is under the direction of the Tailor Guild. With their operation, efficiency is easy. It actually produces more than enough clothing for the city, and the surplus is sold and shipped elsewhere. Other towns have a few boutique shops, but none are open here."

"It smells," Sandy said with a scrunched nose. "And not like coal."

Finn smiled nervously and showed us in. The door opened into a tiny store built into the front. There was no attendant. Uniforms for different uses and in different sizes were piled on shelves on the wall, their prices marked. They looked like they had been there a while.

There were uniforms for a dozen different types of peasant classes—farmers, fishers, and even carpenters. The sound of a dozen people working echoed from the back. To the atelier's credit, the storeroom was much nicer than the outer facade suggested.

Finn led us past the store and into the back of the building. I stopped immediately. Finn noticed, glancing at me. He pulled out a pocket-sized notebook, flipping through the pages.

"This is the assembly room," Finn said. The half dozen tailors and seamstresses stopped and stared at us as he continued talking. "The finalized pieces of the patterns are assembled here."

There were almost-finished patterns draped over mannequins. Tables split the room. There was a window in the wall at the back where a box of freshly cut patterns was being pushed through.

The atelier staff resumed their work. I could feel the frown on my face deepening. In this room, all six of the workers completed the same pattern—more farmer uniforms, if I had to guess. But they didn't complete the entire pattern from start to finish—they were just assembling finished pieces, near the last step of the process.

That meant the experience would be split between each person working on it. It also meant that each person here had to spend the points they earned from leveling on the same pattern so that they could all work on it.

I paused, trying to keep an open mind for a moment.

They most definitely had the capacity to make a dozen or more sets each day. But it was a massive waste of each individual person's talent and skills. Maybe with separation, each person could focus on specific sets of skills—stitching or cutting, for example. But that had to destroy all of their leveling progress by spending their points so frivolously.

"How many people are working on each of these?"

"They typically employ a little over twenty employees in each shift," Finn provided happily.

A creeping dread snuck up on me.

"Let's continue," I said.

Finn led us into the next room. There, a half dozen more workers used skills specialized entirely in cutting, tearing apart sections of monsters. Powerful shears, passable as scissors for the system's purposes, carved through chitin and clearly magical leathers. The leftover sections not needed for the patterns were simply discarded. I stared at the pile in the corner. In Stitch, I had taken every scrap of powerful material, stitching it back together into a cohesive whole that could be used again.

The quality and attributes of the materials used affected the final product. Using pieces I stitched back together instead of whole cuts lowered the quality, but the value of parts of a dungeon boss far outweighed that.

I could tell at a glance that the value of their trash pile was enormous. The entire room smelled earthy. The leather they were using was a vibrant emerald, a mottled pattern like leaves on a tree.

"What do they do with the leftovers?" I asked.

Finn frowned, flipping through the tiny pocket book. By now, it was clear that it had details on how the atelier was run.

"Ah, I believe they just discard it, Lady Gwen."

Each tailor or seamstress worked on only a few pieces at a time. And as for their own outfits, they had some kind of seamstress uniform, likely one intended to improve their skills, but it was made of seemingly mundane material, greatly limiting the ability it had to improve their work.

The trash alone could be enough to significantly upgrade the atelier's workers.

I stared in horror as we continued our tour. It was remarkably, terribly efficient, but for each person to work together like this, they had to waste their points on all buying the same patterns, which cost a point from their personal progression, and would hamper their development toward making new materials. Most of the goods they processed seemed to be shipped in; they pulled them out of large wooden crates of cargo.

The entire process was split into pieces, which allowed them to produce handcrafted works at an incredible pace. Sure, they could craft a dozen sets a day. But only those sets. Over and over. They wouldn't be earning any levels out of this; my own experience from crafting had rapidly leveled out after working with Mom, especially when we used more mundane materials. Only making clothes out of new materials or new patterns helped level.

I could almost be convinced that the atelier was set up to intentionally depress the levels of its workers.

Finn looked nervous at my reaction. He had clearly expected something else.

I approached one of the seamstresses unloading a crate in the back of the shop. I almost stopped myself when I saw that her eyes were red and puffy. She had long black hair that fell around her shoulders and nearly black eyes.

"Hi," she said, greeting me before I could think better of it. She had a curious look in her eyes.

"Are you alright?" I asked.

"Hah. No. I haven't seen you before. Are you with the Tailor Guild, or . . . ?" The seamstress's eyes locked onto Finn.

"I'm a newly Chosen Noble," I said. "I'm Gwen."

My lie wasn't convincing to my own ears, but she smiled. She wore the same uniform as the rest of the employees; it was stuffy and ill-fitting. The inside of the workshop was hot. The ceiling was low above us.

"Lizzie," she said, offering a hand and setting down the basket she had been loading with uncut monster parts. "What are you doing in the atelier?"

"My mom is a seamstress," I said. "I wanted to come check out the shop."

"It's not much," Lizzie said. "Did you need something? Did a special order come in?" She seemed half-nervous and half-excited.

"We're just giving a tour of the city to these new Chosen," Finn said. "Did you have a question, Lady Gwen?"

"What level are you?" I asked Lizzie.

"Level six," the seamstress replied with a smile.

I flinched. How had someone remained at such a low level?

"And how long have you been level six?" I asked.

I felt bad even as I asked it. The question hurt.

"Around three months," Lizzie said. "I got most of these levels pretty quickly when I first started working here. But I haven't gotten another level in a while."

"Do you like it?" I asked. "The work, I mean."

She pursed her lips, leaning on the open crate below her.

"It's not the worst. I got the class from my father's side. There's always work to be done. I know a ferrier. He barely gets enough work some days, despite being a higher level than me. It's certainly better than killing monsters." Lizzie laughed nervously.

I laughed, trying not to show my own nervousness.

The other people in the room were politely ignoring our conversation. It made me uncomfortable. There was a distinct deference in the way people here treated me. I wasn't sure how much of it was due to the odd social rules of a city and how much of it was due to declaring I was a Noble. There would've only been a few dozen Nobles in the entire city to maintain it, all of them lower-ranking than Valjean. Most of the people here probably rarely even saw them.

Stitch had been reduced by the encroaching Wild. When the border town lost most of its houses, people piled together in the remaining ones in the center of the town. A few left Stitch entirely, moving to the city. Only the most stubborn remained in Stitch, refusing to give up their way of life.

"Thanks for answering my questions," I said. "I'll see you again, later."

"Anytime, Gwen," Lizzie said. Then she corrected herself, throwing her hands up between us. "Lady Gwen, I mean."

Finn led the way to an abattoir just a block away. The facility was both larger and nicer than the atelier. The fresh exterior and large windows did nothing for the building's smell, however. The entire block around it smelled like offal.

The front of the warehouse opened wide with huge sliding doors. Inside, horrifying piles of monster corpses filled two wagons. They had been left behind without any horse to pull them.

The wagons of corpses were impressive. There was enough material in there to try entirely new patterns. But they weren't the most impressive sight. That was the monsters hanging from an assembly of hooks and ropes. Each one of them was easily the size of one of the wagons.

Temporary installations of scaffolding rose around them, and a butcher stood at the highest level of each one, swinging all kinds of knives and tools to cut the monsters apart.

The one closest to us was a bug covered in shining black chitin armor. Hundreds of legs hung from its sides. It looked like a hundred more had already been cut free, falling to the ground, where other butchers pulled them away and sliced them open. On the far side of the room was a gigantic, multi-headed wolf monster, its fur an acid green. The butcher working on it looked like he was in an airtight suit. His scaffolding was surrounded by windows, and the sizzling green blood of the monster dripped into a holding tank beneath it.

A bird covered in arcing electricity was attached to grounding cables that buzzed audibly. The static electricity made my hair stand on end.

There was a fourth monster I couldn't see at all. Shadows clung to it. Several bright light fixtures shone toward the monster. Even in death, it seemed affected by some darkness-aligned stealth skill similar to my own. Only patches of scales were revealed where the light hit it strongly.

"Those are . . . bosses?" I asked.

Finn nodded.

"These are the bosses of the four second-tier dungeons. Highly profitable to export, but we can't afford to send our dungeon teams that far every night. They consume a large amount of potions to reach that depth, and there's the wear and tear on their equipment. Not to mention that hired Nobility are often paid by the floor."

Sandy took a step forward, eyes lit up, but Finn raised a hand to stop her.

"Ah, we'll have to wait for the foreman to enter here. The butchery can be very dangerous," Finn said.

As if summoned by his words, the butcher working on the acid-green monster slipped down from the scaffolding. He was indeed wearing a full-body canvas suit. He stopped more than a dozen feet away from us, only taking enough of his suit off to allow us to clearly see his face. His head was shaved bald, regrowing a tiny layer of stubble.

A scar crossed his lip, coming into sharp focus as he smiled like a shark.

"Finn," the foreman said, smiling. "Is there an extra body coming in today?"

Finn shook his head in the negative.

The butcher foreman frowned. He turned to us.

"And you girls are?"

"Sandy. I'm a Lady."

"Ah, my apologies, Lady Sandy!" the butcher said, smiling again. "You've brought us something?"

"Sandy was hoping to tour the butchery," Finn interjected.

"Actually," Sandy said. "I'd love to stay and watch for the entire shift, if that's alright? I have a ton of questions. Gwen . . ." Sandy turned to me.

"It's fine," I said with a smile. Sandy was clearly more than excited to be here. The butchery looked far more promising than the atelier. "I'll head back and talk to Valjean."

"Now probably isn't a good time," Finn had said. He had checked the time on a pocket watch, frowning. He frowned the entire walk.

But I had insisted.

We crossed Foundry on foot to a park closer to the estate and center of town. Children played between the trees and grass, a tiny facsimile of nature carefully sculpted and contained within the city. It was the most of nature many of these children would ever experience. The smell of flowers hung over the little garden, rising from carefully maintained flowerbeds. There were even birds nesting in the trees, singing above the tiny slice of nature in the city.

Parents watched their children around the flowerbeds and wooden playgrounds. The park was large enough to fit all of Stitch inside it. Large enough that you could forget the city surrounded it. A single building disrupted the idyllic park; a tiny bistro that served food for the park-goers. Behind it, a tall hedge blocked off a section of the park, surrounded by metal fencing with sharp tips.

Finn led me directly through the metal gate in the hedges that hid this part of the park. Inside, there were more tables and seats for eating, more trees and plants and plenty of flowers, and there were graves.

Rows of identical tombstones stretched on and on. They were all uniform blocks of stone, identical except for the words on them. Almost every one of them recorded a life that was unfortunately short.

Neither Finn nor I said anything. I walked along the tiny path, reading the stones as we passed.

Ed Smith, Chosen Swordmaster, 18. Liz Brewer, Chosen Warrior, 19. Em Cooper, Chosen Assassin, 18. Robert Fisher, Chosen Mage, 20.

More than half of them were teenagers, barely living a few years after becoming Nobility. Even the birds were quiet here. There were no mausoleums. No great crypt of a Noble family. They were just buried here. Alone.

"Lady Gwen," Valjean said.

I nearly jumped at the address, turning to see him sitting at a table. Olivier gave a solemn nod. There didn't seem to be any anger or spite in his eyes, despite him having fought us only a few days prior. Both Valjean and Olivier were in fine Noble dress; even their daily clothes were more magical than anything I had worked on.

But the third at the table wore full armor with sharp edges.

Only his gauntlets were off, lying on the table beside him along with an empty plate. An eyepatch covered his left eye, underneath an unkempt mop of salt-and-pepper hair. He rubbed a short beard. He looked like a grizzled veteran too old to be in another Noble's employ.

He nodded at us, too.

"This is Lord Olivier and Lord Dorian," Valjean said by way of introduction, pointing at each of them. "We were just wrapping up lunch, Lady Gwen. Was there something you needed?"

I looked around again.

"I can wait," I said.

"Finn, make sure a meeting is penned into my schedule."

Valjean's next bit of free time turned out to be after dinner, following yet another meeting. His schedule was packed, every minute occupied by something.

Finn and Sandy both joined for the meeting.

When we met him, the dishes were long cleared, and instead, accounting books sprawled across the table. A scribe sat on one side of him, transcribing a book with magical speed and mechanical precision. His pen dashed across the page, copying the contents of a ledger, filling in the page from top to bottom.

Valjean ate a teacake from a plate before pushing it toward me. A server stood behind him with a pitcher of hot coffee.

"Snacks? Coffee?" he asked. "I've sent a missive to Lyssandra with the last train we sent out. She is the resident Lady of Hub and will be seeing you to the Academy. I expect a reply in the next few days—then you should have a trip within two weeks."

"I'm starting to think the most relaxing part of your life is killing monsters," I said. "Who drinks coffee this late?" The sun had already set outside.

"Me," Sandy said. The server filled a fine porcelain cup.

Valjean pulled out a pocket watch, stared at the time on it, then put it away.

"The most relaxing part of my day is often the raiding, yes," he said. "You took a tour of our primary atelier and abattoir today, yes? The amount of work they produce is enough to employ every crafter of their classes under the supervision of the guilds. They produce a steady stream of revenue for the city."

"They're holding back your crafters. They could all be so much more," I said.

"Yes, well . . . not everyone is as inclined to go around killing monsters as we are," Valjean said.

"It's not that. The city throws away a huge percentage of the total levels it could gain out of waste. And the rigidity of the streamlined production prevents anyone there from maximizing their potential."

"Tell me, Lady Gwen. What do you suggest?" Valjean rested his head on his hand and leaned forward, staring at me attentively.

The question put me on guard. But his tone seemed sincere. Inviting, even. There was no condescension. I stared back at him, looking for a hole in the facade, for anything that indicated he lacked sincerity.

He chuckled before he continued.

"You've gained many levels in only a few months. A number any seamstress would be jealous of. I'll take your suggestion seriously."

Would he really consider this? Rearranging his production based on my answer? Suddenly, replying felt like an onerous thing. I had plenty of ideas—things I knew would help raise the level of every crafter in the shop, that would give them their own freedom in their work if they wanted it.

People's lives could change from just my answer.

"I think you should start by having your crafters waste nothing," I started.

I told Valjean how they wasted a ton of resources—enough that the crafters could gain regular levels just out of the workshop's trash.

Sandy interjected, talking about how the abattoir did much the same. She started listing how much they threw away; more than a hundred pounds of monster meat, and hundreds more pounds of hides and chitin and other materials.

The abattoir harvested monster parts for alchemy and bones for fertilizer for farmers and leather for tailors, but it threw away much more than it gave to the city.

Valjean nodded along with each point.

Unlike the atelier, the leveling of the butchers in the abattoir proceeded more smoothly and to a higher level. The foreman and the others who butchered the bosses of the dungeons were far, far higher-level than Sandy.

Despite that, only those top few had actually leveled Butchering to ten and gained the ability to accumulate more attributes as they worked.

Foundry wasted time and materials like no other.

"As I understand it, the waste wouldn't make good products, yes?" Valjean interrupted. "For example, the hides the atelier throws away—we couldn't sell gear made out of them, no? The quality would be lower. They would be outcompeted."

"That's true," I said. "But you would still gain the levels from upgrading each outfit. Under the Tailor Guild's setup, your crafters eventually stop leveling entirely. More skills and skill points would mean more efficient labor."

"But the time they spend crafting those must be paid for, Lady Gwen. There is a cost in labor associated. Is the investment worth the increased output? My funds are not unlimited," Valjean said, folding his hands.

I leaned back in my seat.

Valjean looked to Finn. "Do you have an estimate on how many labor hours it will take before the regular output becomes more profitable?"

Finn flipped through the tiny notebook he had. He frowned and shook his head. "I'm unsure, my Lord."

"But you insist it will be worth it?" Valjean directed the question to me.

"Yes," I said, nodding my head.

"If they're just using the scraps and excesses, then it won't interfere with their regular output, yes? I'll pay the cost of labor for this for . . . let's say . . . three months. In that time, I want to see that the revenue reaches at least half the cost I'm paying. Net returns within a year. It would be even better if they can create something either sellable or with a practical use. Finn?"

The scribe was already recording Valjean's statement in a new notebook. He nodded.

"Let's set our first milestone at two weeks, before you leave. I'll check in with you then."

CHAPTER 4

Valjean worked fast. He had been the head of a body of governance for a long time and it showed.

By the next afternoon, he had already solicited the atelier to open an evening shift while the workshop was unused. Four volunteers signed up. All of them were people who, for one reason or another, needed the extra money.

I arrived at the atelier in the afternoon. The sun was low in the sky and the building was long deserted except for the evening shift workers in the back.

They gathered the last few days' worth of the workshop's castaways. Most of it was practically mundane materials; there was so little magic left in the body parts from what the workshop was using that I was tempted to dismiss it all out of hand, but the softer parts could still be used.

The real value came from what Sandy shipped from the abattoir around lunch: low-level monster parts, left behind from monsters mostly harvested for alchemical properties or food.

I stood over the filling wagons next to Finn. Sandy was off at the abattoir while Gerald explored each and every one of the city's forges.

There was one material that really interested me, and we had multiple crates of it.

"What is this from?" I asked, rubbing my fingers across the glittering scales that covered broad sheets of blue leather. They had been poorly cut, ending in odd angles.

"Minor drakes, Lady Gwen."

"There are . . . a lot of them."

The scales looked almost oily. And the huge size of the sheets of scaled leather spoke to the size of them. They must have been fairly large and there must have been dozens. I was getting an eye for the quality of material, too. These monsters couldn't have been weak.

"Their meat is one of our prime exports," Finn said proudly.

It felt odd to be in the reverse of the position I had been in all my life. I was bringing my own caravan of goods. The entire town had always been excited when Valjean brought a restock, despite the mixed feelings he generated. I set the leather down.

It felt good. It wasn't exactly what I had in mind when I set off to maintain my town. I had a feeling that today was something special. A snowball rolling down a hill.

Finn had arranged for porters to bring the massive crates into the back of the workshop.

"Is this everyone?" I asked.

"There should be one more coming," Finn said. The wagon was already riding away.

I frowned. There were meant to be four workers.

"Then we can get started," I said, folding my hands up and walking over to the crates. "We'll need to bring all the tools into one room. Would the three of you help by grabbing the mannequins and all?" I asked.

Before anyone could reply, there was a pounding on the door. I frowned, looking to Finn, who shrugged and left to open the atelier.

Lizzie ran in a moment later, panting.

"Sorry I'm late! I moved across the city," she said. "Long walk! I'm not too late, am I?"

Her face had a mix of fear and excitement.

"Not at all. We're just getting started." I smiled. "We were just about to bring all the tools together into this room."

The four of them got to work. In my last visit to the atelier, this rear warehouse room had been used exclusively for separating and cutting the sheets of tanned leather and cloth that made up the patterns they manufactured.

The last of the workshop came together.

"Alright. I need to know what patterns everyone has," I said.

"Lady Gwen, if I may . . ." one of the tailors interjected.

"Yes?"

"I'm Reese. I've been with the workshop for years," he started. "We're typically much more productive if we split the work up. What . . . uh . . . what are we working on today? Is this a custom commission? None of us have skill points available to acquire more patterns."

"I assumed that was the case. What did they tell you about what you were signing up for?" I asked.

"They just said that it was extra labor hours. A special order from Valjean," Reese replied.

"Alright," I said. "Today I'm going to have everyone finish a pattern from start to finish on their own."

Reese frowned.

"I only have the assembly skills outlined by the Tailor Guild."

"That's fine," I said. "You can do the work manually. I can show you."

"I mean no offense, Lady Gwen," Reese said. "But our craft isn't so easy."

"My mother is a seamstress," I said. "Besides that . . . I'm the one making sure you get paid."

That stopped Reese in his tracks. I sighed.

"So what will we be working on?" Lizzie asked, obviously excited.

I stepped to the unopened crates and popped off the tops.

"Whatever pattern you're . . ." I hesitated. I was going to say "most comfortable with," but that wasn't the best way to earn experience. "Whatever pattern you've crafted the least, that's what I want each of you to work on today."

I reached in and pulled out the sheet of blue leather, earning multiple gasps, including from Lizzie. I smiled.

"The parts I've brought are much more expensive than what you're used to working with. But they'll require some extra work."

I lifted up a few different pieces, showcasing that some of the jagged cuts of leather featured damage from butchers or Nobles or were just too small of scraps to build whole outfits out of.

"How are we going to use those?" Lizzie asked.

"I'll show you." I smiled.

"I want to carve that one up," Sandy said, pointing at the boss monster.

She had just finished demonstrating carving apart four smaller monsters.

Alec, the foreman, rubbed his chin. He couldn't stop staring at her knife.

"It's a big profit loss if we damage it," Alec said. He sounded reluctant.

"I'll just tell Valjean to cover your losses," Sandy said, smiling with a smug confidence.

"And he'll do that?" Alec said.

"Definitely." She oozed confidence. She knew that Valjean would cover the losses if she said he would. She also knew he wouldn't want to and would likely scold her for this. But she wasn't going to damage the monster.

"Then I guess we can let you at it. Where did you get that knife?" Alec asked, still rubbing his chin.

"Friend of mine made it," Sandy said, walking up to where the scaffolding was being assembled. It had to be torn down to hang the giant monster. To her surprise, the abattoir employed a lot of people besides just butchers—there was a class called porters, who specialized entirely in moving things. On top of that, the abattoir actually kept carpenters on shift, who were seemingly able to bend and remold the wooden structures, rarely even needing to bring out tools. They seemed much more versatile.

The entire status of the abattoir was much higher than many of the other crafters' businesses. Not only that, but several of them, especially the foreman, actually significantly out-leveled Sandy. They required that many levels and that much progress to process the monsters pulled out of the dungeon.

Alec walked Sandy through the process of cutting up the monster. He even shared his much higher-level Butcher Vision with her.

With his buff applied, she not only saw the red lines of perfect cuts to optimize the yield, but shifting yellow lines in different patterns that showed alternatives. It even surrounded the shadowy monster with a yellow mesh, making it much easier to see through its stealth effect.

Sandy smiled viciously. With two weeks before they had to leave, she had plenty of time to catch back up to Gwen in attributes.

She just had to do it without anyone noticing that she was a butcher herself.

Gerald piled up metal shavings and discarded, polluted metal. The forgemaster next to him looked nervously at the pile of metal.

"You know," she said, "Buying some more cohesive magic alloys wouldn't be too expensive. Anything you attempt to forge out of these will be extremely brittle."

"Not if I enchant it," Gerald said, staring greedily at the slowly accumulating pile of slag and shavings.

"Enchanting metal of this quality would be a waste!" the forgemaster said. She wore an exasperated look. This was not her first experience with a Noble rampaging through the forge and making demands. Typically, this involved asking for ludicrous weapons or custom orders, or repairs on clearly magical items.

This was the first time she had seen a Noble so obsessed with the forge's trash.

"Don't worry about me. I just . . . can I borrow a forge?"

"Our forges run all day," she said.

"Then I'll work overnight."

Gerald didn't look away from the pile of metal. To him, every single scrap was a treasure.

I woke to a pounding fist on the door of the estate, sliding out of bed in a panic. I hesitated. The insistence and power behind the knocking felt like there was an emergency on the other side. I wasn't sure I wanted to answer it.

But the knocking continued as I deliberated.

An unfamiliar attendant greeted me at the door.

"Valjean has sent a summons," the attendant said. He had a condescending look on his face.

"In the middle of the night?" I asked, aghast.

"It is six seventeen in the morning," the attendant said.

I rubbed my eyes.

"Okay. I need a few minutes."

"I'll be waiting."

I shut the door and waited a moment. I had no idea why the hell Valjean wanted me in the morning. Unless . . . he wanted to bring me with him on a dungeon clear?

Excited by the thought, I used [Quick Change] to get dressed. It only took a few seconds. Then I tied my hair back before opening the door.

I paused again at the open door. The attendant stared at me.

"Will there be food?"

"Breakfast will be served," the attendant said.

I followed him as he led me through the winding guest rooms of the estate halls. Some Nobles lived full time in the estate, coming and going through the halls all day.

We didn't head to the dungeon. Instead, we headed to one of the open training fields behind the manor. Valjean sat at a table, inspecting a sword. His fingers slid along the naked blade. I knew it wasn't his weapon of choice; he was practically never without his polearm. When he swept through the dungeon behind us, he rode on horseback the entire time.

He had leveled a whole floor of the dungeon with ease.

Valjean looked up at me.

"Coffee?" he asked.

I rubbed my eyes.

"What is this?" I asked.

"One of the only convenient gaps in my schedule. Yours is appreciably more flexible," Valjean said. He sheathed the sword and threw it to the attendant, who grabbed it and returned it to a nearby cabinet. "Tell me, how high are your stats right now, Lady Gwen?" Valjean said.

The attendant stood to the side. I looked at him nervously. If I listed off my stats, would he know that they weren't in the range for most Nobles?

"It's alright," Valjean reassured me. "He won't leak the details of your status to anyone. You can summon your weapons here, Lady Gwen. We only have around half an hour. I'll see what I can fit into my schedule each day for your training, as well as some time with Sandy and Gerald."

"Alright," I said. With a sharp intake of breath, I pulled up my status. Then, piece by piece, I equipped the Arachne-Knight set. It was the one Mom helped me make; a suit of shining white chitin armor, harvested and reassembled from the spiders of the second floor of Stitch's dungeon. It was all sharp angles and hard pieces, but the interior was soft and padded.

It was by far my most important outfit; it gave me three points of Thread Sensing, helping propel my single Legendary skill to seven. Thread Master gave me the ability to manipulate string; it was an ability I was still working on mastering.

[Gwendolyn Tailor][Human, Lv18][Seamstress]
[Health: 58/58][Mana: 10/10][XP: 0/10]
[ATTRIBUTES]
▶SPD: 25
▶WIL: 5
▶STR: 11
▶DEX: 42
▶CON: 29
▶PER: 9
[SKILLS]
▶Crafting I
▶Running Stitch I
▶Hand Spinning I
▶Thread Mastery IV
▶Wardrobe X
▶Quick Change I
▶Embellishment III
▶Pattern Mirroring I

‣Always Prepared II
[PATTERNS]
‣Hunter Pattern
‣Shell Dress Pattern
‣Houndsmaster Pattern
[TEMPORARY SKILLS]
‣Bow Proficiency I
‣Shadow Cloak II
‣Tracking Proficiency I
‣Thread Sensing III
‣Thread Mastery VII
‣Parry V
‣Projection III
‣Trapping III
‣Befriend III
‣Wildspeaker I

Wardrobe X was one of my inventory skills. Most classes had at least one, and mine allowed me to store multiple outfits at a time. Not only that, but once I reached tier ten with it, I gained the skills and a percentage of the stats from every outfit I had stored. All of my temporary skills came from the outfits I crafted.

My stats, including the stats from the clothes I was currently wearing, veered easily into the realm of the superhuman. Since I had started wearing the outfits piece by piece and slowly leveling, the difference in my stats over time had been small and subtle at first. It was much more jarring when switching outfits and feeling how much faster and stronger I was.

I listed the numbers out to Valjean.

Valjean nodded along.

"We need to round out your numbers. My specialty is the polearm, but I've gained skill proficiencies in multiple weapon styles. With such high dexterity, you'll want to practice a style that emphasizes finesse. You typically practice with needle swords, yes?"

"I also have these," I said, activating my other inventory skill—[Always Prepared]. The skill summoned a wooden crate that could contain tailoring tools as well as some basic materials. I had loaded it with thread and cloth. It also contained my oversized sewing needles. By using skills ostensibly designed to stitch together cloth and leather into patterns, I could carve apart monsters.

I pulled out the pair of scissors. Valjean raised an eyebrow. I focused on them for a moment, spending a point of mana.

By expending a mana point, I could cause the scissors to expand in size. They scaled up until they were easily the size of a sword. Pattern Mirroring made it so that whenever I cut a monster, an equal cut appeared. The skill was optimized for cutting multiple pieces of hide or leather or cloth, but it didn't discriminate against living targets.

Valjean nodded slowly at the giant scissors in my hand. He very carefully and deliberately reached out, then paused, looking to me for permission to grab the pair of giant scissors. I nodded and held them out.

He frowned as he plucked them from my hand.

"Heavy," he said.

"They don't feel heavy to me," I replied.

"Yes. I suppose your class proficiency makes wielding them easier." He ran his finger along the blade's edge. There were fine details along the outside of the blade, engraved in the metal by Gerald in a state of crafting mania. They were decorations of spools and scissors and a single line of thread tracing all along the blade. Purple cloth was tied tight to the handle to form a grip.

Valjean nodded at the scissors before handing them back.

"They would be more useful if you raised your strength set higher."

"Then I just have to craft a set with lots of strength points," I said.

"For now, let's practice what you do have."

"Are we . . . going to spar?" I asked.

Valjean nodded.

"Training rapiers, please," he said.

The attendant pulled two blades from the cabinet before presenting them to us. I lifted one.

"I'm not sure my skill will work with this," I said.

"Give it a try," Valjean said.

I frowned. For the needles to count, we had to tie a string to the end so that what we were doing was technically sewing. I leaned down to my [Always Prepared] inventory, pulling out a tiny line of thread and tying it to the end. Valjean walked a few paces away, lifting the training sword to me. The edges of it looked sharp. He must have caught my worried glance at the blade.

"These are enchanted to not damage us," Valjean explained calmly. "You can exercise the full power of your skills. Go ahead."

I had never stabbed a person before. I didn't even hold thoughts of eventually overtaking Valjean through force. But now we were pointing swords at each other for a friendly duel.

"Are you ready, Lady Gwen?"

I looked at the rapier in my hand. It was very needle-like. I tried very hard to convince myself it was a needle. Then I activated [Running Stitch].

To my surprise, it worked. The sword shot forward with magically enhanced speed, blurring through the air.

Valjean deflected it. [Running Stitch] kept the sword in my hand. His deflection sent me staggering sideways as a consequence, the force of his simple parry sufficient to throw me off my feet and onto the ground with an "oomph."

"That will be a problem," Valjean said from above me. "Did your skill keep you attached to your weapon? Teaching Nobles to cancel weapon skills is one of the early lessons the Academy will foist on you. Guess you'll have to start learning it early, though."

I stood up, pointing the sword again and readying myself.

"What are you waiting for?" Valjean asked. "Hit me."

I stabbed forward, feinting, then activated [Running Stitch]. Because of the magical nature of the skill, I was able to change directions entirely, bypassing his guard and landing a hit on his side. There was a flash of purple and the sword made a ringing noise. I [Canceled] and stepped back.

"Oh! That was excellent, Lady Gwen. You're a natural," Valjean said. "Great cancel. Now, let's fix your posture . . ."

Valjean correcting me, making me stand straight. I stabbed him again, repeating the feint with the skill. Valjean frowned.

"Lady Gwen, your dexterity is beyond the realm of the commoners. You need to learn to rely not just on your skills, but technique and attributes."

"I don't have a chance at hitting you," I said. Valjean was much faster and stronger than me.

"Hmmm. I thought I was holding back enough." Valjean sighed. "The point isn't winning, regardless. It's getting better. Fighting an insurmountable challenge is one of the best ways to improve."

I attacked him again. He parried me to the ground again.

"Fix your stance. Like this . . . I'll demonstrate."

"Your posture again. Good job. Clean hit."

For the next half hour, Valjean repeatedly beat me into the ground before offering one piece of advice or another. Eventually, there was a chime, and his attendant interrupted.

"Sir, it's time for your morning dungeon clear."

"Thank you, Thomas." Valjean sheathed the practice blade and passed it off. "For you, Lady Gwen, practice your form and posture while working on one of the dummies. And keep up your workshop project. I look forward to the results," he said.

CHAPTER 5

I looked into the crates in the back of the atelier. Sandy had come through after an earlier talk. One of the materials inside of the crates was a caustic-looking leather, covered in fur that was thin and sharply abrasive. The individual hairs were like fiberglass rather than fur. It was mottled acid green and swirled black, rough to the touch. But it had already been processed by the butchers.

It was broken into several pieces. I slowly stitched it together, unable to demonstrate my skills in front of the mundane laborers.

I looked up at Lizzie. She was standing at arm's distance from me.

"Lady Gwen?" she asked. "Can you show me how to do a cross stitch?"

She looked nervous. I smiled, setting down what I was working on and taking hers before walking her through it. Being a seamstress didn't mean having the innate skill to do this work—that was acquired with one individual skill point at a time.

I walked Lizzie—and the rest of the group—through all the various skills they needed to learn. The ones who worked the front had to learn to cut the patterns from the leather. Then they had to learn to join the poor pieces back together. The ones in the back needed to learn to stitch. During their normal hours, the back of house mostly performed cutting and prepping; the thicker and stronger leathers required hole punches and other prep work.

Not to mention the atelier also often did finishing touches or partial augmentations to metal armors.

Once we fell into a routine, we worked for the entire four-hour shift in quiet. Most people were completely outside of their comfort zone, slowing them down even more. It would be days before anyone finished their first set.

At the end of the night, I helped clean up the workshop for the morning shift. I was sweeping the floor after the workers had left when Lizzie walked back into the shop. She stood apart from me, staring nervously.

"Hey," I said.

"Gwen. Lady Gwen!" Lizzie said. Then she paused awkwardly.

"What's up?" I smiled. It was grating that everyone was so nervous because of my perceived Nobility.

"I was wondering if I could stay late and work more."

I frowned and looked around the shop.

"I can't pay you for any more hours."

"That's fine!" Lizzie said. She wrung her hands. "I want to . . . I want to get another level. I'll help you clean, too!"

I chewed on my lip. I could afford a few more hours directing her.

"Okay," I said.

Sandy practically sprinted in circles around the butchering platform, swinging with a giant, enchanted knife as large as she was. She was laughing as she went, cutting into an electrically charged jellyfish that hung from the ceiling, dripping brine to the ground.

The Cloudpiercer Jellyfish was another famous export of Foundry. Its nest featured many materials that incorporated mana-rich alloys. Though it had an aquatic appearance, it actually was capable of flying through open air as well. Its body contained alchemical and enchanting components, and its meat was considered a delicacy that also massively raised magic-related stats.

It wasn't any good for making armor out of, though.

Pieces of it piled up below where other butchers sorted them out, cutting the pieces even further and separating them by use. The alchemical and enchanting regents needed special care and storage, especially without a porter with skills to keep them stable.

She cut into specific patterns and depths; right after cutting into a specific organ, she pulled the knife free and stepped back. A burst of electricity followed, metal grounding rods buzzing as they carried the charge. Sandy braced, holding the rail beside her. Her smile didn't leave her face. Then she continued on.

The work in the rest of the workshop had almost completely stopped as the other butchers stared up at her.

"Was that Butcher Sight?" one of the butchers asked.

The woman next to him punched his arm.

"Lady Sandy is a Noble. She can't have Butcher Sight. It's probably Expose Weakness or Environmental Mastery."

"How does Environmental Mastery let her see the organs?" the man asked, confused.

"I hear it highlights ways to hurt monsters with other monsters. Acid sacks, fire breath. The works," she said. She had an admiring smile. "Lady Sandy is on track to beat Alec's level-twenty record. It's too bad she was Chosen."

A door to an office blew open in the back.

"What are you standing around gawking at? Get back to work!" Alec shouted at the low-level butchers on the floor. He stared up and quirked a smile at Sandy.

Alec would never say no to free labor.

Gerald crackled maniacally at three in the morning. The forgemaster stared at him nervously with bags under her eyes. Gerald didn't even seem a little tired, though.

"That weapon is way too big for anyone to even use . . ." she whispered to herself. Then she shook her head. Not her business. The kid wasn't going to burn the place down. She went home to sleep.

I managed to sleep in that morning. Valjean interrupted my lunch instead.

I had new bruises. Valjean was teaching me to block. Even if the enchantment on the weapon stopped it from cutting or lowering HP, it still hurt like hell.

And my lunch was cold by the time I got back to it.

I could hardly complain. The chefs Valjean employed were on par with Henri—Sandy's dad, a chef who lived in Stitch. Even cold, the meal was still fantastic. It was too bad they didn't have something as extravagant as enchanted plates that kept food at the perfect temperature. That would be perfect for ice cream.

I pushed my way into the atelier's workshop. To my surprise, it was already half set up. Lizzie was hard at work. She had even finished a couple pieces of her set. She didn't notice me come in, focused as she was on her work. I shrugged. I had been the same way; the world disappeared when you immersed yourself in your work completely. Once you found a flow, you started to see memories of the crafters who had worked on the outfit before you.

Eventually, I had to interrupt her to have her move away from the table in the back. I reached out and put a gentle hand on her shoulder.

"Lizzie?" I asked. "Lizziiie," I said.

Eventually, I had to squeeze a little to get her to look up. She blinked, smiling at me with a dazed look. When she recognized me, her smile widened.

"Gwen!" Lizzie said.

I smiled at her. She had worked late into the night, and today she was working before her shift even started.

"Going well?" I asked.

"Actually, I had some questions . . ."

I was still answering Lizzie's questions as the rest of the atelier's late-night workshop session arrived. They got to work right away. Eventually, I pulled away to help the others.

This became my routine at Foundry. A random interruption in the middle of the day—never overlapping with my workshopping hours—followed by working late alongside Lizzie. I was making good progress on my own set. And the bruises healed fast.

It was absolutely no surprise that Lizzie was the first one to complete her set, and consequently, the first one to level.

It was after everyone else had already left. We worked under the greasy light of oil lamps.

"I got experience . . . I got multiple points of experience!" Lizzie said, jolting out of her seat. "Gwen! I got a skill point!" She was absolutely exuberant.

I'd been sitting off to the side, waiting for her to finish. She was in one of her flow states, crafting with incredible speed and care.

"Nice job!" I said. "Now we have to decide what pattern to spend it on."

Lizzie instantly dropped her happiness, grimacing.

"I can't spend it on a pattern. The atelier's track has a specific skill order for back-of-shop workers like me," she said. "If I deviate from it, I won't be promoted on time, and I'll make far less money . . ."

"How much experience did you get by finishing this set?" I asked.

"Three," Lizzie said. There was a little shine of excitement behind her eyes again. "Lady Gwen, *why* did I get three experience? I've made this pattern dozens of times and never gotten three."

Lizzie was holding a completed seamstress uniform.

"Because you made it out of higher-grade parts. Look at the stats and skills on it."

Lizzie paused. Her eyes slowly widened.

"Woah," she said. "Who's going to use this?"

I smiled.

"You are. It's yours now."

"What?" Lizzie asked, staring up at me. Then she looked back down. "I mean, thank you, Lady Gwen. I've never kept anything I've crafted before. It's all mine?"

"Of course." I smiled. "Hopefully the skills on it will help complete your skill set?"

"They will!" Lizzie said. "It has three separate skills! Two crafting skills and a mana-recovery skill that generates mana after I finish enough work."

"Oh? That sounds like an intriguing skill. What's the name of it?" I asked. If I had that skill, I could stop halfway through a dungeon and recover by crafting by hand.

"Mana Thread Shaping. It's rare."

A thread skill?

"Does it give a level in Thread Mastery?"

"I'm not sure," Lizzie said. She would have to put the set on to find out. Thread Mastery was a legendary skill, one you gained by assembling several other skills. I hoped to develop it into one of my most potent fighting tools.

"Lady Gwen, should I really go against the Tailor Guild . . ." Lizzie looked uncertain.

"You'll be able to earn way more levels if you pick a pattern and practice crafting it with different materials," I said.

"That's . . . a good point. But the supervisor will be mad."

"Just don't tell her." I shrugged.

Lizzie looked at me aghast. I forgot most people had a lot of respect for systems of authority.

"Tell me what patterns you have available to pick."

Each level, we seamstresses gained one point; it could be spent on a pattern, a new skill, or leveling an existing, permanent skill you had acquired through the system. Being forced to split half of our points was just another way the system kept us weaker than Nobles, who could invest all of their attribute points and skill points directly into fighting skills.

With every level, a Noble's attribute points inched upward. The rest of us only had whatever came with the clothes we wore. And it was obvious after just a day here that the Tailor Guild wasn't supplying us with the best. It had to be intentional, and thus insidious, how little they invested in the mundane outfits supplied to workers.

Lizzie listed her pattern shop.

[Pattern Shop]

▶ [COMMON] Lumberjack Pattern (Basic)

Grants minuscule bonuses to Strength and Constitution dependent on craft quality and materials used. Grants bonus point to Lumberjack skills depending on craft quality and materials used.

▸[COMMON] Peasant Pattern (Basic)

Grants minor bonus to Constitution dependent on craft quality and materials used. Grants bonus point to first skill in status.

▸[RARE] Robes of the Archon of the Forever Storm (Advanced)

"That one," I interrupted.

"I haven't even read out the description of what it does," Lizzie said.

"Doesn't matter. That's the one. Look at the name. Rarer is always better!" I said.

"It's advanced, though. I might not even be able to craft it."

"I'll help."

"Lady Gwen . . . you're a Noble, not a seamstress."

"You don't trust my skills after all this?" I asked, leaning forward. My hair shifted.

"I do," Lizzie said, hesitating. "It's just . . . at least let me read out what it does."

"Okay," I said, leaning back.

Lizzie continued reading it.

Grants immense bonus to will. Inflicts minor penalty to Constitution and Strength. Grants set bonus skill based on craft quality and materials used.

"That one," I said.

"I don't think I can craft anything a Noble will want to wear," Lizzie said.

"Don't have to. You just need to get levels by crafting it a lot. How much experience do you think it will reward you per initial craft? Five? Ten?"

Besides that, it would be incredible for me. Maybe I would figure out how to be her first purchase. The amount of mana I had was relative to my Willpower attribute. Every point I raised it by would expand my possibilities massively. Also . . . it was a mage set. The skills it could grant probably included straight up magic.

"Pure Willpower doesn't sound that useful," Lizzie argued.

"Lizzie," I said, putting my hands on her shoulder. Her eyes refocused on my face, looking away from a System window I couldn't see. "You're picking that one."

"Alright, Lady Gwen. If you're sure."

CHAPTER 6

I snuck inside Valjean's guard, holding the rapier blade with one hand. With my other, I threw a pile of messy thread from my pocket, pinching a single piece of it and flexing [Thread Mastery] to manipulate it.

It was a surprise I'd prepared for him today. He'd interrupted my workshop hours for this training.

After only a week, I had improved by a lot. And I had started using my own specialties. But this was my first time using Thread Mastery against him.

I smirked as he ignored the knot of thread flying at his face in favor of my sword. The ball of thread expanded into an entire net of thin string. I tugged on it mentally as it grabbed at him. He made a noise of surprise as it jerked him with force, making him flinch, and my sword jabbed into his chest.

"Ha! I got you! Without using [Running Stitch]!"

Valjean nodded. "Good work, Lady Gwen. You can manipulate these strings?" he asked, pulling the makeshift net off of himself.

"Yes," I said, nodding proudly. It was the first time I had hit Valjean without using Running Stitch to enhance the attack to superhuman levels. Even if that meant having to use Thread Mastery.

"Good improvisation. But why throw the string at me? Can you slide it along the ground?"

"I . . . can," I said.

"Then you should try to trip or incapacitate me. That would allow you to land as many hits as you wanted."

It took me another three days before I successfully knocked Valjean off his feet. He recovered with one hand, pushing himself upright before he ever hit the ground.

That same night, Lizzie had finally finished her first set of the pattern she'd bought.

Reese had also started working late after seeing Lizzie's gains. He didn't stay as late as she did, though.

After hours, she changed into the seamstress outfit she'd made herself. With the skills it gave her, she was able to work much faster, halving the time it took to produce the outfit. When she finished it and got the experience points, she practically squealed.

"Gwen! I got an entire level!" she shouted, throwing herself to her feet, then engulfing me in an unexpected hug.

I directed the needle in my hand away from her and laughed, returning the hug one-armed.

"Congratulations," I said.

"What pattern should I take now?" Lizzie asked. Her face was glowing as her eyes snapped back and forth, reading text I couldn't see.

"You should take skills to round out your skill set," I said. "You should focus on skills that let you craft faster. Take another pattern when experience from this one slows down."

"But . . . my leveling . . ."

"That will be fine. You'll just continue crafting your advanced set. It should be easier now that you've done it once, right?"

"Yes!" Lizzie said, practically jumping.

"Are you going to try it on? Tell me what skills it gave you?"

"Try it on? But the skill it has . . . I can do that?" Liz asked.

I just nodded.

She walked toward the mannequin, carrying most of her outfit like it was a monster. She carefully reached down and grabbed the hat before placing it on top of the mannequin.

The set didn't look like anything a mage would wear.

Lizzie had elected to use the clearly magical scaled leather that had come from the butcher shop. After being assembled, the scales were so light blue they were almost white, iridescent stripes of shifting rainbow color visible as you walked around the set. The pants were large and baggy, overlapping two huge platform boots. The shirt covered the skin completely, stretching down until it covered the edge of incredibly tight gloves—a mage's fingers needed to be fully articulated, presumably.

The set had a huge, wide-brimmed hat, but it was missing the pointy top of a proper wizard hat. To finish it off was a thin but large cloak that bloomed outward from the neck, practically a cape.

Lizzie tried it on. Her face was flushed as she stood in the outfit.

"It's so weird," she said.

"It looks cool," I replied. "What does it do?"

Lizzie closed her eyes. She carried an expression of immense focus. Then she raised her arms, and—

It was suddenly dumping water on me. A miniature cloud exploded, like a storm had shrunk down and spread along the ceiling. The entire building shook as water poured out of it, erupting with force. The cloud boiled and flashed with thunder and lightning. Water pooled to my ankles, unable to escape the building. The oil lamp went out.

Then the cloud disappeared.

"You almost destroyed the atelier," Valjean said.

This meeting was unscheduled. Lizzie looked practically mortified next to me. She was as pale as a ghost. I reached over and squeezed her shoulder. I didn't blame her.

Valjean was in full battle-dress. And it wasn't the stuff he wore to clear the piddling dungeon of Stitch. It was matte black metal armor, shaped in spikes and studded with purple gems that seemed to glow. I could tell it was enchanted. Valjean had no helmet on. He didn't look angry, just tired. Even his horse was armored; Truffles wore matching black battle dress and ate from a feed bucket near the sortie building outside the central dungeon.

"They need a new one anyway," I said, shrugging.

Valjean sighed. "I might as well move them into a new building rather than pay to do redo all the flooring. Tell me, Gwen, it's been almost two weeks. Have you made progress?"

"We have." I smiled. "I think I have an answer."

"An answer to what?" Valjean asked curiously.

"Lizzie—Elizabeth here unlocked a pattern that can summon rain."

Valjean nodded slowly.

"And she used it to . . . destroy my workshop."

Lizzie stiffened. Then she bowed and started to apologize. "Sorry, Lord Valjea—"

"We weren't sure what it would do!" I protested.

Lizzie directed a horrified look at me.

"Sure. You couldn't have read the skill description?" Valjean asked.

"Is that what you did the first time you got a magic skill?"

Valjean half chuckled.

"No. I blew down a wall in my dorm room at the Academy."

"See?" I asked. "Anyway, the set has a ton of uses! But mostly, the water it summons could be perfect for putting out fires."

Valjean's eyebrows rose. His mouth opened. Then he stopped, his face fixed in concentration.

"That might actually be worth more than the workshop you've cost me," Valjean said. Then, with a groan, he stood up. He metal armor creaked beneath him. "Let's test it. Olivier?" Valjean shouted.

Olivier turned away from where he was talking to other Nobles.

"Lord Valjean?" he asked.

"I've need of you. Let's go to the dungeon. We're going to set something on fire."

"Certainly," Olivier said.

"How long until you can get the suit here?" Valjean asked, looking at me.

"I have it in my inventory," I said.

"Excellent. Elizabeth, come demonstrate your new pattern," Valjean said, turning and focusing on her.

Lizzie held her hands up, signaling *no* but tripping over her words. She gestured for a few moments.

"Come on, Lizzie!" I said, pulling the set out of my Wardrobe.

"Lady Gwen, you should be the one to—I mean, I shouldn't go into the dungeon. I'm no Noble!"

"This is a great opportunity to show Valjean how incredible seamstresses are," I said, grabbing her by the shoulder and leading her to somewhere she could change. I brokered no argument.

I shot down every attempt she launched at running away. She would be fine! She would be with me. And with four Nobles, even if one of them was Olivier. Who had gotten knocked out by me.

Three and a half Nobles and me.

We trudged into the dungeon, practically dragging Lizzie along. The Nobles even helpfully provided her with a staff—an old-looking metal rod with scars from use and time. Apparently, it was a useful channeling implement for casting mage spells that required no proficiency. She caught a few stares from people on the street around the dungeon, which probably didn't help her anxiety.

The dungeon we entered was devoid of trees but covered in foliage; a hedge maze spiraled around us. The air was absolutely choked with the smell of plant life. The copper smell of blood undercut it, but it was distant. It had been a while since the dungeon was cleared, and the corpses had long been brought away.

Harvesters carrying baskets trailed around the hedge, pulling the multi-colored flowers that grew from it.

"Lord Dorian," Valjean said.

Dorian nodded, replying by freeing a gigantic claymore from the sheath at his side. The sheath was only a few inches long, but the blade that emerged from it was larger than Dorian himself. With two sweeps of the blade, he separated out a section of hedging.

"Olivier."

Olivier drew his bow and fired an arrow so fast that I didn't even see it happen. One moment he was standing there, the next he had a bow in hand. The isolated hedge was on fire.

"Elizabeth," Valjean said, this time turning to look at her.

"Do I just . . ." Lizzie raised the magical metal rod up, holding it between herself and the fire. Her nervousness was visible.

"You got this, Lizzie," I said.

She closed her eyes.

Without the limited confines of the building, the storm cloud that appeared was much larger. It billowed outward before pouring down water. It didn't fall like rain; it fell in great sheets that soaked the hedge entirely.

"Gwen?" Valjean asked, staring at the hedge.

"Yes?" I asked.

"That was a proper spell," Valjean said.

"Yes," I said.

Valjean frowned. A point of contention between us was exactly how powerful commoners could become. Valjean was more aware of seamstresses' skills than most Nobles, having seen us in action. He was aware that Wardrobe granted me the skills of every piece I had assembled. He was probably thinking the same thing I was.

If I made ten separate Mage sets, I could be a powerful mage. And not only that, I could draw from skills of completely separate classes. I'm sure it wasn't unheard of for someone to wear a set that gave them skills from outside of their class. Surely they had discovered the butcher class's ability to reveal weaknesses, for example. But Nobles couldn't gain the skills of ten sets at once.

Valjean's gaze was fixed on the hedge.

"Elizabeth. I'd like to order a hundred."

CHAPTER 7

There was no firefighter class. Each city's fire brigade was assembled of volunteers, often porters who could transport vast quantities of water very quickly until a Noble could arrive and clear the fire—whether with water magic or something else.

Sometimes, they would tear down entire buildings around a fire to contain it, costing the city months of resources.

Lizzie's own house had burned down that way.

The infrastructure savings were potentially enormous. The opportunity was sufficient to disrupt Valjean's entire schedule. He overrode a new construction project and directed the atelier to rebuild there.

Lizzie would have to be involved from start to finish—no other seamstress or tailor would be able to successfully roll that pattern from the shop with its rarity. They wouldn't even get the levels to produce it.

The atelier spun into action to fulfill the orders. Valjean intended to sell several units to other cities. Once its popularity spread, they would order many more.

"So none of the cities have fire brigades?" I asked Valjean between meetings. We had been with him for an hour of rearranging his schedule and arranging to increase the capacity of the atelier.

Valjean locked eyes with me.

"Most of the Nobility is not so open-minded. Even most Chosen look down on the common classes. Most will dismiss this out of hand. Of course, the capitals have water mages on staff, but with enchantment or reinforcement on the most valuable buildings, fire isn't as much of an issue, either."

The Nobility would always find a way to look down on us.

It only took a few days to bring the new atelier to life.

I was invited to the opening.

It was much closer to the city center, the floor covered in a light-colored hardwood. Giant windows let daylight pour in. Bare mannequins sat in the windows, ready to be clothed with new products. Wagons of goods waited outside.

"Lady Gwen!" Lizzie said from inside the shop. She was wearing a Seamstress set, and looked far more comfortable in it.

"Lizzie," I said with a smile.

"Thank you so much!" Lizzie said. "My hourly rate is higher during commissions. I didn't even know that!"

"Of course," I said with a smile.

"So . . . what now? After I finish these sets, I'll have so many levels . . . Should I grab another pattern?"

I nodded.

"Grab a new pattern before the old one runs out of experience. You wouldn't want to have to go kill monsters for levels, right?"

Lizzie shook her head no.

"That last trip to the dungeon was already enough for me. Although . . . it was really pretty in there! A hedge maze in a dungeon. Are they all that pretty?"

"Most of the early floors, yes," I replied. "You'll have to help lead the other crafters since I'm leaving tomorrow," I said.

"That soon?!" Lizzie asked.

"All new Nobles are required to graduate from the Academy if they wish to become landowners," Finn said, stepping up from behind me. "Hello, Lizzie. I'm Valjean's assistant, Finn. I've acquired some resources from the Tailor Guild. I'll help you give a more hands-on approach to the management of this atelier. And once we're done with this order, I'll assist you further."

Finn nodded at me then. "Your bags are all ready to go. Additionally, Valjean has ordered one of the first Fire Brigade sets to be sent to you."

"Really?" I asked. "Where!?"

I practically jumped forward. That set gave real magic! Not magical sight or magical speed. Cloud summoning! It was even more impressive than Olivier's fake fireball.

Finn held up a hand. "You won't see it until after your train ride. It'll be shipped to you and should arrive around the same time you reach the academy. We've sourced some outfits for formal occasions as well, though the stats won't be impressive . . ."

"That's alright," I said.

I had almost finished the Caustic Hunter set as well. It needed a few finishing touches. Since I worked on it entirely during workshop hours, I was forced to not use any seamstress skills in front of the other commoners. It demanded a ton of work, especially since it was in so many disparate pieces, which added a ton to the workload.

And now I would receive a Mage set as well; the extra willpower would extend my mana pool, increasing my ability to fight and craft in a single day.

I said my last goodbye to Lizzie, giving her a hug and promising to write her.

Then we were off to prepare for our train ride to Lyssandra's city, and after that, to the Academy.

Lizzie stared nervously at Gwen's back as she left the shop. She was wringing her hands again.

"What's wrong? Nervous?" Reese asked her.

"No, I'm excited about all the work," Lizzie said.

She kept to herself that there was something . . . wrong . . . with Lady Gwen. She hadn't interacted with a lot of Nobles, and she would never voice it for fear of offending anyone. She liked Gwen fine, of course. Better than she liked other Nobles, even. She was approachable. And kind. And a good teacher.

But she was really, really good at crafting.

Lizzie couldn't stop thinking of walking into the room where Lady Gwen was crafting and watching as her hands blazed at inhuman speed to stitch something together. She seemed lost in that fugue state that all crafters found themselves in, and it took a moment for Lady Gwen to notice her.

And whatever she was using was not a combat skill. Ever since, she had questioned every time Gwen joked about seamstresses killing monsters.

Eventually, Lizzie shrugged and got back to work setting up the atelier.

"We have something special for you," Alec said, his smile vicious as he slapped a hand down on Sandy's shoulder.

"Okay," Sandy said, drawing the word out and looking nervously at the man. He smelled like sweat and alcohol. She reflexively leaned away from him but walked with him as he led her deeper into the abattoir. Behind a freezer enchanted to keep cold and through another door, she found a few of the older and most dedicated staff members waiting.

"I still don't think this is a good idea, Alec," one of them protested.

"And I don't care what you think. Sandy here fits right in with the rest of us."

"What is this about?" Sandy asked, pushing Alec back and stepping away.

"Sandy . . . you have to know something about butchers. Every single one of us has a moment where we think, *Shouldn't this skill work just fine on a living monster?*"

Sandy froze. Several thoughts ran through her head. Had they found her out? Alec smiled.

"Well, they do," Alec said with a smile. "We know you haven't been able to fight since you came here. That's why you love tearing up monsters at our abattoir. But we get the same way. And we can't go around sneaking into dungeons, so we get our fix differently."

Alec led her down a crude tunnel through the floor and into a wider room where more people waited. They shut the door behind her.

Inside a fighting cage, a gigantic, winged serpent slid along the ground, rising and hissing at the spectators. Bettors threw money onto a table.

"So what do you say, Sandy? You interested in a fight or two? We figured it's the best thanks we can give you."

Sandy smiled. "Oh hell yeah."

Gerald looked exhausted across the table, while Sandy seemed exuberant. The three of us hadn't had much time to see each other.

"Valjean is a brutal sparring partner," I said, poking at the food on my plate. I was nervous, and it was doing no favors for my appetite.

"You sparred with Valjean? They made me spar Dorian," Sandy complained. "He *always* had early-morning sessions."

Gerald started snoring, his head now on the table. We ate breakfast outside. Most of our goods were packed.

Cinnamon sat nearby, hooked to a fancy leash. His tail wagged constantly. Occasionally, he barked loudly, making the strangers on the street jump in fright. He was still getting bigger.

"Valjean's schedule is so packed he was fitting in sparring sessions all through the day. And I was running the atelier's night session on top of that."

"Huh," Sandy said. "The abattoir has an underground monster-dueling ring."

"What?" I asked, leaning forward in shock.

"Yeah. I mean, the butcher class eventually killing monsters is a given, but I didn't expect them to just straight up . . . It's literally underground, too. Like under the city."

"That sounds wildly unsafe!"

"It's monster fights. Of course it's not safe."

"I mean hollowing out a section under the city!" I was almost shouting. "Did you . . . Are you gonna . . ."

"I'm not a snitch," Sandy said.

I put my face in my hands.

"Come on. Like we're better!" Sandy said. "They have first aid ready, at least. We walked into the dungeon alone."

"No. Yeah. It's fine."

"What is?" Gerald asked, sleepy but looking up. There was syrup in his hair from where it had dragged over his plate.

"It's nothing," we both replied. Sandy and I made eye contact. I sighed.

"Here comes Finn," Sandy said.

"Are you all ready?" Finn asked.

The sun had barely risen, and our breath was visible in the air. There was just one central train station in Foundry.

Because the city wall was a fixed element of the world created by the dungeon, the rail had to go up and over both tiers of it. That meant the train came in over wooden struts. The rail looked terrifying.

The train looked even more terrifying.

The metal practically shone with enchantment—a fixture on it to prevent the degradation of the Wild from destroying it.

The train looked outfitted for war. Thick steel was marked with old dents, patches welded in like battle scars. Spikes covered the top, preventing anything from landing or roosting on it.

The most intimidating part of the train, by far, was the massive cattle-catcher on the front. Fit for war, it was a spike-covered ramp designed to divert things off the track.

"I'll attend you to Spoke to meet Lyssandra. Valjean would come, but . . ."

"He's busy," I said. I looked at Finn.

Finn led the way inside to guide us through a tour of the compartments. Porters had already loaded our luggage.

Cinnamon hopped up the steps into the train without issue.

"How long is the train ride to Hub?" I asked.

A sister city to Foundry, Hub facilitated trade between every second-tier city east of the capitals. It was called Hub because it was the center for a dozen trade routes, like the middle of a wagon wheel.

"Just over two days," Finn said.

Finn guided us through the compartments. The inside was almost as luxurious as the penthouse; hardwood floors for the tiny kitchen, rich carpet and relaxing sofas. None of the war-torn metal of its exterior was visible. Beautiful wooden panels covered the walls. The windows had visibly enchanted metal bars over them, but they were huge and clear. I just had to not think about why they were a few inches thick.

I wondered if it had any compartments that were even more reinforced. The metal of the train was almost a foot thick, solid and enchanted. And it was wide; the interior was roomy. But this was a vehicle designed to survive attacks from the monsters that roamed the Wilds.

There was enough food in storage for a month, let alone a two-day trip. I assumed that was in case of emergencies. It came with separate bedrooms and was connected to the forward and backward compartments. The segment between the carriages was surrounded by a flexible metal cage.

"The train moves slowly. Don't be alarmed by the bumps. As long as the train is still moving, nothing has gone wrong."

"What bumps?" Sandy asked.

"In order to survive the Wild, the train's tracks are enchanted," Finn said. "As the magic slowly degrades them, it attracts some . . . obstacles."

"And the train just . . . keeps going?" I asked.

"It's great leveling for the operators steering the train. It's a relatively rare class. Only recently seen. Every train driver comes from one of the capital cities, highly competitive placement. Any other questions?"

"Where do they forge the trains?" Gerald asked. Despite how exhausted he was earlier, now Gerald seemed wide awake, eyes sparkling.

Finn laughed. "You can come inspect the schematics in the office, if you'd like. Only a specialized workshop in Crucible can construct them."

"The forge capital," Gerald said.

"Yes," Finn said with a smile. "The natural terrain there is favorable to it—they build huge forges out of the wells of magma."

"Do you have schematics of those?" Gerald asked, already walking to the next cabin.

Finn laughed again. "No. We only have the train schematics, for repairs . . ." Gerald and Finn crossed to the other train car.

Cinnamon jumped up onto one of the seats, shook his head, and immediately covered the sofa in fur.

"Wanna raid the pantry?" Sandy asked.

"Yeah," I said.

* * *

I woke in the middle of the night, the first time there was a "bump." Finn had undersold how severe it was.

The entire train shook. Something roared. I vibrated halfway out of bed before throwing myself forward and pulling back the curtain to peer out the window.

A dozen glowing eyes stared at the train as we rolled past. A monster screamed in the dark, injured from the train. The other monsters pounced on it.

My heart pounded. But nothing approached the train.

No Nobles aboard the train attacked or interfered with the monsters. They took care of each other. And the train kept rolling indomitably forward.

After that, we hit something every few hours as we left behind the safety of the city. I struggled to sleep.

In the day, we ate and hung out around the window, enjoying the view.

I slept no easier the second night, finding myself crawling back to sleep after the "bumps" had stopped. What eventually woke me was the end of the itching sensation brought on by the Wild. I practically shot out of bed.

Out of the window, the edge of the city was cleared much farther back than Foundry's had been. Rail lines ran in every direction, one with another train departing the city. A great black pillar of smoke rose from the top of it.

We slowed down even further as we approached, going up and over the wall and into a trainyard that was far larger than Foundry's. It stretched over multiple blocks of the city, dozens of cargo containers filled with goods being unloaded or packed. Passenger cars seemed exceedingly rare.

The trainyard smelled like grease and burning coal.

We rolled to a stop. We had arrived.

CHAPTER 8

In a crowd of people, Lyssandra stood out immediately. She must have been six feet tall. A dress of purple and black with wide sleeves draped her frame, and a wide-brim hat shaded her from the overcast sunlight. She stared hard at me with dark, analyzing eyes; it wasn't the way someone looked at other people. It was the way someone looked at a good or product.

"Step inside," she said, waving at the wagon behind her.

I half expected the caravan to be bigger on the inside like the priesthood's had been. It was still luxurious; a carriage for a proper Noble. Lyssandra had the bearing of a Noble. She seemed to look down on the world around her.

She let us crowd into the carriage first before she followed. The moment she sat down, the harsh edge to her demeanor fell away. She sighed.

"I read Valjean's missives. You really cleared to the fourth floor of a dungeon?" she asked. She was incredulous. Despite her relaxing, she was still guarded, arms crossed.

"We did."

"And how did you do that with a seamstress class?"

"It wasn't . . . in the letter?" I asked.

"It was. But I want to see it."

"Were your parents Nobles?" Sandy asked.

"No," Lyssandra said. "My mother is a fishmonger. Father is a carpenter."

"The seamstress class gives a variety of skills to enhance its work, which mostly involves cutting into the hardened skin of monsters and stitching their materials back together," I said.

"And that helps you kill monsters?" Lyssandra asked.

"The skills work whether or not the monster is alive. Pattern Mirroring, one of my latest skills, produces a second copy of a cut in a set pattern. Once I reach tier ten with it, I'll be able to damage a monster across its entire body."

Lyssandra nodded along.

"I can demonstrate, if you'd like," I offered, reaching for my bag to grab sewing supplies.

"No," Lyssandra said. "I *know* how crafting classes work. I want you to prove you can do it. How can cutting cloth translate to killing monsters?"

I reached out to [Always Prepared]. The skill dropped a crate of sewing supplies onto the ground between us. I reached down and pulled it open, lifting up and presenting a sewing needle the size of a sword.

"With this," I said, not breaking eye contact with Lyssandra as she looked up from the needle to me.

"I made that!" Gerald said, happy to have something to contribute to the conversation.

Cinnamon barked.

"You're resourceful," Lyssandra said. She nodded to herself. "Good. You'll need that. Your initiative—the zero waste initiative, and the sets you've produced with it—that's good. The results are unbelievable. Dozens of levels across a workshop. Not exactly profitable. But unbelievable. Fantastic, even.

"All ateliers already meet or exceed the demand for their production, especially with low-level materials," she continued. "Creating more high-level tailors won't actually offer an economic benefit; the flood of supply will do the opposite, actually, lowering the value of the highest-ranked ateliers controlled by the Tailor Guild. It would be another story if the Wild degraded goods inside of our cities. However . . ."

Lyssandra rubbed the ring on her finger. For the first time, I saw a smile creep over her face.

"The other towns will be the first to suffer from us undercutting them."

"That's . . . cutthroat," I said.

"Our operations are expensive. Do you know how much we spend to support the Nobility who keep up our towns? Not to mention what we already invest in Nobles working through the Academy to secure stronger positions; those who align with our faction.

"We're barely able to keep the stretch of territory humanity has claimed under our protection, especially in the weakest second-tier cities. The Blooded Nobility have little to no interest in those regions; they're pawned off to promising Chosen. As long as rival factions control the most industrious and productive cities, we won't make any advances in our agenda." The carriage slowed and then stopped. "We're here."

Lyssandra pushed the door open.

We weren't at an estate or a manor or a garden or a restaurant. We were outside a dungeon.

"We can't afford to be anything less than cutthroat. So if you want our support, you have to prove you can earn it. Clear the dungeon. Without leaving it. Stay there for three days. We'll give you the most basic survival kit all Nobles would have . . . but that's it," Lyssandra said.

"Who is 'we'? What agenda are you talking about?" Sandy asked.

Lyssandra sighed. "There are many competing interest groups among the Nobility. Valjean and I represent a young faction of Chosen Nobles who are *trying* to improve the living conditions of the commoners. There's basically no money in doing that, you know?" Lyssandra sighed. "I sound like the Blooded Noble. I know, talking about profit over people's lives. But if you pass this test, you'll prove yourself to our faction. We can introduce you to others in time. Right now, your only task is to clear a dungeon. If you leave the dungeon before it's cleared, I'll assume that means you've given up."

"With no information about it?" Sandy asked.

"If you can't even do that much, how do you expect to be Nobles?"

The dungeon was almost familiar. Half-tended farmland stretched around us. Trees filled part of the field alongside rows of green wheat. Like the dungeon inside Stitch, it was a large field with a centerpiece. But unlike Stitch, the land was covered in rolling hills of golden grass. It was hotter here, almost muggy, and the upturned soil was a rich orange. A mountain sat in the distance. The dungeon's sun glinted off the lake in the center.

The first floor of this dungeon was far larger than in Stitch; this dungeon was in the second wall.

The dungeons in the first wall of Stitch had been horrid vistas that all seemed to align with an element: a wasteland of snow, a burning hellscape, a salted beach; this dungeon in the second wall of Spoke looked the same as the first dungeon I had entered. Just bigger.

It even held buildings—storage warehouses and tiny residences. There was no one inside; they looked long unoccupied and only intermittently maintained. The Wild did not reach here.

We stopped just a step inside.

I activated [Wardrobe] immediately, pulling out Sandy's battle armor. We had crafted her a set of Storm Curtain armor with my mom's help. It instilled a fantastic battle skill—Parry.

"What are we supposed to eat in here?" Gerald asked, looking around.

He was wearing his full set of armor, heavy enough to upturn the dirt at his feet. It was wholly unnecessary a single step into the dungeon.

"Monsters!" Sandy said. "I'm not as good a cook as Henri, but . . . wait, can we start a fire?" Sandy asked.

"They definitely gave us rations," I said. "Nobles probably bring a ton of prepared food for a stay in a dungeon."

The landscape rolled on around us. There was no one tending these farms; they likely just cleared the dungeon daily and mostly left the farms to themselves. The dungeon's accelerated time meant that they could farm year-round and harvest more quickly.

Not only that, but because the dungeon reset, they had to do less work to maintain the soil.

I dropped my bag to the ground. Lyssandra had given us three. "Standard Noble survival kit," she had said. We would get the same at the Academy.

"We should see what we have for supplies," I said.

Quite a lot, it turned out. All three bags came with rope, knives, tools—a tiny axe for cutting dead wood, a flint and steel for starting fires—but none of them came with a tent.

"Are we supposed to sleep outside?" Gerald asked. He sounded shocked.

"We can tie you to one of the branches," Sandy offered.

"Do you think I could climb a tree in my armor?" Gerald looked to one of the distant trees.

"I doubt any of the branches would survive an entire night," I said.

"We need hammocks," Gerald said. He sounded confident and determined.

"Are you going to make one out of metal?" Sandy asked.

"No! You guys make things out of leather, right?"

"Sure. You kill it and we'll do the rest of the work," Sandy offered.

Gerald stared for a second.

"I'll do my best," he said.

Gerald hadn't been overly involved in killing monsters with us. Mostly he absorbed their attacks. Which was appreciated. I couldn't absorb the monster's attacks uninjured. He also created our weapons and equipment—the giant sewing needle I used, the throwing needles, and most recently, a set of enchanted scissors that could grow to monster-killing size on command.

"Really?" Sandy asked. "Alright. You lead the way, then."

"Do we just . . ." Gerald looked off to the center as I packed the bag back up.

"Yeah! Lead the way." Sandy slapped Gerald on the back with a resounding metal thud.

We made our way to the lake. It was slightly downhill, but still, the dungeon was eerily similar to the one at the center of our town. Here in a second-tier city, the dungeon was just one of the outer segments of the walls; three floors that had to be cleared in one of eight dungeons spread around the perimeter of the settlement's walls.

The dungeon was almost the exact same size as the heart of Stitch. My own town's dungeon required an amount of effort that was expended here eight times over every day. And that was just for the side dungeons; the inner wall would have four dungeons that were exponentially harder, while the center would be the hardest of all, cleared nightly by an entire team of adventurers who could level buildings and outrace horses.

Each of them would be supplied with the resources of an entire town. Gear crafted by teams of peasants, of the highest level that amplified the Noble's power. Only the very best of the crafted materials would make their way to the elites. People like Valjean.

We reached the edge of the lake quickly.

"I don't think there's going to be wolves here," Gerald said, looking around as if he would spot an enemy on the horizon.

"Eyes on the water," Sandy said.

Gerald's armored head swiveled to the lake.

It was hard to see anything in the water with the sun glaring off it.

"The monster is in there?"

"It's likely," I said.

"It's not coming out," Sandy commented.

"Can you see it?" I asked.

"Yeah. Here." Sandy passed me a skinning knife.

[Sandy Butcher is offering to share buff [Butcher Vision] with you. Accept?] [Y\N]

I accepted the prompt instantly out of habit. Sandy's Butcher Vision buff revealed the weaknesses of a monster; a set of lines along its back and side where it would be easiest to both split open and preserve the most material for later use.

It worked whether the monster was dead or alive.

At the bottom of the lake some distance away, I observed a set of long, stretching red lines. I couldn't see what it was. The sun's glare burned my eyes as I tried to look past it and see the monster lurking below.

I pulled free one of the throwing needles I kept on my belt. A loop of thread was attached to the end of each, allowing me to use [Thread Mastery] to control it. It was one of the skills I had been working on before Valjean interrupted us.

I was even better at it now.

"I'm going to pull it up. Gerald, are you ready?"

"I'm ready!" he said. He summoned his shield—a gigantic block of enchanted steel several inches thick—and stabbed it into the ground in front of him, leaning against it. I stepped to his side and threw the needle into the water.

Water splashed up as I threw it with preternatural force and accuracy. The entire form of the monster, revealed by red lines, flinched upward.

"Hit! It's coming." I stabbed Sandy's knife into the ground, losing vision, and pulled out my enchanted scissors.

[Mana: 9/10]

Each activation of the scissors lowered my mana. As did each use of my skills.

"It's here!" Sandy shouted.

Gerald shouted over the splashing. A red pulse shot out from Gerald's core in all directions. The monster—an alligator—turned instantly, slamming into Gerald's shield.

Gerald's enchanted set rebounded damage to anything that hit it. The alligator's teeth scraped ineffectually along the shield, and flailed backward.

I stabbed down with the scissors, aiming for the red line that Sandy's buff had revealed, and activated [Pattern Mirroring].

The skill consumed another point of mana. I pulled on the pattern of the Shell Dress. [Pattern Mirroring] multiplied my cuts. Where I stabbed down into the alligator, a second cut erupted on the other side, blood leaking out as I moved with inhuman grace to repeatedly close the scissors over the alligator.

A giant wound tore open on each side of the monster. It flinched back. I heard Sandy sprint up behind me, but before she reached me, I lifted the scissors up.

I didn't activate a skill or use any special ability. I just stabbed downward into the head of the alligator. It stopped moving instantly.

"Is it dead?" Gerald asked. He was behind his shield, in a position where he couldn't see the alligator. The doorway to the next floor glowed to life in reply. It stood just off the lake shore.

"It's dead," I said.

Gerald looked around his shield at the corpse of the alligator. It was a mix of mottled green and brown.

"Do we have to eat that?"

"Lizards taste good," Sandy said, almost defensive.

"Is the whole dungeon going to be this easy?" Gerald asked.

"Don't say that!" Sandy shouted. "You'll jinx us."

"We're still on the first floor. It only gets harder as we go deeper," I said. "And we don't know how many floors the dungeon has. Sandy, we should—"

"Yeah," she said, needing no reminder to lean down and begin to field dress the alligator. I didn't know the details, but her butcher skills meant the meat would be safe and preserved. At least for as long as it would concern us.

"What if the monsters on the next floor are bugs again?" Sandy asked.

"What are the odds?" I asked. "Gerald, could you lead the way?"

"Will it be dangerous?" he asked, looking at the entrance to the next floor.

"It won't be totally safe. Which the entrance to this floor was, by the way," Sandy said, staring accusatorily at Gerald's heavy armor. He had a tendency to overreact to the threat of dungeons.

"The dungeons are all dangerous. You can't blame me for being prepared," Gerald replied. But he ripped his shield from the ground and made his way to the archway that led to the next floor. The shield was too wide to fit through the doorway. He tried turning sideways, then tsked before recalling the shield to his inventory. It disappeared in a flash.

With as much time as Gerald had spent at the forges of Foundry, I had half expected to see him with a new suit of armor. I supposed he probably wasn't able to mine his own ore. There was likely much less to spare from the forges.

We crossed through the threshold to the second floor.

Walls swept forward away from us, choking out the sky. We stood in one canyon, on the precipice above a deeper one. Caves pocked the sides. Trees and brush clung to life in the sandy walls. The ground shifted under our feet.

Gerald stopped only a few steps in, holding up his shield.

The walls around us seemed practically unassailable, giving us only a thin view of the sky above. The deep blue contrasted with the red and orange cliffs rising around us. The wind disturbed dust and rocks; it rained pebbles.

Below the precipice, there was a smaller canyon cut into the earth. Plants grew there, though there was no water to be seen. Steep ramps led down to it.

Five smooth orbs of shining black and purple crawled around below. From here, they looked small, but I guessed they were large up close. Each of them had a set of horns; the sharp ends didn't point forward, but to the side. They looked like they might be for ramming rather than stabbing.

"On the second floor of the Stitch dungeon, there was a dark forest full of spiders in the tall trees. Looks like it's bugs again," Sandy said. "Gerald, you want to eat these instead of alligator?"

"No!" he half shouted.

Sandy patted him on the back, and he stepped forward, moving away from the entrance as we stared down into the valley.

"The dungeon has weird sets of patterns," I commented. "Bugs again. Those things look huge."

I sighed. I wouldn't be able to make anything good out of them.

They looked to be at least as large as the wolves in Stitch's dungeon had been. Pitch-black beetles featuring horns that split in two crawled around, crunching on the few remaining plants that clung to the bottom of the canyon. Ice formed in the shadow cast by the canyon's side, left behind from a chilly desert night.

We slid down into the canyon—literally. Scrambling down the rocky slides, we hurtled into the shaded area of the canyon's inner wall.

"Gerald, you go first," Sandy said. She was half-hunched, not taking her eyes off the distant beetles.

Gerald took a deep breath to steady himself.

"I've got this," Gerald said, resummoning his shield and moving behind the massive wall of steel.

He was lucky he had a true Noble's stats. Either of us would have been exhausted carrying that hunk of metal forward. Gerald stopped occasionally and glanced around to make sure he was still heading the right way. I didn't blame him.

I stood to his left while Sandy stood to his right, both of us a bit behind him. As soon as we neared the first beetle, it let out an insectoid screech and charged.

"Ready?" I asked Sandy.

"Ready!" she said.

The beetle opened its shell, revealing wings that buzzed in a horrid high-pitched noise. It sounded like an entire swarm, lifting itself up and up . . . and then stopping just an inch above the ground, hovering angrily and strafing in midair. The beetle blurred, slamming into Gerald's shield with a crunching thud. There was a flash of purple light as Gerald's enchantment's activated.

The beetle landed a dozen feet away, dazed. Its horn was chipped. It retracted its wings.

I stepped forward, planning to run and stab it, when Sandy put a hand on my shoulder. I had been so focused on that individual monster that I didn't see the other four all charging through the dusty valley.

There was a series of metallic bangs as insect after insect impacted Gerald's shield just to be flung back in a flash of purple.

"Guys?" Gerald asked, sounding panicked. "I don't know how long this enchantment will last . . . Guys?"

CHAPTER 9

"Shit," Sandy said, swinging at one of the bugs as it recuperated and charged Gerald's shield. Her butcher knife bit into chitin before sliding away from the rounded edge of the bug.

Without using my skill, I tried to stab one of the insects before it hit the shield, aiming to conserve my mana. But floating in the air, they were fast and agile, and diverted from Gerald toward me, forcing me to duck back. I gave up on conserving mana and activated [Running Stitch].

The enhanced thrust of Running Stitch pierced chitin with ease, spilling acid-green insect blood across the sand.

In the end, we burned mana and skills to slay all five of the titanic beetles. The three of us panted in the harsh sunlight. I covered my eyes from the glare glinting off the shells of the bugs.

"Alright, Gerald. Collect our dinner," Sandy said, still winded.

"You're joking," Gerald said, turning to Sandy. Then he turned back to me. "She is joking, right?"

I smiled wryly.

"You did say you didn't want to eat the gator."

Gerald looked at the bugs.

"You jinxed us," he said to Sandy.

She shrugged.

"I used up more than half of my mana," I said, frowning as I stared at the field of corpses. This fight shouldn't have been so hard, but the monsters were unfamiliar. "We need a better plan to fight them."

I rolled a corpse over. They had tiny, buggy limbs, a dozen of them decorating their underside, ending in sharp points covered in dirt and sand.

"A tripwire, maybe?" Sandy asked, leaning over to inspect the bug with me. Gerald stayed farther back.

"They fly just above the ground when they charge. Just a trip wire isn't enough," I said. "And I don't know if we'd be able to pull aggro one at a time . . ."

I poked it again.

"But maybe I could place the tripwire and then manipulate the thread to catch them?" I asked. "I need more levels of Trapping. That's what I should work on while I'm here."

"Don't you need to make a whole outfit for that?" Gerald asked, puzzled.

"Yeah, but we do have three days."

"You're going to craft one in here? In the dungeon?"

I knocked on the chitin shell of the insect.

"I bet this is good material."

"You want 'em?" Sandy asked. Before I even replied, a set of floating butchering tools—or at least the ghostly image of them—hovered in the air above her.

Harvesting the bugs took only seconds by Sandy's experienced hand. In Stitch, Valjean had kept a flow of half-field-dressed monster corpses, trickling Sandy's level upward, which gave her plenty of experience for working on a ton of different monsters.

"We don't need the . . ." she looked up at me, tentatively asking if I wanted anything else from . . . inside the monster.

We had previously collected acid from spiders, giving it to an alchemist who took up painting in her spare time.

I shook my head in the negative. "Just the shell," I replied.

Gerald and I brought the monster corpses to her while she worked, and then we had six husks of beetles ready to work with.

We left them in the center of the second floor.

"Let's at least scout out the third floor," I said.

The third floor of every dungeon was a boss with some kind of mechanic. In Stitch's dungeon, there was a bright purple bear that couldn't cross over running water. At least, not quickly.

We would have to discover what the mechanic of this dungeon was on our own. If we had visited Lyssandra's city first or known about the challenge, we could have read up on it. The entire town's dungeon would've been documented, I was sure.

But a real Noble claiming a new territory around a Wild Dungeonheart wouldn't have that option. Founding your own city would involve exploring an untouched dungeon. That was what Lyssandra wanted to see—if we were truly up to the task of being proper Nobles.

So to the third floor we went.

At Stitch's dungeon, the doors between floors had remained closed because no one had maintained the dungeon; eventually, the barrier that resisted the degrading property of the Wild would have sunk back into the dungeon, and the entire town would've crumbled away.

Here, the door to the third floor was ready and open. It was likely that Nobles had visited this dungeon as recently as yesterday.

We stepped through a bone-white archway at the end of the valley and into a muggy heat.

The distant horizon was occluded by smoke, as if there was a distant forest fire. Around us were dead and burnt trees, bending in the wind, and dozens of tiny mountain peaks over craggy stone. Almost no foliage clung to life in the heat of the crag. Overhead, dark clouds swirled menacingly. But there was no rain.

In the dungeon of Stitch, the third floor had been a sunken arena, far and distant from the boss. Here, in a third-tier dungeon on the outer ring of a second-tier city, we entered and immediately stared into the eyes of the boss.

A gigantic black goat stared menacingly as it crunched on a dead plant. Its horns curled backward. Static electricity flashed and arced along its fur. It sparked so much it looked almost like a half-invisible forcefield glowed around the goat.

Yellow eyes glared at us, unblinking. It was almost done eating the tiny amount of foliage that remained.

"Gerald, get your shield," I said.

"Lightning?" Sandy asked. She sounded excited, though; dressed in the Storm Curtain set, she had insanely high Lightning Resistance. It was probably higher than Gerald's, even with his armor.

The goat continued chewing. It swallowed menacingly.

It bleated. The flickering aura of electricity dancing on its fur disappeared as its horns began to glow brighter and brighter.

A second set of eyes opened beneath the top two, bright yellow with barely any sclera visible.

And then the goat charged.

It was a streak of lightning across the crags, appearing below us in an instant. It didn't attack Gerald's shield—Sandy was in front of him.

And when it approached, I saw her [Parry].

The skill was built into the Storm Curtain armor she wore; it was designed for it.

The monster's horns crashed into the gigantic, modified butcher blade that Gerald had made for her. The sky rumbled.

Lightning flashed into the [Parry], exactly where Sandy's blade had made contact, and the skill parried that, too.

The goat rolled down the cliff, fur singed and bleating.

"Nope, absolutely not," I said, sliding down the cliff to try to end this and kill the monster in one go. We were not dealing with a goat that could smite us.

I still didn't know what the monster's actual mechanic was, outside of the lightning, and I didn't want to find out, but as I stabbed down with [Running Stitch], I did anyway.

When the monster hit the bottom of the hill and began to stand, the sparks dancing around its body reappeared, and when I stabbed toward it, a shield of sparking electricity and light blocked the attack. [Running Stitch] slid off the side of the monster.

The goat bleated. The side of its face was damaged from the entire charge of lightning being reflected into it. The monster stood . . . and ran away.

I turned and ran back up the tiny mountain toward the archway.

"Back out!" I said.

Sandy nodded, and Gerald was already running as we crossed out of the gate and back into the second floor.

"What was that?" Gerald asked.

"The goat is immune to attacks except for the moment after it charges. Or at least, really resistant to them. It felt like Running Stitch hit a wall. I don't think we can break the shield."

"Did you *see* that!?" Sandy asked, ripping her helmet off. "I parried *lightning*. Way more impressive than the lava."

"That was terrifying," Gerald said. He had resummoned his shield from his inventory and stared at the archway behind us.

"The monster isn't coming up the floor," I said. "Come on, let's grab these bug shells and go make dinner."

"We're done, just like that?" Sandy said.

"We need more mana and a better plan," I said.

The alligator corpse, already field dressed, was right where we'd left it on the first floor. I helped Sandy tie a rope to it to drag it. Gerald helped us carry the insect shells.

"Where should we make camp?" I asked.

"The ground is kind of wet," Sandy said.

"That tree?" I asked, pointing.

We headed over to a gigantic tree on the first floor. Sprawling branches wide enough to sit on stretched above us. Sandy started gathering rocks for a firepit.

I inspected the rations that came with our packs. They were some kind of hard-packed dry food. It was like biting into a rock. I threw them back into my bag dismissively.

"Give me your travel packs," I said.

Sandy and Gerald handed me theirs, and I slung them over my shoulders. The weight accumulated quickly. I turned to the tree.

I tested the bark experimentally. It was easy enough to bury my fingers into its cracks. My Dexterity had hit superhuman levels long ago; I scaled the side of the tree until I reached a branch, then I pulled out the rope from my bag and hung the packs.

"What are you doing?" Gerald asked.

"Keeping our packs off the ground," I said. It was common sense. "We have food inside them."

"Do you think the alligator is going to go for those?" Sandy asked from the ground. She was shoveling dirt out of the firepit using her monster-killing knife.

"Hey! You're going to dull the edge . . ." Gerald complained. He hadn't noticed until that moment.

"Isn't it enchanted?" Sandy asked, her expression genuinely perplexed. "It can take it."

"You guys are insane," Gerald said. "Are you going to get the tents out?" He looked up at me when he asked.

I peered down at Gerald from a tree branch. The tree was devoid of leaves; their crumbling remains littered the ground around him, crunching under his footsteps.

"Tents?" Sandy asked.

"Yeah! We . . ." Gerald stopped. "We don't have tents, do we?"

I smiled at him.

"You want to be on the ground with the alligator?" I asked. "It's going to respawn in three days."

"In three days?" Gerald asked. Then he froze. I could imagine his expression behind his armor. "We're staying in the dungeon the whole time. Isn't that dangerous?"

"We've done it before. It's no big deal."

Gerald's head went side to side nervously. "I'm climbing up," he said.

He tried to repeat my climb, but his metal gauntlets tore gashes in the wood, unable to support the massive weight of both his body and the plate armor that covered him.

"I don't think that's going to work," I said.

Gerald clenched his hands multiple times, looking around again.

"Boo!" Sandy shouted behind him.

Gerald didn't react. "Very funny. Okay, I get it."

Gerald recalled his armor to his inventory. He still looked incredibly tense. I didn't blame him for being afraid of the monsters. That goat on the third floor even shook me.

As I watched Gerald climb the tree, I felt pride instead of derision. He slowly and carefully sat next to me, staring down.

"Courage isn't not being afraid," I said. "It's being able to confront fear."

"Can I have some rope to tie myself to the tree?" Gerald asked. "I don't want to fall."

I handed him a line of rope wordlessly before slipping down to help Sandy build a fire pit. We had to gather dry wood; the dead branches under the tree wouldn't last forever. I helped gather branches for the fire as the sky started to darken in the dungeon world. Gerald eventually climbed down and helped gather more wood and flat stones for cooking on.

"Is this still not enough wood?" he asked.

"We need enough for several nights," Sandy said. "It can get really cold in the dungeons."

Eventually, the pile of dead wood was almost as tall as I was. Gerald even dragged over a felled tree.

I looked between the husks of the insects and the alligator leather. We would need to build a makeshift tanning rack. It was time to spend the points I had.

Three entire levels had accumulated without me investing any points in either patterns or skills.

Good quality made better clothing and armor as well.

Every time I selected a pattern, the system presented me with three options. Once I spent my points, I would get different options.

[Pattern Shop]

▶[COMMON] Seeder's Uniform (Basic)

Grants bonus to Constitution and Strength. Grants set bonus skill based on craft quality and materials used.

▶[RARE] Scavenger Pattern (Advanced)

Grants bonus to Constitution and Perception. Grants Scavenger skills depending on craft quality and materials used. Scavenger skills allow the user to locate and harvest Resources more easily.

▶[COMMON] Nomad Pattern (Basic)

Grants bonus to Constitution and Speed. Grants skill that reduces resource consumption and improves human endurance depending on craft quality and materials used.

None of what was available interested me. Instead, I looked at Crafting I. The skill ostensibly didn't offer me any advantages in fighting as I upgraded my level in it. At the time, I didn't really have the privilege to invest in it, and I hadn't estimated how much it would be worth.

When Sandy's general skill, Butchering, reached level ten, she started gaining permanent attributes from each harvest. I suspected that Crafting would do something similar.

But I needed to invest nine entire levels to find out.

I would have to craft a lot of patterns to make up for it. I doubted I'd have the extra time to build anything else in just three days.

I dumped all three points into Crafting.

When I had first received my class, I had felt the gaze of an alien presence too large to understand. I hadn't sensed it again since. There were a lot of odd things about the system—it was magic, obviously, even if we often used it to do mundane things like stitching.

But every time I assembled a pattern, the memories of the first person to craft from the pattern and embed it into the system would fill me as I worked on it. I wondered what conditions the human nomads lived in.

Because, as far as I knew, no human could survive long-term roaming the Wilds; at least, not a Noble. Their armor and weapons would break down eventually, no matter what enchantments they used to make them endure longer. So where did these nomadic humans live? In the dungeons?

"Have you ever heard of someone having a Scavenger class?" I asked Sandy.

Sandy shook her head. "I haven't heard of most classes," she said with a shrug.

On the first night, we stayed up late, discussing our approach to the third-floor boss. Before we risked fighting it, we needed to mitigate the amount of resources we spent on the second floor. I fell asleep to the sound of the crackling fire.

* * *

"The alligator's not back?" Gerald asked, walking carefully around the pond.

"Course not," Sandy said. "The dungeon restarts every night, for the floor above it—that would be outside the dungeon for this floor. So the door to leave the dungeon back to Spoke is closed. Takes three days from our view. But the floor below us also resets every night."

I nodded along.

"So we're going to go down there and kill the bugs every day?" Gerald asked. "I'm not even getting experience from them."

"They're probably just not worth any," I replied, taking the first step into the second floor of the dungeon and stopping to survey the monster-filled valley below me. Sand sailed in the slow and rolling winds of the dungeon.

"We need to practice killing them so that we can do it more efficiently," I said. A wooden box fell to the ground as I activated [Always Prepared] and retrieved my two sewing needles. The night before, I had tied together a tiny, thin thread—leftovers from what we had harvested from the giant spiders in our own dungeon.

"You think this will work?" Gerald asked. "You'll not have your needles."

"I'll still have my throwing needles. And the scissors," I replied.

"I'm here, too," Sandy said, holding out one of her knives as if to indicate that she, too, could kill monsters.

I changed into the Hunter set to maximize my levels in Trapping. The set gave me a skill from the hunter class—an improved proficiency with laying traps. It was also extremely hot and heavy.

This second pattern I had made from the bear-like monster, the boss of the Stitch dungeon's third floor, and in its wet and rainy climate, it had been perfectly comfortable. Here, the sun beat down, and it was sweltering in the cloak.

I slid down into the valley and got to work regardless.

I stabbed one of the two needles into the ground before me, then crossed the valley until the line went taught and stabbed down the second.

A near-invisible line of thread crossed the distance between the two needles. I kept my eyes on the beetles while I worked. They dug around, chewing on the sand-filled valley's scraggly plants.

The Trapping skill nearly sang to me. I shifted the needle, pulling the line up, then looked up at Gerald.

He nodded to me and put the shield between himself and the closest beetle. Yesterday, when we had aggroed one, the rest came.

"Ready?" I asked.

"Ready," Sandy said.

I switched into my outfit with the best stats for fighting before launching one of the sewing needles, flinging it out like a dart. The string tied to its end unspooled.

It thudded into the side of a beetle only a stone's toss away. I hadn't expected to actually pierce the bug; I had expected the needle to bounce off its chitin shell. Instead, the needle sank inches deep through the chitin.

It made a horrible hissing noise and started to fly, hovering over the ground and shooting toward me.

I stepped back. Gerald braced his shield. I readied the giant pair of scissors in my hands.

The bug's wings clipped the thin wire string, sending it tumbling into the ground. The beetle rolled on its back.

Sandy stabbed down with her knife with razor precision, splitting the bug in two.

"It worked!" I shouted.

"I hope it works on the rest of them!" Sandy shouted back.

The other five beetles were already flying toward us.

Gerald braced his shield, but there was practically no need—four of the five remaining beetles slammed into the wire, tumbling onto their backs, their wings broken.

Sandy activated her skill, beheading the beetle that managed to fly over the line.

We cleaned up the beetles with ease, then harvested the shells.

"How's our mana?" I asked, looking over at Sandy.

"Basically full," Sandy said. "Got at least two Parry uses left."

When we did our final clear of Stitch for the quest for town ownership, we were chugging what amounted to mana potions in the form of soup made by Sandy's dad. We didn't have that luxury here; none of us had a cooking class or anything that we could use to make restorative items.

We had to make every drop of mana count.

Luckily, we only had to clear one dungeon, and only to the third floor.

Sandy took her Storm Curtain helmet off, shaking her head to release her hair. Then she bent down and started cutting apart the beetles.

Gerald dismissed his armor, and I stared at him. He practically never took his armor off in the dungeon. He was becoming more comfortable.

Still, it directly contradicted the look of concern and disgust on his face as he watched Sandy work, cutting the beetles into sections like butchering any other animal. She threw the bug meat onto the soil.

"Sorry, we're not eating those? Are we?" Gerald asked.

I laughed.

"I get attribute points by butchering lots of new creatures now," Sandy said. "I got it when I reached tier ten on one of my skills."

Gerald looked queasy at the sight. I could hardly blame him. It was grisly. Sandy worked without any of the careful attention she used on our shared hunts; she hacked and cut into the bug without remorse, scattering broken pieces of leg and less-useful chitin.

It only took a few minutes before she was done, rising to her feet and wiping her forehead.

"Woo. An entire point in speed." Her smile was grim, but present. I handed her Storm Curtain helmet to her. She slipped it on.

"Onto the goat," I said.

"Wait." Gerald interrupted before I could walk forward. "I . . . think I can do more this time."

CHAPTER 10

Storm clouds boiled above us on the third floor of Spoke's outer dungeon. We stared down a very angry goat.

It was chewing on . . . something. I could be convinced it was chewing a mouthful of rocks judging by its robotic crunching.

Its eyes were an electric yellow, glowing in the dimness of this half-lit dungeon world.

It roared in the way a goat does, its second pair of eyes splitting open, and lightning danced around its curling horns. Then it charged.

Sandy [Parried] and we ran to catch up with its body. Gerald ran with heavy thudding, carrying hundreds of pounds of plate steel with apparent ease. I nearly stopped as I saw that he had dismissed his shield.

He raised both hands above his head as we stopped before the downed goat, and in his clawed hands, a mace appeared.

It looked almost crude. The metal was pig iron with an uneven texture, the end a giant bulbous shape of roughly forged iron. I doubted it would remain in one piece if it wasn't enchanted. And it was *huge*. The head of the mace was as large as Gerald in his armor.

He huffed, and the mace slowly fell toward the goat. It was more like a helium balloon than a proper steel weapon. It landed with a soft, inaudible bonk while the goat's shield was still disabled. I held up my scissors to charge in, unsure of what Gerald's enchantment on the weapon would do.

The goat's shield reappeared with a flicker of sparking electricity, an impermeable barrier that pushed the mace back just a touch before it hit the goat.

Then the ground beneath the goat exploded. Shrapnel and stone shot into the air as the mace suddenly amplified several times in weight, shooting upward and out of Gerald's hands. The goat made noises of rage beneath the mace.

The three of us stared for a moment. Wind whistled over the desolate terrain of craggy peaks and dry earth. Lightning rained down onto the mace, slamming down into the goat, whose voice was now mixed with terror. But its own shield didn't disappear. The earth was torn to pieces where it flailed its limbs, sending waves of dirt and dust up into the air.

It wasn't getting out from under the mace.

"So . . ." Gerald said. "Is it going to die by its own lightning?"

"When did you make a giant mace?" Sandy asked.

"In Foundry!" Gerald said. "All that time at the workshops?"

"It *looks* like it was made in Foundry," Sandy said. "How long will the enchantment last?"

Gerald stared at the mace. "I think the lightning is charging the enchantment. So . . . a while? They wouldn't let me have any of the good metal." Gerald took a hesitant step forward as he spoke. "Do we . . . attack it now?"

"I think we leave," I said. "Let the dungeon reset."

"But my mace . . ." Gerald said.

The lightning hitting the mace intensified, yellow arms striking the ground around it. I felt my hair charge with static electricity.

"It'll be here when we come back," Sandy said.

We turned and left through the portal door. All of our expeditions to the third floor had ended remarkably quickly, only a step through.

"Sorry, guys," Gerald said, despondent as we crossed into the second floor.

"No, you did great," I said. "We can definitely use this . . . we just need a better way to do it."

"Like if Gerald attacked while it charged me instead of me Parrying. Do you think you can make it heavier mid-swing?" Sandy asked. "That *is* what the mace does, right? Makes itself heavier?"

Gerald nodded. "I'm . . . not sure if I can increase the weight mid-swing. I can try."

"Tomorrow, we should grab the mace and practice," I said. "We have time to get it right. And then maybe I have a skill that can help us."

I made the Hunter outfit twice—once out of the Darkness-aligned wolves from the first floor in Stitch, and once out of the light element bear boss of the third floor. The first-floor version granted me stealth skills, letting me hide, and the third-floor version gave me a skill called Projection— one that allowed me to create a facsimile of myself.

If we used those together, I could probably get the goat to charge at a fake target.

"Don't we only have a day left?" Gerald asked.

"No. We still have three," I said. "It hasn't even been a day on the outside since we entered. Three days will pass outside the dungeon before the door to the city opens back up," I said.

Sandy gave us each a serving of the smoked alligator jerky she had made the day before. We had enough that we wouldn't be forced to make rations.

As I ate, I started working on a set of armor scrapped together from alligator leather and bug chitin. It would be anything but comfortable . . . and ugly to boot. I mostly focused on cutting leather pieces for padding; the material was hard, stiff and inflexible. I would take its skills and attribute points and shove it away in my Wardrobe, never to be seen again.

The next morning, our third day in the dungeon, the alligator respawned and we ate fresh alligator for breakfast. It would still be another twenty-four hours in dungeon time before the gate opened.

We were preparing for our first serious try at killing the goat. The last two had been experimental. Now we had a plan.

I set up two levels of tripwires for the beetles. Today, none of them got around us.

We'd set up the alligator leather to tan on the second floor. Leaving it overnight made it faster. Much of it was ready now.

But first we descended again to the third floor.

"Are we ready?" I asked, standing outside the gate to the third floor. The goat was always waiting, always ready to charge us.

Sandy lifted her giant knife, nodding in assent. Gerald gave a stiff nod, too, hard to recognize through the thick plate armor.

"Are we sure the club will be there?" Gerald asked. "And the goat will be gone from under it?"

"We're sure," Sandy said.

I counted down.

"Three . . . two . . . one . . ."

I sprinted left the second I ran through the gate. With a mental tug, I used [Shadow Cloak]. Darkness stuck to me, solid and inky, its veil of darkness surrounding me. The effect could be dispelled by mundane light, but as long as I remained at least semi-occluded in shadow, I was practically invisible.

It worked perfectly under the cloudy sky of the third floor.

The goat wasn't even looking my way as I sprinted forward. It patted at the ground and tossed its head, horns sparkling as it stared down Sandy.

Gerald ran to my right, scooping up his mace.

The goat charged Sandy. She [Parried]. The goat rolled backward, slapped by its own lightning.

Gerald ran toward me, almost comical as he carried a mace larger than he was above his head.

"Gwen!?" Gerald asked, panicked.

"Here!" I said.

He stomped over and leveled the mace. I activated [Projection] and ran out of the way.

Projection left behind a hazy image of myself standing, a working decoy.

Gerald stared nervously at the goat as it stood, still facing Sandy.

"Get its attention!" I hissed to Gerald.

The goat rose to its feet, then charged Sandy again, crossing the landscape in a brilliant flash.

"Gerald!" Sandy said, voice rising and panicked. We only had two Parries. The goat rolled back toward Gerald. It was slightly uphill from him.

"Hey, uh—ugly!" Gerald shouted, slamming the mace down into the hill. The ground exploded from the force, and dirt and stone rolled down toward Gerald. Gerald backed up, but the goat was looking his way now.

There was just one slight problem. It was preparing to charge into Gerald and not the projection. I panicked, hesitating. I couldn't tank the attack for him. Maybe Sandy could, but she was on the other side of us. I activated [Projection] again, but the goat took no heed of the new decoy.

Should I get the goat's attention myself?

I was still panicking when the goat charged.

A bonking noise echoed through the third floor of the dungeon. Gerald swung the mace, the weight increasing mid-swing.

There was a distant splat.

Sandy raced to get behind Gerald.

"Gwen?" she asked.

"I'm here!" I replied.

We all waited.

But nothing came. Multiple minutes passed.

[+4 XP]

"It's dead?" I asked. I dismissed [Shadow Cloak], feeling my shoulders suddenly relax. The two Projections of myself had already flickered out by the time we got the experience notice.

Sandy made a noise of relief.

"I hope it's in one piece," she said.

We hiked across the rugged terrain of the third floor. Though this was only a three-floor dungeon, each of the floors was much larger than the ones in Stitch—likely because it was in the outermost wall of the city Spoke. The central dungeon would go deeper and deeper, growing with the city as it was cleared and harvested.

Craggy gray rock and gravel crunched beneath my feet over dry earth as we headed in the direction the goat had been flung. Gerald had managed to send it soaring in an upward arc. We found it in a puddle of its own blood. Interestingly, its coat still sparked.

I got zapped the first time I touched it; the magic coat of the monster released charged, accumulated static electricity. Though, the sparking magic on its fur dimmed afterwards. The charge slowly built up as I pulled my hand away.

Sandy tied a rope to it and dragged it back after field dressing it.

"You did amazing, Gerald," I commented idly as we ascended the dungeon. "But you can probably put the mace away, now."

"Oh. Right!" Gerald said. He recalled the mace. "In the end, it wasn't too tough."

"You're a proper Noble," Sandy said. "Our stats won't match yours as easily."

I continued staring forward. The goat boss gave us four experience points. Enough that I would level if I killed it two more times. I could level again if I killed it another five times.

On the first floor of the dungeon, three days would pass for every day on the surface in Spoke. Today was just our second day in the dungeon; we could kill the goat exactly seven more times. But why stop there?

If we bypassed the first floor and started on the second, we could kill the dungeon boss twenty-one times.

"Oh no," Gerald said.

"What is it?" Sandy asked, crouching low and clutching her knife. Her head whipped back and forth.

"She's planning something," Gerald said. "Look at her face."

I smiled.

Lyssandra tsked, pouring over accounting books in her stately office. Accountants and assistants worked through piles of books. Spoke operated as a major trading hub; it produced far fewer goods than Foundry, instead making a profit through careful regulation of tariffs. Like Foundry, it had taken massive loans to build its rail network. Spoke's rails, however, were much more extensive, connecting a dozen towns to its own beating heart.

Lyssandra was already halfway to paying them off purely through careful management of her domain.

"We still need to increase tariffs on dungeonborn imports across this entire category," she said, flipping through an account book with superhuman speed and unerring accuracy.

"Doing that will massively reduce our textile output," an accountant across from her complained.

"It will be worth it," Lyssandra replied. Then she stilled as a knock on the door interrupted her. She mentally flipped through what it could be. Most events that would permit someone to solicit her mid-meeting were emergencies.

There was one recent event she was waiting for news on, however, but she found it incredibly unlikely. Gwen's party should not have cleared the dungeon boss on the first day. If Gwen was smart, they would likely spend the first six days or more simply preparing for the boss on the third floor. They would need every advantage they could get to fight the boss head on.

Lyssandra closed her eyes and hoped that Valjean's latest prospects hadn't died.

"Come in," she said, eyes still closed.

"Reporting to the Lady Lyssandra." The Noble who entered was an older man, scarred and thin and reedy. He wore clothing that didn't seem to befit Nobles at all; leather fur hung in strips from his armor. His hair was an oily black that dripped around his shoulders, but his close-cropped beard was a messy salt and pepper.

Ak was the first of the three Nobles assigned to secretly watch over the group in the dungeon. She couldn't actually let them die, of course.

"How bad is it, Ak?" Lyssandra asked.

Ak paused. He looked confused for a moment. Then he shook it away. "Reporting . . . The sixth dungeon was successfully cleared to the third floor."

Lyssandra was still tense, braced to hear how bad it was. It took her a moment to process his reply.

"What?" she asked. "Repeat that, please."

"The sixth dungeon has been cleared by the vagrant Nobles invited by the Lady Lyssandra," Ak said.

Lyssandra slumped back in her chair.

"On the third day?"

"On the second, my Lady. The vagrant Nobles use . . . unique weapons. I believe it endowed them an advantage."

Lyssandra leaned forward now, rearranging the stack of books in front of her. She rapidly searched through dozens of them.

"Did I send them to the wrong dungeon?" she asked.

"The dungeon manifest is here, ma'am," one of the accountants said, shoving a leatherbound tome toward her.

Lyssandra flipped through it, confirming that this was the dungeon with the Stormhorn—a dangerous species of goat. One that had killed many lesser Nobles early in their careers. In the deeper floors of central dungeons, they could become regular mobs, faced in entire hordes, but to new Nobles they represented a massive challenge even as individuals.

"How injured are they?" Lyssandra asked, looking up. She stood. "Do they need the attention of a life mage?"

"They are uninjured. However, I believe environmental stressors are degrading their morale. It remains to be seen whether they have the steel to persist."

Lyssandra relaxed again. Very few Nobles were ready for the reality of roughing it in the Wild or dungeons. Very few humans ever spent any time outside the safe zones provided by the dungeons—and for good reason. Besides degrading everything that made humanity what it was, the Wild was full of dangerous monsters. So it should be no surprise that most would find themselves uncomfortable.

"Good. Good. Let's see if they have that as well, then." She leaned back, rubbing the circles under her eyes. "Valjean is a crazy bastard."

CHAPTER 11

The material from the goat was hard to work with. It seemed to slowly accumulate electricity, discharging it whenever it was touched. Eventually, we figured out that grounding it with some metal let it discharge steadily into the ground, preventing any sudden shock.

We moved our camp to the second floor. There weren't any fitting trees here, but we roamed farther from the valley and found a tiny cave in the rocks.

And we found out that the goat meat was, in fact, fantastic.

I tipped my little canteen of water all the way back, drinking it empty. We were nearly out of water after three days here; this little environment hadn't produced any rain at all.

"We're almost out of water," I said.

"We should stay on the first floor," Gerald complained.

"No way," Sandy said.

It had been three days since our first kill of the goat from our perspective, and we had killed the goat again each night that followed.

"We need to do something," Gerald complained. "So thirsty. Can't you make more waterskins?"

I looked at the little canteen.

"I think if I did all the water would leak right out."

"I can make one," Sandy said. She plopped over into the dirt next to us. "But you're not going to like it."

"Please," Gerald said.

"Sure. Next time we kill the goat."

We went to the first floor first, refilling the canteens and water cans we'd brought with us in the small stream.

We killed the alligator and Sandy field dressed it. Gerald was becoming increasingly comfortable in his role as a fighter, even gaining some confidence in moving forward to attack the goat. He still made it very clear he didn't like it.

He just wanted to work a forge. I could respect that. But he stepped up now, when it mattered.

We finished off the rest of the dungeon for the day, killing the bugs and the goat and cooking a dinner out of gator. Sandy presented us with two organs after. Gerald flinched back from them.

"I'm not eating that," he said.

"They're not for eating." Sandy rolled her eyes. "They're—"

"Waterskins," I said, staring at them. I carefully took one of the organs, cringing at the squishy texture. "I'll tie some leather into shape around them. Thanks!"

I stared at the waterskins for a long moment.

"No more ideas!" Gerald said.

"I'm just thinking that I could probably make us more than just sets of clothing," I said aloud.

"Like what?" Gerald asked.

"You'll see."

On the third day, the three vagrant Nobles hadn't exited the dungeon by morning. When Lyssandra's lunch came around, there was still no report of their success. She sat at her desk, face scrunched.

"Should I tell the chefs to bring lunch to you in here, ma'am?" one of Lyssandra's assistants asked.

"No. I'm going out for lunch today," she said, standing.

She headed to the dungeon.

She had expected the three "Nobles" to give up. Or at the very least, pull off a miracle against overwhelming odds. The basic supplies they gave to Nobles clearing the dungeon didn't exactly provide comfort or quality. They would have had to find water and suffer through eating those rations.

They should've raced out of the dungeon the first opportunity they got. But instead they were still down there. Lyssandra crossed the city on foot, stewing in her thoughts. It meant she would be late for her next meeting. But that was okay.

Based on Ak's frequent reports, the three Nobles weren't injured.

Lyssandra slipped into the dungeon unimpeded. She followed the trail of the three young Nobles, staring at the remnants of their camp at the tree. Scraps of cut rope were piled on the ground. One of them had embedded alligator teeth into the tree in the shape of a diamond.

But there was no sign of the three of them on the first floor. She descended, a sliver of worry steadily building despite all the reports and confidence of the guardians she had watching over them to prevent any real and serious injury.

The second floor was even hotter than the first, making it uncomfortably stuffy.

She didn't bother summoning a weapon. The monsters here, even on the third floor, were little more than the bottom of the food chain to support the real dungeon monsters on the levels she'd cleared.

She could crush the beetles on this floor with her bare hands.

When she stepped onto the second floor, she stopped immediately, taken aback by the structures she saw near the cliff. And the rising smoke of a fire. With a deep breath, she strode toward them.

There was a set of makeshift tents constructed out of fur-covered hide and wood poles. Lyssandra paused as the wind picked up one of the flaps of the tents, releasing a sparking noise as electricity arced off the side and to the ground.

Sandy, Gerald, and Gwen all jumped at the noise, turning to look at her. They sat on hastily carved wooden benches, smoking alligator meat over an open fire.

"Lyssandra!" Gwen said, excitement on her face. "I thought you'd be busy. We were going to head out after we cleared the dungeon one last time."

Gwen's eyes glanced to the side. There was a fresh corpse of one of the goats from the third floor, half-butchered.

Lyssandra looked around. There were half-filled bags littering the camp. Not just the ones they brought with them—they had crafted more, filling them with monster bones and hide.

The three of them were dirty and harried. The little camp smelled of sweat. All three of them smiled. They were enjoying a pleasant, self-procured lunch. The three of them had not just cleared the dungeon–they had farmed it. Lyssandra schooled her expression, calming her face.

"Is everything okay?" Sandy asked, clearly unnerved by Lyssandra's calm inspection.

"Everything is fantastic," Lyssandra said, strained. "I just expected you to manage to kill the dungeon boss perhaps once. Not . . . how many times did you kill it?"

"Seven," Gwen said, smiling. Her smile disappeared a moment later. She continued in a strained whisper. "We're not . . . We don't have to . . . Are there material taxes for what we kill?" Gwen asked.

Lyssandra sighed. "The materials are too low quality to worry about.

You'll have to pay a tax if you exchange some of the material for coin, but otherwise . . . no." Lyssandra smiled. "I'll help you pack up your camp. Ak."

"Ak?" Sandy asked.

The three of them jumped as a man seemed to step out of thin air beside Lyssandra.

"Yes, my Lady?"

"Fetch us a wagon to carry all these supplies."

Ak gave a polite bow before disappearing again.

Lyssandra turned back to Gwen. "So, tell me about your stay in the dungeon. I want to hear about your strategies. And your mistakes."

I recounted each of our fights with the boss to Lyssandra on the wagon ride back.

Disassembling the tents and blankets took some work, especially since they were still shocking to the touch if they weren't grounded. We kept a string dangling to the ground. Lyssandra's facial expression kept changing. At first, she was more and more alarmed, but then she seemed to settle into a calm hope, occasionally asking questions or giving advice on how charging monsters were normally handled.

"Being able to use the skills from almost a dozen different sets of armor is an incredible advantage," Lyssandra said. "I would focus on expanding your Wardrobe so that you are equipped for most situations you might find yourself in. Once you have the resources, you can also drag along more sets physically."

"So . . ." Sandy interrupted. "This was an evaluation, right?"

Lyssandra sighed. "You three passed. More than passed. Blew my expectations out of the water. Valjean, you know him—I could hardly trust what he said about you. I expected less. It was wrong of me. Though many things he may be, all positive, a good teacher has never been one of them. I'll arrange the train ride to the capital soon."

Sandy looked over at me. She was suspicious. That was obvious. It sounded too good to be true. She always was the most cynical of the three of us.

"And until then?" Sandy asked.

"Valjean spent time helping you learn to fight, did he not?" Lyssandra asked.

I nodded in assent.

She sighed in disappointment. "He spent no time at all teaching you manners."

"Manners?" Sandy practically sneered at Lyssandra.

"Etiquette. Noble etiquette. The Academy presents itself as a meritocracy—a place from which the strong graduate with greater advantages. It's possible to earn your way into owning land after graduating. But incredibly difficult, compared to someone who graduates with high marks."

"And that requires etiquette?" I asked.

"Valjean has told you remarkably little. The Academy is not a real meritocracy that tests your skill; the generations who have come before you have left resources behind for their descendants. The real game is a social one. Graduation can be completed at any time once you have completed the mandatory credit requirements; the final test is nothing more than submitting one hundred merits. Graduating at the top of a class will give you merits. Every class, every skill, and every piece of equipment you acquire will cost you merits. Your room and board will steadily consume the merits you receive from graduating classes. The school is expertly established to prevent any student from reaching this number on their own.

"This way, those who are adept at fighting but poor at leadership can graduate easily and early, while those who are poorer at fighting are forced to learn and study more, forming the backbone of the nation's economic policies."

"Then . . . what? We have to get good grades and then we get to own land?" Sandy asked.

Lyssandra shook her head. "Lesser drakes live on the Academy's floor. Presenting the body of a lesser drake is worth one hundred merits on its own. However, no individual Noble can kill a lesser drake. And you'll need one each."

"We have to convince a team of Nobles to work with us," I filled in.

Lyssandra nodded. "A team that won't betray you and leave you behind. The established factions will all be competing for the lesser drakes. And you don't actually have to kill one, you just need to be the person that turns its body in."

There was a pause.

"So Nobles steal other teams' prizes," Sandy said.

Lyssandra nodded slowly this time. "It takes months or years of grinding your power to reach the point where you can kill a lesser drake on your own. Because of this, many Nobles spend years in the Academy. It's by design. Theoretically, though, you could graduate in as quickly as three months. The Academy is not just designed to facilitate knowledge and power among the Nobility, but also acts as a way for young Nobles to build their social networks. The teams that go with them to kill the lesser drakes often swear oaths as vassals of the lords, ladies, or lieges they follow, forming the foundation of each house's knights.

"Every faction in the Academy is eager to raise their own heirs to the strongest position, raising not just their own social position, but their military strength as well. If you want to have any chance of integrating with Blooded Nobility and finding a team capable of helping you graduate, you will need to master the expected social etiquette. It's a good thing we have two weeks until you leave."

Over the next two weeks, Lyssandra's training, while it involved no combat, was far more punishing than Valjean's.

ACT 2

CHAPTER 12

Lyssandra's estate was different from Valjean's. It was dark, paintings and tapestries covering the walls. She kept flowers in every hallway. Every window was tall and rounded, mixed with purple glass that stained the light entering the tall halls of her manor.

Like Valjean, her schedule was packed day and night, overseeing the many affairs of the city. But she insisted that we had to learn etiquette. We sat alone in a dining room under the glare of a motherly woman. Governess Victoria's hands were folded over a thin wooden rod ending in a rounded tip.

The governess of Lyssandra's estate was responsible for tutoring the Noble children who lived in the city. Even Chosen Nobles' children would almost all be born as Nobles. They would have to have their etiquette drilled into them from a young age.

And Spoke had plenty of Nobles; dozens had to live in every second-tier city to maintain the dungeons, clearing them to push the border that held back the Wild and kept the town safe from the world's seeming hatred of humanity.

"I am Governess Victoria. For the next two weeks, your every meal will be with me. Food will not be served until you know how to sit properly. Dessert must be earned by completing dinner without any infractions."

Sandy glanced at me. That tactic probably worked great on literal children. Gerald scratched the top of his head.

"Okay," Sandy said.

I rested my hands on the table.

"Sit straight. Hands off the table."

The governess's rod painlessly tapped my hands, and I reflexively pulled them off the table. She tapped Sandy's back, making her sit straight.

"Feet on the floor," she said, poking Gerald.

She circled the table three times before she was satisfied with our posture.

"Good," Governess Victoria said.

We had been in the room only a few minutes and hadn't eaten since the dungeon. We had, however, been given time to get dressed in stiff, uncomfortable, formal Noble clothing.

The governess raised her hands and clapped.

A door at the side of the hall opened. And in strode two orderly rows of children.

Sandy groaned.

The governess tapped her on the back of her head. Every time the wand poked one of us, it made us sit up straight, like a doctor testing our reflexes.

The children walked into the room with perfect footsteps, spreading out and each taking individual seats at the table. They waited, observing us in silence.

It was disconcerting how well-trained they were. They all sat with perfect postures.

"Good," Governess Victoria said, and she clapped again. This time, servers walked in, in a synchronized motion, stacking plates across the table. And plates . . . and plates . . . and forks.

So many forks.

In the end, there must have been almost a dozen utensils at each place setting.

"Choose your fork, children," the governess instructed. I reached for the wrong one and received a tap. "Each utensil is designed to accompany its meal," the governess said.

The children all knew the rules. None of them received any taps.

Throughout the meal, we were continually corrected on our posture and utensils. When breakfast was finished, the governess asked questions that drilled the knowledge of the students.

"Which Noble house established and rules over Eastport?"

"Which mage bloodline produces water element mages?"

"In which cardinal direction lies the city of Spoke from the city of Eastport?"

And on and on. I was stunned at how easily and readily the children answered the questions, having memorized dozens of geographical locations as well as the names and bloodlines of what must have been hundreds of Noble houses.

We didn't get any treats after breakfast.

Between breakfast and lunch, we attended cram classes, memorizing maps of the country. Multiple maps showed the many cities of the kingdom. The western edge constantly changed, the details fuzzy, though the eastern border of the ocean was well charted.

"Why is the western edge so . . . irregular?" I asked.

"Roaming calamities rule the western edge of the continent. Each one can require a team of a hundred Nobles to kill—monstrous entities that have broken out of floor after floor of the dungeon to live on the surface. Scouting expeditions to the western coast of the continent have met varying levels of success, often routing around the monsters that make it their domain.

"Regular patrols keep anything truly destructive away from the eastern edge of the continent and the port cities that harvest ocean dungeons and trawl fish."

The entire eastern edge was well defined, with port cities and local dungeons marked. Untamed dungeons were scattered through the maps, marked by little pin dots. Some even had information on what was in the untamed dungeons, with a few rare dungeons being valuable enough to occasionally send Nobles to clear despite there being no city there.

When lunch came, the children put us to shame again. Between lunch and dinner we had remedial math lessons. A few of the parents in Stitch split up teaching letters and math, but nothing advanced. Sandy and Gerald struggled to keep up with some of the concepts.

"Letters can't be numbers," Sandy complained.

We only enjoyed a tiny amount of free time, almost all of which we spent outside, escaping the confines of Lyssandra's estate, before an attendant summoned us again to more classes and etiquette.

We also had to memorize the names of dozens of Noble factions and topics to avoid about them. Our lessons were even tailored, including the names of a few prominent heirs who would be attending the Academy this year, jockeying for power in their own houses, and which ones we should avoid offending.

When I fell asleep, I felt like my brain was on fire.

Breakfast.

Classes.

Lunch.

Classes.

Dinner.

Repeat.

* * *

"What led to the increase in economic prominence of the city of Eastport and its near ascension to the third tier? Jacques?" Victoria asked at the dinner table. Our main course had been taken away. And now we were answering questions to a pop quiz. The constant questions after dinner meant that the children mostly discussed the answers while they ate; what amounted to Noble gossip spreading among children.

"I don't know, Governess," Jacques said. He stared down at his palms.

"There is nothing wrong with not knowing, as long as we know that we do not know. Sandy?" the governess said.

"The city of Eastport is ruled over by the House of Storms, who deflect the horrifying storms that would otherwise ravage the eastern coast," Sandy said.

"Correct," Governess Victoria replied. She looked over to Sandy. "What are the economic ramifications?"

"The House of Storms enabled cities to prosper on the east coast," Sandy said.

Victoria clapped. New plates were brought out. They loaded mine with freshly baked, soft cookies.

I looked over. Jacques was only a seat away from me. He was barely older than a toddler. And he was crying.

I slid one of my cookies onto his empty plate.

He had answered three questions wrong today. But he was under a lot of pressure. His dad was currently on a deep expedition in a dungeon, on one of the primary teams responsible for clearing the center dungeon of Spoke monthly.

Jacques cried harder, but he grabbed and ate the cookie.

Bedtime.

Breakfast.

No children.

"Do you feel prepared for the Academy?" the Governess asked.

This was different.

"No," I replied.

Sandy looked around the room.

"Oh. It's been two weeks already," she said.

I hadn't even gotten a chance to use all the goat leather looted from Lyssandra's dungeon.

"Lyssandra . . ." I said. She wasn't here. She was also off clearing the boss of the city's central dungeon.

"She won't make it to see you off," Victoria said. She smiled wryly. "But you've done as well as you could. Crammed well. The next train to the capital will be arriving soon. We need to talk about your first days at the Academy."

"Will there be dinner etiquette?" Sandy asked.

"Worse," Governess Victoria replied. "The orientation to the Academy also functions as the debut for several prominent Nobles. The first formal meetings between students happen at a function ball. Your initial rank in the Academy is seeded, and those in the highest positions stand to earn merits. Winning a duel will increase your initial ranking, and thus, your initial merits. It will be imperative for you to avoid offending anyone, and to avoid attracting attention in order to avoid being challenged to a duel by a Blooded Noble."

CHAPTER 13

The train ride to the capital was even bumpier than the train ride from Foundry to Spoke. The train was bigger and faster; it was the only rail with a wider standard than the rest, and it headed dead north, direct to the Academy.

The human kingdom had three capitals, one for each of the King Candidates—local Nobles who ruled over each third-tier city, all with power pushed to the limit. The kingdom was locked in a political struggle over which one should occupy the highest office. With none of them able to claim primacy, they instead settled for split control, rather than an outright fight.

Whichever city advanced to the fourth tier first would decide humanity's ruler.

Despite all being called Kings, they weren't all men. But when they claimed a city of the third tier, the system had designated them as such.

I had no idea how that worked, but I guessed I would find out when I got to the Academy.

The train rode over the walls of the city and away into the wilderness. We even stopped in a second-tier city along the route, trading goods and people before heading farther north.

When we reached the third-tier city, the railway didn't go up and over the wall. Instead, the wall opened to let the train through.

The wall of the city towered above us, looking for all the world like a mountain. Buildings piled on top of each other. The train rode through an open tunnel, a spine of stone archways supporting structures above us. The smell of smoke rolled back into the train, cramped and constrained by the spine that held up the city.

The city was built up, rather than out, in the confines of the castle fortresses. Humanity had taken advantage of the ability they gained to manipulate the nigh-invincible structures created by the dungeon.

The train stopped for what must have been an hour in a gigantic, multilayered switching station. I sat by the window in the dining car. Sandy sat down next to me eventually.

Out the window was a direct and precipitous drop into the city below; there was no wall or guardrail to stop us.

We were almost there.

When the train rolled forward again, it moved faster. It must have disgorged and exchanged its cargo—or mounted more engines to pull the train.

Whatever the case, we didn't stop at the capital before heading forward.

It didn't even stop at the entrance to the dungeon; it plowed straight inside.

Outside the window, I saw sprawling farmland that stretched into the distant horizon. Roads split away, dividing the farmland into massive fields of different crops. Most notably, orchards full of trees bearing brightly colored fruit were being picked at by dozens of workers.

The other thing that stood out were the buildings. Not temporary shacks or warehouses for goods; there were entire villages visible in the distance, homes for farmhands who must have lived in the dungeon for expanded stretches of time, aging three times faster than those just a floor above.

Irrigation troughs poured water from massive silos. Steam engines burned next to pipes that pulled the contents of entire rivers, redirecting them for irrigation deeper in the dungeon.

We passed onto the second floor quickly.

Sprawling mountains rose in the distance. Teams of workers mined at exposed veins in great quarried sections of the mountain, standing on erected scaffolding.

Entire factories were at work, cutting apart gigantic blocks of marble and granite in open yards. A train sat lifeless on a track.

The third floor contained a sprawling savannah. Gigantic ranches held herds of animals. There must have been a dozen different species visible in the fields; they couldn't all have been sourced from here. At this floor, each night at the surface would take nine days. If it took nine months to raise an animal for slaughter, they could do it in one here. The dungeon refreshing would restore the land for grazing.

There was something comforting about the sight. The tiny settlements in the dungeon reminded me of home. Going far out into the Wild had made me more and more uncomfortable, the ever-present itch building up as the train rides took me days from a dungeon and human settlement.

It was almost unnerving how going deeper into the dungeon made me more comfortable instead.

On the fourth floor, a torrential rain fell. There was no industry here; just mud and swamp. Walls surrounded the train, blocking my view of the environment. They seemed worn with age.

We passed onto the fifth floor. I had never been to the fifth floor of a dungeon.

"Try not to fall out," Sandy said.

I leaned back from the window. I had been nearly pressing my face to it.

The fifth floor was a small island. Gray clouds hovered in the sky. Docks stretched out into the water, fishing boats rocking in the waves. The buildings were fortified. There was another train here, and a crane dropped raw fish into an open top cargo container. Hundreds of workers acted as if they weren't deep in a dungeon, going about their daily work without fretting.

I wondered how many lived here and how many rode the train in each day.

I felt the change acutely on the sixth floor. I could just tell. There was no edge to this world. It would go on forever.

A gigantic forest was being logged for timber. Teams of people in armor and bearing weapons—presumably Nobles—waited at the ready while lumberjacks felled monstrous trees.

The sixth floor had the itch of the Wild.

"Do you feel that?" I asked, taken aback.

"Yeah," Sandy said, staring out. "It doesn't feel like a safe floor."

There was no industry here. But there was life.

The safe floors were floors where no monsters spawned. Time passed on them at the same speed as the surface; you wouldn't be trapped for days if you reached this point.

An entire tiny city bustled around the sixth floor in spite of the presence of the Wild. The city seemed industrious; the clothes people wore looked similar to the other dungeon work uniforms: utilitarian outfits with no frivolities or decor. Due to the ever-present decay, almost every building was either enchanted or bore the evidence of frequent repairs. Almost everything was built out of metal and stone.

"Do people *live* here?" I asked, taken aback.

Gerald wandered into the dining compartment. He silently sat down in our booth and stared out the window.

Beyond the sixth floor, the dungeon became truly dangerous; this was where a team of no less than twenty Nobles would work together to clear each floor in succession, rotating groups to recover in order to clear the floor within a single day.

There was no more industry. No more signs of life. Just walled fortresses. One of the floors even opened into a sprawling underground cavern. Gigantic fans pushed air back out through the gate.

The ninth floor was the next safe floor, again covered in the pervasive itch of the Wild. The city here was much smaller than the one on the sixth floor, but more than enough to establish a barracks and resupply. There still must have been more people living here than in the entirety of Stitch.

On the twelfth floor, we reached the Academy. The train released a high-pitched whistle as it began to slow. The brakes squealed over the metal.

We finally arrived.

Unlike the harsh industrial buildings on the safe floors, the Academy was a fully functioning city, almost the same size as Foundry or Spoke.

It wasn't just Nobles who lived here. It must have taken thousands of commoners to make the city run.

We unloaded our luggage in the gigantic train station. The walls were stained from coal smoke; the entire building smelled.

There was something altogether more comfortable about this floor. Maybe the presence of the Wild on the previous floor had simply brought it into starker contrast, but I felt that there was something different.

"Lady Gwen?" a thin, wiry man asked as we were still pulling luggage from the train. He was dressed in an official-looking uniform.

"Yes?" I asked.

"Lady Lyssandra sent me. I'm to show you the way."

The attendant led us across the city and back toward the gate. The entire fortress-compound was kept in remarkable condition; I couldn't help but notice how every fortification seemed to be built out of a smooth, shining white brick that was marred by no imperfection.

"The entire city is open to you when you're not in class," the attendant said. "You'll get a comprehensive tour later, but for now Lyssandra wanted to pass on some information to you. The city contains multiple crafting workshops: ateliers, abattoirs, and the like. You can trade in currency or accumulated merits at most of the shops. Curfew only applies to time spent outside the fortress wall. That's when the Academy begins to recall most of the Nobles on patrol outside. You can have your term suspended and even be incarcerated if you're caught outside the wall after curfew."

I nodded along.

"Where are we staying?" Sandy asked.

"Your housing will be in the Academy dorms. The most basic options have a very low merit cost. I recommend finding a way to earn money in the city and renting from someone other than the Academy. They offer luxurious rooms for a high merit price. The living quality in the dorms may seem lackluster after spending however many months in Noble estates.

"Lyssandra has also emphasized that you should not reveal details of your classes. Especially Gerald."

I looked askance at Gerald. He was the only Noble I had heard of who also had a crafting skill, but other than that, there was nothing obviously extraordinary about him. Anxiety built in me as we were led to what would be our new home for the following months.

The dorms weren't what I expected.

They were built into the wall of the compound, the windows visible as we approached the building over the open cobble street.

The attendant led us to a front desk inside the building.

There was a crowd of young Nobles in matching uniforms behind the desk, scuffling about quietly, whispering as they tracked us with their eyes. They looked like they could be students themselves, or had just recently graduated. A man behind the desk scribbled onto a piece of paper.

Glowing text was embedded in the wall above and behind him. It read, *To build an empire that will forever prosper.*

The room was almost barren aside from the desk—no other furniture. Scuffmarks on the wooden floor showed that it had been pushed out. The entire place was kept remarkably isolated and sterile.

The Academy's sheen and dedication to raising Nobles as students felt like paint over the real nature of the place. It was a gilded castle, a bulwark of humanity forced down the throat of the dungeon. The city inside did not hide the militant nature of its existence; there was more fighting power consolidated here than anywhere else I had ever been.

"Names?" he asked.

"Sandy, Gwendolyn, and Gerald," the attendant said.

"Rooms . . . B227 . . . C228 and . . . B301," the man behind the desk replied. He pulled out keys from somewhere in the desk, laying them in front of each of us.

Three people walked out of the crowd to show us to our rooms. Gerald was led in one direction, while Sandy and I were led in the other. The farther we moved down the halls, the closer together the doors became.

"Are you two students here?" Sandy asked.

"Graduates," one of the women said. "You're both Chosen then? The school has a great post-grad program. You can level here, build merits and experience before looking for other work."

I looked the attendants over with a more appraising eye. They were Nobles. I wondered how many of the people here were—it felt like a waste of the country's Nobility. Our town—and many others like it—rotted away, while Nobles stayed within the better living conditions of the Academy.

The amount of care given to the students—giving each an attendant who showed them the way—struck me as odd. But there was obviously more to it; the fact that we ran into no one in the hallways nor at the desk was clearly intentional. The school was separating every last student until the debut tomorrow.

We must have been some of the last students to arrive. There was no way everyone had stayed isolated from each other for however long they waited for the new term to start.

The hall curved as we traveled forward, the dormitory built into the very walls of the fortress. Glowing stones lit the interior. It was inhumanly quiet.

"Do they pay you in merits?" Sandy asked.

The woman frowned, then nodded. "They do. We get wages, too, though. Look into it once you graduate!" she said.

We reached a spiraling staircase that expanded out into multiple directions, hundreds of rooms built into the walls. They had to accommodate more than just students. There was practically an entire town here; every Noble needed dozens of people to produce and craft for them, and this place had hundreds of Nobles.

On the second floor, the doors were pressed together, the rooms tiny. The guide pressed the key into my hand.

"Showers are that way," she said, waving down the hall. "There's some on every floor. Orientation will be in room H101. That's building H—you'll find it. It's the ballroom. It will be first thing in the morning. Come prepared. Dress sharp."

She handed me a map of the campus, clearly made by a cartographer. My location was marked with an image of a pin. Then she walked away. Her shoes clicked against the stone halls. The building was warm; it didn't seem like it should be. There was no ventilation system; it must have been entirely magical.

The room doors were only a few feet from each other in this part of the building. The room was tiny—I could tell before I opened it. I dreaded learning what it would be like to stay here. I slid the key into the lock and braced myself to open the door.

I turned the key and stepped into room 227.

The closet had barely accommodated my luggage. There was just enough room to stand on one side of the bed, which was pushed against the wall. A desk sat at the end of the room, scarred from time and usage. The room was much longer than it was wide, forcing me to awkwardly turn sideways to navigate it. The air was old, stale and stuffy.

I had slept better on the train when it was running over monsters.

The Academy seemed intent to instill a sense of unending isolation. We were separated upon arrival, unable to see any of the other attending Nobles. Then we were separated further at admission, the school going so far as to avoid letting anyone meet in the halls.

For those who had grown up in Noble society, the Academy functioned as their debut. It was, for many of them, a singular opportunity to build an impression of themselves. For some, those children of Nobles destined to inherit huge holdings and vast quantities of bannermen, it was a chance to bond with the future generations of their closest allies. For others, the Chosen, it was their first introduction to Noble society. And a half dozen opportunities for them to put their feet in their mouths.

For me, it was an inconvenience.

The entire point of becoming a Noble was to uplift my hometown of Stitch. In all honesty, the idea of merely attending a school to earn a certificate that let me protect my town sounded less ludicrous than killing monsters each night. I was willing.

I was instructed to stay in my room until orientation. Breakfast was delivered to my door. A cart blocked my view of the hall. My shower was scheduled so that I wouldn't run into anyone else in the hallway. They'd given us a uniform for attending classes. The stats on it were fantastic, but it boasted no skills or resistances. Finally, around noon by my estimate, an attendant, acting like a handler, guided me from my room to the ballroom.

The entire walk was filled with an oppressive sort of ambient noise, the kind you only find in old buildings; ancient wood creaked and groaned as heat made the building expand and cold made it shrink.

Instead of doors, windows showed a sky so dark it could be confused for night. Rain pounded against the panes, the sound overwhelming everything else in the hall.

The hallway grew wider as we moved away from the dorm rooms. It grew as wide as a city street, large enough to fit wagons. The ceiling was recessed into darkness above us.

The handler—or guidance counselor, or whatever—stood to the side of the ballroom door and curtsied at me. I almost curtsied back but stopped myself. The door opened.

Sandy stepped into the ballroom. Just a single step. Then she stopped.

A hundred sneering Nobles turned to her all at once, the weight of their gazes burying her.

Her clothing was stiff. The door shutting behind her was like the sound of a coffin lid locking. She didn't move.

Behind her in the hall, she heard the footsteps trail away. She stared forward. She ignored the people smiling at her, inviting her to approach. Someone took a step toward her.

She turned around and left.

When the door swung inward, I wondered if it was enchanted. A hundred voices boiled out, like heat rolling off the forge. It took me a moment to realize I wasn't just imagining it; the air rolling out of the room really was hot. And wet.

I knew orientation would be excessive. I'd braced myself further after learning that it was the debut event for many Nobles, their introduction both to Noble society, and to each other.

Still, I wasn't prepared for this.

I froze at the entrance.

For a moment, I thought we were at the wrong door. The room was huge, almost a stadium, around a central field full of trees. A sprawling glass dome above showed the cloudy morning sky, the noise of tempestuous rain fighting against the sounds of a tiny orchestra in one corner.

A few people shot looks my way, but they just as quickly looked away. They were huddled in groups, sometimes three or four, sometimes eight or nine or ten.

A hundred glances pricked my skin like needles, locking me in place. I was sure of it; they would all judge me and find me wanting. They would all know I wasn't a Noble.

When I looked up, I didn't find anyone's eyes looking my way. I realized, belatedly, most of these people knew each other. Chosen who were selected in a city would probably meet the children of the Blooded Nobles who lived there.

It felt isolating. Like I was the only person who'd come here alone.

I didn't see Sandy. What I saw was the way the little groups huddled together, cliques already long formed. I moved into the room, stepping to the side of the door and out of the way. It was darker in the corner. No one was looking my way here. Most of them were sending nervous glances toward the center of the room.

The little cliques hung around at tables covered in snacks and food, and the room smelled like coffee. Commoners bustled through the room, replenishing trays and taking them away through side doors.

A balcony rimmed the entire room above us. Silhouette figures leaned down over the railing. Staff—maybe teachers or evaluators of some kind. They were barely visible from here.

In the center of the massive room was an arena.

It was like someone had ripped out a chunk of a rainforest, complete with towering trees and blooming plants. Light seemed to spill outward from it, like the air itself was enchanted to glow. A glowing white circle represented the arena's edge.

Above it, hovering in the air through effort of enchantment, and probably extraordinarily expensive magic, I saw my name. Gwendolyn. It was fourth from the top, which shocked me for a moment, before I saw the numbers next to each of the names.

The display was a scrolling leaderboard. The top three names had the numbers one, two, and three after them—the highest currently ranked nobles of this year. My eyes lingered until the door opened again. I was unsure whether it was showing the number of the latest person to enter, or if it just showed the name of whoever was looking at it. My own number was 203.

I scanned the room again, debating whether to approach one of the groups and say hello.

The choice was ultimately taken out of my hands.

"Hi!" I nearly jumped as a girl my age spoke to me. She smiled. I smiled back, staring at the house emblem proudly pinned onto her school uniform. She was standing in a circle of other Nobles; almost all of them smiled encouragingly.

"Hello," I said, offering a smile.

All of the uniforms were the same—stiff and ill-fitting—but now that I looked, I saw that many people had found ways to customize theirs. A pin of their house's crest was worn by almost everyone in this circle.

"I'm Lady Marisicia."

"The fishing house," I said, stumbling over my words as I stepped into the group.

A girl to Marisicia's left scowled, but she herself just laughed.

"Yes. We produce more than a third of the entire nation's fish—though it doesn't feed many people far away from us. Nobles from all over come to my city to sample it." She spoke the lines like they were rehearsed, something she had said over and over. She still sounded remarkably proud. "You should come visit sometime after we graduate."

Marisicia was all smiles, warm invitation and open hand. No one in the circle seemed hostile. She definitely wasn't from Valjean's and Lyssandra's political faction, but she still spoke to me kindly anyway. She didn't know who I was. And she was being nice.

"I would love to," I said. "I'm Gwen—I'm, uh, from the frontier."

I flushed. The girl who'd scowled raised her eyebrows, no longer scowling. Most of the group were holding glasses of what looked like wine. I wasn't sure if it was actually alcohol. That sounded like a terrible idea. Actually, I didn't know how alcohol would affect stats.

"Have you ever seen a calamity?" another one of the girls asked, tilting her head. "Father says that the frontier is full of calamities and monsters. A barren wasteland unsuitable for life."

"No!" I said, before calming myself. "Where I lived was beautiful. Completely peaceful. No calamities. It's very . . . calm, compared to the cities. There's only a few dozen people in the entire town."

Half the group gasped at that.

"You're serious? It sounds so quiet," another person said.

"Will you move to one of the cities once you graduate?" Marisicia asked, smiling.

"No," I replied. "I want to go back to my town."

"Why return to such a small, isolated place?" one of the girls asked. "It's so much easier to carve out a future in the city."

I paused for a moment, thinking of how to reply. What could I say to explain to them how I felt about my town? I watched as the group occasionally darted their eyes back toward the arena in the center of the room.

"I know everyone there," I said, stumbling over my words. "And not just in a people-I'm-comfortable-around way. In the frontier, we have so little that everyone shares. Everyone knows and cares for each other. It's like a big extended family."

"Eugh," one of the Nobles said. "My own family is huge enough for me."

"I was always taught that the quality of life in the frontiers fails completely," Marisicia said, searching my face. "Without concentration of capital and resources, it becomes increasingly difficult to provide for people. Less land to farm with a smaller dungeon, and a lack of access to factories to produce goods that enhance the quality of life."

"That's true, in some ways," I said. "Life in the city is . . . less personal. I remember three winters ago, several houses burned through their entire stockpile of wood. So we hosted in the town center, burning a single fireplace for a dozen people. Bob made everyone tea, and we played board games through the night on an old table. We wouldn't have had happy memories like that in a city."

"That's true," a Noble on my left replied. They had bright, green eyes, and freckles that seemed almost gold in color. I wondered if they were artificial for a moment. "But in a city, you wouldn't have run out of wood."

I frowned. "That's not guaranteed either, is it? You still have to rely on the city's industry to work. How many Nobles do you trust to put the quality of the lives of its people above their own economy? What city do you come from?" I asked.

"I'm Annabelle of House Gloomwood," she said. She glanced nervously to the side. "I—"

A few Nobles in the crowd gasped.

"House Gloomwood? I thought that the last heir met a calamity in a western expedition!" Marisicia interjected.

"They . . . did," Annabelle said. "I am an adopted daughter."

A few of the Nobles nodded. Before any other questions were asked, we were interrupted by an announcement.

"Duel: Lord Gerald, Chosen, has been challenged by Lord Adrian, House Ironheart. Duel accepted."

The voice boomed across the ballroom, followed by an audible noise as every person in the room turned to the arena below us.

Gerald was having a really bad day.

He couldn't say no to the duel. That wasn't allowed. Lyssandra had repeated over and over that it wasn't acceptable.

He couldn't win. He knew that. His opponent knew it, too.

"Why?" Gerald asked, staring across the center of the arena at his opponent.

Adrian Ironheart smiled and waved at someone in the crowd. He spun around, offering greetings and acknowledgment to a dozen people before turning to face Gerald. He had long, dark, curly hair that framed his face. His features were sharp, and his skin had a slight tan. His eyes were a smoky gray. And his smile was forced. The pained look in his eyes broke the illusion as he waited.

Gerald didn't know what Adrian was waiting for until it happened.

There was a rush of air, suddenly cold, that blew across Gerald's face. All sound from the crowd cut off.

"No offense. But you're Chosen. You wouldn't understand," Adrian said. He still had a pained smile on his face. But it didn't look like he was pretending to be happy anymore. It looked like he had swallowed something bitter.

Gerald was sick of hearing that he wouldn't understand. It was his first day at the school and he already hated it.

He wanted to be at home, working the forge. Continuing his father's profession. He hadn't wanted to be Chosen. He had been lucky to be gifted with a class that allowed him to carry on his family's legacy. Here he was, enduring the words of a condescending prick instead.

The arena at the center of the ballroom emulated a tropical environment. Even the ground was covered in thick, vined plants that coiled on the floor, providing tripping hazards. Trees bent inward at the arena's edges, fighting for soil and sunlight within the magical dome that constrained the dueling pit.

The needs of the school and the needs of the trees diverged. From far away, it looked like a perfect tropical section of the world cut away. From up close, it was clear that they bent and moved to compete for sunlight.

"What wouldn't I understand?" Gerald asked. "Being forced to do something against my will? Because that's what you're doing right now. I don't even want to be here."

Adrian paused. He looked surprised. Then he laughed. "No, no. You're right. I'm being uncharitable." He tilted his head back, looking up at the tallest tree. Its branches spread outward, leaves choking out the trees below it. "I'm titleless. Heir of nothing. My family's entire dynasty has already been sliced up and allocated to my brothers and sisters. I'm going to have absolutely nothing when I leave. So I have to do well in the Academy. If I can outperform my siblings, I may be able to bump myself up in the chain of inheritance. And if I fail, I can go find my own dungeon to claim."

Adrian glanced up to the ceiling. There were letters above the arena projected in midair, held there by a magical enchantment. They flashed and changed.

Gerald had never seen anything like it.

Pure magic, projecting letters in midair, and not through the system. Just hovering light. How advanced were the enchantments of the cities? If not for the circumstances, Gerald would've stared forever to study them.

[Duel starting in three . . .]

The flashing display began to count down. Gerald stared at it, watching the letters change, trying to figure out how it worked. Each letter was actually a composite of a bunch of little lines that approximated its form.

He searched for the source of the projection. On the walls, to the side, he spotted a contraption of metal boxes.

[Two . . .]

Gerald tracked his eyes back to the countdown. He wished he could choose what his enchantments did. He wanted to make things like this. Enchantments that made life better for everyone.

[One.]

Instead, all of his enchantments revolved around combat.

Gerald felt his face heat up. Around the arena, he felt hundreds of eyes resting on him.

Adrian kicked off the ground, rushing forward. A rapier appeared in his hand, summoned from his inventory.

[Go!]

With a mental tug, Gerald summoned all of his armor. He still only had the one set, though the burning urge to forge another was starting to creep forward in his mind. He needed to find a forge he could use on the school's sprawling campus.

Adrian's rapier danced across Gerald's armor, purple light sparking as he stabbed and slashed. Adrian's sword danced with light of its own. Gerald staggered backward in the heavy metal, raising his arms to block.

Every swing and stab and poke into Gerald's armor triggered the enchanted ability it held, rebounding the damage onto Adrian.

Gerald watched through a layer of plate steel as Adrian grew increasingly frustrated. Dozens of cuts opened along his arms. A line bloomed across his face, a tiny drop of blood leaking out from him. He backed away.

"Come on! You can't be serious. What kind of skill is this?" Adrian asked. His expression was still controlled. But he was starting to get angry.

Gerald lowered his arms. The metal creaked.

He hadn't known how to forge something to be comfortable. The metal grated awkwardly against his skin. It wasn't padded on the inside, so it sapped the heat from his body, radiating it into the air.

"I told you I didn't want to fight," Gerald said.

Adrian scowled. "I've never heard of a skill that damages the attacker like this. What are you, a porcupine? Come and fight me!"

"It's not a skill," Gerald said. "It's an enchantment."

Adrian blinked. "I thought you were Chosen."

"I am," Gerald said.

"Where did you get enchanted gear then? The expense—I mean . . ."

"I made it," Gerald said.

Outside of the arena, the onlookers watched in confusion as the two dueling Nobles suddenly stopped and held what seemed to be a calm discussion with each other.

"Did someone sponsor you? Who would waste such a high-level enchantment on such a shabby set of armor?"

Under his helmet, Gerald scowled. His forging was the one thing he had to be proud of.

"Take that back," Gerald said.

"Sorry—I didn't mean the armor was a waste on you," Adrian said. "This is a show. It's theater! We have to give people a good fight. Not just me beating on you while you defend. Even if you have no chance at winning. I won't receive any merit for beating up a defenseless person."

"I said take that back," Gerald said. "This is good armor. It's my armor."

He had spent hours toiling over it, bringing it up into his room piece by piece, shaping it perfectly to fit him and only him.

"It's not, though. I know good armor. Our family works closely with the Smith Guild—I—who sold that to you?"

"I *made* it," Gerald said.

There was confusion in the crowd around them. Gerald saw it—people talking and pointing and laughing. He was still standing in the spot he was in when the duel had started. And Adrian stood across from him, asking questions instead of fighting.

"Then who enchanted it?" Adrian asked.

"I did," Gerald said through clenched teeth. He was starting to get angry.

"Only a Divine class would be able to—Are you making fun of me?" Adrian asked, taken aback again. He squinted. He looked like he'd just had an idea. "I'll break your armor to pieces."

In a flash, Adrian crossed the field. His sword glowed. It *dinked* as it scraped against Gerald's chest plate. Adrian flinched as a matching cut ripped his shirt.

"You and that terrible, ugly, useless armor!" Adrian punctuated the words with slashes.

Gerald summoned his gigantic pig-iron mace and swung.

He had practiced for days in Lyssandra's dungeon, but he was now weeks out of practice. So he activated and deactivated the enchantment that lightened it with ease, swinging it with enough speed to displace the air in a *woosh* of power.

Right before it hit Adrian, he suddenly slid backward over the ground. It was like he was a puppet and someone had yanked the strings backward.

The mace hit the ground with a catastrophic thump, sending up earth and dirt that splattered over Adrian and Gerald both. Gerald turned to face Adrian from his new position. He was slow in the armor. He wasn't sure if that was Adrian's own skill, or some protective feature of the arena. He guessed it was Adrian's, since the duel didn't end. The semi-translucent barrier still surrounded them.

Adrian stared in shock. Then he schooled his face back into the mask of confidence.

"So you *can* fight back!" Adrian said.

Gerald stepped forward. In that same instant, Adrian shot out to his left. Gerald's armor was gigantic, bulky plate mail, while Adrian still wore only the school uniform, and he outmaneuvered Gerald with ease. He was simply feinting with the blade now, realizing he was unable to cut Gerald. So instead he led him around in a circle.

Gerald, frustrated with being dodged over and over, recalled his armor. It disappeared soundlessly. Adrian's eyes widened, then sharpened, sensing the opportunity, but Gerald was already leaping toward him.

He swung.

It was simple. A straightforward motion, Gerald's fear of fighting temporarily lost in the heat of the moment.

Adrian leaned away from the blow, ready to dodge. The mace accelerated.

A mesh of purple appeared over Adrian at the moment of impact, not dissimilar from the enchantment Valjean's training weapons used. The mace stopped, all inertia absorbed by the purple mesh. The same mesh locked Gerald in place, stopping him from moving.

[Duel: Victory for Gerald Smith, Chosen.]

The voice echoed across the room. There was a flash of light from above, on the high walkway around the massive ballroom. Gerald felt the strain leave his muscles. For his part, Adrian stood, brushing off the dirt that had gathered on his clothes. He made a noise of disappointment.

As Adrian stood, Gerald observed that all the cuts that he'd sustained had disappeared. Gerald stared up to where the light had flashed above him.

"They keep a healer on task for the arena duels. It's good training for some of them, apparently," Adrian said.

Gerald continued staring up, chest heaving.

"Come on, we're holding up the line," Adrian said.

"What?" Gerald asked.

Adrian threw an arm around Gerald's shoulder, dragging him away from the arena.

"You did great in there," Adrian said.

Gerald pushed him off, stomping away.

"Gerald! Sorry about what I said. I was just trying to get you to fight back!" Adrian followed Gerald as he stomped out of the arena. "You're dragging mud onto the ballroom floor."

Gerald looked down. His armor had torn apart the dirt and grass, and he'd tracked muddy footprints behind him. He scanned the room for Sandy or Gwen again.

He didn't see them.

"Your class is impressive," Adrian said, continuing to trail him. "You beat me without using a single skill."

I beat him, Gerald thought, turning to look at Adrian again.

They were still catching glances from the Nobles around them when the next duel was announced.

Gerald walked to the corner, leaning against the wall under the balcony high above. It was a shaded little alcove. For some reason, Adrian was still following him.

"No hard feelings?" Adrian asked, staring around the room. He waved to someone.

"Sure, whatever man," Gerald said.

Adrian spun, putting out a hand to shake.

Gerald looked him up and down, then tentatively shook his hand. He looked back to the arena.

"My rank jumped a hundred spots," Gerald said. There was alarm in his voice. The last thing he wanted was to have to duel more people.

"No one will challenge you—it's fine," Adrian said.

Two Nobles walked over to join them, forming a loose circle. One of them wore a pin colored white and cyan. She fanned her face with a hand fan of gold, white, and blue, patterned with dragons. She looked at Gerald like he was a bug, then looked away.

The second was a huge man, his face already smiling as he approached. His hair fell in red curls just above his shoulders.

"What the hell was that, Adrian!?" the man shouted.

Adrian smiled bitterly.

"Gerald was far stronger than I expected him to be. Gerald, this is Elara of the House of Storms, and Cedric, a member of one of our branch families."

"Charmed," Elara said. She didn't even look at Gerald. She was watching the fight in the arena, eyes cold and calculating. It made Gerald uncomfortable. She looked at people the way his father looked at burning steel.

"I'll say. You beat him without even using a skill? Your stats must be insane!" Cedric said. "Duel me next!"

Gerald's eyes widened. He opened his mouth to speak, but Adrian interrupted him.

"Gerald's a bit tired. Couldn't get much sleep—debut anxiety," Adrian said. He smiled at Cedric.

"Ahhhh!" Cedric said. His arms fell on Gerald's shoulders, staring down at him. "Do not worry! With skills like that, you'll graduate in the top ten with ease!"

Gerald had no idea how Cedric was in the Academy. He looked like a fully grown man. He even had the shadow of a beard growing in.

"So you threw the fight for him?" Elara asked, turning to stare at Gerald rather than Adrian.

"People will think what they want," Adrian shrugged. "Most of the people here don't know me, so they don't know . . ."

"That you've enjoyed such an extensive education," Elara said.

Adrian smiled.

"But won't that look bad? Since he didn't use a single skill? What did your rank drop to?" Cedric asked.

"High three-hundreds. Near the very bottom," Adrian said. "We have all year to boost the rankings up. Being ignored is much better than starting at spot ten."

"Wait . . ." Gerald said. "You always intended to lose?"

He was almost as offended as when Adrian had insulted his armor.

"No." Adrian shook his head. "But a win against you wouldn't have pushed me any higher in the ranking. It would've demonstrated enough skill that people wouldn't have challenged me easily. The goal was to find a fight that would dissuade challengers. I don't think I succeeded at that. But now that my ranking is so low . . ."

"No one will challenge you for it," Gerald said.

"The ranking is only valuable if you fight for it," Cedric chipped in.

Adrian sighed and leaned against the wall next to Gerald.

"So Gerald, you said you forged that armor yourself?" Adrian said.

Gerald sighed, happy they were finally asking him something he actually wanted to talk about. He didn't notice the way Elara froze, standing completely still, nor the way that Cedric's smile suddenly became strained.

"Yes," Gerald said. "I know it's not much. You've all seen better. It's the best I could make in the frontier. No mana-alloy or magical composite. I'm sure if I made it here it would be more impressive."

"Why don't we find out?" Adrian asked with a smile. "Our family works very closely with the Smith Guild. I can probably work out some favors and get you a forge here."

Gerald nodded along. He flexed his fist. His class's desire to craft itched at him. He had been getting better at holding it back, especially as his stats rose, but it was still ever-present. He had told Sandy and Gwen they would figure something out after arriving together, but this couldn't hurt, right?

Gerald nodded. "Sure. When?"

"How about right now?"

CHAPTER 14

The Academy used every last scrap of space it had. It was a bastion of safety in the heart of a dungeon. Unfortunately, that turned the place into a labyrinthine maze. Buildings were built tall atop each other, walkways cresting the sides of factories and classrooms, bridges in the air connected raised stone roads. The school's campus, luckily, was built mostly around the wall at the edge of the fortress. It must have been the first thing built.

The architects seemed almost prophetic in how they prepared for the expansion of the city, containing most of the school to the looping wall. They also seemed almost sadistic, as this meant massively long walks through the empty corridors.

After Gerald's duel, the anxiety of waiting for someone to challenge me next had been the worst part of the debut last night. I searched for Gerald after his duel, but he slipped away through the crowd before I could reach him. The students had piled around the arena, forcing me to elbow my way through them.

And the Nobles' stats had made that hard.

In the morning, I found I had received a packet under my door that contained a list of my classes, a map, and my rank in the school.

Following the map, I made my way to my first class. As I walked, the wall towered over me; intimidating, carefully designed archways rose on either side into a darkened top, and light filtered in through windows high in the walls. They didn't afford a view of much else besides storm clouds.

I almost walked past the door I had been looking for.

C001 was etched into a plaque embedded above the door.

Beside it, a familiar-looking Noble crossed his arms. He had an annoyed look on his face, eyes fixed on the ceiling. His hair was black and curled, falling around his shoulders. A giant of a man with bright red hair stood beside him.

I could almost place his face. It was so, so familiar. But right now wasn't the time. I wouldn't know anyone in this school anyway.

I nodded at them. The giant man's eyes tracked me as I pushed the door open a crack.

The wind ripped the door out of my hand. It slammed open with a crash, revealing a skybridge that led to a building across the way. Birds flew away from the noise of the door.

A laugh poured from the giant man.

The smaller man turned and looked at me, his features sharp.

"Late to class?" he asked.

The moment he spoke, I remembered where I knew him from. This was the man who had dueled Gerald. I hadn't heard their conversation, but I was sure that Gerald wouldn't have challenged anyone.

"You're Adrian," I said, grabbing hold of the door handle. I looked from Adrian to the sky bridge the door opened to, considering if I wanted to sit and talk to him. I decided I didn't have time. I might have been late already.

His face lit up.

"Oh? Are you from one of the branch families?" he asked.

"You're an asshole," I said.

I stepped through the door and pushed it shut behind me, alone for a moment on the sky bridge. Wind whistled through giant stone columns, and the Academy stretched around me. Gray clouds choked the sky.

In the distance, a jungle canopy rocked in the wind. Huge flocks of birds circled. And far, far away, so distant it was just a speck on the horizon, something much larger flew above the trees.

The Academy itself was alive below me. Buildings were stacked on top of each other, great stone edifices piled high until they resembled skyscrapers, complete with second roads that ringed around them, raised a story in the air.

I had been so enraptured by the view that when the door opened behind me my heart nearly jumped out of my chest.

"Hey, wait up! Do you know a Gerald?" Adrian asked.

I stopped, turning back to look at him on the bridge. "What?" I asked.

"Do you know a Gerald Smith?" Adrian said. His eyes scanned me. He looked to where the pin would have rested on my lapel; the spot that all the Nobles affiliated with houses or factions placed theirs.

"He kicked your ass last night," I said, scanning his face. Adrian winced. "Yeah, that's my friend."

The giant man behind him let out a belly laugh. "He did!"

"I don't want anything to do with you," I said. I didn't know whether they wanted to mock us or search for information to use to beat him next time, and I didn't care. I stepped past the two of them and threw the door to my own homeroom open.

It opened directly into a classroom of raised seating oriented around a teacher.

But not just any teacher. I froze in place as I stared at a familiar face. When Valjean had said that they had agents in the Academy who could help us make our way inside and graduate, I hadn't expected any of them to be teachers.

My shoulders tightened.

"Lyssandra?" I asked, staring at her where she stood drawing on a blackboard.

"Gwen Tailor. In this classroom you will always address me properly as Lady Lyssandra or Professor Lyssandra. Take a seat, and tell the two boys behind you to take their seats as well. They have been harassing students all morning."

Like every Noble in the academy, Lyssandra wore a pin on her uniform's lapel. Three, in fact. One of them seemed to represent the Academy. A second for Spoke, the image of a wagon wheel. The third I didn't recognize; it was a symbol of a torch.

"So you *are* Gwen!" Adrian said, excited.

He followed me into the classroom. The other Nobles were congregating in little cliques, and only looked up before turning away. They were taking notes—copying from the board, I realized.

Lyssandra was drawing a map of the campus.

"Welcome, late arrivals. Adrian. Cedric," Lyssandra said. "Take a seat and begin filling out your first assignment. I'm hoping you'll familiarize yourself with the campus . . . and not be late for any more classes. The inside of our little Academy is quite labyrinthine. Your initial trip to your homeroom orientation should have demonstrated that. You'll be making a copy of the map yourself."

There was a pencil and paper on every desk, along with an unlabeled map of the academy. The paper included instructions to label the map with the location of each of our classes, and asked a bunch of questions—Where would you find x facility? Where would y event be held? Where can you put in z request?—that were all rather basic and designed to accommodate newcomers.

It did not mention anything outside Academy walls.

Leaving the fortress was allowed, but only so many students could roam outside the wall at once, and you were required to report your leaving and take a pass with you so your location could be tracked.

The moment I answered the last question and stood to turn in my assignment, Adrian stood as well. He submitted his own paper only a moment behind me and followed me back toward my seat.

He tried to gain my attention by repeatedly sending glances my way. I ignored him as best I could, not even looking at him. He tapped my shoulder.

"What?" I asked.

"Can we talk?" he whispered, then looked around the classroom.

The students were much more interested in the discussion between me and Adrian than they had been about my knowing the professor. I wondered how many different Noble factions maintained relationships with their teachers in the Academy.

"Sure." I shrugged, eager for him to leave me alone so that I could continue on with my day.

"Outside, I mean. It's about Gerald."

I scowled. If he meant to start more trouble with him, I would throw him off the sky bridge. Still, I stomped through the door before turning on him.

"What do you want!?" I half shouted the second we stepped outside. "You practically assaulted my friend and got beat down and now you want to come to me for, what? To turn me against him? To find his weaknesses?"

"What? No!" Adrian said, waving his hands and pleading. "No. I need your help. Do you . . . do you know about his class?" Adrian whispered the last part.

"Yes, I know his class."

"I don't know if you do. He—he can craft," Adrian said. "Last night, I asked him to show me, and brought him to one of our forges. But he started and then never stopped. He's been at it for hours. I was up all night watching him, but then I had to go to class. I need your help. We can't snap him out of it."

"What?" I asked. "Gerald . . . went with you? After you *fought*? Voluntarily?"

* * *

Adrian led me away from the class and down the stairs, stepping into Academy City proper. Skybridges crisscrossed above us, leaving trails of ice in the shifting shadows that hung over the city. Puddles gathered in worn walkways and corners.

"Are we . . . just allowed to ditch class like this?" I asked, looking over at Adrian.

He shrugged. "There's just orientation classes today. Reviewing syllabi. Even more reason for you to come snap Gerald out of this. Has he done this before?"

"He loves his work," I replied.

He had always had a manic fascination when crafting, going stir-crazy if he didn't get to work on something.

The foot roads inside Academy City were cramped but kept nearly spotless. There was no mud despite the rain. I didn't see many people who looked like students, but almost everyone on the roads carried themselves with regal bearing, even if they appeared to only be doing chores.

Adrian led the way up a winding staircase path that looped around the back of second story buildings. We stepped out of an alley and onto a main road. Adrian's hand slammed onto my shoulder, whipping me back.

"Whoa there!" a teamster steering a wagon forward yelled. The man whipped the reins and scowled at us.

"Sorry!" Adrian said, smiling and waving. The man whipped the wagon again, trundling forward at an incline up the road. Warehouses and storefronts lined the road, and his wagon was piled high with wooden crates.

We crossed the road before shooting back into another alley.

Dozens of entrances opened on balconies above the alley, each uniquely decorated with plants and tapestries. Clotheslines hung over the roads, whipping in the wind. People leaned over the railings, smoking.

"Why did you challenge Gerald, anyway?" I asked finally, breaking the tense silence between us.

Adrian side-eyed me as he continued leading me through the alleyways.

"The answer I gave him didn't impress him," he said.

"Let me guess. You're a broke and struggling seventh son of a family set to inherit nothing and have to make a power grab at the Academy," I said.

"I'm a fourth son!" he replied, sounding defensive. "But . . . yeah."

"Why pick a new Chosen then?" I asked.

"To show off! And hopefully intimidate challengers."

I laughed.

"Hey! I couldn't have known what kind of class he had."

"You really think the class is the reason you lost?" I asked. "Or did you just underestimate him? You Nobles have a tendency to do that."

"You're a Noble, too," Adrian said.

I grunted.

The smell of iron and smoke hung heavy in the air as we moved toward an industrial section of the city. Adrian led me to a narrow alleyway down several flights of stairs. We had climbed and descended half the Academy before he unlocked a back door to a building and stepped inside.

There were guards posted at the door. One of them put a hand on a sword and squinted at me. He was well equipped. Ready to fight. He wore an extremely expensive and carefully crafted wool coat in a rich blue color. The outfit looked tacky. The stats on it must have been incredible.

"She's with me," Adrian said, waving.

"You said to—"

The scar on the man's lips crinkled as Adrian cut him off with a wave. "I know, I know. Make sure no one at all comes inside," Adrian said. "Keep that up. Except for me and her."

"Yes, sir," the guard grunted.

The man and I stared at each other as I walked past him. Adrian unlocked another door.

"What are you doing, keeping Gerald in a prison?" I asked. "Two locked doors and a guard, really?"

Adrian side-eyed me then waved his hand out when we stepped inside.

Crates sat piled against the walls below shelves full of ingots. There was a sound of hammering metal coming from the other side of the room, interrupted by laughter.

Adrian grimaced and led me through the warehouse. The walkways were half-blocked by crates that we had to turn sideways to step through.

"Aren't you afraid of a fire in here?" I asked.

"Huh?" Adrian said, turning to look at me.

"It's impossible to walk through here. And you have piles of wooden crates in the same building as your forge."

"The storage crates will be made out of magical wood harvested from the dungeon or reinforced by carpenters to resist fire. At least most of the time. Sometimes a crate gets confused. But it's no big deal. Most smiths get resistance to heat early into leveling."

We dropped the conversation as we reached Gerald.

He was wearing a full set of armor, save for the helmet. A *new* set.

He stared with manic glee as he deformed and reshaped a helmet in his hands. The metal was still burning hot. Gerald's face was covered in soot, and bags hung under his eyes. He dunked the helmet in murky water, sending steam up across the room before putting it on.

Then he fell backward and landed on his back with a crash.

"He'll wake up soon," I said in the hallway outside of Gerald's room, my arms folded over my chest.

"Uh huh. It's none of my business. But if he ends up injured or sick, I'm snitching," Marcus said. He was an attendant Noble in the school's postgraduate program—one I had inferred, through subtext, was friendly with Adrian's House Ironheart.

"He'll be fine!" Adrian said, smiling with boyish charm. Adrian turned to me. "He'll be fine, right?"

"Yes," I said. "His, uh . . . manias . . . typically resolve after he . . . expresses them like this."

We had been told not to reveal the details of our classes. But I was starting to think that they didn't explain why well enough. If being a Noble who could craft was that special, Valjean and Lyssandra should have pointed it out immediately. Unless they thought that downplaying it would keep us from broadcasting it.

Looking back on it, their reactions to learning about Gerald's class had been odd. But I'd thought nothing of it at the time; Chosen were pretty rare, after all, so I had attributed their surprise to the combination of a Chosen emerging at the same time that a few crafters cleared the dungeon.

Marcus gave us a weird look, then shook his head.

"I don't want to know. Thanks for the merit, Addy," Marcus said, walking away from us.

He had helped us drag Gerald across the city to his room. He didn't wake up even after an hour had passed; I didn't know how long he would be exhausted for. Adrian had suggested it may be mana exhaustion and could last most of a day. I had used [Quick Change] to pull Gerald's new set of armor to my inventory. The skill belonged to the exclusive domain of seamstresses and tailors.

We wouldn't have been able to carry him into a wagon without it.

"Lunch?" Adrian asked. He pulled out a pocket watch. "We still have time before our next class."

"It's not even noon," I said.

"Late breakfast, then," Adrian replied.

"Only if you're paying," I said.

Adrian led the way.

"By the way," Adrian asked, "what skill did you use to remove Lord Gerald's armor like that?"

Sandy hesitated outside the door to her fourth class of the day. She checked the plaque above the door. It was the correct room this time. The only issue was that it wasn't a classroom.

It was a gigantic, circular tower that jutted from the side of the Academy fortress. The wind tousled Sandy's hair as it whipped by. The giant structure was just at the entrance to the city, an arena that reached for the sky above her, constructed of rough stone stained by dirt and rain. Lichen ate at the stone.

The main entrance was a story up—the first entrance she had found was on the street below, reserved for wagons going to the basement. The guard there hadn't let her through, though he did give her directions to circle around, up two flights of stairs, and into this human-sized entrance on the second level.

Sandy stopped hesitating and ripped the door open, then stepped inside.

The room was almost empty. At one end, someone dressed as a teacher—wearing the glittering metal pin she had noticed on all of them—stood and instructed two guards. The guards carried crates that contained monsters, loading them into a caged arena in the center of the room.

Rows of desks surrounded the raised arena.

It reminded her of the one the abattoir in Foundry kept beneath the street.

"Sit down together," the teacher said, his voice booming from across the room without even looking at Sandy.

Sandy looked around the room. There was only one other student present. For a moment she was hopeful that she might find Gwen or Gerald.

Instead, she locked eyes with a woman with raven-black hair and a calculating gaze. She looked the epitome of a cold and guarded Noble. Cold wind whistled through tall, thin, open windows in the arena-tower-classroom.

The woman looked Sandy up and down with a perfect poker face. Sandy felt like she was being stared at with her own Butcher Vision buff. Or whatever the Noble equivalent was.

"I'm Elara," Elara said, smiling up at Sandy. "Of the House of Storms?" she continued.

Sandy eyed her warily as she sat down next to her.

"The work for this class will be mostly group projects," Elara said.

"I'm good at working in a team." Sandy nodded. She was still squinting at Elara. This was the first class that had actually had any kind of team activity.

The two before this one were just boring orientations.

"That's great," Elara said, smiling.

"What are we doing in this class?" Sandy asked.

"Many Nobles . . . especially Chosen . . . find themselves ill-prepared the first time they are confronted with a monster from the Wild or dungeons. This is a controlled environment to build the necessary mental preparation that no tool can replace," Elara said.

The desks around the arena were grouped together into little clusters of three or four with space between. More people started to filter into the room, gradually filling up the other seats.

Eventually, a third student filled the last desk between her and Elara. She carried a metal rod that looked like it had seen years of use. The metal was discolored around the handle, the once-shiny chrome now a matte gray from what seemed to be decades of fingerprints. The woman's hair was buzzed short.

"I'm Elara," Elara said, smiling up at the new girl. "Of the House of Storms?"

"Oh! Hi! I'm Ash," the girl said. She leaned her staff against her desk, turning to reach out a hand to Elara. The staff fell to the ground with a noisy clatter.

Elara returned the handshake, looking her up and down before reaching down to pick up Ash's staff.

"And you are . . . Chosen, yes?" Elara asked, presenting Ash's staff to her.

"Oh! Yes! Sorry!" Ash reached up and ran her hand through her buzzed short hair. "And you're Elara and . . ."

"Sandy," she said. Her arms were still folded as Ash reached a hand out. Sandy uncrossed them and shook her hand. "I'm Chosen, too. No need to be so nervous."

Ash smiled between them, clutching the metal staff she carried. Sandy recognized it. In orientation, one of the things the students were offered were weapon rentals. Sandy didn't bother looking at them—she still had the gigantic knife Gerald had made her.

"You do magic?" Sandy asked.

"I . . . I do." Ash paused, clutching the staff. "I only have one spell. And you?"

"'Doing Magic' isn't the proper way to refer to a mage," Elara said. "We practice one of humanity's highest disciplines."

"What spell is it?" Sandy asked.

"It's rude to ask a mage what spells they have. Ash, dear, you'll get plenty of spells in time. The levels come quick for people like us. We mages stand far above the average Noble."

"Thank you!" she said. "My spell is Force Bolt. It requires Focus and consumes most of my mana with one go, so I don't get to practice it much."

"What level are you?" Sandy asked.

"Level one."

"Oh, dear." Elara paused, seemingly taken aback. "Did you receive your class right before orientation?"

"No." Ash started turning red. "I just—we couldn't—"

"It's fine to not want to fight monsters," Sandy said. "I'd much rather be in an abattoir right now."

"An abattoir?" Ash paled.

"My mother was a butcher," Sandy said, smiling.

"It's not that I was afraid," Ash said. "We couldn't afford the pass to enter the dungeon—or to rent Focus. And it's not like I could just go wander the Wild."

Sandy blinked.

"Magic is still a great class to have, yeah?" she said. "It will be fine."

Sandy watched out of the corner of her eye as a porter lifted up one of the steel crates and pulled it into the arena at the center of the classroom. The teacher followed them up, standing with his arms behind his back and staring down.

Sandy thought it was odd how much the Nobility looked down on each other. The porters were both younger, but almost everyone here was still a Noble.

The porters were transporting small monsters. They had caught Sandy's eye because they were so familiar: the very same crystalline golems she had encountered in her own dungeon.

Sandy was paying rapt attention when the teacher started speaking.

"Quiet down. Quiet. I know you've all had a nice, tedious, boring day so far, so I won't bother with theory and paperwork and maps or a long preamble lecture. I am of House Stonehart. You may call me Lord Evan. Sir Stonehart is also acceptable. Elara to the arena please."

Elara stood without a word, walking confidently up the staircase and through the metal door. The second porter shut it behind her, while the teacher and the first porter remained inside the arena.

"I take it your family hasn't spared any expense in your training," Stonehart said, loud enough for everyone to hear. His voice was deep and resonant, booming through the entirety of the circular arena classroom.

"No, sir," Elara said.

"Good," Stonehart replied. "It is the duty of the Nobility to slay the monsters that the dungeons create. What you must know is that no matter how harmless a monster looks, you must remain on guard. Stay paranoid and hold nothing back. Because these monsters, and the Wild itself, beyond the bounds of our cities, hate us.

"They hate humanity," Stonehart said, pacing around the edge of the arena as the porter pulled forward the tiny cage. Inside was a bright cyan crystal golem. It looked around almost inquisitively, making a noise like a windchime. "And they hate the Nobility most of all. We are natural enemies. As a Noble, you must always be ready to kill to protect."

The porter released the cage door. Many members of the class began to whisper as the monster staggered out, looking at first confused. Sandy kept her arms folded. She knew exactly what these things were. She had fought them.

A staff appeared in Elara's hands. It was clearly finely crafted, the metal engraved with hundreds of tiny patterns. It was a shining black.

Elara extended her staff. The monster turned and charged her, releasing a noise through the entire room that sounded like nails on a chalkboard. Half the class threw their hands over their ears, including Ash.

"That one's new," Sandy said to Ash.

Then the sound cut off entirely. The golem floated up into the air, seemingly unable to move. Elara's back was to Sandy, but she could hear her grunt. The sound in the room seemed to echo out, making everything in the arena audible.

Elara kept one hand extended, holding up the magical focus rod she was using to channel her mana. Then she raised her other hand and closed a fist. Her arm shook. The sound of glass crunching, cracking, and then shattering filled the room. A bubble of force compressed on the floating golem until it shattered to pieces.

Elara let the staff lower with a gasp. What hit the floor was mostly dust and broken shards.

Students started to clap.

"Wasteful," Stonehart admonished, cutting the applause short. "It's good that you are quick to action. Speed of violence is important for Nobles. I would expect anyone with your family's training to be able to do the same. You can learn a lot about another Noble from how they fight. Elara here is wasteful. Just because your family has a class of high-capacity mana users does not mean you should waste resources on flashy moves. Remember that even within the walls of the Academy, you are in a dungeon, and dungeons are never safe. Elara, aim to kill an enemy with minimum effort. This isn't a class for social games."

Sandy wished she had magic like that, wasteful or not. Fighting monsters with knives didn't come close.

"Next," Stonehart said.

Ash scooted out of her chair, holding her clearly well-used magic rod, and walked up into the arena where the porter had already switched the cage to let the next monster out. She was pale as a ghost as Stonehart began to lecture.

"For those of you without the training of a Noble house . . . which will be many . . . your first experience in combat will be less than a Noble's. Twenty-five percent of all Nobles entering our program are Chosen, without the lineage and retained generational knowledge of how to best operate their classes. Each year, more than twenty percent of all graduates are Chosen. While this sounds like fewer graduate each year, in actuality, when weighing the advantages that Blooded Nobility are born with, it is a great mark of pride on the tenacity of our nation's Chosen.

"When you are confronted with an enemy, do not hesitate." Stonehart waved a hand and the cage opened.

Ash stood dead still and stared as the crystal golem trundled out. Then the monster screamed and charged her. She pointed her focus at it, concentrating. The monster charged her. She broke, running around the arena and trying to maintain the direction of her staff on the monster.

A bolt shot off, slamming into the metal mesh that surrounded the cage with a high-pitched impact.

Stonehart sighed as a few Nobles erupted into laughter.

Ash fired again, another shot missing. Aiming while moving seemed difficult. Stonehart stepped forward, snatching the golem's leg and holding it upside down. He extended an arm, holding the golem in the air while it flailed ineffectually. It cried out in a noise like tinkling bells.

There was a disappointed look on his face as he stared down Ash.

"Strike the target," he said.

Ash stopped and panted, but nodded, raising the staff.

"[Force Bolt!]"

The golem exploded into pieces that scattered across the arena. Sandy felt her eyes widen. She wouldn't have guessed the spell to have that much impact.

"Good aim," Stonehart said, dropping the half-broken skull of the crystal golem. "Next time, be ready to fight the moment the monster is released. And we will see which of you in the audience will be laughing when it's your turn."

Ash returned to her seat, gripping the staff and staring at the ground. Sandy watched her. She trained her gaze down onto the desk, fingers death-gripping the training staff.

"You alright?" Sandy asked.

"Yeah," Ash said.

"Your magic was impressive," Elara chimed in.

"Thank you," Ash said. She breathed out. Then she relaxed. "Thank you, guys."

"My turn," Sandy said.

There was a stone staircase leading up into the cage arena. The teacher smelled overpoweringly like smoke, like he had been sitting near a fire, and the porter stared at her. Her golem was green.

Sandy had gotten a few upgrades after the last fight in the dungeon. But the most important one was to her inventory.

Stonehart looked at her.

"I'm ready," Sandy said. Then she activated her inventory skill.

In front of her, she saw ephemeral floating images of the tools she had stored in her inventory. Tiny knives for throwing, cutting, and field dressing sat on either side of the gigantic, monster-tooth-embedded knife Gerald had made for her.

Her golem stumbled out of the cage one step at a time.

Sandy's hands closed around one of the weapons produced by [Butcher's Tools], the inventory skill of her class. The monster's weak points lit up red. Uneven lines scattered through the crystalline structure of the tiny monster.

Sandy swung for one on its head, crossing the distance between them in three long strides before the monster even made it out of the cage.

With her constant butchering after her skill reached level ten, her baseline stats were no longer anything to scoff at, even without preferred equipment.

She hacked through the golem's head in one clean sweep.

The golem didn't take a third step, crumbling into a pile on the ground.

Stonehart's eyes widened just a little. Sandy offered a smile.

"You should have your weapon ready before the fight," Stonehart said. He didn't seem unhappy with Sandy, though.

She lifted the weapon up, letting it disappear into [Butcher's Tools].

"Yes, sir," Sandy replied.

"Her decisiveness is something you should all seek to emulate," Stonehart said to the room. "Great job . . ."

"Sandy," she offered. Then she stepped down out of the arena.

"Next!" Stonehart said.

Sandy stepped back to her seat.

"You did amazing," Ash whispered. "I couldn't imagine having to fight a monster up close like that!"

"You should get used to it," Elara said. "You won't always be fighting at a distance. It's important to invest in skills you can use at close range as well as far."

Ash nodded along.

"Maybe we can all practice together sometime?" Sandy asked. "If we're going to be on a team together?"

Elara put a finger to her chin.

"That isn't a bad idea, you know. Give me a day or two to talk to some friends of mine. They're probably already putting something together."

CHAPTER 15

Out of all of my classes, Practical Combat was the one that I was both the most nervous and most excited for. The class took place in a tower staged off the wall with open windows exposed to the weather, filling the classroom with a chilling wind.

The class was clearly designed to force us into groups; I took a seat in a row of three. I recognized one of the two people I sat with; the girl named Annabelle I'd met at the debut. Looking at her, I was even more sure that her freckles were odd; in the cloudy daylight, they seemed almost metallic, reflective.

The man sitting next to her had short-cropped blond hair. The open seat was in the middle.

"Hi?" Annabelle said. I was staring at her face too long.

"Hey! I'm Gwen," I said, extending a hand.

"I remember," Annabelle said. She was staring at me with a concerned expression. "You can call me Anna."

"I'm Victor," Victor said without preamble. He stared toward the front of the class.

"How are your first days of classes going?" I asked.

We made small talk until the class started. People filed in and took seats. The instructor—a Sir Stonehart—barked out advice at each of the Nobles as they fought. Many of them were clearly fighting a monster for the first time in their lives. They weren't very threatening. Far less so than the wolves I had fought for my first kills; they were the tiny, crystalline golems with nubby limbs and smooth heads.

Victor fought with enthusiasm, wielding, of all things, a whip. A single snap of his arm and the golem exploded to pieces. His eyes lit up, and he was excited when he returned to his seat.

When it was my turn to be called up, I was anxious that the instructor would inquire about the nature of my weapon; we hadn't made any effort to disguise the giant sewing needle as something else.

My concern diminished after seeing the myriad weapons the other people in the room used. Many of them seemed to be custom or handcrafted, though they could all damage an enemy. The Blooded Nobility, however, carried a variety of high-quality weapons. They struggled the least against the monsters. Watching carefully, you could tell that their attributes were far higher than a human's baseline.

I stabbed the golem, leaving it in pieces on the ground.

"Excellent, precise strike. Your name is?"

"Lady Gwen," I said, offering a half bow to the instructor.

"Observe Lady Gwen's spacing. She keeps the monster at the farthest range of her weapon. You all should note it. Next."

Annabelle frowned as she stared down at the caged monster. The expression was readable on her face.

She crossed the arena in a flash of gold, the golem exploding in a solid punch, and then she returned to her seat next to us without saying a word.

"Clean kill," the instructor commented meekly. For every single person before her, he had some specific comment to make—mostly things to improve, but in a few exceptions he observed something the student did well.

He looked befuddled by whatever skill Anna had just used. I had never even heard of anything like that skill, but that didn't say much. I hadn't heard of much of the Nobility's powers.

The class continued on.

When a student failed to kill the monster, the instructor intervened, capturing it until they could finish the job.

When every last person had slain one of the golems, the class continued with a series of questions and answers. Every student was forced to contribute something. The instructor asked how they could kill it in the future with less effort; how they might fight against three of this monster at once; against ten.

With my work for the day over and a pile of assignments in my hands, I headed back to the dorm to shower before crunching them out. I found a note attached to my door that interrupted my plan.

Mail for Lady Gwen from Lord Valjean. Storage 38C. See front desk for key.

I dropped my homework in my room then brought the note to the front desk, trading the note and signing the key into my possession before retrieving a packed parcel.

I opened the wooden tote to a pile of letters from Stitch as well as a package from Lizzie, and practically sprinted back to the dorm.

To the Lady of Stitch;

The new Foundry atelier is amazing!

In the time since we last saw each other, I have gained six levels and two additional patterns. They both show great promise. I hope to be able to send you more once they are refined.

The atelier has received an additional fifty orders; more are expected in the coming weeks as the utility of our items in the hands of commoners is further demonstrated.

I pray for your outstanding success in the Academy and your swift return.

Signed Elizabeth Tailor

Written by Finn Scribe

I put on the outfit and spun around, wishing I had the pattern myself. I remembered I once passed up on a skill that allowed you to copy a pattern by destroying it. I regretted it. Who knew when I would see it again?

The mage outfit was uncomfortable. The quality was inconsistent. It was stitched together from dozens of cut pieces of leather and rearranged into something coherent. Layers of cloth that hid the imperfections meant it was stuffy and harsh to wear. But it was all mine.

I still needed to finish the Caustic Hunter set that I had started work on back in Foundry; there'd been no time during Lyssandra's cram sessions, and there would be no room in this tiny dorm room to do any real work. I needed a workshop.

Over the course of my stay in Lyssandra's dungeon, I had gained two whole levels. I had also gained two levels in my last clear of Stitch. After learning that Sandy gained permanent attributes every time she crafted something after her core Butcher skill reached tier ten, I started leveling my Crafting skill to pursue the same.

It would take me a whopping nine levels of investment, but I was convinced that it would lead to permanent stat increases. And gaining those extra levels would be easy now, because I expected that this mage outfit might let me complete entire outfits in a single day.

[Gwendolyn Tailor][Human, Lv20][Seamstress]

[Health: 40/40][Mana: 70/70][XP: 0/10]

[ATTRIBUTES]

▶SPD: 22

▶WIL: 35

▸STR: 5
▸DEX: 16
▸CON: 20
▸PER: 14
[SKILLS]
▸Crafting V
▸Running Stitch I
▸Hand Spinning I
▸Thread Mastery IV
▸Wardrobe X
▸Quick Change I
▸Embellishment III
▸Pattern Mirroring I
▸Always Prepared II
[PATTERNS]
▸Hunter Pattern
▸Shell Dress Pattern
▸Houndsmaster Pattern
[TEMPORARY SKILLS]
▸Bow Proficiency I
▸Shadow Cloak II
▸Tracking Proficiency I
▸Thread Sensing III
▸Thread Mastery VII
▸Summon Rain IV
▸Projection III
▸Trapping III
▸Befriend III
▸Wildspeaker I

The biggest things I was lacking were space to work and raw materials. I still had leftovers from the goats harvested in Spoke's dungeon. I needed to find a way to acquire more material, whether it meant leaving the city and hunting in the woods with Sandy or purchasing the materials directly from the city.

The dungeon monsters on this floor would be no joke.

But maybe I could earn money to buy materials by selling custom commissions. I would just have to find a way to convince Nobles to purchase from me.

I knew just the person who had already demonstrated a willingness to trade favors with other Nobles and a broad social network. I just needed to track down Adrian.

I needed a way to get started. I needed the support of a faction.

I needed Lyssandra's help.

But first, I headed to dinner. There was a mess hall connected to the dorms that served meals included with the merit cost of the room. Simply maintaining a passing grade in your classes was enough to offset the price.

I sat down at a lonely cafeteria table. The other Nobles avoided it. Sandy was the first to find me. She sat down across from me as I poked at the food.

"How is it?" she asked.

"Not good," I replied.

"You think they have a more upscale place if you get better grades?"

"Worse," I said. "They have whole private restaurants."

"Oh?" Sandy asked.

"I skipped a class today and visited one."

"What? Did Lyssandra pay for it? And she didn't bring me?"

"No—it was the Noble who challenged Gerald last night."

"What?" Sandy asked.

"At the debut. Where were you? I couldn't track either of you down."

"I . . . left immediately," Sandy said. "Walked in. Turned around. Walked out. Not my thing, really."

"You can do that?" I asked.

"No one stopped me." Sandy shrugged. "What happened to Gerald? You hung out with someone who fought him? How beat up is he?"

"Gerald won. Neither of them are very beat up."

"That's odd," Sandy said. "How did that . . . What happened?"

"Gerald went with him last night and gave in to the crafting mania. He ended up awake all night. I skipped classes to try to pull him out of it, but he finished right as I arrived. Passed out on the spot and Adrian arranged some favors to drag him home without anyone noticing," I said. "Speak of the devil . . ."

Adrian and Gerald appeared right behind Sandy. I hadn't even noticed them approaching. Adrian was all cool smiles, but Gerald looked half-asleep still, rubbing at his eyes.

"I also arranged some favors to gather all of Gerald's homework for the day. And already completed, too," Adrian said, coolly sliding into the seat next to me. Gerald sat down across from us, yawning.

Adrian set down a stack of completed papers.

"Oh, cool, all the answers," Sandy said, thumbing through the pages.

"On the house," Adrian said, spreading his hands.

"Why are you here?" I asked, staring Adrian down. "Were you just waiting outside Gerald's room for him to wake up?"

"Of course not!" Adrian said. "I paid someone else to do that. I wanted to bring him his homework in person."

Gerald looked over the page with half-mast eyes.

"Thanks, Adrian," he said. "And thanks for last night."

"My pleasure," Adrian said. "So, Sandy, Lady Elara tells me you were interested in joining an extracurricular practice team?"

"Hm?" Sandy said, looking up from the stack of Gerald's already-completed papers. "You know her?"

"We're good friends. I assume the three of you are a package deal? How about this: tomorrow, after classes, bring all three of your teams, if you can convince them. We have training weapons and space for sparring."

"And what do you get out of this?" I asked.

"A loyal group of friends, of course," Adrian said. "A very, very interesting group of friends."

Adrian held his hand out toward the pile of completed assignments Sandy was browsing. She hesitated before handing them back. From the bottom of the pile, he slid out a pile of maps, marking a location for a warehouse he rented in the city.

"You're very prepared for this." I squinted in suspicion. Adrian had information about us that he hadn't gotten from me. He was aware of our class teams' members. He knew all of Gerald's classes. He hadn't mentioned Gerald's team, though. It gave me a pause. "Gerald . . . who are your teammates in Practical Combat? Do you know?"

"I didn't make it to any classes today," he said.

"Cedric and I saved you a spot on our team," Adrian replied. "Your class schedule might be slightly off. They should send you a new one soon."

In homeroom the next day, the word *EXPEDITIONS* was written across the blackboard.

"Excursions out of the Academy must be signed. A Noble guardian will accompany any excursion deemed unsafe. If the guardian must intervene at any point, you will forfeit all material gains from your trip. Practical Combat and Practical Dungeoneering will both feature multiple assignments requiring you to register for excursions. You do so here in homeroom."

Lyssandra continued, "Additionally, the combined final for both classes will involve an expedition. That will require you to find and join a team. You should have noticed your seating arrangements in Practical Combat."

In the middle of Lyssandra talking, the door to the classroom swung open. She clenched the piece of chalk she was holding.

Adrian walked in, clearly late. Lyssandra said nothing, but irritation was plain on her face as he crossed the classroom and fell into the seat right next to mine. He offered me a smile. I looked back at the worksheet for today.

It mostly covered what Lyssandra was already saying aloud. I did my best to ignore Adrian and pay attention to the lecture.

"Want to skip classes again today?" he asked.

"No," I said, trying my best to stare harder at the homework.

Adrian yawned and leaned back in his seat. He looked at the paper in my hands. He leaned over my shoulder and read it.

"I could get you the answers if that's the concern," he said. He wasn't even whispering.

"Adrian Ironheart. Gwendolyn Tailor," Lyssandra said.

I grunted and looked up, then did my best to remove the scowl on my face and smile.

"Yes?" I asked.

"You . . . stay after class today," Lyssandra said. "And you, Adrian. Get out. Come back on time tomorrow."

"Yes ma'am," Adrian said, standing up and marching theatrically out of the classroom.

The rest of the class detailed where to rent equipment for expeditions, going on to mark some of the closest monster dens and the more dangerous ones farther away. Each monster corpse would be worth a merit or two, and the closest and safest were reserved for the new, lower-level students to clear. There still wasn't enough for everyone.

A boy in the back of class raised his hand. "Couldn't we just hunt monsters to get enough merits to graduate?" he asked.

"Yes," Lyssandra said. "That's known as one of the many unofficial tracks to graduation. You'll have to ask your peers about it; the Academy does not endorse a course that dangerous. It is a great way to find sponsorship in another Noble's city or offers to become a vassal and bannerman."

"What if I want my own city?" the man asked.

"And what would you do with it?" Lyssandra asked. There were giggles from the back of the class. "Fighting is among the least important duties the Nobility must discharge. To receive a first- or second-tier city from the state and not a lesser house, you'll need a higher title, which you can earn by completing more necessary credits. Back to the lesson at hand . . ."

Lyssandra continued surveying the map and the various monster dens around the city. She drew a ring around the little figure of Academy City, marking how long each trip to one of these would take. As they grew farther away, they became an entire day's march through the jungle.

Class wrapped up. Students filed out of the room.

I waited nervously. When the last student exited, Lyssandra seemed to deflate with a sigh. She smiled.

"Sorry about that. The first few days at the Academy are always busy," Lyssandra said. She folded her hands. "I'm sure you have a lot of questions."

"You have a city to defend," I stated plainly.

"The church and state reward us generously for working in the Academy, especially if we raise talents. Not to mention that talents that join houses as vassals expand our own effort. The protection of Spoke will be covered," Lyssandra said. She crossed the room and sat on the desk near me.

"What do you teach here?" I asked. "I mean, that's worth so much. No offense."

"In the almost decade I've run Spoke, it's risen as a prominent center of trade south of the nation. Several prominent houses have begun to send their heirs through this Academy specifically to enjoy private tutoring and my lectures on trade and tariff. With the advent of the rail network spanning the major cities two decades ago, trade has steadily risen across the nation. Almost every Noble house is trying to raise merchant heirs," Lyssandra said. She looked distant for a moment. Then she turned and scanned my face. "You need a workshop," she said.

"I . . ." I did need a workshop. It was one of the things I most needed to talk to Lyssandra about. "I'm not in trouble? I mean, that's not why you kept me after class?"

She smiled knowingly.

"That boy could be a great asset for you while you're in the Academy. He is wealthy, especially in merits. Most of his Noble house and Vassal houses attend a different Academy, which means there is very little oversight on the resources and connections they maintain here."

"He seems like a . . . privileged layabout. You know he's paying other students to do his homework for him?"

Lyssandra waved the concern away.

"Adrian Ironheart is anything but lazy. You will likely see tonight exactly how hard he works. He has had private mentors for years, to the point that the first year's worth of material at the Academy has no value for him. We knew that Gerald's class would eventually leak, but this is far from the worst case. We thought under-emphasizing how . . . unique . . . his class is . . . Well, we didn't want you to catch the attention of another faction before entering the Academy. Combination crafting and combat classes are rare, to say the least.

"You should use Adrian as much as you can. Squeeze every last concession you can from him."

"So, the workshop?" I asked.

"Ah, for that, I know the supervisor of the Academy's atelier." Lyssandra reached into a pocket in her uniform and passed me an ordinary-looking key ring. "If you did your homework from the first day, then you should know where it is. Not every room in it is used. Much of it was built for future expansion that never came. Just . . . don't mind the supervisor. She can be prickly. I also need to warn you . . . do not mention me around her."

I clutched the keys.

CHAPTER 16

We killed another golem in Practical Combat. After the first day, this one went much faster. With half an hour left in class, the instructor started discussing initial skills and fighting for Nobility.

After class, I headed to the training arena that Adrian rented. Sandy was already waiting outside, wearing most of her Storm Curtain set.

"Ready to kick some Noble ass?" Sandy asked.

"Are they in there?"

There was shouting on the other side of the door. Adrian was yelling something.

"Sounds like it," Sandy said.

"You mean you haven't opened the door to check?"

"I was waiting on you," Sandy said.

The entrance to the warehouse was below a crisscrossing section of sky-bridges, in a back alleyway with poorly maintained cobblestone.

We were interrupted by murmuring from behind us. Anna strode down the alley, constantly looking down at a map and back up.

Her head snapped up. She always wore low bangs. Even when fighting, she never tied her hair back.

"Gwen," she said, searching my face. "And . . ."

"This is my friend, Sandy," I said. "I know her from back in Stitch."

Anna frowned.

"Humans have an incident rate of turning into Nobles just above two percent. I thought you were from a frontier town? Its population shouldn't number more than a few dozen," Anna said. The words were clinical. She turned to Sandy. "You were both Chosen from the same town?"

"All three of us. Us and Gerald, I mean," Sandy said.

"Two percent?" I asked. "I thought it was lower than that. It should only be, what, one percent?"

"So they say," Anna said, still frowning.

Exactly how many Nobles died each year for the rate to be two percent? The door swung open.

"You're here!" Adrian said, his face a smile. I saw Victor at his side with his arms folded.

Inside a crackling arena, Gerald and Cedric were boxing barehanded. Every punch released a crackle of purple light; it was the same enchantment I had seen used in training weapons.

"Uh . . ." I said, staring at the two of them fighting.

"Come inside!" Adrian said.

The three of us were the last to arrive. Once we entered, there were ten people in the room. The two strangers from my own Practical Combat class, Anna and Victor, grouped up next to me. Most people were staring at Cedric and Gerald boxing inside of the central arena. The warped field appeared to mute sound.

Cedric clearly had every advantage in their fight. His form was better, somehow more professional. His reach was longer, boxing in and out of Gerald's attacks, feinting and jabbing.

But he still didn't look like he was winning. Gerald would block at the last second, sliding back, but taking no damage, then cross the arena in a flash before returning Cedric's blow just as hard, despite the amateurish form.

There was a layer of foam on the ground. A tall, thin window let in light from the afternoon sun, occasionally disrupted by the shadows of people passing on the street a level above. A pile of shelves occupied one side of the room; they looked new, and they were loaded with goods.

On the other side of the room was a massive wheeled case of enchanted training weapons, folded open to reveal an entire arsenal equipped with almost any common weapon you could think of.

On top of my own team of Anna and Victor, and Gerald's—very suspicious—team of Cedric and Adrian, there was also Sandy's two team-mates; Elara, a blooded Noble mage of the House of Storms, and Ash, a Chosen mage.

It didn't escape my notice that almost everyone here was Chosen. Adrian, Cedric, and Elara were the only members of the Blooded Nobility.

The others must have had teams from their own families and factions.

Cedric eventually wore out Gerald, who tapped out.

Marcus walked to where a pillar rose from the floor, grabbing and shifting an array of gemstones on the top of it. The buzzing field wound down.

"It will only run for a few hours a day before it needs to be recharged again," Marcus said.

"That's plenty," Adrian replied. He had pulled towels from two of the shelves and thrown them to Gerald and Adrian.

"Suit yourself. I'm heading out. If you need anything else, you know where to find me," Marcus said. "I'm prepping for an expedition, so leave a note if I'm not home."

With that, he crossed the room and left. An awkward pause followed.

Adrian clapped his hands. "Alright everyone, welcome to Study Hall," he said. "I'm Adrian Ironheart for those unfamiliar. I've rented this building and this equipment for us to use."

"Why?" Victor interrupted. He folded his arms, leaning back against the wall. "Out of the goodness of your heart? I'm not signing up as anyone's vassal."

"Of course not." Adrian smiled. "I could tell you that we simply need someone to train against. I could tell you that as a lesser heir of my family I'm not afforded the resources for private training. Both of those would be lies. The truth is that Study Hall is a longstanding tradition of the Academy known among the Blooded Nobility. The nine of us here will hopefully form the foundation of our expedition group. But to get there, we need to train."

"Your competition are likely doing the same," Elara said. "If not today, they will be headhunted for sessions by the end of this week or next. Most of them won't be half as willing to afford as many resources to Chosen."

Sandy was grimacing. Gerald was on the floor, pressing the towel to his forehead. I had never seen him fight much. Back in Lyssandra's dungeon he had barely been willing to fight without his armor. He caught my stare and smiled up at me. I nodded at him.

"We have years of experience and private mentoring," Adrian said. "We're willing to pass on what we know to you all. For free. The catch is that we need allies to complete expeditions to accumulate merits and, ultimately, to graduate. We're not seeking vassals. Based on everyone's skill, we have some suggestions for who should fight who first tonight."

Adrian looked over to me.

"I want to fight you," Victor said, interrupting whatever Adrian was going to say next.

Adrian had a look of surprise on his face. Then irritation. He schooled it quickly, turning it back into a smile.

"Alright." Adrian's eyes had a manic edge to them. "We have training weapons available. You can pick whichever you'd like," he said, approaching the wall and pulling free a rapier.

He twirled it in his hand before stepping into the arena. Victor, once again, went for a whip.

Once they'd both stepped into the arena, Elara adjusted the control panel and turned it on. Adrian held his rapier extended toward Victor. For a moment, there was a bit of darkness in his face. It disappeared, replaced by that constant mask of smug, charismatic confidence.

"This is that thing again," Gerald said. He walked toward me, but he wasn't necessarily speaking to me. He looked to Elara. "Making a statement."

"Yes," Elara said. "Poor Victor."

His whip flashed forward.

Adrian parried it without moving.

Victor blinked, then started whipping rapidly. Adrian must have been using a skill—he perfectly met and deflected the whip each time. Victor slowly came closer and closer. A vicious smile bloomed on his face as he redirected his whip at the last moment. The whip wrapped around Adrian's rapier.

Adrian pulled backward. Victor stumbled forward.

Adrian backhanded him. He hit the ground hard, disarmed, his face red. Elara disabled the arena.

"That hurt," Victor said, rubbing his face. "I thought it was supposed to . . ."

"The arena will prevent any damage that lowers your health. Minor damage doesn't do that."

"I . . . that wasn't fair," Victor said.

Adrian smiled.

"Would you like to go again?"

Victor lost another two rounds. Each time, Adrian never moved from his position, at most turning to face Victor as he circled him. The whip never hit him. As I watched on, I realized that Adrian wasn't using a skill.

He was just that good.

How long had he practiced to be able to do that? Parrying a whip was surely in the realm of the superhuman. Or maybe it was some kind of passive skill like a weapon proficiency.

Either way, it meant that Adrian was leveled.

I wanted to beat him.

"Most of you will likely only be in your first few levels. It's normal for

Blooded Nobility to be guided through several early levels to gain an advantage in the Academy," Adrian explained. "After a few weeks of practice, we can schedule our own expeditions and help you level faster than just by relying on Practical Combat courses. There is plenty for you to gain here," he said.

Every word and action was designed to woo us toward working with them. A few others sparred before eventually it was my turn.

"Elara and Gwen?" Adrian said.

"A real mage," I said, looking over.

Elara wore a smug smile.

I tied a string around one of the training rapiers.

"What's that?" Elara asked, curious. She had her hands folded. She was using her own focus—the magical staff that channeled her spells, or enhanced them somehow. I bet it gave her attributes, too.

"It's for good luck," I said.

"Superstition," she said.

I smiled. "I didn't grow up around real magic."

We stood opposite each other over the arena mats as I played with the rapier. Adrian watched me intently; likely because he was a fellow rapier user. The sword was sufficiently needle-like to activate my skill, but I couldn't say that I actually preferred it over a needle. A bladed edge opened up more ways to damage monsters, but I was worried about handling it.

Maybe there was a seamstress skill that would prevent damaging myself with my own tools, similar to how a smith's could handle burning metal or tools, but I didn't have it yet.

Elara held out her focus. There was a crackle as the barrier came to life around us. Excitement and fear boiled inside me in equal measure; I had never fought a mage. And now I was about to fight someone with real magic.

Elara lifted the focus and then stopped.

"Attack me," she said.

It felt like one of those cheesy segments where someone was being set up to prove a point. I knew better than to hold back.

I needed speed. I used [Quick Change], switching into the Aracheknight set and out of my school uniform. Elara's eyes widened a bit at it. Switching equipment out of an inventory was nothing special, but everyone else had fought in their school uniforms.

The Aracheknight set gave me a boost of fifteen points in speed.

I crossed the arena in three steps, my sword shooting forward and right as I finished assembling the armor.

[Running Stitch] dragged my hand with supernatural speed and strength.

It ground across an invisible barrier, screeching like metal on metal. I didn't [Cancel]; the attack continued, trying to pierce the invisible barrier around Elara's face as I stepped to the side.

She gestured forward with her focus.

A wall of invisible air picked me up and threw me backward. I landed hard, pulling myself together and back to my feet quickly. Elara wasn't done. She continued waving her focus at me. It only took a moment before the next invisible force slammed into me.

I couldn't even see the attacks. I needed to think quickly. The invisible projectiles she pushed forward were like magical barriers; they had to be physical or they wouldn't stop attacks. If the same spell attacking me was the one she defended herself with, which seemed to be the case, as her initial barrier is what had hit me, then they likely also disrupted everything in their path.

Along my belt I carried a row of sewing needles with long threads attached to the end.

I grabbed a handful and threw them toward the ceiling with supernatural strength. A few bounced and fell, but others stabbed into the wooden rafting. I saw the people outside the arena flinch.

One of the strings was brushed aside as Elara's next projection flew toward me.

I ducked under it, running forward and grabbing the throwing needles on the ground.

When I raised my arm, Elara flinched, using her focus. She was probably summoning a barrier that would block any needle thrown at her.

I threw the needles to either side of her, leaving the string across the ground. She turned to face me as I circled her, raising my rapier. But it was a feint.

[Thread Mastery] worked just well enough to let me wrap the threads on the ground around her ankles and pull. It wasn't enough to knock her off her feet, but it was enough to slide one leg back. I stabbed forward into her invisible barrier. She took a step back and tripped. [Running Stitch] drove the rapier into her neck.

A flash of purple erupted at the tip of the blade; it stopped at the skin. I paled, flinched back.

"Sorry!" I said. If these weren't training weapons, I could've killed her.

Elara looked up at me, shock plain on her face. I lowered an arm to help raise her to her feet.

"That was . . . good," Elara said, almost begrudgingly. "Excellent work, Lady Gwen."

"Thank you! You, too. Your barrier magic is really cool. How much mana does each one of those cost?"

The field around us collapsed.

"I think I just lost my deposit," Adrian said. His arms were folded and he was staring at where I had embedded needles in the rafters.

I blushed.

"I don't think it's that bad," I said, grabbing hold of a thread and pulling the needle loose. Old, split wood splinters fell at the same time as the needle.

Adrian sighed.

"He's being dramatic," Elara said. "We were never getting that deposit back."

Sandy and Adrian fought next. He had apparently recovered.

Sandy used her speed and [Parry] with incredibly accuracy, pushing Adrian back. With her larger blade, she eventually overpowered his rapier and tapped him for damage.

"Impressive," Adrian said, smiling in spite of his defeat. "I do have to ask, though—where did the two of you get those gear sets?"

Everyone else in the training session had been fighting in just the school uniform. Elara, Cedric, and Adrian had access to gear without a doubt. The other Chosen, however, wouldn't. And they were paying rapt attention. I hesitated over how to answer. I obviously couldn't reveal that I wasn't a Noble. However . . . maybe these people represented my first sales channel.

I was jealous of how much Adrian could accomplish by throwing merits around. I needed to start earning currency of my own.

"I have a . . . connection. For making custom gear," I said.

Adrian nodded.

"You were clearly trained to fight by the Nobles of your locales. You know, I actually heard about a powerful gear set being produced down in Foundry. It only came to my attention because my family controls so much of the smithing. Just a fun rumor. Is that related to your connection?"

I paused.

"Yes."

"And you're able to get access to more equipment while inside the Academy?" Adrian asked.

I nodded once.

"I see," Adrian said, thinking.

"For a price, of course," I said, before he got any ideas about trading favors. "The raw materials, labor, the workshop . . . and extra for discretion." I was making it up as I went.

"Our expedition team will need equipment," Adrian said. "If we bring back monster parts, you'll be able to supply your connection. We can sell whatever they don't want for merits or currency to pay for the rest."

I scanned the room. Every face was looking at me expectantly. Could I make eight more gear sets for everyone here?

The answer was definitely yes. And if we had the chance to study the lesser drakes that functionally acted as a final project for graduation, I could probably find an armor set and materials specifically to resist them.

"Yeah. We can make that work."

After Study Hall—the colloquial, and allegedly, widespread term used for afterschool practice groups—I headed to find the atelier that Lyssandra helped me reserve time in.

It was on the upper level of a wide open street, a multistory building accessible from street level. I opened the door and retail employees working a late shift looked up at me.

"Here for a pick-up?" the worker asked. He looked exhausted. He was currently sweeping the floor.

Mannequins in glass cases, surrounded by metal bars, displayed outfits. The goods here were valuable.

If it wasn't for the glass case, I could likely reach right through and use Quick Change to loot the pieces.

These were sets designed, visibly, for mid-level Nobles. They radiated power in a way that you could sense. No expense was spared in their design. Which probably meant a ton of resources were wasted. My eyes lingered on armor that looked like it was cut from a dragon. Or from multiple dragons, thick red scales over leather over enchanted metal beneath.

"Not here for a pick up," I said, lifting the keys. "I, uh, have a package waiting for me in the back."

The employee looked me up and down.

"I'll have to get my manager."

He stood the broom up against a table and turned around. Before he could reach the back of the shop, a door opened, and Lyssandra strode out.

I blinked.

It wasn't Lyssandra. But she looked close enough for them to be twins. The woman sighed, striding out of the back of the shop and staring at me with heavy eyes.

"She's with me," she said. "You can go home for today. Thank you."

"Alright, Viv."

The employee didn't need to be told twice. He looked at me a second time, then back to Viv, then he left, turning the sign around to "Closed" and locking the door before stepping outside. He pulled on the door to check it.

"Pleasure to meet you, Viv," I said, extending a hand.

She looked me up and down.

"Call me Vivienne," she said.

I hesitated.

"Lady Vivienne?" I asked.

She shook her head no. "Vivienne Scriver."

"Are you, by any chance, related to the Lady Lyssandra?"

Viv grimaced. "She's my sister, yes. We aren't exactly on the best of terms. And why she thinks it's a good idea for a crafter to pretend to be a Noble is beyond me. Though, she was right in that my particular job has given me a more favorable view of your activity."

Vivienne turned and stomped deeper into the building.

"What?" I asked.

She didn't reply, continuing to walk away.

I followed after her a second later.

How many people knew? Though, I supposed people were likely to trust their own flesh and blood. I shut the door behind me. Directly behind the front room was a storage area with shelves lined with goods. There were more patterns on secured mannequins as well. Viv was already descending a set of stairs in the back.

The next story down was dark. Very dark. The back hallway that connected the rooms was full of half-empty crates and boxes and smelled like dust. We were still stories above ground level, but it felt like we were crawling through a cave, guided only by the light that crept in from the hallway above us. Vivienne led me to the end of the hall, which brightened considerably from the light escaping under a door.

"Key?" she asked. I handed it to her. The door slid open, creaking to reveal a workshop covered in a layer of dust. The hardwood floors were gorgeous but grimy. Floor-to-ceiling windows gave a view of streets below and buildings across the way.

"This is nice," I said. "But . . . I can't have anyone see me crafting." I stared down at the street below.

"The windows are tinted." Vivienne sighed. "This floor is almost entirely unused. The ones below it are active but we've never needed to spill over up here. Cleaning it is up to you. You're welcome to it at any hour." Vivienne passed the key back to me. "Just don't be noisy enough to disrupt any of the work."

"You said your last name is Scriver, right?" I asked, curious. "You're not a seamstress?"

"Lyssandra and I come from a long line of scribes," she replied simply. "I help manage the atelier in this Academy on behalf of the Guild. It's a considerably more expansive operation than those in a minor city and I won't have you mucking about in it.

"Stick to this workshop, work quietly, and don't disrupt our shifts, and I'll ensure a completely blind eye is turned to this room. Understand?"

I nodded yes.

CHAPTER 17

Classes ramped up. So did training.

The monsters started to get bigger in Practical Combat. The first four days featured the tiny, crystalline golems which represented no real danger to the students.

It was Friday when they released the wolves.

"Annabelle," Sir Stonehart called my teammate to the front of the classroom. I had seen her fight a lot by now, in Study Hall. She didn't demonstrate much at all in class. All four monsters had been taken out with the same technique, with the same form, struck the same way and defeated in a single blow. I didn't know what her class was; she rushed monsters barehanded with a trail of burning light behind her.

In Study Hall, she used brass knuckles.

The entire class was quiet as she was called to the stage, the first of the students to fight the wolves. She said nothing, just stared forward with the same bored expression. Out of all the students in Study Hall, she was the only one who had turned down every invite to dinner or hangouts after. She was also the only one to ever have missed a day.

I knew almost nothing about her.

In the cages, wolves identical to the ones in the heart of Stitch gnawed at the bars of their cages, forms of muscle bulky beneath thick black fur. They were absolutely rabid, foaming and leaking drool where their teeth cut marks into the metal of their cages. Their eyes were a brilliant yellow.

Anna stared at them with the same bored expression she used on the teacher.

"When facing a real monster, it is important not to cower. You must take the offensive. And you must not be caught by surprise."

The porter carrying the cage for the first wolf opened it at the word "surprise."

The wolf howled as it stepped free from its cage. It was injured; they had likely damaged the monster when capturing it. Anna tensed the same exact way she always did. Her muscles bulged, visible where her sleeves rolled back. With a calm, steady exhale, she stepped forward.

She left behind a golden blur as she raised her right hand and brought it down with a sickening crunch. The wolf hit the floor and died. The fight was no different than her fights against the golems.

It was just as quick and just as brutal.

The instructor paused for a moment.

"Efficient technique."

Much of the rest of the class struggled to fight the wolf, with a few of them even receiving bites from the monster. The instructor was fully capable of stopping that from happening; he was letting it happen on purpose before stopping the wolf from inflicting serious damage.

Like a vicious form of exposure training.

I ran a needle through the monster's head without any issue.

"Impressive force," Sir Stonehart commented.

Of the entire class, only a handful received positive comments.

At night, after Study Hall, I had been slowly working on converting the leftover materials from seven entire goat kills into sets. The materials were hard to work with; I had to ask Vivienne for help to figure out how to use the workshop.

The advanced atelier had all kinds of fancy equipment, much of it buried unused in storage or under pop-up panels in the floor. This included grounding cables that drained the slowly building electricity from the goats' fur.

The dense black fur constantly accumulated a static charge, a magical property seemingly embedded in the material. The smaller the piece, the slower it accumulated, and the lower the maximum charge.

It would have been a waste to use it on the Hunter pattern. I didn't have a better pattern to spend it on, and I needed to do something to continue leveling while working through classes. Our Study Hall team still wasn't ready for expeditions yet.

To maximize the experience I gained from the high-level resources and hopefully make the most of the set, I had to invest it into the Houndsmaster pattern. I doubted it would reward me with useful skills, but the attributes alone would hopefully make up for it.

I almost finished the first set. Both it and the materials now stayed in the workshop instead of my own bedroom. When I first lifted the remaining goat leather from my luggage, the shock had cost me three health, and left a tiny scorch mark on the floor.

I moved a rug to cover it.

I'd likely finish the Houndsmaster set after Study Hall tonight.

Elara came up with a way to counter my hanging strings after only two more fights. She was able to project thinner, faster barriers, and moved much more frequently in combat, making it harder for me to set up my traps. I still won more than half our matches, especially once I started using Stealth mid-fight.

Most of us ended Study Hall covered in sweat. But it wasn't the only thing that changed.

Adrian had brought in more furniture. Tables for working. When we weren't sparring, Elara, Adrian and Cedric helped with everyone's home-work. And not just buying it, either—they actually taught the basic concepts.

"Gwen?" Adrian asked as soon as I entered.

"Yeah?"

"Do you want to try sparring with Anna tonight?"

I looked over to her.

So far, Anna had easily defeated everyone she sparred with in a single shot. She had worked her way through almost everyone in the room. The only people to give her trouble were Adrian, Cedric, and Elara of course.

Even then, she maintained a near perfect fifty–fifty win–loss record against them.

"Sure."

It sounded exciting. Could I beat her?

After the first night of Study Hall, Adrian had the ceiling covered in a layer of foam as well. It meant I could throw my needles wherever I wanted.

I wasn't shy about preparing the battlefield beforehand. What I really needed to do was to spend some time to add something to the bottom of the threads—more needles, or some kind of weight to manipulate for attacks using Thread Mastery.

I raised my training rapier to Anna, who stood in the same pose she used every time she launched her attack.

When the field fuzzed to life, she shot forward, unstoppably fast, a rush of gold shooting toward me.

I used [Running Stitch].

Anna shifted to the left, sliding over the air. Her eyes widened by the smallest margin as my arm followed her with superhuman speed. There was a flash of purple. Anna kicked off of me, sending me back with a grunt, then landed on the other side of the arena.

Her head tilted to the side in an uncanny movement.

"What was that?" she asked.

"It's my skill," I said.

"It must be new," Anna said.

"Uh . . . no." I blinked. "I've had this skill since before I came to the Academy."

Anna shook her head. Even in combat, she wore her hair down.

"That's not what I meant. Show me it again?" Anna said.

She stood and entered her pose. I shrugged and waved to Adrian that we were going again. He gave me a thumbs-up.

"I think that kick is going to leave a bruise," I said. When Anna kicked off me, it didn't take any health away. "Was that a movement skill?"

Anna nodded her head slowly.

The more time I spent in the Academy, the more I noticed how strange Anna's abilities were. She was both confident and powerful. I was starting to be able to determine whether or not someone had started leveling just by watching them fight. And Anna had clearly leveled.

We fought again. This time, I was more proactive. The moment the fight started, I ducked low, grabbing the network of thread on the ground and creating a tripwire. Anna jumped over it—and me. I threw a needle past her, tugging on the thread to wrap it around an arm. She grabbed it and pulled, bringing me forward and off balance.

I activated [Running Stitch] preemptively. This time, before Anna even reached me, she jumped, kicking off midair. There was a flash of gold where her foot hit the air and she landed some distance away, staring at my needle—rapier.

My [Running Stitch] deactivated and we stared at each other for a moment.

"Interesting. Your skill's pursuit has a limited maximum range? Or is it active as long as you're near me?"

"I'm not sure."

"Let's find out."

Anna rushed me. A new cast of [Running Stitch] brought my sword up to meet her again. She backed just out of range. I followed her, running forward. My rapier dashed toward her. She dodged in flashes of gold light.

"It can run indefinitely?" Anna asked, calmly dodging each attack and walking back. "Fascinating."

Anna blurred.

I felt Anna's blow through the purple shield as she shot forward. The world turned upside down. I slid across the mat. Everything flashed purple. The barrier around the training area fuzzed out, and I could hear talking from the other side, though it was muffled as if it came through a thin wall.

"Oh! Sorry!"

I wheezed, trying to recover my breath. She stood over me, hair hanging down like a halo around her face. I took her hand and rose to my knees, leaning over. Then I checked my status. Despite how badly that hurt, I didn't lose any health.

The barrier wound down. Anna looked genuinely concerned. She patted my back.

"Come on. I'll help you over to the bench."

I leaned on her as she helped me take a seat. Adrian stared with visible concern. Anna cringed.

"Sorry, again," she said.

"It's alright," I said. "What level are you? If you don't mind . . ."

"I can't tell you that," Anna said.

"Fine. But you owe me for that one." I rubbed my ribs.

"I'll do a day's worth of homework for you," Anna said, smiling wryly.

"Come to dinner with us," I replied. I was fascinated by Anna's skills and background. She had clearly been through a lot. I wanted to know more about her. Besides that, we needed to build a rapport with our entire team. She was the only one not engaging in our other team-building exercises.

Anna looked uncomfortable about it.

"It's okay," Sandy said. "Adrian pays."

"Alright," Anna agreed.

I recovered from my bruised ribs by working on classwork. Realm management and economics involved reading and writing reports from a huge, multi-volume textbook that discussed the economies of various cities. This volume was only a few years old.

Our Study Hall session was interrupted by pounding knocks on the door. I looked at Sandy who shrugged, then over to Adrian, who was tense. He crossed the room, opening the door just a sliver to answer.

"Ah," Adrian said, opening the door the rest of the way.

In walked Marcus.

The Noble was one of Adrian's foremost connections at the Academy, not only helping us secure this warehouse but also getting Gerald home after finding him a forge.

Marcus was in bad shape. He practically limped into the room. His hair was now buzz-cut short, and he had a black eye. Bandages slipped out of the edges of his clothes—not a Noble Academy uniform.

"You look like you got trampled on," Adrian observed, shutting the door.

"Enchantment still working?" Marcus asked, brushing past Adrian. He manipulated the controls for the enchantment, turning off the noise. Training had ended for the night; whatever attack Anna hit me with had drained too much of its power to continue using it.

Marcus walked into the fizzling field and shouted his lungs out. It sounded very far away through the sound suppression in the training field.

It was an awkward moment. The room stared on. A second later, he limped back out.

"Sorry about that," Marcus said. "I need your help."

The comment was directed specifically at Adrian.

"What are you working on?"

Marcus sighed. "Special Environmental Hazards: Advanced Hunting Three."

Adrian nodded along.

"What did your team decide on?"

"We're hunting an electrical monster a full day's march away. We didn't expect electrical attacks to bypass our protections. Can you help?"

"I can ask around," Adrian said. "Meet us for dinner tonight."

Marcus scanned the room. Then nodded.

"Same place as usual?"

Adrian smiled. "Yep. Dragon's Den."

Not everyone came to dinner every night for our little group session. Plenty of people had to catch up on homework. For several Nobles, their first introduction to math was in Economics class. It was not a good environment for learning fundamentals.

It was still simpler than algebra, though.

"How is your Economics class going, Anna?" I asked. She walked with me and Sandy to the Dragon's Den—the diner that Adrian frequented. It wasn't a first-class place—it was a favorite of Chosen and even commoners.

"It's fascinating to see the way our Nobility manages the realm. Their economic theories are . . . interesting. The impact that stratified classes have on functional economics is fascinating."

Yeah, she wasn't having any issues.

"Did House Gloomwood give you economics lessons?"

Anna hesitated.

"Yes. They were more than generous in my upbringing."

It was cold out in the late evening. The sun was setting beyond the wall, but oil lamps kept the city alive. Industry was constantly bustling here. Noble teams often used the Academy as a resupply point and a place to acquire new gear; it was the last stop before a deeper dive into the dungeon, and to maintain a third-tier city, the dungeon dives never ended.

Gerald wasn't with us tonight. He was headed over to the workshop that Adrian had helped him secure.

I wanted to ask Anna what class she had. But she would probably reply by asking what mine was. If she answered at all. She was sketchy about her stats. She seemed almost traumatized.

"So . . . you're a mage," I said.

"You're a fencer," she agreed.

I wasn't good at this. Luckily, we were already at the Dragon's Den.

"Adrian, I want the roasted drake again," Sandy said.

"You didn't eat the whole thing last time. You took it home! Where did you even store that?"

"I need another," Sandy said.

The Dragon's Den was, in a word, sticky. Dozens of people crowded the multistory haunt. The bottom floor featured gambling tables of dubious legality; but the law was what the local Nobles decided, for the most part, and this place was filled with young Nobles new to their way of life. The center of the building was a huge, open column, with every floor above looking down over balconies. The glass roof at the top was dirty, letting in stained light.

The entire place was orange from oil lamps and alive with the noise of a hundred conversations. It took us several minutes to reach an actual table we could sit at, finding one available on the third floor after stopping every few steps for Adrian to greet someone or another. We brushed away the trash that was left behind by the previous diners. The serving staff hadn't gotten there before us. I stared down into the crowd below. Shouts and jeers rang out around a roulette table.

"Can I steal some of your roasted drake?" I asked Sandy. I was tying back my hair. This entire place was way too gross.

But the food was *good*.

"Sure!" Sandy said. "Only if you share your dish with me."

"What should I get?" I asked, resisting the urge to lean on the table.

"Another roasted drake." Sandy nodded sagely.

"No!" Adrian interrupted a conversation he was having a table away from us to shout back.

I laughed.

"Is there a menu?" Anna asked. She spread her hands on the table.

"Server!" Adrian shouted over the crowd. "Menu?" he asked.

An employee rushed over, pulling out a notepad—a scribe, rather than an actual server—and began to write everything that was currently available. Their hands blurred over the page, and in a few seconds, they had finished. When they tore the page free, they tore the pages under it, too. A copy of the menu appeared on all the pages.

It was probably a similar skill to my own Pattern Mirroring, applying the labor across multiple pages.

The server smiled.

"What can I get for you today? Drinks?"

"There's no roasted drake today?" Sandy exclaimed.

"We're all out." The server hesitated. "There may be more tomorrow?"

The menu of the Dragon's Den wasn't set. They acquired huge quantities of meat from the many abattoirs in the city, and what they had available changed from day to day, and even from hour to hour.

When we ordered, the scribe copied our order to a notepad. I knew from asking last time that the order was being transcribed to another page inside the kitchen, where they would start preparing the meal before we even finished ordering.

It was a little cool.

After the server left and everyone in a two-mile radius had greeted Adrian, he sat down and turned to me.

"Gwen," he said.

I already knew what this was about.

"Marcus's request," I said. "You don't have connections to get equipment?" I asked out of curiosity. I was more than willing to fleece every last merit I could out of Marcus. And Adrian.

Adrian smiled wryly.

"I do. But what I would be acquiring would be top-level gear—sets made for people with dozens and dozens or even over a hundred levels. And the cost for that . . ."

"You want me to get something cheaper."

Adrian took a long drink. It was beer. They served alcohol to the often freshly eighteen-year-old students in the Academy who had just unlocked access to vast magical power. It felt like a bad idea.

"Yes. Something cheaper and highly specific. I could get something cheaper by sending mail back home, but the travel time makes it unpreferable. So . . . can your connection make something with lightning resistance?"

I already had something half-made.

"Not for free," I said.

"Five merits."

"Deal."

Adrian blinked.

"Gwen!" Elara shouted from across the table. "You're not supposed to accept the first offer. He's ripping you off!"

"Oh," I said. Right. Negotiating. "Ten merits!"

"You just said five," Adrian said.

I had window-shopped the atelier. Five merits would be enough to buy the raw materials for another entire set. With some creative crafting, I might even be able to squeeze out a set and a half.

With ten merits, I could almost afford three sets. I was mostly focused on the levels I would afford.

"Seven," Adrian said.

"Deal," I said.

"Gwen!" Elara said. She was losing her composure.

I smiled. With seven merits, I could also buy two mana potions. When in the mage outfit, they could restore my mana to full—enough to work much, *much* faster. With two in a day, I might be able to complete seven sets in a week.

"But this is three merits off, since it's a deal for a friend. What . . . kind of set should it be?" I asked. "Skillswise."

"Marcus is a rogue." Adrian said. "He mostly uses knives. Or ranged weapons. But anything with high lightning resistance will work."

I glimpsed over at Sandy for a second. Her Storm Curtain set had insanely high lightning resistance—but that pattern was crafted by my mom, not me. I couldn't recreate it.

"I can make that work," I said.

Food arrived a few minutes later. Cedric was among the most talkative of the three Nobles; he constantly rambled on about his Practical Combat class and tried to guess at his classmates' classes, comparing them with stories of Nobles from back home.

Marcus arrived when we were halfway through eating. He grimaced when he presented a stack of tokens to Adrian.

They were round and visibly enchanted; the physicalized tokens that represented merits. Adrian smiled.

"Thirteen is all I can do."

"For a friend? I'll only take ten. Come eat."

Adrian pushed three of the tokens back before taking the rest in two handfuls. One, he pushed to me. He pocketed the remaining three.

"Hey! You *can* afford ten!"

"Broker fee," Adrian shrugged.

I should have asked for more. As a matter of fact . . .

"Two more merits and I can make sure my contact has it done by Sunday."

"Really?" Marcus asked. He fetched the two tokens from his pocket. Adrian reached for them.

Sandy practically snatched them out of his hand and handed them to me.

"I'll bring them here Sunday?" I asked. I looked to their faces for approval. Adrian gave a slow nod.

Marcus left a few minutes later, declining Adrian's offer of a free dinner. He was heading home to sleep. Judging by his appearance, he still hadn't gotten a full night's rest.

"What's Gloomwood's city like?" I asked Annabelle.

She hesitated before replying.

"Gloomwood Mills is a prominent second-tier city. They export magical lumber harvested both from the Wild and the interior dungeon worlds. Sawmills cover the city, making it noisy at night."

"Uh . . . oh. Do you sleep during the day, then?"

"No," she said.

"I heard that the forest there is beautiful," Adrian chimed in.

We made small talk over dinner. I remembered that I still had a mana potion to buy before the end of the night.

I stood up when I remembered.

"Adrian, where can I buy a mana potion this late?" I asked him.

"There's a ton of twenty-four-seven shops that will have them," he said.

"A small potion will restore more than fifty points," Elara said. "How high have you raised your mana pool?"

"Not very. That will be more than enough."

Anna stood up and bowed.

"Thank you for the dinner. I will see you all Monday at Study Hall."

"What are everyone's weekend plans?" Adrian asked.

"Catching up on Economics," Sandy replied.

"I'm taking supplemental combat courses," Victor, a member of my team during Practical Combat, chimed in.

Adrian gave him a funny look. "That's not the best use of merits."

"I want to start hunting soon," he replied.

That was the end of the conversation. Our Study Hall had talked about doing our first expeditions on the second weekend. Most of our group was nervous about it rather than excited.

Elara recommended a shop that would have the potions I needed. I had expected an adventuring shop on the scale of the atelier, filled with equipment and weapons and potions. What I found was more like a pawnshop.

Low-grade secondhand gear fought for shelf space alongside mixed lots. Crates that once held perfectly organized glass vials were half empty; replacement bottles had been haphazardly shoved in to the empty slots.

I leaned down and stared at the potions on the shelf, keenly aware of the shopkeeper leaning over the front desk to stare at me.

There were a dozen different colors of potions; verdant, swirling green labeled as an antivenom to a specific snake found fifteen miles east of the Academy, sparking yellow that said it would *reduce* electrical resistance, and deep purples. Some of the bottles were stained with alchemical liquids, like the crates had been damaged in transport.

They were priced at a number of silver coins *or* a merit token. The entire Academy City accepted merit tokens as currency. It was little wonder that large Noble houses could accumulate so many; they could simply run business and offer services inside to build them up.

I plucked out two mana potions that were available for a single merit token. They included the name of the shop and the specific alchemist who had made them. Those names didn't mean anything to me, though.

Alchemist families could grow to rival Noble houses; they were one of a few classes whose rarity and power afforded them the political capital to influence the policy and rule of local Nobility.

Economics class did not speak highly of the alchemist houses.

The shopkeeper stared suspiciously at me. He pulled some device out from behind the counter, holding it over the merit tokens, which began to glow. He nodded, satisfied, and I walked out and headed to the atelier.

I crossed the Academy in the dark, pulling on my magical outfit only once I slipped inside the atelier's private workshop. The employees no longer second-guessed me at all, now that they recognized my face; they didn't even dare to question the actions of the Nobility.

With the magic outfit in my Wardrobe, I inherited only ten percent of its power; that meant that my current willpower was only nine; base five combined with ten percent of the Archon set's effective points of forty-four after my seamstress bonus was applied. That meant that I had eighteen mana to play with; two points for every point of willpower I had.

With the outfit on, and after applying the bonus I gained from stats as a seamstress, my mana pool reached one hundred points.

I stared at one of the two mana potions I had purchased with reverence. It was in a tiny glass vial, just larger than one of my fingers at the neck, with a body shaped like a star. The price tag was still on it.

Back in Stitch, we had relied on Henri's cooking to restore our mana. Sandy's dad was a great chef, but I didn't relish drinking so much soup to get through a dungeon clear. Even if it was delicious.

I popped the cork out and brought the bottle to my lips with incredible care.

The potion tasted like acid and blueberries, sickly sweet and somehow bright as it passed down my throat. It tasted like fruit, and like light, and like power.

My breathing was rapid by the time I finished drinking it.

In the Archon set, my total dexterity was much lower than in the Aracheknight set. But that didn't matter if I could use my skills for every last piece of crafting.

My first commission.

I looked at the half-finished set of a Houndsmaster outfit. I had been crafting this set for myself. I wasn't focused on the grade of the final equipment; the quality would have an impact on the stats and skills in the end. I had been focused only on completing it to level faster.

But now that I was working on a commission, I should make the highest-quality piece I could.

I sorted out the best and most whole pieces of the goat leather, attaching them to the grounding cables that discharged their magical electrical charge.

Then I began to cut whole pieces from the cloth, making the finished pattern significantly higher quality than if I stitched together multiple disparate pieces. I wasn't actually going to waste anything; every last scrap would go back into making more outfits for myself.

Having a pool of over seventy mana was more than worth the tradeoff of losing my dexterity. Unlimited use of Pattern Mirroring and Running Stitch meant that most of the set was done by the time my mana dropped to nineteen points. I didn't even notice that night had come a long time ago. The atelier was completely empty now, the shop upstairs long since shuttered.

There was one thing I had to test.

Piece by piece, I changed out of the Archon set, slowly lowering my willpower.

My mana stayed above my pool limit. It would have been a risk to test this with the entire contents of a potion bottle. The health pool worked the same way, but I wasn't going to risk some fifty points of mana.

Instead, I just risked one point. A smile crossed my face.

Tomorrow, with a mana pool above seventy and the highest dexterity score I could manage, I would finish the entire Houndsmaster set I was crafting. My heart raced in my chest. If I could continue fielding commissions, I'd be able to complete a set every day and a half. That would be multiple levels per week if I could keep it up. And at the same time I would be earning merits.

This was my first commission; the thing I had dreamed about when I was a little girl. I dreamed just as often about fighting monsters.

And now I was going to do both.

ACT 3

CHAPTER 18

Quality Assessment: Great!]

[Houndsmaster's Uniform (Uncommon, Lightning) completed!]

[Generating Skills . . .]

▸Shock and Awe V

▸Lightning Resistance 50

[ATTRIBUTES]

▸SPD: 0

▸WIL: 0

▸STR: 25

▸DEX: -5

▸CON: 25

▸PER: 0

[+10 XP] [Level up]

[Bonus experience rewarded for first craft of this pattern at (Great) or above!]

▸Shock and Awe V

While mounted, generate an increasing lightning damage buff based on speed and inertia. Discharged to inflict bonus damage at the first attack or skill used.

The set was absolutely gorgeous. Since I wasn't struggling to make use of every last scrap, the entire process was smoother and faster. There were fewer weak points where uneven pieces were stitched together and reinforced. And the quality reflected that; it raised the stats, too.

Of course, I *would* use every last scrap, just on my own sets. Even if I didn't use a set I crafted, I still gained experience. And once I gained Crafting X, I would gain attributes every time I finished a set.

With access to enough raw materials, I could level incredibly quickly. I stared greedily at the Houndsmaster uniform I had made for Marcus. As soon as the set was finished, it no longer accumulated a constant electrical charge. Instead, the magic was pressed entirely into the pattern, used for the buff instead.

I started picking up the scraps from the floor, wincing as they bit me with electrical charge, before adding them to a metal bucket tied to a grounding wire. I had looted the bucket out of a supply closet.

At this rate, I would need a Lightning Resistant set to craft with high-tier Lightning attribute materials. The elemental alignment of the monsters clearly affected the skills and sets they generated. The Fire element Houndsmaster set I had made before had skills to talk to and befriend animals, not to mount them.

And I had gained an entire level. I looked down at the scraps on the table.

It was still early morning; the weekend wasn't over yet. I didn't have to deliver the finished Houndsmaster set until evening.

There was still time left before my meeting.

I still had a set of my own to finish. And I could do so before the time I promised to deliver Marcus's.

The finishing touches came smoothly and without issue, especially with the practice of having already crafted the set twice. I had left the pieces hanging on the second mannequin in the room, grounding cables discharging the magical material.

As I fell into a crafting fugue state, the memories embedded in the pattern bubbled out. Trying to understand what happened in them was like trying to remember dreams. Scratch that—it was like running my fingers through water, trying to scoop it up, even as it slipped through my fingers.

The most powerful memories in a pattern still left an impression.

When I made the first Houndsmaster pattern, I had seen a camp deep in a dungeon, full of seamstresses. I have even seen them fighting.

The memory that bubbled out of this pattern was different. It was peaceful. It was the memory of a seamstress riding on the back of a lizard the size of a house. She stitched together patterns over the top of a gigantic style. The lizard swiveled his head back. The swell of fear I felt almost disrupted my crafting. But then the seamstress reached into a bag and fed the monster with smoked meat. She scratched his nose. The monster turned around and continued trundling forward through an ancient-looking Jungle.

[Quality Assessment: (Fine)]

[Generating Skills . . .]

▶Shock and Awe II

▶Lightning Resistance 50
[ATTRIBUTES]
▶SPD: 0
▶WIL: 0
▶STR: 15
▶DEX: -10
▶CON: 15
▶PER: 0
[+5 XP]

Halfway to one more level. And I had a skill point available.

Most sets were composed of five pieces; each piece rewarded a trickle of experience. The more I crafted a set, the less experience I got. The same was true for monsters; I couldn't level perpetually killing the same monsters. I had to kill bigger and bigger ones. And I had to craft bigger and better sets.

Maybe it was time to diversify my points. With merits coming in from other Nobles for commissions, which I was sure they would be soon, I could complete more crafting than ever. I could practically power level if I got enough commissions.

I could complete two sets over a weekend, and one every few weekdays, all while balancing school work.

Maybe it was finally time to invest in crafting skills; I might reach Crafting X faster if I had more skills like Running Stitch that allowed me to work with preternatural speed. That, and I had a hunch that part of the quality of my last work was tied to how much more use I made of my skills.

I opened [Skill Shop].

▶[COMMON] Cross Stitching I

Enables system assistance with a new stitch type. Additional levels increase proficiency.

▶[UNCOMMON] Unweaving I

Grants user the ability to recycle items into base materials. Additional levels increase the amount recycled.

▶[COMMON] Alteration I

Aids user in retrofitting clothing to increase its quality and repair it. Additional levels allow user to upgrade old equipment to higher levels.

[Pattern Shop]

▶[Rare] Factory Worker's Coverall Pattern (Intermediate)

Grants large bonus to Constitution. Inflicts penalty to Perception. Grants set bonus based on craft quality and materials used.

▶[Rare] Storm Archer's Raiment (Advanced)

Grants large bonus to Strength, Dexterity, and Perception. Inflicts penalty to Will, Constitution, and Speed. Grants Bowmaster skills based on craft quality and materials used.

▶[Common] Lamp Lighter's Uniform (Basic)

Grants large bonus to Speed and Constitution. Grants Movement skill based on materials and craft quality.

Cross Stitching seemed like a valuable skill to get. Eventually. But not right now. Right now, my choice was obvious.

I only wondered how much a bow would cost.

The set sounded alarmingly similar to the Storm Archon set that Lizzie had acquired. I suspected the skills that it gave me would be completely different; not only did the set not reward willpower, and even penalize it, but a bowmaster would have completely different skills from a mage.

Olivier wasn't a mage either, though, and when I looted his inventory, I had gained access to a skill that was real, actual magic.

[Ignite Projectile.]

If I was lucky, I would unlock something similar.

I was out of time; I had to get to my meeting with Adrian and Marcus at the Dragon's Den. I locked the door to the workshop behind me after packing up the set for Marcus; the set for myself was absorbed directly into my inventory.

Late at night on a weekday, the city felt more alive than ever. Stalls selling goods overflowed from the fronts of buildings. Young Nobles offered to sell goods for merits. They advertised high-end magical weapons, practically shouting up the street. I only had to take a single look to know that they were secondhand goods, worn from the degradation of the Wild and likely used for years before being hawked here.

It was startling exactly how many Nobles roamed the streets when there was no class. They looked like they didn't know where to go or what to do. Many of them were Chosen, likely from border towns, and probably had never seen a city this large.

And vertical.

The Dragon's Den was even more packed. There must have been more than a hundred people in the restaurant.

I had to elbow and shoulder my way through them, all the while carrying the crate that contained Marcus's outfit.

I had no intention of showing off my inventory skills. I was already pushing it with how much I revealed in Practical Combat, and in Study Hall.

"Gwendolyn."

The word was forceful. It wasn't a shout, but it was still loud enough to hear through the din of the Dragon's Den.

It was Elara. She was tucked away in a corner booth. Empty cups piled up around her. The Nobles near her carefully avoided her. She had homework spread across the table.

For most people, doing homework at the Dragon's Den was a terrible proposition.

Elara, however, maintained a magical barrier over her homework.

"Elara," I said, offering a smile.

"I see your connection finished the commission in time," she replied without looking up. I recognized her homework; it was for Economics class.

"Yeah," I said. "Can I, uh, set this here?"

"The barrier will hold," Elara said.

I set the crate down. It floated inches over the table, atop the translucent barrier. I didn't blame her for creating it. The Dragon's Den was sticky, if nothing else.

"Is Adrian here?"

"Just me today," Elara said, still paying attention to her homework.

"I thought you guys paid someone to do the homework for you," I said.

Elara scrunched her nose. "Who could get a better score than me, even paid? The grade you get is based on the viability of your proposal, but that changes from teacher to teacher. There's no one I can pay who would carefully research the teacher and formulate a precise and perfect proposal." She waved the discussion away with one hand. "Coffee?"

She pushed one of the cups of coffee on the table between us toward me. I picked it up and considered it. Did she buy this much for herself?

"This late at night?"

At least it was thoughtful. Elara returned to looking at her homework without answering. I took a sip. The coffee was stale and freezing cold. I set the cup back down. Thankfully, Marcus found us only a few minutes later.

"You have it?" he asked. I slapped the top of the crate.

Marcus's teammates flanked him as he took the crate.

"Really is a rush job. I'm going to be sweating in this," he said, holding each piece of the outfit and turning it around. "What skills does it have?"

"Shock and Awe," I replied. "It's a skill for mounted combat."

Marcus made a clicking noise with his tongue.

"I wonder how far I can stretch the definition of mounted combat." We shook hands. "Thank you."

"Feel free to come back for more," I said, smiling. It was the first time one of my products would be bought and used. Even if he had complained about the quality.

Marcus folded the clothes back up. "Tell Adrian we're heading directly back out for expedition."

I watched the three of them leave, the smile never leaving my face.

"Want to stay to do your homework?" Elara asked.

"All of mine is done," I said, then hesitated. Elara froze, her pen standing still. That was clearly a social invite. She still wasn't looking at me, though. Was it the pretense of being above Chosen Nobles that she couldn't drop?

But she was obviously desperate enough to be working with the Chosen. Despite all the wealth Adrian threw around, including bribing teachers and paying to have his homework done, he didn't seem to have many friends here.

I wondered how Elara had ended up in the same situation.

"But I can stay and kill an hour," I said.

Homeroom covered the second tier of monster dens around the Academy. Lyssandra drew a smaller circle, beginning to detail some of the most commonly hunted.

Alongside them, she marked recurring resource nodes: rare mana-alloy metals, groves of alien trees, and quarries of replenishing stone.

But the most notable thing of the day was the gigantic circle to the northeast of the Academy: a huge, scratched out ring that she marked *exclusion-zone* and then didn't explain.

One hand shot up in the classroom, waiting for permission to ask a question. Then several more. Lyssandra put the chalk down.

"The exclusion zone is a region of anomalous danger. It contains the ruins of an old fortification, and no Academy student is permitted to go there. The entire area around the location is highly hazardous and students should do their best to avoid it."

The hands went down.

"Sometimes, direct force is not the best way to fight," Sir Stonehart lectured from the front of the class.

He sat on a crate, holding a lit cigarette. The crate held a wolf that kept alternating between gnawing at the bars and barking, forcing Sir Stonehart to talk louder. He was practically shouting. The wind today didn't help either.

"At the end of this week, you will fight your first monster in the wild."

A third of the class perked up, a third looked panicked, and the last third, including me, barely reacted at all. Victor perked up. Annabelle looked panicked. I thought her reaction was odd, but I couldn't ask her, as the teacher continued talking.

"Spend this week not just fighting, but learning how this monster fights. Each team of three will be expected to track down and kill one of these monsters in the open. Let's get started."

The first few students who killed it too fast got scolded. The next few kited over the monster in circles around the arena, dodging its attacks. Or getting bitten by it. The teacher made noises of disapproval each and every time.

Then it was my turn.

I did my best to pretend I was really in danger, letting the monster jump toward me a few times. I wasn't going to take a bite to sell it, though. Eventually, I ran my needle through it.

"Good. Do you see how Gwen fought the monster for as long as was safe to learn its attack patterns?" Sir Stonehart said. "Monsters are not truly thinking beings like you and I or their degraded descendants in the Wild. They can be intelligent. They can even be sapient. But they will always obey their patterns. Learn them. I want to see more of the same from the rest of you."

Maybe I overdid it.

The week continued like that. The challenge with the monsters didn't change. Eventually, in the middle of the week, Marcus barged into Study Hall with his teammates behind him.

"Gwen! Adrian!" he shouted. There was a smile on his face.

He was wearing the Houndsmaster uniform I had made him. The outfit looked odd covered in black monster-goat fur and caked with blood.

"Marcus," I said with a smile. "How did it go?"

"Amazing, thanks to you!" he said, picking me up in a crushing hug and spinning me around.

I pulled on my Aracheknight set from my inventory and he set me back down.

"Sorry!" he said.

His two teammates looked around the room.

"We were wondering . . ." Marcus said, looking to his teammates behind him.

I beamed, though they couldn't see it under my helmet. "Ten merits each," I said.

One of Marcus's teammates, a girl with fiery red hair, spoke up. "T—ten? You only charged Marcus nine!"

"That was the friend discount."

Marcus's teammates looked at each other.

"Can your supplier make a set that's ice resistant?"

"Definitely," I said.

"And I need it by this weekend!"

"That's—" I interrupted myself before I could say "easy." Then I sucked in a harsh breath. "Might cost a little more."

"No way!"

I shrugged.

"Suit yourself."

Marcus's teammate closed her eyes.

"Alright. Next weekend then. We can push it back."

At the end of the day, I had twenty-five tokens. A quarter of what I needed for my own graduation. Of course, I wouldn't do that without Sandy and Gerald graduating, too.

And I had to spend most of these.

Graduation was a one-time cost. It gave me the right to own my land, to become a titled Noble.

But currently, in the heart of the Academy, I could turn every one of these merits into precious, precious levels.

Because of my seamstress class, every level I gained gave me another two-percent bonus in the stats I gained from my sets, plus the ten percent inherent to my class.

At level forty-five, I would have the effective stat gain of two complete sets, between the stats shared by my Wardrobe X outfits and the outfit I was wearing. At ninety-five, I'd have the power of four. Not to mention that if I rushed to level Crafting to ten, every single set I crafted would stack on more attribute points.

And I could it all without leaving the city. In fact, I suspected that I could level even faster than a Noble!

All the shops were closed for the night. I looked through the atelier's stock, but I couldn't just pilfer materials. They were carefully accounted for. And locked up.

There were plenty of ice-resistant materials in the atelier, make no mistake; they were locked in boxes hanging from the ceiling by strings. A layer of ice covered the outside of them. Giant buckets sat below them for when the condensed humidity on the surface of the containers melted and dripped down.

Just like the goat's electrical fur, the white hides inside the glass boxes maintained their magical properties despite being sheared off their former host.

I had to skip one of my classes to visit the shops when they were open. A materials supplier who harvested monster parts walked me around a warehouse. The ice-resistant hides were contained in enchanted cabinets that neutralized their hazardous magical properties.

The warehouse floor featured dozens of similar cabinets. Some hung from the ceiling. Some had metal bars all around them. They were evenly spaced, the same distance from each other, like dozens of pillars rising up from the smooth stone floor.

The materials supplier wore a very durable-looking outfit. It looked almost as powerful as some sets of Noble armor, accompanied by a hard hat and goggles. He was smoking, which I wasn't sure was safe around the enchanted materials.

"What will it run me?" I asked.

"Twenty pounds for fifty square yards."

That was enough for a set and a half.

"In merits?"

The man took a puff of a cigar.

"Run you ten."

"I'll pay you five," I said.

"Call it seven."

I really didn't want to buy any materials from the man. I would much rather have gone hunting for them myself. But we wouldn't have enough time to start an expedition outside the city until Friday. And I doubted the Academy would even approve of one.

"Seven and you deliver them for me."

"Deal."

CHAPTER 19

On Friday, all our classes were canceled to accommodate an all-day Practical Combat class. We were directed to a new "classroom."

The instructor had said that the class would take place outside. It was mostly true. We were directed to the back of the Academy to a massive section of untamed land. Although in fact it was quite tamed—artificial, contained and controlled. Fenced in to prevent the monsters that spawned in the dens across this floor from slipping into it. They called it the Range.

There was a security checkpoint to cross the city wall and enter the area.

The security checkpoint also acted like a miniature defense point itself. Bored-looking young Nobles hung around in combat uniforms, holding weapons and leaning against the walls. The room was divided in two by giant metal bars, the doors to pass through them guarded by no less than four Nobles at all times. It was a little overkill considering the caliber of monster we would be fighting today.

On this side of the fortification, there was a veritable armory. Securely separated from the easily accessible part of the room were rack after rack of glowing, enchanted weaponry, and even sets of armor on mannequins.

One of them looked close enough to reach out and use Quick Change on. If there weren't so many people watching.

Outside of that were plenty of rental weapons—used, old, worn and scuffed. A line of students waited to receive one for class today.

Everyone from Study Hall had already rented something higher quality, thanks to Adrian, while Sandy, Gerald, and I had our own weapons. Though I didn't see either of them here today.

I did, however, find Annabelle and Victor. We grouped up near the edge of the room and waited for class to start. Victor was practically standing on his toes, excited to go in to fight.

It was more than just my class attending; I saw plenty of faces I didn't recognize. And plenty of people were wearing sets other than the school uniform; it was expected for today. There were even locker rooms for changing.

"Everyone group into your teams!" Sir Stonehart shouted. "You won't be let through without a team of three. If you have less than three, join another group and hunt together."

Every single group of three was expected to bring back an entire wolf themselves. That meant that any group that took on one extra person took on double the work with only a third more power. Most groups were reluctant to accept any new members at the last second for that reason.

We filtered through the line into the gate and passed to the other side of the room.

"The sooner you're ready, the sooner you can get started! Get through the lines!" Sir Stonehart shouted.

There were students still changing or waiting in line to rent weapons by the time we passed through the gate. A moment later, the reason for the excess count of Nobles became evident; every team was grouped again into sets of three; nine total students, paired with an older Noble and given a section of the Wild that they would be allowed to roam in.

"Go outside the confines of the Range at your own risk," the Noble partnered with our teams said. "Knowing your own limits is important. If you're in trouble, scream like you're dying."

I doubted our team would have any problems. Still, for some reason, Annabelle looked the most nervous out of the three of us.

"Let's get going," Victor said. The other two teams were less eager.

We were lingering near the exit. Most of the Nobles were staring warily out of the gate.

The exit led immediately to steep stairs that led down to the ground. The distant heights of a fence of metal rods were visible over the tree line.

Nobles pushed past us.

Victor shouted a cheer and cracked his whip, causing Nobles behind us to flinch and a massive flock of birds to shoot out of the closest part of the tree line.

"Off the stairs!" an older Noble shouted behind us, shoving Victor down.

Annabelle and Victor both wore their school uniforms. That wasn't a problem for them since they could manually allocate attributes. After the last two weeks of killing monsters, they should have gained a handful of levels.

We headed down a well-worn path in the Range. Only the area closest to the exit was clear cut, plants hacked back and trees culled young. The plants of the dungeons grew voraciously and competitively, requiring constant clearing.

We'd only taken a few steps before the canopy began to choke out the sky. The worn path was clear of foliage, but it constantly made ingresses out to the terrain.

Annabelle visibly calmed down once the fortress was no longer visible.

"You okay?" I asked her.

"Yes," she replied, definitively.

"Where the hell are the monsters?" Victor said, cracking his whip again.

"They'll all run away if you keep making so much noise."

"Huh?" he said, turning back to look at me. "Sir Stonehart said that they attack us as part of their pattern. They should be hunting for us right now."

"Those monsters aren't from around here. They're captured or bred somewhere else, obviously, or the school wouldn't be able to let us kill hundreds of them per week," I said. "Because this isn't their natural environment, they won't just be hunting us down. They should be trying to run away and return to whatever dungeon they came from."

Annabelle nodded. "They look like tier-zero monsters," she said. "If I had to guess, they're either bred on a deeper floor for leveling or captured at the outermost ring of tier-zero dungeons. However, if they are second- or third-generation monsters, their behavior could be erratic. I suspect we may not end up fighting an individual monster. In fact, if the monsters' pattern causes them to flee, they may also group up and hide at the edge of the Range."

"What the hell is a tier-zero monster?" Victor said. He raised his whip again, but grunted in annoyance instead of cracking it.

"That would explain why teams are mandatory," I said, thinking aloud. "You think this is a trick? A way for the teachers to help the students realize how unprepared they really are?"

"It has to be," Anna said. "We're not hunting one wolf. We're probably hunting a pack."

"That's an entire pack!" Sandy shouted as her team broke through the foliage and into a clearing. The wolves weren't all the plain black she'd seen before. Some of them had white or even red-brown coats of thick fur. All of them had huge fangs, extended claws, and bared teeth.

They charged her.

Between the team of Elara, Ash, and Sandy, she was the only front-liner. Ash moved uncertainly, aiming her focus and dropping it repeatedly as Sandy swung wildly, skill-enhanced swings carving apart wolves and forcing them back, but they were quickly surrounded.

There were seven. Three of them were injured. They surrounded them, circled behind, and snapped at their heels.

Elara shoved them back with invisible barriers, pushing them into the trees.

"Ash!" Elara shouted. "Use your magic! Show the pride you have as a mage!"

Ash steadied herself.

A bolt of force struck the side of one of the already-injured wolves, causing it to howl. Sandy leapt on the opportunity, jumping forward to flank the wolves in front of her. She was a butcher in an abattoir, a storm of slashes doing deadly work as she carved the monsters apart.

Ash fired again. Then the wolves reoriented and charged her.

Adrian was a blur as he combined movement and combat skills, his rapier buzzing like a needle as he carved through the necks of a half dozen wolves in seconds.

Their group were the first in for their time slot inside the Range.

The remaining wolves formed a cage of tooth and fang around him. He panted for a second. The wolves circled him hungrily. But Adrian waited patiently.

Gerald charged in a moment later, wearing a full set of new armor. His every step landed with a heavy thud. He slammed directly through three of the wolves like a juggernaut, swinging a gigantic mace that left them broken on the ground. Cedric came in behind him, cutting through two remaining wolves.

Adrian pulled rope from his bag, tying the wolves together to the long line Gerald was already carrying.

"Next area! Go, go!" Adrian said, running forward.

Killing just a few wolves wasn't enough for him.

He wanted all of them.

"The monsters are up ahead," I said, letting [Shadow Cloak] roll off of me. "You were right, Anna. There is a whole pack of wolves.

Victor jumped as my stealth ended, but Anna just eyed me evenly.

"Let's get in there!" Victor almost shouted.

"How many?" Anna said.

"Nine. They'd completely overwhelm us."

"Should we look for an easier group?" Anna asked.

"We can handle them!" Victor said. "Think about all the levels we could get today."

"Victor is right. We just need to do some preparation," I said, pulling the throwing needles from my belt.

I tied them into pairs, throwing them into opposite trees to create trip lines.

The fine thread I was using for the throwing needles was the ultra-strong thread made of the spider webs from the second floor of Stitch's dungeon. The material was barely magical, but it remained resistant and strong enough to be used aggressively.

"What's the plan?" Anna said, observing me carefully laying the trip-wires under the guidance of my Trapping skill.

"Victor, do you think you can grab the monsters' attention and lead them backward through the tripwires?" I asked.

"Of course!" he said.

"I'll use my Stealth and Threa—" I interrupted myself with a cough. "I'll use my Trapping skills to catch them in our wires. Anna, you and Victor can work together to finish them."

Anna nodded.

"I'm going back into Stealth. Victor, go ahead. Make sure not to trip on the wires on your way back."

Victor immediately tripped over an ankle-height wire.

"I'm fine," he said, brushing himself off.

I shook my head. He would be all right. These low-level monsters weren't much of a threat, and if I had to, I could jump in and finish off any that attacked him.

Victor, to his credit, did not blindly charge into the clearing where the pack of wolves were. He crept up slowly. The monsters were on high alert; they probably heard and smelled all the Nobles entering the Range.

Still, Victor got within stone-tossing distance before they noticed him.

He stepped forward and his whip flashed with a skill I had never seen him use.

The long whip flashed white, bending unnaturally as it cracked, targeting multiple enemies and hitting them hard enough to send them rolling over. A sneer was on his face. He turned and ran, ducking under and jumping over the tripwires I had set in the forest.

I ran with him in Stealth, ensuring he wouldn't be caught out. When he reached the end, his face returned to a panicked expression.

"There's so many!"

I squinted at him. Was that an act?

I didn't have time to study him further as the wolves burst through the foliage all together. I pulled on the loose threads. The tripwires popped out from the trees, and I manipulated them with [Thread Mastery], entangling the wolves further and leaving them vulnerable.

Only one of the eight wolves made it to Victor; he cleanly struck it down before striking it multiple more times. It stopped moving long before he finished attacking it.

Anna rushed in as soon as the wolves were entangled, taking them out one at a time. I let [Shadow Cloak] fall away and crossed my arms as the two of them tore into the wolves.

Victor was panting by the end, but smiling.

"Now what?" he asked.

"Now we turn in our classwork for the day," I said. "Let's tie these together and drag them back."

Sandy shoved her arm into the wolf's way just as it pounced toward Ash. She winced as she took the bite. Then she took the monster's head off.

Gerald sat on a mountain of wolf corpses. He was guarding them. They had killed almost every wolf in the range. The older Nobles scheduled to oversee the class today stared angrily at him. Most of them had left the zones they had been set to guard.

Gerald, Cedric, and Adrian had rushed out first, sweeping the wolves from closest to farthest away. There weren't actually enough left for every team to graduate. Many of the teams persisted in hunting anyway.

But most of them lined up to buy the wolf corpses from Adrian's team.

"The price is the price. It's one merit. You can afford it! If you can't, you can sign here." Adrian presented a legally binding contract that he'd just happened to be carrying.

"I can't afford to—I won't agree to this!" the Noble standing across from him said. He raised a sword.

"Oh? You want to fight? Welllll . . . we did just get some levels from killing all of these."

The Noble paled and took a step back. Adrian smiled. That was, of course, a lie; these wolves weren't even worth a single point to him.

"You could also just fail the class for today," Cedric chimed in, walking closer to the group of Nobles. He towered over them and rested his hands on his hips.

"I—No. I'll sign the contract."

"Great!" Adrian said.

CHAPTER 20

In Study Hall right before the weekend, we weren't getting any work done. It was noisy, and sunlight filtered in through the windows. Adrian had picked up food for all of us and we were making a mess of the tables where we typically did homework. Everyone was celebrating finishing class for the day—mostly uninjured.

We were trading stories of how many of the monsters we had each killed.

"You did *what?*" I asked, aghast.

"Yeah, we killed . . . almost all of them," Adrian said with a shrug. "It was a lot of work. But Gerald's strength stat being so high helped."

"But . . . wouldn't the other students fail?"

"Oh, most students fail their first field test. The real point of the exercise is teaching Nobles that when they're up against odds they can't beat, it's better to run away and live to fight another day."

"But all the levels they'll be behind . . ."

"Most students spend years in the Academy," Elara said. "There's typically a minimum level to apply to be a knight errant—an unvassaled knight working in the employ of another Noble," Elara explained after seeing me stare vacantly at the term.

"I see. So no harm, no foul."

"Yes! Everybody wins."

"Adrian sold the bodies we collected for merits," Gerald interjected.

"What?" I asked, shocked again.

"Technically, I *traded* the bodies. For future merits. With interest!" Adrian smiled. "Everybody wins."

"The teachers allowed you to do that?"

"Oh, I got written up for it. Extra homework assignment and everything. Even have to do it myself and not pay someone."

I rubbed my eyes. Adrian was crazy.

"Still, I'm surprised all three teams here managed to actually hunt their packs. I don't think I can claim full credit for that. You're all amazing."

"Don't you know it," Victor said, leaning forward.

"Victor. Have you ever thought about becoming a vassal?" Adrian asked.

"Hell no. I'm going to run my own city."

Adrian smiled at him before looking back at me.

"I heard you got additional commissions for your connections. Nice job," he said. "What are you planning for this weekend?"

"This weekend?" I said, looking between Sandy and Gerald, who nodded. "We're planning on trying our first expedition."

Adrian's eyes lit up.

"Just me, Sandy, and Gerald. Sorry."

Adrian didn't seem too distraught at being excluded.

"That's still great. Do you know what you're hunting?"

"Winged snake," Sandy said.

Adrian looked confused.

"It's kind of low-tier for you if all of you are confident enough to clear a wolf pack. Make sure to buy antivenom for it."

It was big. Very big. Long. Which meant a ton of materials for crafting a set. And most of its combat abilities involved quick movements. Not to mention the venom in its fangs. I was hoping for sets that would give me movement abilities, like how Annabelle could kick off the air.

"We'll also be scouting for what else is in the area. We . . . haven't really done any kind of long-haul hike like this."

"Ahhhh. That's smart. Getting used to the environment. We'll do camping trips for Practical Combat, but not until halfway through the term," Adrian said. "Good luck."

"Cold cold cold cold." I took my hands off the metal box and shoved them into my uniform pockets to try to warm them up. Then I switched into my Aracheknight set to try to use the gloves to distance myself from the chill coming off the box of supplies I had purchased. They had been delivered to me at the atelier.

On the bottom floor.

Which meant I had to drag them through the empty workshop and up the stairs, all the while leaving a trail of water where the frozen humidity remelted. After stopping to warm my hands up, I continued up the stairs, into the cramped hallway, and finally, into my little private workshop in the back of the atelier. I set the box up.

It was still frozen. This wasn't going to work. I looked up at the ceiling.

I needed to grab a stool to open the ceiling panels, revealing ropes that could hang hazardous materials to store them. It took me a while to find the ceiling panels, pop them open, and hang the box, but once I did, ice was no longer accumulating on the floor around the box and melting.

I nearly jumped out of my skin as the door pounded behind me.

"GWEN!" a voice shouted.

I opened the door slowly.

Vivienne, the scribe who oversaw this atelier, stood behind it, furious. Scribes acted in many different roles: accountants, bookkeepers, assistants . . . and I guessed as supervisors as well.

"Yes?" I asked, wincing.

"You damaged the floor across the entire workshop. Is that—" She leaned around me, staring at the box hanging from the ceiling. "Hazardous materials? We have a cart for that."

"I'm sorry. Can you show me how to move this properly? I'll do better next time."

Vivienne paused. She closed her eyes and steadied herself, visibly calming before letting out a puff of air like a suppressed laugh. "Yes."

[Quality Assessment: (Ragged)]
[Generating Skills . . .]
▶Poison Touch I
▶Poison Resistance 10
[ATTRIBUTES]
▶SPD: 0
▶WIL: 0
▶STR: 0
▶DEX: 15
▶CON: 0
▶PER: 15
[+1 XP]
▶Poison Touch I
[All of the user's nonmagical damage sources are enhanced with a chance to inflict the poison debuff.]

The Caustic Hunter outfit was finally done. I knew the quality would be bad, but I still grimaced at the final numbers. I had assembled the piece mostly after hours in the Foundry atelier and almost entirely without using any skills while doing so. Still, the skill would be a boon.

I was getting to the point where low-level patterns with low-quality production weren't worth the attribute points. It was better to spend the same effort leveling.

There was only another half hour or so before Sandy, Gerald, and I were meant to meet up and prepare for our first excursion outside the wall.

The prices of monster materials were ridiculously prohibitive. If we could hunt the monsters ourselves, and find enough customers for commissions, we would be swimming in merits.

I stored the outfit in my inventory. Then I pulled on my Mage set. I knocked back a mana potion before storing the Mage set away again in favor of my school uniform.

My mana store remained far above the limit of the set.

Registering for an excursion outside the wall involved an entire process.

Sandy and Gerald were already waiting when I got there.

"Gwen!" Gerald exclaimed as we entered the crowded office. Employees—Nobles doing desk work—stood on one side of a counter. A line formed around them.

"Take a ticket and wait," one of the Nobles said as I stepped in.

"She's with us! Come sit down," Gerald said.

I sat next to them, blinking at the sheer number of Nobles bound for beyond the walls. Even the students who had obviously attended the Academy for years weren't exempt from the process. They stood patiently in line, chatting with each other.

It took another half hour before we were called to the front.

"Names?"

"Gerald, Gwen, Sandy. Year one students," Gerald said.

The Noble on the other side scribbled notes before handing over three badges.

"These are enchanted to be tracked. Crush them if your life is in danger. The cost for rescue service is a hundred merits. You can earn back a negative balance through direct employment with the Academy." The Noble suddenly looked up at us, dead serious. "Do not overextend or put your lives in danger. Or you'll end up working here."

"Got it . . ." I said.

"Are you taking tags today?"

"Tags?" I asked.

Tags, it turned out, were the Nobles' answer for how to transport the bodies of monsters. It hadn't really occurred to me how difficult it would be to transport an entire monster body home. And most of them didn't bring butchers with them.

Some of them did, though.

The tags came in three colors: Red tags would mark the monster to be retrieved, butchered, and sold, adding the value earned to a balance that paid out in merits. The cost of butchering, retrieval, and managing the sales were all recovered from it.

Blue tags had the monster brought back to the city and preserved.

Green tags had them returned to the city, processed, and preserved.

"Who buys green tags?" Sandy asked.

"Monster meat enthusiasts." The man behind the counter sighed. "Have you heard of the Delicious Dungeon Club?"

Sandy shook her head.

The school had several extracurricular and recreational bodies and clubs; the Delicious Dungeon Club was one of them. They especially enjoyed eating the monsters they killed themselves.

"If we return a blue tag, do we get the down payment back?"

"No returns."

I guessed I could buy it and save it for later. The tag was a lot like the gigantic badges, though designed to be stabbed directly into a dead monster. It cost an entire merit, though most of that was earned back after the body was collected—if it wasn't destroyed. Which wasn't guaranteed, as there were few things as attractive to other monsters as monster corpses.

After registering our excursion, we had just one more stop before heading out of the city. The fourth member of our team: our expert tracker, master monster hunter, and all-around good boy.

I knocked on the door to Lyssandra's miniature estate in the Academy.

It was a house. A condo, maybe. They must have only been called estates to assuage the egos of the Nobles who lived in them.

There was a bark before the door opened.

"Cinnamon!" Sandy shouted even as the dog pounded down the stairs and tackled her. She petted him.

She was already in the Houndsmaster uniform I had made her. Her Storm Curtain set was in my Wardrobe.

Lyssandra came down the stairs in casual wear, stirring sugar into a cup of tea.

"Are you heading out already?" she asked, looking curious. "I heard about your results in Practical Combat. Good job. If you hadn't passed, they wouldn't have let you beyond the wall."

"Thank you," I said.

Between the tags, mana potions, antivenom potions, and the supplies we purchased for sleeping overnight in the wilderness, I had spent my entire store of merits; my balance was down to zero.

Cinnamon carried our gigantic pack of supplies. He was growing bigger and bigger; he was almost the size of a horse. I wondered how much Lyssandra was paying to feed him.

The Nobles at the checkpoint to leave the Academy stared curiously at Cinnamon but didn't say anything. I heard lots of whispers about a tamer class being rare, though.

We took one step into the wilderness outside the Academy, and stopped.

An entire world stretched out before us.

The world felt less magical after two hours of hiking. It had rained recently, and the ground was mushy. There were endless muddy trails made by the Nobles and monsters that must have roamed the wilderness. We walked along them, over the plants, slowly moving uphill and keeping our eyes to the forest, watching for monsters.

We stopped when a bird landed on the trail in front of us. It strutted back and forth, looking at us patiently. It was about the size of a chicken. We paused, unsure whether to fight it or continue on. It crowed a few times.

Cinnamon pounced on it before any of us could react. There were a few seconds of crunching noises. His tail waggled with extreme enthusiasm. Before any of us even turned to stop him, he turned around and barked happily, eyes sparkling as he walked up to Sandy and demanded pets.

She scratched his chin.

"Good boy."

"Cinnamon has the right idea. We should eat lunch," Gerald said.

"In the middle of the jungle? You don't want to find a clearing first?" I asked.

Gerald shrugged.

"It's all low-tier monsters around here."

Sandy and I exchanged a glance. Only a few weeks ago Gerald was too afraid to be in the dungeon without his armor. He was acclimatizing quickly to life as a Noble.

Out of the three of us, he was the only one who was actually Chosen.

"Let's at least find somewhere dry," I said.

We continued on, eventually stopping beneath a giant, ancient-looking tree where the ground was almost suitable. We pulled out prepared meals. The shops around the Academy sold all kinds of goods to prepare adventurers on excursions. In Dungeon Economics, they constantly reiterated which workshops needed to produce which goods to keep a dungeon-diving team in optimal condition.

But for students or knight errants who lived in someone else's territory, just buying it would do. I splurged for slightly more expensive food than ration bars and thanked myself for it. We had to pull the pack free from the massive pile of other goods. Cinnamon enjoyed the break from lugging, too, running in circles around the giant tree. He stretched against it, expanding giant claws that dug deep furrows into the bark.

There was an audible popping noise.

I looked to my left.

A gigantic squirrel appeared. It was colored with patterns of spiraling purple and green. It reached down, grabbed my bag of food, and—

"Hey!"

It popped out of existence a moment before Cinnamon would've hit it, taking my bag of food with it. Cinnamon cried as he sailed over the spot where the squirrel had been. I stood quickly.

"Where did it go?" I asked, looking around the clearing.

"Cinnamon!" Sandy said. "[Track.]"

Cinnamon's head shot up. Sandy stood.

"Oh crap. Gerald, get the pack!"

Gerald looked between us, but hesitated only a moment before closing the rest of the supply pack and hoisting it. His armor appeared on him in a flash.

Cinnamon shot toward the tree, jumping at the bottom and barking.

I pulled a throwing needle before I even saw the monster. The squirrel was up there, digging around in the bag. When I threw the needle, it disappeared again, and Cinnamon shot off.

We followed after him.

He tore through brush and foliage chasing the squirrel.

It was nearly ten minutes before the squirrel ran out of mana for whatever teleportation skill it had been using and we finally caught up with it.

Cinnamon, of course, caught up with it first.

We were all panting by the time he caught the squirrel.

"Wait . . ." I said, winded. "Don't let him . . . eat it."

"Cinnamon! Leave it. Good boy."

The squirrel was soggy.

"Can you . . . ?"

"Yeah," Sandy said.

She field dressed it. Cinnamon whined the entire time. Sandy piled up the leather and placed it into another bag before throwing the rest to her dog, who crunched down happily.

"Where are we?" Gerald asked, looking around as he set our pack down.

CHAPTER 21

The sun was basically right above us in the sky. Which didn't help at all. I tried to remember which side of a tree moss grew on. Nature skills weren't taught well anywhere here. Because most commoners simply died in the Wild. I was sure Practical Combat would include more navigation skills later in the term. But we hadn't covered it yet.

Sandy was trying to talk Cinnamon into leading us back to the Academy, but he mostly seemed confused by the question. Also annoyed by having the pack back on his back.

"Let's pick a direction and walk in it," Gerald said. "It beats waiting here."

I touched the badge on my neck. I couldn't afford to go a hundred merits under.

Cinnamon barked, tail wagging playfully, then began sniffing the ground.

"It's okay! Cinnamon has this," Sandy said. "Good boy. Yes you are!"

Cinnamon sniffed the trail and led the way forward.

We followed behind.

It only took half an hour for us to return to a trail. But it wasn't exactly the same. There was fresh grass growing on it, like it wasn't trekked often enough to reduce the path to dirt. Even the roaming animals and low-level monsters should have roamed enough to do that.

The forest grew darker and more imposing as we went farther down the path. Even the sky seemed to darken, clouds boiling black overhead.

Eventually, we stopped.

The three of us stared at a hazy field that blocked the air, but one that was all too familiar. Inside this dungeon, all the way down past the safe zones, there was a bubble of the Wild's influence.

"What the hell?" Sandy asked, reaching out and touching it. Her fingers passed through to the other side. The entire area was eerily quiet; there was no birdsong or even insect noise.

I leaned down. The grass and plants inside of the bubble went wild.

"I think . . . this might be the exclusion zone," Gerald said, touching the bubble.

"The what?" Sandy asked.

"Lyssandra mentioned it in homeroom. There's a section of land outside the Academy we're supposed to avoid at all costs. She said there were dangerous monsters here," I said.

But that couldn't have been true. Because there was nothing here. So what was it actually hiding? Was it just that the Wild was particularly dangerous? And why was there a beacon of the Wild here?

"Gwen . . ." Sandy said. She was staring at me. I was staring back. I didn't realize how hard my facial expression had grown. "There's no way—Gerald won't want to."

"We should explore it," Gerald said, crossing his arms.

The answer startled both of us. It was totally unlike him.

"What? Aren't you guys tired of people telling you who you are and who you'll have to become? Wasn't that the whole point of us coming here? They're obviously lying about whatever this is."

"It might be dangerous," Sandy said.

"Can you ask Cinnamon to watch for threats?" I asked. "I'll move ahead using Shadow Cloak."

Sandy looked uncertain, but she leaned down and talked to her dog anyway. He barked happily, his tongue lolling out of his mouth.

"We can do it," she said.

I nodded, then hesitated. "We just go in, take a look around, then leave. The first sight of a monster we see, we run away," I said.

"Agreed," Sandy said.

"No problem there," Gerald said, arms still folded.

With a mental tug, I pulled on [Shadow Cloak] and stepped into the Wild.

It had been weeks since I felt the itch of the outer world beyond humanity's fortifications. And it was in full force here.

The path zigged and zagged, winding around. I only stayed some thirty feet ahead of Sandy and Gerald. Cinnamon's ears were pressed to his head.

But there were no monsters. No insects, no birds.

No noises.

The tree line cleared after half an hour's walk in.

The road led directly into the mouth of an ancient, dilapidated fortress. I froze, staring up at gray walls embedded with vines and lichen.

"What the fuck?" Sandy said, nearly making me jump. I dismissed [Shadow Cloak].

The front door was opened inward. Dirt and gravel piled up inside the entrance.

"Lanterns?" I suggested.

Sandy dug through the pack before pulling one out, holding it up and shedding light across the area.

"Let's stay close to each other."

We crossed through the open door that was far too tall for a human and into the domain of the fortress. It quickly opened back up on the other side, exactly like a human city. Except it couldn't have been, because the Wild should have reduced all of this to dust.

When we found the crystal golems outside of Stitch, the Wild had reduced their workings to dust as well. Man or monster, the Wild seemed to hate all living things. But it clearly hadn't degraded this fortress.

Buildings—rows of houses with the roofs long decayed and collapsed in on themselves—stretched on. Each one was huge, far beyond human scale, with a massive door in the front.

"It's a city for giants," Sandy said. We moved cautiously toward the center.

Even the cobblestone roads were scaled up.

As we neared the center of town, we realized why there were no dangerous monsters here. It was because there were only corpses. They looked weeks old. The bodies of gigantic monsters lay broken and burned, scattered through the city and piled across the road. No beasts of prey feasted on the remains; they rotted in the streets. The Wild did not consume them.

I knew what we were heading toward. I just didn't want it to be true.

At the center of this town in the middle of the wilderness was an empty stone archway. It was pure white and organic; there were no seams. It wasn't made of brick but rose straight out of the earth.

A dungeon gate, empty and offline.

And outside it the corpse of a monster larger than any building. Its scaled leather was rotting mush. Its skull was visible beneath the sagging layers of its face. It wasn't a drake. It was a dragon. We all paused to take it in before approaching the dungeon gate.

The dungeon gate wasn't closed; during the nights when a dungeon operated in accelerated time and reset, the dungeon gate would be blocked by a wall of wild, warping energy.

"Why is it off?" Gerald asked. He pressed a hand to it. "That's not right. This doorway . . . if it led downward, and was off, it would be sunken into the ground?" It was a fact, but it sounded like a question.

"Yeah. This doorway has to go up. To a higher floor of the dungeon," I said. "The question is . . . what did all of this?"

Every floor of a dungeon only had one entrance and exit. That was the rule. When we cleared the dungeon, it produced the barrier that held back the Wild.

The *dungeons* created the barrier that protected humans from the world. The same malignant force that destroyed monsters.

"Let's leave."

We left the exclusion zone quickly, heading directly away from the lost city as quickly as we could before we found a normal trail. There were signposts marking how many miles we were from the Academy.

And many more signposts saying to avoid the trail and general direction toward the exclusion zone.

"Are we going to tell anyone what we saw in there?" Gerald asked.

"We shouldn't," Sandy said.

"We should tell Lyssandra."

Even Cinnamon seemed more reserved. We talked far less during the next segment of our hike, heading off toward the den of the winged snake monsters I wanted to pursue. My thoughts churned.

If that dungeon entrance simply led to the floor above us, then it would have been open. Or, maybe it would have been closed. But it wouldn't have been *off*. If it was a dungeon that went deeper, it would've been partially embedded into the ground. It wasn't any of those things.

Human settlements, and monster settlements, should have been wiped away by the Wild. Everything we had that survived the Wild was enchanted. It felt like I had just discovered evidence of aliens.

It took a few hours to reach the den of the winged snake monsters. We stopped far away from it.

"Stay here," Sandy said, talking to Cinnamon.

He sat. She took the pack off of him anyway, leaving it next to him on the ground.

The winged snake den was a hill covered in holes that presumably led down to burrows for the snakes. They opened out of the side of a cliff face like a bug nest.

I pulled out my scissors. Snakes sounded like bad targets to hit with a needle.

"Let me go first," Gerald said even as Sandy and I were stepping up to the nest.

"Are you sure?" I asked.

"Yeah. They won't bite through my armor."

Gerald was wearing the new armor set he had crafted. I still wasn't sure what the abilities on it were. His previous armor set featured a bounce-back damage ability that reflected damage to his enemies. We hadn't yet fought together while he wore his new set.

To my surprise, Gerald didn't summon his shield either. He just waltzed right up to the snake den.

"Come out!" he shouted.

A white and blue snake head popped out of one of the holes. Huge fins spread around its face as it extended a tongue and tasted the air.

We braced for an attack.

It shot out through the sky, multiple wing-like fins glowing with mana as it slithered out of the den it was in and into another.

I started lowering my scissors.

"Is it not going to come fight us?"

As if on cue, the monster shot out of a lower hole and straight toward Gerald. Its gigantic mouth opened and extended, fangs sinking down toward Gerald's head. He screamed for a moment, staggering back, but the fangs didn't penetrate his armor, instead scraping over the metal.

Gerald grabbed the snake's bulk with both hands and slammed it into the ground.

The snake must have been thirty feet long. Whatever magic it used kept it floating in the air. Sandy and I charged it from opposite sides.

My scissors clamped down, cutting open the monster's scaled armor, but failing to cut straight through it. Sandy ran along its side, opening a long, shallow wound.

The monster thrashed, slipping free of Gerald's grip and back up in to the sky. It shot back into its nest.

"Are you okay?" I asked Gerald.

"I'm fine," he said. "Get ready. It's coming again."

The monster shot back out.

This time, instead of trying to cut its scales, I went straight for its wings. It ignored me again, diving for Gerald, and I cut one of the magical fins from its side. A horrible hiss resounded in the tiny clearing around its nest as it started to rotate uncontrollably.

The monster hit the ground and thrashed, hissing, and turned back to its den.

Gerald grabbed its tail under an arm, stopping it. It thrashed and spun.

I dropped the scissors, pulling free a tiny throwing needle. I ran to the monster's head and used [Running Stitch] to punch through its hard scaled leather and drop the monster dead.

[+4 XP]

"Nice work, Gerald!" I said.

He nodded in his armor, staying oddly quiet as he stared at the monster corpse.

Sandy got to work, pulling out a variety of knives to begin to carve through it.

"I'm going to need better tools soon," she said.

"How many merits do they cost?" I asked, half hesitating. I had to invest in my team, too.

"Unsure. We'll have to stop by the abattoir. Find out how much they pay for each of these monsters if we drag them back, too. Maybe we can find a way to make extra merits if we bring the monsters back a different way."

I squinted.

"What do you mean?"

"I mean that the abattoir in Foundry can't be the only one butchering live monsters. I think every last butcher has had the thought at least once. And I bet they're willing to pay well for it."

We ended up with a pile of dripping snake leather that we added to our supplies.

"If we had the stuff for it, we could store up the venom to use for tipping archers or poisons. Need harvesting supplies, too."

"Our shopping list just keeps growing," I remarked.

We hunted two more of the snake dens. There was only one snake at each, which meant someone had cleared them out just the day before. More and more should have respawned into each nest, but with so many students fighting over sources of experience and merits, we were lucky there were any left at all.

Once we figured out that removing the wing-fins destabilized the monster, the fights became much easier. We tried to minimize the damage to the fins as much as possible; they were almost definitely the most valuable part, practically glowing with magic.

Luckily, unlike the high lightning- and frost-attributed materials, they didn't seem to have any hazards.

[+4 XP]

[+4 XP] [Level Up] [Excess Discarded]

I put the point into crafting.

[Crafting VI]

We had roamed far from the Academy to reach the monster dens, but the sun had only just set. In the end, we hiked back through the night instead of camping. The increased endurance from our growing constitution turned the nightmarish proposition of a hike into a calm walk.

I walked with Sandy back to Lyssandra's residence—the dorm was too small for Cinnamon. The door swung inward; she answered with a horribly bright candle that must have been made of some magical material.

"You're back early."

"Lyssandra, I need to tell you what happened on our excursion," I said.

"Tomorrow before dinner. I'm going back to sleep," Lyssandra said.

"It's important!" I said.

Cinnamon pushed his way inside, sniffing at Lyssandra's candle.

"Did anyone die?" she asked.

"No, but . . ."

"It can wait."

Sandy strode into the abattoir with unusual confidence. She stopped and crossed her arms, looking up at the butchers at work. She smiled. Their handiwork was fantastic.

Just like Foundry, the main floor of the abattoir was focused on harvesting gigantic, high-level monsters. Unlike Foundry, they possessed a great amount of equipment to do so here. And they ran all through the night. Huge, seemingly magical lights kept the workshop running.

The sound of mechanical buzzing filled the shop as enchanted contraptions operated. A butcher used manual controls on a gigantic, industrial buzzsaw to split open a monster with twelve legs, gigantic talons, and a fur-covered carapace.

Troughs in the floor occasionally had water pumped through to bring away pooling blood that sometimes sparked, bubbled, or even steamed. In other places, it was collected into gigantic metal receptacles. Sandy watched as a butcher pulled one of the metal cylinders away, closing the top shut with a wheel that turned to lock it tight. Then she slapped a sticker on it, leaving it in an area marked *Alchemical Supplies*, the letters painted directly on the concrete floor.

The industrial abattoir was a thing of beauty to her.

"This area's restricted." A woman with a scar across her nose walked up to Sandy, hands in her pockets. She wore a brown apron full of butcher tools of all sorts. A name badge read Rosalind.

"I'm Sandy," she said, holding out a hand. "Sandy Butcher. I'm Chosen."

Rosalind shook Sandy's hand uncertainly, eyeing her up and down.

"One of our own. Looks like the upgrade is treating you well. What can I help you with, Lady Butcher?" Rosalind smiled, a light in her eyes as she watched Sandy admire her handiwork. Only other butchers seemed to really understand.

"I just did my first hunting trip," Sandy said. She was still watching them work on the monster.

"Blue tagged?" Rosalind asked. She was noticeably excited.

"Nah," Sandy said.

Rosalind frowned.

"Hey," Sandy said. "You willing to buy material directly? If it's uh, prepared?"

"Butchers can always do a better job. Get more material, less damaging cuts . . ." She trailed off.

"What if I bring you . . . even less-damaged material?"

"What do you mean?" the forewoman asked.

"Something still alive."

The forewoman squinted. She took a step back. She eyed Sandy up and down. "This a prank? Or you with the guard?"

"I'm the most honest Noble you've ever met," Sandy said.

"An honest Noble? Ha." The forewoman looked her up and down again. She turned her head, contemplating. "I'm not saying we would buy anything of the sort. But . . ."

The forewoman reached into her leather apron, pulling out a white tag marked with a black cross, and handed it to Sandy.

"We can take a look."

CHAPTER 22

I couldn't get any work done in the morning while I was waiting to meet Lyssandra. Evidently, neither could Sandy, because I found her pounding away on Lyssandra's door when I approached her apartment.

Lyssandra, half asleep, opened it to let us inside.

Her little estate was maximally decorated. Paintings covered almost every inch of the wall. Several dog beds were piled on top of each other in the corner of her living room, covered in dog hair.

Lyssandra led us to her kitchen and poured herself—and us—coffee before saying anything.

"We—"

Lyssandra waved a hand to stop us before sipping her coffee.

"But I—"

She stopped us again.

I begrudgingly drank the coffee. It could wait a few more minutes.

"Okay," Lyssandra said.

"We went into the exclusion zone."

"There's a dead dragon near a dungeon gate in the center of it."

Sandy and I both talked at once. Lyssandra froze. She set her cup down slowly.

"What?"

"We got lost in the woods."

"And then we saw the Wild inside the dungeon."

I was already regretting my decision to be more forthcoming with the adults supporting me as I withered under Lyssandra's stare.

"What about the other monsters there?" she eventually asked.

"All dead," I said. "For weeks."

"Shit," Lyssandra said. She stood. She sat back down. She put her face in her hands. "Shit."

Cinnamon barked.

"What *is* the exclusion zone?" I asked. "Why are the buildings inside not destroyed by the Wild?"

"There are buildings inside?" Lyssandra asked.

"You . . . haven't been inside?" I asked.

"The exclusion zone is defined by the priesthood. I knew there were monsters inside. It's a monster den—the monsters should respawn, they shouldn't—The Wild was present? In the dungeon?"

"Unmistakably."

"And it didn't destroy the monsters?"

"No."

"They were too old to harvest," Sandy said.

"The priesthood—my only interaction with the church was when they came through our village to activate our systems. I expected churches in Foundry or Spoke or . . . in the Academy. There's not—there's no worship," I said.

"They have monasteries in the capitals," Lyssandra said, rubbing her face. "But they are highly isolationist. They regularly interact only with the highest echelons of Noble society. They are considered one of the strongest bulwarks against the Wild's encroachment and culling the calamities that roam the far Wild."

"And this exclusion zone?"

"The priesthood will know what is going on with it, despite how little they share with us," Lyssandra said.

"But what *is* it? It looked like a dungeon gate. And not a dungeon gate that goes farther down, but an unopened one leading up."

Lyssandra paused, considering her reply. She sighed.

"You must not share what I am about to tell you. You are not meant to know it. *I* am not meant to know it."

We nodded.

"Within the world-scale dungeons there are often shortcuts that allow you access to a deeper floor. They are considered extremely dangerous and often protected by guardian bosses—something like the dead dragon you saw. But they're not dangerous for the bosses—they're dangerous because they can often cross an entire continent. Many of them will turn on only once. Almost all of them will open in the vicinity of another dungeon entrance."

"So the dungeon worlds are interlinked?" I asked.

"Frequently, but not always," Lyssandra said. "Many Noble teams have been lost after choosing to explore one of these shortcut dungeons. Even when a corresponding team reopens the gate a day later, they do not return. We suspect it's due to these skip floors often having serious time differences. Or the threat of monsters deeper in."

"So where does the gate in the exclusion zone come from?" I asked.

Lyssandra paused. "I don't know."

"But it could open from a different continent entirely in the floor above it? So are there . . . people out there?"

"There are things out there," Lyssandra said. "And the Wild hates them less than it hates us."

Lyssandra had to report it—anonymously, of course. I left her to that.

Sandy took Cinnamon out on a walk, and I left to continue work on my second commission.

I decided to make my new pattern. I hadn't actually practiced it yet, so the quality of the final product might be reduced, but I had to make it eventually.

I went through my normal routine of switching into mage gear, drinking a mana potion, and switching back to gear with high dexterity for crafting. It felt a little silly to be producing so much in armor.

I decided that I would look for a higher-level crafting set. If I could get a few more seamstress skills, I could dramatically improve my time crafting.

Vivienne had shown me more of the workshop's equipment; there was a section of the floor where a panel could be lifted to reveal a copper fitting. It was meant for a metal mannequin or a conductive rod of a metal work-shop table. A system downstairs was adjusted to push hot steam through the pipes.

I dragged furniture onto them and clicked them into place; the steam was already flowing after starting the device downstairs. Instead of building heating enchantments throughout the entire building, they used one central heat enchantment and steam power to distribute it, turning the cost and time of enchanters into the cost and time of carpenters and architects.

It felt a lot less magical. But it worked. The table rapidly heated it up.

I opened my case of freezing leather. Cold air burst out into the room. The case was hanging from the ceiling, minimizing the spread of its deathly chill.

As quickly as possible, I dragged a sheet over and threw it onto the heated table, letting it counteract the magical chill coming off the leather.

I stared at it for a moment. Condensed humidity melted and dripped off the side of it. I let out a contented sigh, activated [Pattern Mirroring], and got to work.

My regular hand scissors could barely cut the leather. I fished out the enchanted set Gerald had made me. I hadn't actually tried using them while they were downsized.

They sheared through the leather with ease.

I needed to buy more proper tools.

The Storm Archer's Raiment was very different visually from the other sets I'd made; it looked closer to Lizzie's Storm Archon set than anything I had crafted before.

It featured a huge, wide-brimmed hat to keep the rain out of the wearer's eyes, and a half cloak that flared around the shoulders, deflecting water but not consuming as much material as the Hunter pattern's full cloak.

I carved the leather into shapes, punched holes through it, and stitched it back together. The collar of the half cloak rose to the nose, until only the eyes and ears of the wearer would be visible. It was a set made for fighting in stormy dungeons.

It reminded me of the train ride to the Academy and passing through the dungeon floor with the rain storm.

The memories I had of the seamstresses making the set featured views out of glass windows in high stone towers of storms that blotted out the sky.

By the time evening came, I had already completed a few pieces of the set. I took the rest of the night off, meeting up with Sandy to eat sandwiches in the Academy's park. The swathe of artificial nature was built atop the roofs of several connected buildings but featured old trees growing from the lifted earth. I wondered if they were using magic to keep this structure stable, considering all the weight.

Valjean leaned back with a groan.

"When you're ready, Lord Valjean."

Finn stood with a quill in hand over a set of fine parchments; paper made from magical pulp designed to survive long trips through the Wild. Each one was marked with the header of a different Noble in the surrounding cities.

"How many units has our atelier sold, Finn?"

"Six hundred thirty-two, Lord Valjean."

"Good. Begin the letter."

Dear Lord, Lady, or Liege. I hope this letter finds you well. I write to you from the heart of Foundry about a new economic initiative that has bolstered our city. In just two weeks, this initiative has created dozens of levels across no more than two workshops.

We have gained the levels of years in the work of weeks.

That is not the whole of the reason I've contacted you, of course.

In the four weeks preceding this day, our workshop fulfilled over five hundred private orders from outside Foundry. It has fully repaid the entirety of my invest-ment in labor and training costs to produce it. In the days to come, we await hundreds more.

Furthermore, we believe that the current economic plan, which restricts the basest skill of crafters—be it Crafting, Butchering, or Scrivening—is wrong, and that these skills should actually be prioritized within a workshop.

The details of my economic initiative follow . . .

Sir Arthur was the oldest of my teachers. He taught Dungeon Economics. He had a wiry, spry build that didn't fit the scars visible on his arms and face. He often wore rolled-back sleeves that revealed the tattoos and yet more combat scars. His hair was always a gray and black mess.

I took notes with the rest of class.

"Levels are not the only consideration to factor when managing a work-shop," he plainly stated. "Not all levels are invested evenly. Many skills that workers may pick might enhance the worker, but not the workshop. In the modern area, we split workers into tracks, often with the assistance of the accompanying guild that oversees their class. While workers may be inclined to level their crafting skills, these primary skills of their class do not actually enhance their practical output.

"And that cost in levels can take months or years to be recuperated."

Sir Arthur droned on. I groaned.

"Did you have a question?" he asked.

"No," I replied.

It took me until Wednesday to finish the archer set.

The boots were knee high, designed to slog through rainy conditions and water tight over baggy pants. The top was loose fitting with long sleeves; the entire set was clearly for hunting in some stormy dungeon, and the memories embedded in the pattern as I crafted it agreed.

As the set neared completion, the constant chill it emanated lessened, the magic of the material being redirected into each piece's attributes and skills.

It was done.

[Quality Assessment: (Good)]

[Storm Archer's Raiment (Rare, Ice) completed!]

[Generating Skills . . .]

▶Strike Twice V

▶Bow Proficiency V

▶Ice Resistance 50

[ATTRIBUTES]

▶SPD: -5

▶WIL: -5

▶STR: 35

▶DEX: 35

▶CON: -5

▶PER: 35

[+10 XP] [Level up]

▶Strike Twice V

[For a modest mana cost, imbue projectile with a heavy electrical charge. On contact with an enemy, inflict lightning damage with a chance to stun.]

▶Bow Proficiency V

[Grants proficiency with and additional damage from a bow.]

I blinked. The finished craft had given me a level directly, despite only being good quality. I doubted the next instance would do the same. I leveled Crafting to seven.

Homeroom was idle time the next day; time to complete assignments for other classes. I scribbled on Civics homework that discussed the common law from city to city.

Adrian didn't show up until halfway through class.

"Good morning, Teacher," he said, striding into the room with a casual smile.

Lyssandra nodded at him and returned to reading a book at her own desk across the classroom.

I set my pen down, waiting for Adrian to sit next to me.

"Marcus's teammate's set is ready," I said.

"Perfect. Bring it to Study Hall and I'll make sure they're there to pick up."

Practical Combat continued with the dark wolves. Many of the students seemed much more timid after their experience last Friday.

My team was among the only teams in our class who had actually killed the monster. Once every last student had killed another wolf, Sir Stonehart interrupted the usual proceedings to lecture.

"I hope you see now how imperative it is to join an extracurricular Study Hall. There should be no shame in running away. The shame only comes when you bite off more than you can chew. Many of you had to have the monsters pulled off of you by an experienced Noble. You lost potential experience that day, and your peers are pulling ahead. Take it to heart and prepare more thoroughly."

Marcus's teammate picked up the Ice Archer suit at Study Hall.

This time, I brought an entire mannequin, placing the suit on it.

"Looks good," Marcus's teammate commented. She put a hand to it. "Still a little chilly to the touch. What skills does it have?"

"Archer skills," I said plainly.

She tsked.

"Doubt I'll be able to make use of it. But the Frost Resistance?"

"Sixty," I said.

She smiled and pulled the hat off, putting it on.

"Looks funny, too. Tell your contact I said good work."

Marcus's teammate left happy.

I didn't receive a new commission immediately despite setting up the display so ostentatiously, but I had faith more commissions would come.

After Study Hall, I took account of the materials I had.

I had the scraps remaining from the lightning goat from Lyssandra's dungeon. I also had scraps remaining from the ice-resistant set. I had a handful of gem hearts from crystal golems, and I had everything we had collected from the flying snakes.

I had never crafted a set out of so many disparate pieces. I wasn't confident I could complete it in just a weekend, especially without an extended mana pool. With no reason to rush, I couldn't justify spending merits on it.

Unless there was another way to get a full mana pool.

Just like dungeons, when humans rested overnight, we recovered all our health and mana. I had the crazy notion to sleep in the Archon Storm set.

They were the least comfortable pajamas I had ever worn.

CHAPTER 23

I woke up sore, missing my hat, and overflowing with power. The first thing I did was recover the hat from the tiny space between the bed and the wall. I had thrown off my blankets in the night and still managed to sweat in the mage robes.

They were completely waterproof. Which was awful when sweating in them.

I was still giddy staring at my status screen. Laughter bubbled out of me as I pulled my hat back to my head before sending it away to my Wardrobe.

I wouldn't need to spend any more merits on mana potions. Because this morning, I woke up with almost a hundred mana available.

Getting through classes today was harder than ever. I couldn't look away from the windows, my foot tapping against the floor. I found myself pulling up the mana total every few minutes, greedily awaiting Practical Combat.

Despite so many of the class suffering minor wounds last week, no one had any bandages or scars. At night, humans healed—everyone knew that. It made me wonder how the many grizzled veteran Nobles I had seen accumulated scars at all. Monsters that could leave wounds so deep they were embedded in a person even after they healed were beyond my reckoning.

Mental scars, though? Those were easy to get. Half my Practical Combat classmates were back to acting timid and reserved.

The Chosen Nobles who had never fought had been fearful on the first day of Practical Combat; they hadn't truly *understood* then as they did now. They had never fought, never been wounded. And as the class had continued, they had built up a false sense of confidence. That confidence had been broken Friday for most of them.

It was easy to feel immortal. Especially when you were overflowing with new magical powers. This was likely the most turbulent time of their lives for many of them.

And Nobles grew fast. They didn't have levels from crafting, but each of them were able to allocate attribute points with each level gained, and each of them gained skills only for combat. Several of them were catching up to me quickly. Especially since I gained nothing from the low-level monsters killed in Practical Combat.

Except, hopefully, today.

The monster in the arena was big. Bigger than a wolf. But it was slow. It was orange and tan and smooth, with an armored hide. The entire class watched eagerly as the first student stepped into the cage. The porters ducked out of the arena after freeing the monster; that was a first. The instructor stood inside of the cage still, ready to intervene.

A young Noblewoman stood across from the monster. She carried a long, bladed pike.

I leaned forward in my seat, watching eagerly as the pike-wielding Noblewoman circled the monster. The gigantic, armored armadillo sniffed at the ground. With a shout, the girl charged forward. Her weapon flashed as she used a slashing skill.

The monster dodged, rolling into a ball with deceptive speed. Instead of diving forward, the Noblewoman paused and took a step back and away from where she was standing. It was good, too, because the monster used a skill of its own.

It shot forward through the space where the Noblewoman had stood a moment earlier. She spun around, ready to swing.

But the monster didn't stop when it hit the wall. Instead, it continued up the wall, rolling faster and faster around the arena.

The Noblewoman inside spun in circles to try to keep up with the monster. When it was behind her, it launched from the wall and slammed into her back. She gasped and staggered forward as the monster bounced off of her before landing on the ground.

The monster took a moment before it moved again. The Noblewoman was still recovering, too. She clung to her pike, recovering from the impact that had almost knocked her off her feet. When she stepped forward, pike extended, the monster moved again. Again, it spun around the cage before slamming into the Noblewoman. She grunted, prepared for the impact.

This time, when the monster lay stunned on the ground, she activated a different combat skill—one that drove her across the arena in a brilliant flash. It looked a lot like Anna's techniques, without the burning gold light.

The Noblewoman drove the pike into the monster's head; once, twice, and it was dead. She stabbed it a third time, panting.

Sir Stonehart nodded.

"I see you've developed multiple attack-based skills," Sir Stonehart commented. "Movement and utility skills are also imperative for developing Nobles. If you had either, you wouldn't have struggled so hard."

The next few students struggled as well. But they all approached with caution. A few had skills that let them deal with the monster; one student with a sword and shield turned to brilliant white marble, like a living statue. The attack bounced off of him.

Victor flashed around the arena, sliding over the ground with the same odd movement as his whip, dodging the attack and retaliating. Another student turned half transparent and the attack phased through her.

I felt a brief pang of dread. The Noble students in this class were developing skills like this after only weeks of activity. Exactly how strong would the Nobles get?

I had to spend weeks and hours of effort and labor to acquire my skills one by one. Even the skill I planned to use today and the extra mana I had were thanks to others helping me.

There was no time to relax. I had to continue working hard, not just hunting monsters, but crafting out of them. I wasn't sure if the extra levels I gained would be enough to outpace the extra work I needed to do.

Sir Stonehart nodded his head in seeming appreciation at the fresh caution each Noble showed. Many stopped outside the cage or stood nervously. They were more serious than they'd ever been facing down the monsters.

When it was my turn, Sir Stonehart eyed me and the needle-thin sword I carried warily.

The monster plodded forward toward me, long snout sniffing the ground inquisitively. It recoiled as it caught something it didn't like. I held the needle-sword in front of me with a smile.

I currently had Sandy's Storm Curtain set in my Wardrobe. She had the Houndsmaster set in the meantime. The Storm Curtain set's Parry skill was one I couldn't use often due to the cost on my mana.

But that was before today.

Today I had all the mana I could ask for.

The monster rolled into a ball, sliding forward, then backward. Then it accelerated to its side, shooting up and around the cage and rolling in circles around it.

They must have picked this monster specifically to surprise the students on the first day of class after the field day. Most of them had reacted well to it, except for the unlucky student to be called up first. Halfway through the class, most of the students already had strategies prepared to deal with it.

Only a few who had overzealously invested in offensive skills suffered, and even then, they were able to overcome the monster by virtue of being stronger and faster.

As for me?

When I heard the monster leap off the side of the wall with enough force to make the metal groan, I activated [Parry].

My body turned as if pulled by invisible strings. The monster, whose bulk was almost as large as I was, slammed into the thin blade. It continued to spin as if it had hit an impassable wall.

I flicked the blade with no more force than a twitch of my wrist and the monster was sent spinning across the ground. It let out a shocked noise before I stepped forward, driving the needle directly into its head with a smug smile.

[+4 XP]

This was the first time there was something worth fighting in Practical Combat.

Sir Stonehart nodded appreciatively but said nothing.

I cleaned my blade and sat down, staring up as Anna finally took her turn.

When the cage opened, Anna crossed the arena in a flash of gold, using the exact same move she had used every single day in Practical Combat—except Sir Stonehart caught her fist in his own hand. There was smoke coming off his palm.

"The lesson today is about using utility skills," Sir Stonehart said.

Anna stared up at him. From where I sat, I saw her eyes glowed brightly enough to splash light onto his face.

"Yes, sir," she said, stepping back. The monster rolled forward. The porters exited the arena.

When the monster shot off the arena cage, Anna stepped to the side. There was no skill activation. Just a flex of attributes that touched the line of superhuman.

The monster shot past, rolled onto the ground, and stopped.

Anna looked to the teacher. He hesitated, then nodded.

She shot forward and crushed the monster's head.

Sir Stonehart frowned.

"Stay after class," he said. He spoke quietly. But no one here had baseline perception.

The last few students killed the monsters one at a time. When they were done, Sir Stonehart discussed some of the utility skills that had been used. He seemed especially proud of the student who had chosen the Stonehart skill—the one that had turned him into a marble statue.

He was also eager to point out the skills' weaknesses.

"Victor, if the monster was attacking you with a homing skill, then your movement technique wouldn't have dodged it," he said. "You have to time that skill as close as possible. A dangerous game." He turned to address the Noblewoman who had turned transparent. "On the other hand, Ethereal Moment fixes you in place. It's a good use of this skill, but against wide attacks, you might find yourself in danger the moment it ends."

The teacher went on to talk about more of the class's skills before the day ended.

Victor was practically jumping on the way out of class.

"Ready for Study Hall?" he asked.

I felt myself smile. I could show off my Parry skill today.

"More than ready. Let's wait for Anna?"

Victor turned, frowned, and leaned against the wall outside of class. The rest of the students slowly filtered out in little groups. Many of them had formed their own Study Halls by now. We caught a few curious glances. Anna followed a few minutes later, looking irritated.

It was novel.

She almost always had an expression of boredom on her face.

"You okay?" I asked.

Anna glared at me for half a second before relaxing her face and nodding.

"Coming to Study Hall?" Victor asked. "It'll be good to blow off some steam."

She nodded again.

"What was that all about?" I asked.

"Sir Stonehart thinks I've disrespected the spirit of the class by using only one move over and over," Anna said. She looked at her hand, flexing her fist.

"That's stupid. Fear the woman who has practiced a punch ten thousand times, not the one who has practiced ten thousand punches, right?"

"That is . . . insightful," Anna said.

"Your skills are almost as flashy as mine," Victor said. "I can't wait until I get something like that. What's it called? Wait, don't tell me. I want it to be a surprise when I get it."

Anna stayed quiet on the walk to Study Hall, but her agitation slowly faded.

Study Hall was packed today; all nine of us were there. Ash, the Chosen mage from Sandy's team, had a black eye, and was holding ice to it. Sandy patted her on the back.

"She caught an attack right in the face," Sandy said, noticing me looking.

"You alright?" I asked her, sitting down on the row of tables. A few bags spilled loose papers out over the table, loose schoolwork forgotten in favor of Practical Combat training.

"I'll be fine tomorrow," Ash said. She gave a pained smile.

Out of everyone in the class, she seemed like she wanted to be here the least. I smiled and sat next to her.

"You struggle with the monster?" I asked.

Ash nodded. Ash was a mage like Elara, but Elara had years of training and a heritage to lean on that let her cover her own weaknesses from the beginning. Ash, on the other hand, struggled to express her magical talents fluently. Elara had had years to study the applications of her family's class—one perfectly passed down and refined across generations, each individual skill and level picked in advance. She must have already had a dozen levels—if not more—before reaching the Academy.

Ash had no such benefit. She was struggling through learning to apply force mage class skills. Her abilities centered around applying a burst of force and kinetic damage. I had seen how she struggled to deal with moving targets in Study Hall. But she needed a lot more levels to gain the skills to deal with it.

"I got a utility skill," Ash said.

"Oh?" I asked.

"It's called Killing Field."

"That . . . sounds dangerous?" I asked.

"It's not," she said. "It just creates an area like a swamp. Trips up your feet. I thought the fight today would be no problem, but . . ."

"The spell only applied to the ground in front of the monster," Sandy said. Ash nodded.

"I see. And it shot up the wall and out of your area of affect. Can you cast it on a wall?"

"That was the first thing Sir Stonehart recommended. But it costs so much mana," Ash said. She clutched the staff in her hand. Then she sighed.

The arena on the other side of the room warbled to life as Adrian and

Cedric sparred. Both of them used swords and small shields—different weapons than what they used against the rest of the class. Their swordplay was highly refined—they were a dance of flashing blades and bucklers slapping into each other.

"Want to practice your new spell on me?" I offered after a minute of watching. The two of them could spar for minutes at a time before landing a blow.

It seemed like a waste to train so much against other humans.

Ash hesitated, staring at my face. Her hair was growing back in—she had shaved it bald before the Academy, clearly, and hadn't had time to shave it again since.

"Yes," Ash said, voice determined.

"I want to see if I can Parry magic."

We took over the arena after Cedric and Adrian.

Ash raised her staff between us, her face fixed in determination. Light warped subtly as it passed through the warbling barrier of the training zone.

The bolt of force hit me before I had time to realize. I blinked as I was pushed back with a flash of purple. The barrier wound down.

"Try again?" I asked.

Ash nodded. She didn't seem any more confident despite having hit me dead on.

"Your magic is invisible. That's a pretty big advantage, isn't it?"

"So is Elara's . . ." Ash trailed off.

"I don't think that's the norm, though." Most skills and abilities had very large, visible telegraphs. "I think you could be amazing fighting from stealth. Ready?"

Ash nodded.

This time, I watched her more closely, looking at every move she made. And I circled her. It took her a second to discharge her skill. Her hands twisted uncomfortably on the staff. Her breathing was faster, as if she were exerting herself. And her eye twitched.

I [Parried], catching an invisible bolt of force that I redirected back at her. The redirected bolt wasn't invisible—it was a mass of boiling and distorted air that slapped into her, damage mitigated by a purple flash.

The barrier powered down.

"One more time, Adrian!" I said.

He frowned.

"I know I'm hogging it. We're done after!" I assured him. "Ash needs it."

Adrian nodded at that. The training barrier wound back up. Every time it was used, it got a little weaker, needing down time to regenerate its protective property. Using magic like this exhausted it quicker. But Ash really did need it—way more than Elara, the other true mage in our group.

"Ready?" I asked.

Ash nodded and lifted her staff. But I wasn't just sitting still this time. I rushed her. Her eyes widened in alarm as she lifted the staff up and held it in a different position; I cast [Parry].

I felt the skill hit her Killing Field and not stop it. Maybe it was because it was area-of-affect magic, or maybe there were other qualities at play; whatever the case, I was trapped in a quagmire of thick air that grappled with my ankles as I tried to rush toward her. Ash stood still for a moment before remembering to kite backward. When she cast her next [Force Bolt], I [Parried], but instead of flinging it toward her, I threw it downward experimentally. The two magics dissipated with a noise like shattering glass, my legs free as I dashed forward and tapped her with the rapier. It flashed purple.

Ash looked disheartened as the arena powered down.

"That was good," I said. "Quick thinking with the spells!"

I was still jealous of proper mages.

"Me next," Victor said, tapping a foot.

I smiled wryly.

"Sure."

"Thank you, Gwen," Ash said with a nod, stepping out of the arena and toward the table we reserved for doing homework.

So far, Victor had struggled to hit me even when I didn't have practically unlimited mana. That didn't stop him from throwing himself at me anyway.

"Show me how your new skill works," Victor said.

The barrier fuzzed to life around us as Victor took a spot across from me. I lifted my sword, ready to wipe the cocky smile off his face.

His whip cracked and flashed toward me, enhanced to superhuman speed by a terrifying skill. It was a gunshot, explosive force erupting as I calmly slapped it away with [Parry]. The smirk did drop from Victor's face after the second or third exchange. Each time, the whip blew backward, slamming into the barrier with explosive force. It didn't slam back into Victor as I intended; the force of his whip was odd and didn't move in straight lines, instead cracking forward and to the side. It maintained that even when [Parried].

Victor cracked his whip forward again. I [Parried] a fourth time, but as I did, his entire body flashed white. He slid along the ground, using his mobility skill to pivot behind me in a moment. With a crack, I staggered forward. Purple light flashed over and behind me.

"Got you!" Victor said.

It took me a second to recover my balance before looking back at him in shock.

"Again," I said.

Victor's smug smile wasn't wiped away.

We fought again. This time, he managed to slip around me mid-[Parry] and hit me in only three blows. I hit the ground and stalled, pressing my hands into the soft mat foam on the floor.

In only a few weeks, the Nobles at the Academy were catching up to me. Their classes, their skills, everything about them was designed to enable them to fight. Every one of their skills was focused on buffing themselves. My own skills were split in a dozen separate directions, a significant amount of my recent investment going into leveling Crafting.

The system inherently gave them the ability to fight harder, better, and faster than it did for me. I had over a dozen levels above Victor and he was still catching up.

"You okay, Lady Gwen?" Victor asked.

I realized I was glaring at him before schooling my face.

"Yeah," I lied. "I'm fine."

I needed to finish my mobility skill set. I needed to dump all the merits I was acquiring into leveling faster. I needed skill points to craft faster, to level faster, to kill monsters faster.

I had to keep up.

That night, I started work on my own version of my new pattern.

Even after the excessive practice with Parry, I still had more than fifty mana left over. Enough to do what I normally did ten times over.

I went over the resources I had remaining as I planned to create a new set of the Storm Archer's Raiment. The main component would be the leather from the flying snakes we hunted outside the Academy.

The snakes had magical wings of translucent film; I planned to make the pattern's cloak from them.

Having crafted it once before, I was very confident in merging together practically every scrap of material I had left. I still had pieces of the electrical goat's leather remaining as well, which would add some lightning resistance.

And make the inside very comfortable. I wasn't planning on making anything as uncomfortable as Lizzie's Storm Archon set. If I ever had to sleep in the field, I wanted to have my best stats.

Thinking of Lizzie, I needed to send her a letter and ask how she was doing. There was constantly something on my to-do list that got in the way of that, though.

Like today, playing catchup with Nobles.

I got to work, using the scaled leather of the snake as a base. The monster was long and thin, which meant I had to start by stitching multiple sections together, using Running Stitch to punch a hole straight through the magical monster leather. I worked to make sure every seam was as tight as possible.

Then, I had to cut the pieces into the largest shapes of the pattern, cutting apart pieces I had just brought together, before stitching the pattern together. As I fell into a crafting fugue, I swam through dreams and memories of the times this outfit had been crafted previously. Often in huge, ancient-looking towers.

There was one memory that stood out of a tailor working on the deck of a ship. A drizzle of rain fell across the deck—and his face. An ocean stretched on behind him until it fell out of the distance. I blinked, coming back to consciousness and out of the memory.

The crafting fugue left me fully aware of everything I was doing during it; the memories played over it like dreams, borrowing the expertise of all the crafters before me. It was rare for a scene to be shocking enough to shake me awake. I had never seen the ocean.

It was gorgeous.

And I saw the same images of an endless sea over and over the rest of the week. At night I sparred.

Victor was the first to start to catch up to me. He wasn't the only one. All of the Chosen Nobles were advancing in skill and power so fast that I didn't have a chance of catching up. All of them were gaining mobility and utility skills simply as a matter of leveling up and selecting them.

As for me?

I worked even harder to finish the Storm Archer set.

Of course, I also leveled up Wednesday. In Practical Combat, Sir Stonehart threw stronger monsters at us, which meant even I was feeling the benefits. But that point went into crafting, which did nothing for me yet.

The investment would be worth it. It had to be worth it. But it still

didn't feel like it as my classmates caught up to me. They should have leveled, too, after all.

I just needed two more levels for crafting to start giving me permanent
attributes every time I completed a set.

I just needed to complete this set to catch up in combat classes, even
though I had lost months of advantage in weeks.

I just needed to work harder.

CHAPTER 24

When I finished the set, it was late enough into the night that the street noise had fallen quiet. Academy City's nightlife rose and ebbed in waves; every three days, the gate to the surface opened, and trains rode through the Academy, bringing goods in and taking others out. For every day outside, three passed here, meaning the Academy could produce more and faster.

It went without saying that the Academy wasn't the only reason for this place. This floor churned out goods and resources, far more than it consumed, and it imported trainloads of food and living monsters. Today the city was on an ebb; the streets were full of shadows, oil lamps dimming hours after their refill.

I slumped over in a chair, recovering.

The mobility set was done. It had been assembled from practically every resource I had left.

The Storm Archer set was like the Hunter set in many ways; it was designed for a single person navigating a dense environment full of rain. It was entirely waterproof, layers of leather creating a barrier for tromping through muddy terrain.

The cloak fell over its shoulders and ended at the elbow. It was made of translucent wings with hard ridges; like a bat's wings, but made of crystal. The rest of the pattern was created with white, scaled leather, smooth and watertight to the exterior. The scales had a light blue shimmer when you caught them at an angle.

The top of the cloak flared upward, shielding the face from whatever water wasn't stopped by the massive, wide-brimmed hat. I used [Embellishment] to change it from a circular hat to a triangular one.

I just liked how it looked alongside the angular cloak.

Besides that one visual flair, you wouldn't realize how much the outfit had been Embellished. I put most of the effort into making the inside comfortable. The outfit was lined with warm goat fur, plenty to keep me warm in the event I ever waded through a storm myself.

I was hoping it was enough to raise the quality higher than ragged. I closed my eyes. When I opened them, I finally called up the system and looked over the sheet for the finished set.

[Quality Assessment: (Fine)]

[Storm Archer's Raiment (Rare, Light, Lightning) completed!]

[Generating Skills . . .]

▶Flash Step III

▶Arc Bolt V

▶Lightning Resistance 15

▶Light Resistance 25

[ATTRIBUTES]

▶SPD: 0

▶WIL: 0

▶STR: 35

▶DEX: 35

▶CON: -5

▶PER: 35

[+10 XP] [Level up]

[High-quality materials have altered the stats of the completed set.]

▶Flash Step III

[The user teleports a short distance blocked by line of sight. Cooldown scales with Speed. Distance scales with skill level.]

▶Arc Bolt V

[Conducts a bolt of electricity to the target, discharging damage. Discharging through the air reduces the damage.]

One more level. One more point into Crafting. Just one more level to go, and I could race to keep up with the Nobles. I was so prepared for archery-related skills that it took me a moment to process what the skills I received actually were.

I shot up in my chair.

"Magic."

Real, actual magic. Not an enhanced projectile. Not a cloud of rain for putting out fires, either.

Excitement bubbled out of me. But not at the prospect of using it on monsters.

I was going to fry Victor at Study Hall on Monday.

And I could kill a few new monsters on Saturday. But I could do that whenever.

Work into the witching hours.

Sleep in a mage uniform.

Wake up half dead and full of mana.

My new routine was killing me.

Breakfast at the Dragon's Den could almost convince me it was worth it.

"How big are the birds these come from?" I asked, poking at my plate of fried eggs. They were *huge*. And the spice on them made my tongue burn. In a good way.

They were clearly monster eggs.

"Dunno," Sandy said. "Think they have a ranch of these somewhere? Some kind of giant birds. Dunno what they'd even feed 'em."

We scarfed down food, making the most of our morning. I drank a carafe of coffee. Then we rushed out of Academy City and into the wilderness beyond it.

"What's our destination this time?" Gerald asked, squinting to stare out over the clearing surrounding the Academy. The sun peeked harshly through autumnal clouds.

"Out of the city's line of sight," I said, excitedly rushing forward.

"To where?" Gerald asked.

"You get a new skill?" Sandy asked.

"Yes!" I said, excited to try out a literal lightning bolt. I obviously couldn't test it inside the city.

We rushed along a trail and beyond the city's sight.

"Shouldn't we have an actual plan for where we're going?"

"I do!" I said. "We're heading half a day north after."

"After what?" Gerald asked.

I stopped in a clearing next to the trail and looked around.

"Right here should be fine," I said, stopping and setting down my bag. The grass alongside the trail was almost dry. It was at least free of mud.

I called up [Always Prepared], the heavy wooden box falling to the ground before me, and pulled out my sewing needles. I pointed one at an old, dying tree.

I didn't even need to change out of my school uniform to activate the skill, but a stray thought stopped me from casting.

"What counts as a mana focus?" I asked.

My sewing needles only worked with sewing skills when they had a string or rope at the end; mages' focuses were much the same; specially crafted devices used to channel and enhance magic. Many mages had skills they were unable to use at all without a focus.

I looked over to Gerald. He shrugged. "I haven't gotten one as a . . . pattern. They're typically mana alloy or enchanted—wait, did you get a mage class skill?"

I smiled at him, pointed at the tree again, and mentally tugged on my connection to the skill I had from the Storm Archer's Raiment in my [Wardrobe].

The sewing needle in my hand glowed brighter and brighter, accumulating a magical energy I could feel as a tingle beneath my palm. Then it released it all at once with a crack, a bolt of blue, white, and yellow arcing out of the tip of the needle—and directly into the ground beneath me.

"Aw," I said.

"Whoa!" Sandy said, pulling Cinnamon back from barking at the sudden display of light and sound. He whined as she scratched under his chin.

Gerald squinted at the spot on the ground the lightning had made contact with.

"Not very long range," Gerald said. "I wonder if . . ."

I stared at him, feeling excitement build up for a moment. Gerald always had moments like these before he got sent into a crafting frenzy. His face started to light up. Then it fell.

"Nope. I have no inspiration," he said, shrugging. "I'd love to craft you a focus if I could."

"Maybe we can find you some motivation," Sandy suggested.

"I know just the place," I said, leaning down into my bag and pulling out the map.

About six hours north, there was a deep den of monsters—an open dungeon in the world—which featured monsters not dissimilar to the giant armadillos we had fought in class. These ones had scales instead of thick leather hides.

Monstrous pangolins the size of horses lived there. Their skills focused on hardening and defense, and I was hoping that the outfits made from them would give similar skills.

We just had to be able to kill them.

We stopped for lunch halfway through the trip. The entire hike had been at a slight but constant incline. I practiced [Flash Step] a few times as well. It shot me several feet forward in an instant with a popping noise and a flash of light. The mana cost was only two; far lower than I expected. With the enhanced mana of my terribly uncomfortable pajamas, I could cast it dozens of times in a day.

The trees grew monstrously larger until they were as wide as houses, vast swathes of the wilderness being choked by darkness. Shapes moved across the canopy.

None of them came for us.

I used [Tracking], searching for the red trails of monsters. With the skill's pitifully low level, I was only able to see very recent and very close trails. But we eventually found the first of the monstrous pangolins' nests.

A circular tunnel double my height dipped into the ground below.

I turned to Gerald. He was already in full plate.

"Are we sure we're ready for this?" he asked.

"We have to be," I said. "Are you guys even getting experience from Practical Combat? We have to keep up."

Sandy stared down into the tunnel. After a moment, she nodded.

"I need to butcher more. We need to find a way to get out of the city a few times a week, too. My classmates are already catching up to me."

"We have to split our skills between crafting and fighting, and our time between study and practice. We're basically working full time to try to keep up, Gerald. We have to be ready."

"I'll go first," he said after some hesitation. He stepped up to the entrance, then stopped again. "I won't be able to swing my mace in here."

Gerald summoned his shield.

"Hold on—take this," Sandy said, summoning a knife and sharing Butcher Vision with him. Then she lit a lantern. Gerald nodded. He carried the massive bulk of his enchanted shield with one hand. Notably, the shield no longer matched his suit of armor.

His first suit had been enhanced with the ability to rebound damage. This second one was crafted soon after he joined the academy. I still wasn't fully certain what it could do, but any thought of asking him disappeared as we descended into the tunnel, earthen walls choking out the sky and noise around us.

The sound of songbirds fell away as we descended into damp earth. Instead, there was a calm, rhythmic scraping from deeper in the tunnel that slowly grew louder as we proceeded. Any attempt at conversation died in my throat. I switched into my Aracheknight set, ready to mentally call on Parry the moment I needed it.

The tunnels were huge. As wide as a road, an entire wagon would fit within. And they fell away to darkness on either side of us.

Eventually we came to a place where the tunnel split in two. Sandy and Gerald looked to me.

"Left," I said, the word echoing and louder than I intended in the dark.

We continued forward until we approached another split in the tunnel. The sound of the scraping was still distant, farther in. If we just kept left—

A monstrous arm burst from out of the dark and roared. And it wasn't just a roar—magic rolled over us, a buzzing tingle in my skin.

[Willpower too low to resist Stunning Roar. You have been stunned.]

I froze for just a moment, but that was long enough. A pangolin that looked more like it belonged to elemental metal than earth rolled in front of us—literally—before uncoiling and sliding. Its massive tail whipped, slamming into me and sending me backward. I gasped as I was slammed back into the earth, unable to Parry, unable to retaliate—unable to do anything.

Cinnamon whimpered somewhere. I threw myself forward the moment I could. Sandy was back in the dark, too. Without Butcher Vision, I couldn't see the monster.

A flash of purple revealed it for a second. It roared again.

[Willpower too low to resist Stunning Roar. You have been stunned.]

I stopped in place, sucking in a breath. I could still breathe. I just couldn't move. The monster was slapping its gigantic arms down into Gerald's shield, each blow releasing a purple flash that revealed it.

The stun ended. I started forward again.

Gerald was now dancing with the monster, moving left and right to block its blows as the steel pangolin pressed him backward into the cave, fighting in the dark.

"Guys?" Gerald asked, his tone panicked. "Gwen! Sandy! Help!"

The monster screamed again. I was stunned.

I needed more willpower. I needed—a thought occurred to me. I couldn't move, but I was still thinking. In the seconds between being stunned, I reached out to the system and swapped into my highest willpower set.

[Stunning Roar resisted.]

[Running Stitch]

My needle bounced off the scales of the monster. That almost never happened; the enhanced power of Running Stitch pierced through almost any material. I dreaded the thought that I would need to level it.

The attack wasn't for nothing, however. It carved a thin gouge along the massive scales. Each one was almost the size of my torso. It also put the monster's attention onto me. Gerald stepped back as the steel pangolin turned its full height toward me. Sandy caught up now.

"Gwen, that thing has almost no visible weak points! Only the tiny sections at the bottom of each scale!" Sandy said, panicked. "And its mouth!"

"Shit!" I said, dodging backward as the monster started running toward me. "Shit shit shit!"

Gerald bonked the monster on the side with his club. Inside the cavern, he couldn't swing it fully—the length was massive. He could still use its enchantment to make it gain weight. The pangolin shook the attack off, shaking back and forth with its massive bulk, before pressing me back to the wall.

I almost forgot that I had a teleportation skill now. I activated [Flash Step], teleporting toward Gerald. There was a cooldown before I could use it again. The monster roared. I resisted the stun. Sandy, Cinnamon, and Gerald were frozen.

There was a tiny weak point at the bottom of each scale. I could work with that. I twisted around, activating [Running Stitch] and stabbing into the bottom of one scale.

The monster screamed. It was louder than its magical roar. It made my ears ring in the little cavern. I stabbed a needle longer than my arm into the tiny weak spot between the monster's scales.

I may as well have not bothered. All I did was piss it off. The monster slapped me away a second time. My remaining health dropped precariously as I rolled across the ground. The needle was still embedded in the monster's side.

The monster lurched before prowling toward me. Sandy slammed a gigantic butcher knife into the side of its face, blood spilling out and pouring over one of its eyes as I rose back to my feet and threw myself toward my needle with [Flash Step].

The monster rolled into a ball and shot forward. A moment later it made a noise of pain as it rolled onto its side, driving my sewing needle deeper into it.

"We need to damage it somehow," I said, half panicking.

"Use *magic*!" Sandy shouted.

"I would have to be close enough to—"

I stared at the monster. Its forward roll had embedded the needle into its side. Thinking quickly, I switched partially back to the Aracheknight set, pulling the throwing needles from my belt and lobbing them toward the monster even as I ran closer. The pangolin was already pushing itself to its feet.

Casting [Thread Mastery] and holding the spider-silk threads attached to the ends of the needles, I manipulated the smaller needles through the eye of my larger, handheld one. Most of them missed. But two landed.

The pangolin got to its feet. I wouldn't make it in time to be in range to cast the spell. But maybe I didn't have to be.

I pulled on [Arc Bolt].

It was a sudden, half-assed thought. The lightning before might have not reached its target because of the lack of a focus. Or maybe the lightning was just naturally attracted to ground. But I gave it a better ground this time—the thin wires connected to the metal rod embedded in the monster.

The wires in my hand flashed with color and the cave filled with the smell of burning spider silk—one I hoped I would never have to smell again. But the monster fell back to its stomach, landing hard in the cave. I ran forward, holding my other sewing needle in my left hand.

Every time the monster tried to stand, I activated [Arc Bolt] again, bringing it back to its belly. Gerald and Sandy tried to run forward, but the monster repeatedly used [Stunning Roar] even while unable to rise.

[Running Stitch] drove my second needle through its eye without any problems. But that wasn't enough. The monster started to stand. I let go of the two threads I was holding—they were literally burning to pieces any-way—and gripped the needle with both hands.

Then I channeled [Arc Bolt] directly into its skull.

CHAPTER 25

Level up!]

I panted as I fell to my knees, gripping the sewing needle. Cinnamon was the first to catch up to me. He barked at the monster's corpse a few times before charging forward to take an ineffectual bite at its face. His teeth gouged lines in the metal-like body of the monster.

"Are you alright!?" Sandy asked, running forward. Gerald joined a moment later.

"Not to rush you . . . but we need to get out of the cave," Gerald said, nervously staring behind himself.

"He's right," I said. "We can recover outside of here. If there are more pangolins in this den, we're dead."

I switched into my set with the highest strength.

"Let's drag this thing out."

It took a moment to tie rope to its legs. The three of us pulled it as quickly as we could, leaving a trail of blood behind us on the cave floor as we rose up and into the jungle. We didn't stop there. We continued forward, steeped in silence.

"Maybe we should run forward and recover," Gerald said.

I glared at him.

"There's no way we leave this behind after how hard we . . . after how hard Gwen worked to fight for it," Sandy said.

I stopped and sighed.

"Gerald might be right," I said, turning around.

We were already a decent way from the pangolin nest. The only problem was the trail of broken foliage we were leaving behind. Cinnamon was sniffing excitedly and walking back and forth in front of us. He barked when we stopped; he seemed uninjured.

I sighed.

"Maybe this was too advanced a hunt."

Sandy nodded grimly.

"I need more skills. But I don't have access to a Wardrobe or Noble skills." Sandy waved at Gerald. "We need another solution."

"There has to be a way," I said, falling flat onto the forest floor. The adrenaline left me all at once. "We almost died," I said.

And then I put my face into my hands. "How are we supposed to do this?"

"Slower," Sandy said. "And together."

"There's no way for us to keep up like this," I said.

"Have you tried . . ." Gerald started, cringing back as Sandy and I both locked onto him. I waved him to go on. "Have you tried looking for like-minded crafters in the Academy?"

"You think there are crafters in the Academy who hunt monsters?"

"Well, no—not ones who hunt monsters. Just ones who can help. Like Henri's cooking. An alchemist maybe who will trade for material . . . Though, Sandy did say there were other butchers who . . . Maybe they would know a way."

Sandy's face lit up. "Maybe they would," she said.

"But would they just tell you if they did?" I asked, staring at the pangolin.

"Maybe they wouldn't," Sandy said, but she sounded more excited rather than less. Her eyes scanned the horizon excitedly.

"What is it?" I asked.

"If other butchers are hunting monsters, they almost definitely wouldn't openly talk about it. If they know another way to get skills I'd almost definitely have to earn their trust to learn it. So maybe that's what we do. I think Gerald is right."

"I am sometimes," Gerald said, nodding.

"And we get their trust how, exactly?" I asked.

"I think we start by capturing some live monsters for their arena," Sandy said. "But first . . ." She looked back at the massive steel pangolin.

It was time to butcher.

I stayed on guard in the woods while Sandy started her work. Then I ended up helping. The massive scales were fused to the monster, each one magically reinforced by the monster's own body. It was like cutting apart metal rather than prying them off.

It was long, messy work as Sandy used skill after skill to more efficiently rip the monster apart.

"Do you want these scales?" she asked, panting as she held up one of the gigantic metal scales with a single hand. I looked it up and down before shaking my head no.

She flung the scales into the wilderness. Gerald leaned down and tapped a fist against one.

"These are almost metal," he said.

"You think you could use them?" I asked.

Gerald shook his head. Very casually, he tossed the scale to the side. It went sailing up through the air in an arc before exploding into the ground. Gerald turned away from it. He didn't even seem to notice how fast his own strength was growing. He was a few levels ahead of most of the Chosen Nobles coming in, but Gerald was growing fast.

It took half an hour for Sandy to finish. She'd had to climb atop the monster to split it open, and all of us helped to roll it over.

We were left with more material than we could use.

"I think I could make a few sets out of this," I said. The leather was so thick I would have to split it into pieces—or use a skill to compress it. I had seen my mom use skills like that, stitching threads into directions that didn't exist.

But any point I invested in seamstress skills was a point I wasn't investing into increasing my combat ability. I bit my lip.

We ended up tying slabs of leather and carrying them like backpacks. There was more than I could reasonably use myself, but the material would likely give defense skills. Maybe even a stun like the monster's roar or another form of crowd control.

"We should head to the flying snake dens," I said.

Sandy and Gerald shared a look.

"Gwen . . . we should head back. That fight was . . . close."

"I know," I said. "That's exactly why we need to hunt more. We have to keep up. And we have to go out and hunt again exactly because that fight was so close. Something to get our confidence back, I think."

It's not like I wasn't scared, too. Now that the adrenaline had worn off, and I looked back on the fight. That monster was the size and power of a dungeon boss in Stitch. Here it was just living in a hole in the ground.

Sandy closed her eyes for a moment. "I'm almost out of mana," she said. "You know what we need? An alchemist."

"Alchemy is strictly regulated and products are tracked. No one can produce unlicensed potions," I said, rattling off knowledge from classes.

"Wait, really?" Sandy said, eyes wide. "Damn. So Terry was breaking a law?"

"Yeah. But we could afford more mana potions if we had more credits."
I sighed. We needed to make progress on too many fronts.

"Well . . . do you think you can capture one of the snakes alive?"

"Definitely not. And not today," I said. "Let's just . . . do an easier hunt."

We headed from the pangolin den toward the much more familiar flying snake nests. It was already afternoon when we got close. But before we actually reached the snake den, a sight on the horizon stopped us.

A controlled pillar of smoke rose above a clear section of grassy prairie. The smell of wood smoke drifted over us.

"Someone already cleared it?" Sandy asked.

"Or they're fighting now," I said. "Let's go see."

The monster camps were all known locations—it wasn't too uncommon for two groups of students to run into each other. We sped up a bit—not jogging, to conserve our stamina, but walking faster until we crested a hill and looked down at a campfire. A circle of stones held a contained fire while a half dozen Nobles laughed and ate.

They were cooking snake meat over it.

It only took a moment before one of them noticed us, pointing up the hill at us. He shook the shoulder of a tall man with white hair who was leaning near the fire pit and laughing. The man looked our way, a smile still visible on his face as the other whispered into his ear.

The entire atmosphere of the little Noble party changed, the emotion lowering to a chill.

They had definitely already killed the snake monsters; their corpses lay on the ground. Most of them were frozen solid, encased in blocks of ice that had been hacked apart—presumably to pull out the parts of the snakes they were currently eating. When I looked closer, I realized the white-haired man was using one of those chunks of ice for a chair.

He squinted at me before standing, the smile returning to his face, and waved at us to come toward him.

I took a step back.

"I don't like these guys," Sandy said.

"What's the big deal?" Gerald asked. "They're other students, right?"

He started walking toward them, much to my alarm. I looked at Sandy. She shrugged.

We walked into the group of Nobles.

The man—who was clearly the leader of the group—was older than us. It must have been his second or third year in the Academy. He was also clearly an ice mage. Rather than the Academy's uniform, he wore what looked like a hunting uniform—an almost-formal one, complete with a sport coat. It looked magical. And expensive. The smile on his face didn't match the venom in his eyes.

"Gerald of Stitch!" the man said. "I've heard about you."

"Yeah?" Gerald said.

"I'm Oswaldo. You can call me Oz. And this here—" He waved his hand behind himself at the people around him, "—is Soul Night. The name of our Study Hall. We're a group of all Chosen mages." Oz said that last part proudly.

"That name is corny," Sandy said.

Oz frowned.

"You and your . . . *teammates,*" Oz said the word with disdain, making eye contact with Gerald and Gerald only, "are new to the Academy. It's your first year, after all, so you didn't know. I will explain it for you: You can't just go around taking monster dens so loosely."

Oz's expression returned to a smile as Gerald glanced between me and him.

"Not this shit . . ." Sandy said. "You want us to, what, check in with everyone else before we take a den?"

Oz and a few of the men behind him laughed.

"Yes. It's all posted on the student bulletins!" Oz said.

"No," I said.

"Excuse me?" Oz asked, turning to look at me seriously for the first time. The expression on his face was ugly.

"She said piss off," Sandy said.

"Yeah. You can't go around claiming monster nests like you own them," Gerald said.

Oz looked angry.

"Soul Night clears the snake dens every week. Because of you, there were only four in the den instead of five. You're leeching our resources."

"Are you still low-level enough to level up from those?" Sandy asked. I laughed. Just a little. Oz locked onto me.

"We will clear whatever camps we want," I said. "Like Sandy said, piss off."

It was creepy that no one in his little cartel chipped in to say anything. They all just gave us angry expressions. It felt like a cult.

Oz's expression flashed through a variety of faces before landing on a fake smile.

"Then don't blame us for what happens. We'll see if you change your tone when we steal every monster you hunt."

I blinked. Were they really that petty? Oz departed with a nod, walking back into his makeshift camp. The atmosphere was tense. Several members of the student organization—Soul Night—were staring at us harshly.

"Let's go," I said. We turned to walk away.

"Gerald!" Oz shouted after us. I turned to see him lifting his focus—a white cane. "Watch out! There's a monster behind you!"

A spike of ice condensed on his cane and he flung it forward—toward Sandy.

I used [Parry] with the back of my hand, slapping the bolt of ice away from Sandy. It shot back with the same force and speed it had been ramming toward us with—but I didn't aim it at anyone.

The bolt of ice hit the fire pit and exploded, sending dirt and burning wood over Oz before erupting in a second explosion that created a cloud of obscuring dirt.

"Oh. Oh no."

"Are they alright?" Gerald asked.

"They're Nobles! They'll be fine! We need to run!" I said.

And then I turned and ran.

I didn't stop running until I was halfway back to the Academy. I could've kept going, too. My lungs disagreed, but my legs were still fighting. I stopped to recover for just a moment and then sat down in the grass.

Sandy and Gerald followed a moment after, all three of us staring back in disbelief at the fact that another group of students had just attacked us.

"We should tell someone, right?" Gerald asked.

"Who, Lyssandra?" Sandy asked.

"Adrian," Gerald said.

"Both?" I asked.

CHAPTER 26

Oz's arm shot out and captured Tristan's wrist in an iron grip. He frowned, brushing burning mud from himself with his other hand.

"Calm down."

"She just lobbed a spell at us!" Tristan complained. "Let me."

A trail of fire circled Tristan's raised focus.

"It was just a slowing spell," Oz said.

"They didn't know that! They just tried to kill you. We can't not respond."

"We will," Oz said. "Tomorrow, we can watch the entrances and race ahead to clear any den they're heading to. There's a few groups like this every year. They just have to learn it the hard way."

"Fine," Tristan said, ripping his arm out of Oz's grasp. A curling snake of fire still circled his extended focus—a piece of wood that looked thoroughly charred. "Are we going to tag these?" he asked, looking back at the snakes.

Soul Night had a mix of students in their second and third years. With years' worth of leveling and skill development, most of which they reinvested in themselves, they had absolutely no need for low-level monsters. More than anything else, they killed them as a way to relax. Or to cook their own favorite meal.

"No. Burn them."

They didn't leave even a scrap behind.

"Was it more of a cone? Or a beam?" Elara asked, leaning over curiously. "Was it glowing?"

"I didn't get a good look at it," Sandy said. "On account of it being thrown at my face."

"It was kind of a . . ." I made a pointed shape with my hands.

"That sounds like Ice Chain," Elara said, leaning back.

Adrian's face was grim.

"The Chosen factions have gotten bold. But I'm not sure it's a good idea to go fight them."

"What? They try to kill us and you want to go . . . fight them? Like a vigilante?"

Adrian shook his head.

"Ice Chain is a crowd-control spell—it's not damaging," Elara said, folding her arms over the table and leaning forward again. "Tell me, what did you do to make them so upset at you?"

"We cleared a monster den they said they had claimed," I said.

Adrian nodded. "You didn't check the student board?" He had half a smile on his face now.

It turned out this was a common occurrence. Adrian's own team had met us at the Dragon's Den, which had rapidly become our own meetup spot. He'd been out on a hunt of his own—one for higher-level monsters with Marcus's team, which meant faster leveling.

I'd considered asking to join, but I knew there would be a price in credits or favors. And I would have to answer a lot of questions about why we wanted to field dress and take parts of whatever we killed home ourselves. Unless we could come to an agreement with the local abattoir, but that was a problem for later.

Adrian led us to the student commons—the part of campus reserved for student relaxation. It was an area I had never visited. Everything in it cost merits—expensive food that would boost your stats; expensive gear and equipment, though cheaper than what was for sale at the shops; and expensive tickets to medicinal spas or alchemical treatments. Everything you could think of was available down a strip of manicured land with a green park in the center. To either side were even more expensive apartment complexes aimed at students.

"Most of the people who live there are fourth- or fifth-year students," Adrian provided. "Many of them have taken on teaching roles already. The rest are lifetime Noble teachers."

Tall lanterns showered light, dissipating the shadows around the student commons. Light glinted off the armor of the dozens of Nobles crowding the place. Teams removed their armor, cleaning off monster blood in the grass.

Adrian led us to the series of semiofficial corkboards that separated the outdoor area. Plexiglas covers sat over boards stuffed with notes and notices. A few students lingered around, but at this time of night, it seemed mostly empty.

There were notices related to monster expeditions; long-haul hunts that could last weeks. Many of them even went deeper into the dungeon. Others just ranged far away from the dungeon Academy. And as we progressed farther along the boards, we eventually came to a series of maps. Little emblazoned logos rested next to marked den locations.

"Isn't filling this map from one of our homework assignments?" Sandy asked.

Adrian smiled wryly.

"It's part of why they don't direct you here until later."

Sandy had already taken a notepad from a bag and was beginning to madly scribble down locations. Gerald looked to Adrian, who shrugged, before he started taking notes, too.

The homeroom assignment covered a small portion of monster nest each day, and by the end of the class you would have a completed map you were required to turn in. Occasionally we even got tests asking for which monster locations had what monsters, and the approximate level to be handled solo or as a team.

Lady Lyssandra—my homeroom teacher—had said that it was important to be able to map out a dungeon even without a cartographer, especially once you took control of your own land and had to deal with the upkeep of world floors like the Academy on your own.

I squinted closer at the little metal pin stabbed into the map. It read *Soul Night* across the bottom.

"So, what, these groups just claim locations like this? And the Academy *lets* them?"

"The Academy doesn't enforce it," Adrian said. "The students do. If you want help from the other student organizations, you have to respect the structure or you'll be deprived of opportunities for expeditions that could give you faster leveling."

"Those wouldn't do as much for us anyway," I said, thinking about how difficult it would be to convince an entire team to let us keep the body parts from a monster. Or to field butcher it in front of them.

"Of course. You already have us," Adrian said with a confident smirk. "Typically, you'd struggle to find a Study Hall with resources if you ignored the rules like this. But I'm not on the best terms with the other Nobility already. I'm a very late son in my family, so my access to the family's resources are limited."

"They don't seem very limited," I said, squinting at him.

Adrian held up his hands.

"This is actually not the Academy my family usually sends students to," he said.

"But . . . this is *the* Academy," I said.

"It's only one of three. Each of the three Capital cities, and each of the three King Candidates have their own Academy."

"And they just call them all 'the Academy'?" I asked.

"Formally, yes." Adrian shrugged. "The point is that I don't have leverage and connections with existing student bodies here, so I don't have anything to lose by pissing off Soul Night. Funnily enough, they are a group that formed from pissing off other established groups. It's why they're all Chosen. But it seems they've fallen in line to uphold the very same structure."

His smile was bitter. I looked over all the monster dens. The steel pangolins were not actually taken by any group. But I had no intent to go fighting them again. Besides that, I already had enough material from one to make an entire outfit.

Dozens of the other locations were claimed.

"Soul Night only knew we'd cleared it because we went back," I said, thinking aloud. "So we can clear any of these as long as we don't go there twice."

"Good criminals never return to the scene of the crime," Adrian said. He was still smiling.

I gave him a raised eyebrow.

"So you're . . . okay with us pissing off half of these Study Halls?"

Adrian shrugged. "It's not a problem for me. Cedric, Elara, and I group with Marcus's team on expeditions, so we won't face any struggles to find teammates for higher-level runs. It's your prerogative, of course—but if I thought sticking stringently to the current social order was the fastest way to grow, I wouldn't be in this Academy halfway across the nation."

Lyssandra said a lot of the same things Adrian did.

"If they used only noncombat spells, the Academy is unlikely to do anything. Small fights between students are expected—as long as there's no property damage."

It seemed like a highly irresponsible stance to take toward an entire academy of young adults who just got vast magical power. But what the hell did I know.

As for responding to Soul Night, we had come up with a plan.

We were just going to kill the snakes anyway. And they could eat shit.

Soul Night cleared the nest once a week, waiting for the monster dens to be full so they had a small, consistent stream of credits. So we could just snipe them every day. Soul Night would have to skip clearing other monster nests to interfere.

We were sure they wouldn't do that—after all, they had to go level themselves, and these students wouldn't be leveling at all from monster den so close to the Academy.

We left early in the morning, making sure we were ahead of anyone else. The checkpoint on the way out was actually busier than any other time of the day, with a few teams splitting off ahead of us. We were still all on the lookout for members of Soul Night.

A few steps out of town and through the torn-up mud path, we stopped and looked up, seeing an owl of transparent mana screaming as it circled us. Then it shot away.

"What was that?" Sandy asked.

"Some kind of scout spell?" I asked. "Are they actually going to . . . ? This is ridiculous. Let's go. We can probably beat them to the monster den."

We found the den of the flying snake monsters with a still-smoking corpse outside. The entire thing was ruined. A red tag was stabbed into its side.

Another screaming owl waited above the lot for us. I grimaced as I looked up at it.

"Seriously?" I shouted, pulling out a throwing needle and lobbing it at the screaming bird. It was definitely some kind of scrying or seeking spell. It flew away, and I reached out to the enchantment on the needles a moment later, recalling them to my hand.

"What now?" Sandy asked.

I thought back to the map. There were dozens of monster nests that no one had marked, especially low-level ones closer to the Academy. Even lower than the snake monsters.

"There should be a wolf den . . . that way."

We rushed forward through the wilderness in time to find a member of Soul Night still there. Bursts of slicing wind leapt from his focus, carving into the trees and cutting the last monster apart. He turned and looked at us from under a hooded mage robe.

With a smile and nod, he waved his focus again—rapidly. The monster corpses exploded into pieces. He carelessly slapped a red tag into one and then started running—far faster than any of us. A bird screamed above us.

We repeated the same dance a few more times before stopping, always reaching the monster dens too late.

"What a piece of shit," Sandy said.

I groaned. They really were going to do this. And it was only one or two of them at a time, different members—so they weren't all wasting time screwing us over. The rest of them must have still been hunting actual monsters.

"Let's go back," I said. "We can be better prepared next weekend."

Between the distance and navigating the wilderness, we had wasted basically an entire day. Not only that, but the screaming owls continued to harass us as we trudged back to the Academy.

"What if they do this again next weekend?" Gerald asked.

"It wouldn't be our first time sneaking into a monster camp," Sandy said.

"We just need the right equipment," I said, smiling.

All we needed was a den of Darkness monsters—or to purchase the leather to make more equipment that would unlock the Shadow Cloak skill.

In the meantime, I still had more projects to work on. I needed to decide what to put the leather from the steel pangolins toward. And I needed a thread that could take the electrical power from Arc Bolt without burning up.

"Gerald," I said, thinking of something. "Can you make metal wire?"

"Sure. I can try."

CHAPTER 27

Practical Combat classes still involved the relatively small armadillos that rolled up into balls and flung themselves around the arena. And they were still worth a trickle of experience. Not enough for me to level up this week.

I didn't see Gerald Monday. I sent a questioning glance to Adrian at Study Hall. After a few matches, he sat next to me and Sandy at the table.

"He's crafting again. Lots of . . . wire," Adrian said.

"When did he start?" I asked.

"Last night. Whatever it is, it's taking quite some time. He tucks it into his inventory and passes out right on the workshop floor. Then when he comes back, he gets right back to working."

"Is he even eating?" I asked.

"Yes," Adrian said. He looked uncomfortable. I was grimacing, too.

"It sounds like his crafting mania is getting more intense," I said.

"It might be," Adrian said. "I'm unsure of the mechanics. Classes like his . . . are rare."

I saw Gerald Wednesday. He was too tired to participate in Study Hall—instead, he sat at the table catching up on homework from the classes he'd missed.

"You okay?" I asked him.

He looked up at me. Despite how visibly tired he remained, the smile on his face carried genuine excitement.

"I'm good!" he said.

"What'd you make?"

"I'll show you later."

Once Sandy was done sparring, she sat down, looking between us.

"What's the plan for the weekend?" she asked.

I shook my head.

"We can't afford the Shadow materials we need to . . ." I hesitated, ". . . commission a third set of stealth gear for Gerald. So we need to get more merits. Would you be okay in just stealth gear?" I asked Sandy.

She frowned.

"Only if we're hunting something small. My attributes aren't enough to fight anything really big. Not yet."

I nodded and pulled out a hastily written map and some notes. Sandy looked over curiously.

I had scrawled a caricature of Soul Night's logo. There was also another Study Hall's logo nearby.

"Those two monster dens are that close?"

I nodded.

"They are. I've looked into the monsters here. Both of them are types that are very easy for lightning mages to clear—a Water element bird nest for one, and some tiny, nearly docile monsters for another."

"Won't we just piss off both groups if we take them?" Gerald asked.

"Soul Night are all mages," I said. "I think . . . we let me kill all of the monsters in these two camps. And I'll do it only using Arc Bolt."

"So that it looks like a mage cleared them. The other group will blame Soul Night. And they'll busy themselves competing with each other," Gerald said, thinking aloud. "But you said you only have two stealth sets?" he asked.

I nodded. "Only two of us will be able to go."

"There's another problem," Sandy said. "Soul Night red-tags all their monsters since they're hunting them for merits. This rival group could just wait at the abattoir for them to be picked up. They'd be suspicious if they weren't tagged."

"You're right," I said, frowning. I hadn't considered that.

"Why don't we just bait Soul Night into clearing the camps ahead of us and take the tags off the monsters they're on?" Gerald asked.

"I . . . didn't think of that. That's a great idea. But it would mean we would have to split up. Sandy will have to go with you and return to me stealthed. That means you'll be alone out there to make your way back. Are you going to be okay like that?"

Gerald hesitated. Then he nodded.

He was becoming more confident. Less afraid. That was the point of the Academy, but it was still shocking how fast and effective it was. We'd only been here a few weeks.

"We'll have to go when it's dark enough to use the stealth," I said. "Or stick close to the tree line."

"Let's make a plan," Sandy said.

* * *

I hadn't worked on any patterns that week. I wanted to. I stared at the pile of high-level monster leather.

It was uniformly gray and flat, dozens of pounds of refined material lying across the floor. I would've killed for something like this just weeks ago. But today I just couldn't bring myself to work on it. So instead, I tied the metal wires Gerald had made me to the ends of my throwing needles, busying myself with the work. The wires would carry the magic electricity of Arc Bolt without burning up, though I couldn't throw the needles into the monsters for fear of leaving evidence of nonmagical damage.

I was going to frame Soul Night for stealing a den. We would see how they liked competing against other Nobles for their own resources.

Before the weekend came, I still had made barely any progress on another set. I built the foundation for a new Hunter set from the steel pangolin leather, but I worried about adding too much and overpowering the Shadow materials I needed to get a stealth skill.

When I had crafted the same set from a Light element monster, I instead got a skill that produced a transparent copy of me. The other skills just weren't what I needed currently.

I did, however, level up again—in Practical Combat. The tenth and final monster gave me the final drop of experience for Crafting X.

[Crafting X]

[User gains 10% of stats, permanently, from any finished, crafted set. Portion of stats gained is split between workers on the same pattern based on total amount of contribution. Maximum of ten uses per pattern.]

I froze inside of the cage arena in the middle of class, my heartbeat spiking.

"Lady Gwen?" Sir Stonehart asked. The concern in his voice was rare for him.

I felt my face flush as I realized I had frozen in the arena.

"I'm fine. Sorry," I said, rushing out of the arena.

Level ten changed everything. I could keep up with the other Nobles. But to do it, I had to craft faster. And I'd barely managed to craft this week. I had spent hours staring at a half-empty mannequin, dreading confronting Soul Night again this weekend. Even with a plan, the odds were constantly stacked against me. Against us.

If you were crafting alone, it would be incredibly hard to even reach level ten or eleven—the required number to fully upgrade Crafting. But the longer you took to upgrade it, the more potential stats you lost in everything you crafted. Most of the crafters in the city would have never brought it to level ten in their lives, especially with the direction provided by the crafting guilds. It was even more blatant now that I was seeing it from a Noble's perspective.

If it wasn't for the demands of the crafting organizations, a person could craft alongside their parents or other crafters when they turned eighteen, investing their points into crafting and reaping experience from hard effort.

The current system kept the economy moving in exchange for holding everyone else back.

I was so lost in my own thoughts that I snapped up when I zoned back into what Sir Stonehart was saying.

"As to why there was no special class today, it is because you'll be receiving special homework instead. This weekend, you're expected to head outside the Academy's border, visit a monster camp, and return. You are allowed to do this in groups. Next week we are going to range far from the Academy and back, practicing hands-on survival skills. Instructors from each course will accompany us, teaching Domain Management in the field."

A week-long camping trip was going to throw all my plans into disarray. I definitely wouldn't be getting any crafting done during it. I sighed. Right as I unlocked Crafting X, of course.

That night, we only stayed at Study Hall for an hour.

"You three leaving?" Adrian asked, walking over to us. He was covered in sweat from sparring.

I nodded. "We're going to head out early in the morning," I said.

We needed the darkness as cover to use Shadow Stealth.

"Trying to dodge Soul Night?" Adrian asked. "I already looked into it. I was planning on bringing this up later. They've had at least three people guarding the gate from the moment curfew ends. I was thinking, if you wanted, you three could accompany our group. The experience will be split between more people—but we're hunting much bigger monsters."

"Thanks," I said. "But we have a plan."

Adrian raised an eyebrow.

"Well . . . stay safe," he said.

As much as I would appreciate trailing along for free experience, it meant missing the experience from butchering and the crafting materials from whatever we hunted. In a way, it would probably slow us down more than it helped us.

"We will." I smiled.

No one in the Academy except for Sandy and Gerald were aware of the true range of skills I had access to. I hadn't even used Flash Step or Thunder Bolt in Study Hall yet. No matter how tempted I was. It would be so easy to channel the spell back down Victor's whip.

But I couldn't have anyone know I had a Lightning magic spell before the weekend. I wouldn't risk any of them leaking it.

Despite turning in early and heading back to my room, I struggled to fall asleep, staring up at the ceiling. Tomorrow, we would fight a group of Nobles. It wasn't that different from what we did in Stitch—evading Olivier's tracking, stealthing behind Valjean.

My heart wouldn't stop racing at the thought.

But I wasn't afraid. I was excited.

We met up in the morning—far from the wall. We found a cafe open in the early morning. One that was atrociously expensive.

You could open a tab up on a single merit, so that was what we did.

The cafe looked down over the trainyard on an open balcony covered in lovingly tended plants. Vines twisted around the metal guardrail, their flowers closed in the still-dark morning.

I nursed a cup of coffee, Sandy and I sat quietly, staring over the edge at the train station. Today was an arrival day for one of the freight trains transporting goods. Among other things, cages and cages of still-living monsters were being unloaded from massive cargo cars. The price of importing so many monsters for Practical Combat must have been enormous.

"They must have a ranch for growing monsters somewhere," I idly commented.

There was no way they were pulling this many monsters out of the dungeon and keeping them alive in containment. Those floors needed to be cleared, and I didn't think just pulling the monsters out would work to upkeep the dungeons.

Gerald finally arrived, half asleep but with a goofy smile.

He held a gigantic lantern in one hand, the light pouring over the entire cafe. I blinked at it.

A central ball was held between a cage of wire mesh cables, bright blue and pouring out light. It shifted like liquid inside the cage.

"Is this what you made?" I asked.

"Yes!" Gerald said.

"What does it do?" Sandy asked.

"The light inside is its remaining charge. It cancels out hostile stuns for everyone in its light," Gerald said.

It was one almost perfectly designed to counter the circumstances of danger he had found himself in with the steel pangolins just a week ago.

It was also huge. We would have to wear it as a backpack rather than hanging it from a belt.

A server finally approached, interrupting us. "My Lord? I have to request that you extinguish your lantern."

"Oh—sorry!" Gerald said. The lantern disappeared, presumably into his inventory. I squinted at him, making sure it didn't miniaturize or something similar.

We finished up breakfast, Gerald ordering last since the two of us had already eaten, and then headed to the checkpoint.

Outside the wall, we didn't find a screaming owl. Instead, there was a figure made of shadow trailing us.

"Creepy," Sandy said loudly.

"Do you think it transmits sound?" I asked.

Sandy shrugged.

Classes hadn't covered scrying spells yet. Adrian had talked about them after we asked about the owl—how they were very important for teams on long missions. But the scrying spells for each class worked differently and had different weaknesses.

"Follow the plan," I said.

Sandy nodded, pulling the hood of her Shadow-aligned Hunter set over her head. She didn't use Shadow Cloak yet.

We all jogged forward into the tree line—where it was even darker. Gerald kept a regular lantern burning in the meantime. The person-shaped shadow kept disappearing and reappearing, trailing us. Once we were under foliage, I activated [Shadow Cloak]. A moment after, I activated [Projection].

A copy of me ran forward with Sandy and Gerald. The real me turned and began to run as fast as I could toward the designated monster camps.

Hopefully, Soul Night would be none the wiser.

CHAPTER 28

They're finally coming?" Tristan asked, turning with excitement visible on his face. His eyes practically burned as he looked back at Soul Night's shadow mage. "What are we waiting for? Let's go."

He broke into a sprint, racing to cut off the stupid first-year students. If they had any brains at all, they would try to hunt different dens than the same one each time. The only reason Soul Night hadn't simply cleared the den every day before they could was the thought that they would go and clear something else.

Clearly, they weren't that smart. The first-year students seemed to be more stupid than ever. Tristan had learned his lesson about the social order of the Academy right away.

And with a few more levels, he knew he would surely gain an offer to be a knight of a prestigious family—even if he only ended up with a single border town under his direction, he would hold out until he got a worthy offer.

He was too good to be wasted as a landless knight errant, after all.

A spark of magically controlled fire hovered over his head, a fire element illumination spell guiding his way. Even though he was a mage, his enhanced attributes were balanced into his other stats as well—he ran with superhuman speed and dexterity. Even far away, the group of mages easily outpaced Gerald and Sandy, arriving in time to kill the flying snake den.

They left it a smoking ruin in minutes.

Tristan smirked, crossing his arms and leaning against the rock, waiting.

"We can leave," the shadow mage said. He was staring at the charred snake corpses. "You wasted the bodies."

"They'll still be worth a quarter of a credit," Tristan said, flicking out a red tag at the shadow mage. It was one of several on a leather belt hanging from his shoulder. The shadow mage caught it and pinned it down into the monster. "Let's stay. We should beat these brats into the ground and teach them a real lesson instead."

"Oz said—"

"I don't give a fuck what Oz said," Tristan snapped.

A few minutes later, the first-year studentwarrior—Gerald, Tristan recalled—burst into the clearing at a light jog.

He leaned forward with a smear on his face. A trail of fire appeared, swirling around his right arm. Then he waited for the other two.

Gerald stared at him, eyes hidden behind a full plate of armor.

"Where are your friends?" Tristan asked, still sneering. He turned to the shadow mage at his side. "I thought you said all three of them were together."

"One of them disappeared. Probably a stealth skill. But the other two were right here!" the shadow mage said. "I saw her a moment ago—right before she burst into the clearing."

"Where did your friend go?" Tristan asked, lifting his arm to fling the bolt of flame forward.

Gerald stared at him, saying nothing. There was a tense moment of silence.

Tristan flinched, looking behind himself at the noise of a crunching leaf. There was nothing there.

Gerald turned and ran back into the forest.

If Tristan and the other mage were paying more attention, they would have noticed their red tag had gone missing. And not just the one on the monster.

But they weren't.

Tristan was about to snap forward, shooting after Gerald.

"Wait, if there's only one of them, this has to be a distraction," the shadow mage said.

"So maybe we should just beat one of them up!" Tristan said.

"No, the other two are probably clearing a camp. He's just a distraction," the shadow mage said.

Tristan grimaced. "What was the last camp they cleared?"

The shadow mage pulled out a map.

"They approached us from the north . . . so here." The shadow mage pointed to the den of the steel pangolin. Then the two of them shot off.

A den of birds was a first for me. I expected maybe a craggy hill covered in nests, as that was what most monster dens were. Instead, there was a towering tree rising out of a lake, with huge nests of straw cradled between massive spiny branches. The wood looked magical. The bark was translucent, like crystal.

And there were furrows in the earth that were clearly from someone cutting the tree down and hauling it away. Very recently, too. The tree must have also re-spawned each night along with the birds.

I got closer to the lake. The sun was only just cresting the horizon, dipping the world in streaks of red and orange. The second I touched the water, one of the birds made itself known. It was covered in dense brown feathers. I stopped and stared at it.

The bird screeched, launching straight up into the air, before diving back down into the lake with a splash. My eyes widened as crescents of water shot away from the bird as it splashed. I activated [Flash Step], blinking to the side as the blades of water tore through the earth and cracked into the trees. I couldn't stab it with a needle even though it was close enough to reach.

I needed to use Arc Bolt on it immediately. Using any other spell or skill would leave wounds that would make it obvious Soul Night hadn't killed it. They were the only group comprised entirely of mages.

The throwing needles on my belt had an upgrade today. Two of them were tied to each other like a bola, secured with a metal wire that would conduct Arc Bolt without suffering damage.

I threw the needle behind the bird.

Between my enhanced stats and practice, I landed the throw on my first try.

Thread Mastery worked on metal wires. It was harder than with regular thread, but I pulled both metaphysically and physically. The wire wrapped around the bird, pinning a wing to its body. I sent electricity down the connection with [Arc Bolt].

The wire glowed hot, releasing a flash of blinding light so bright I averted my eyes.

When I looked back, the bird was cooked.

It had been a while since I killed a low-level monster. I forgot how easily they were downed with one shot.

Steam bubbled out of the lake where the burning-hot wire touched the water. I pulled the needle free, cleaning it off before tucking it back into my belt. Sandy arrived only a moment later, the shadows falling away around her to reveal her holding a cut belt loaded with red tags.

I stared at the belt. Then stared at her. She stabbed a tag down into the monster at her feet, smiling wickedly.

"You stole a whole belt of them!?" I asked. Then I squinted. "Can we sell those?"

"They're registered to Soul Night," Sandy said, shaking her head in the negative.

"Then what are we going to use them . . ." I trailed off. Sandy's smile didn't disappear.

It only took us a few minutes to rush to the other monster nest; it was a large mammal, almost like a squirrel. I killed it, we tagged it, and we rushed back to the Academy proper.

In stealth, of course.

Gerald was waiting for us at the checkpoint. Alone. He had a worried expression as his eyes took us in.

"You get away from them okay?" Sandy asked.

"They didn't chase *me*," he said. "Are you two okay?"

Sandy and I exchanged a glance.

"They didn't come for us either?"

Gerald shook his head.

"Then I've no clue where they went."

Marcus dumped a monster corpse into the receiving room of the abattoir.

He was pissed. He'd interrupted his hunting day for this.

He was a member of a Study Hall called the Teeth—a conglomerate of families based in and around the southwestern mana range, where the local cities almost all sat embedded in the cliff faces of great mountains.

A scribe on duty shuffled out from behind the desk and took in the monster. Their gigantic mop of blonde hair bobbed over thin, wireframe glasses. A moment later, they pulled out a tiny bestiary from their pocket, flipping to the exact page.

"Sapphire skybird, worth . . . one tenth of a merit," the Scribe said. "Red tag? You won't get a full discount for retrieving it yourself, you know."

"Not mine," Marcus said. "Need to know whose tag it is."

The scribe shut the book, looking Marcus up and down again, hair bobbing.

"Right," the scribe said. They took a look at the monster before looking back to Marcus. "The tag, if you would?"

Marcus grimaced, pulling the tag out and passing it to the scribe, who took it in a gloved hand.

The non-Nobility were still squeamish around monster corpses. Even those who worked in an abattoir.

The scribe lifted the tag, reading a number on it before carelessly tossing it back toward the corpse. They removed the glove, throwing it in a bin, before walking to a wall of books. They pulled one free, finding the name logged with the purchase of the red tag.

"This was sold to a . . . Tristan, Chosen mage," the scribe said, turning around. They flinched at the darkened expression on Marcus's face.

"Thank you."

Marcus returned to his team, meeting them at another monster camp farther afield. In a craggy field, monstrous golems of stone and crystal competed to consume the natural mineral nodes, growing larger the longer they survived.

"Well?" Sera asked, kicking her feet as she stood on the corpse of a gigantic, quadrupedal golem of glowing stone. She was chewing on an energy bar while Ophelia carved into the golem's core.

Since the fist-sized core was the only piece of value, it was more profitable to bring it home than to tag the entire monster. Ophelia pushed themselves up with a grunt, turning around to listen to what Marcus had to say.

They pushed their hair out of their face.

"It was Soul Night."

Ophelia spat on the ground. Sera smiled, leaning forward.

"Oh, that's fun. Again?" Sera asked. "I thought they learned their lesson last year."

"Apparently not. The red tag belonged to them."

"So what's the plan?" Ophelia asked. They rested a hand on the weapon at their side, staring into the distance thoughtfully.

"Let's get the other teams together. Then we can wipe all of their camps at once. The day's still early."

CHAPTER 29

I drank cold coffee with a distinct lack of enthusiasm. I was not a napper. In the roaring hustle of the Dragon's Den, Sandy, Gerald, and I caught up on homework.

With Soul Night dead set on cutting us off, we gave up on farming resources for the weekend. The constant practice sessions and late crafting had put me behind on homework anyway. Good grades were still important to graduation—they determined how many credits you got from passing each class.

"I need my favorite back on the menu," Sandy said, looking up from where she was finalizing the map she had copied from the student commons. The finished map was the homework assignment and final project for homeroom.

"We can go hunt for it ourselves," I said.

The Dragon's Den bought leftover meat from the abattoir, which turned over a frankly ridiculous quantity of monsters. Not only was there the massive number harvested on the floors both above and below the Academy, as well as outside of its walls, but there were also those brought in exclusively for student training. Which meant the menu—and its prices—shifted rapidly.

Wherever the best cuts went, it wasn't a place we could afford. The Dragon's Den just had what was left.

"Gwen?" Adrian swept toward our table from out of the crowd in the Dragon's Den. Cedric followed close behind him as always. There was a look of fierce pride on his face today. "Sandy. Gerald," he said, nodding toward them.

"Adrian! Cedric!" I said, smiling. There was a note of acute distress on Adrian's face before it leveled out.

"What did you guys do?" Adrian asked, pulling up a chair.

I looked over at Sandy. She was smiling back at me. Her evil smile was better than mine. Gerald was looking away from all of us.

"Well . . ." I started. I explained that we stole the tags from Soul Night—not how—and used them at a nearby team's monster den.

Cedric burst out laughing. Adrian cradled his face in his hands.

"That was Marcus's team," Adrian said.

"Oh," I said. "Uh . . ."

Adrian seemed pretty intense.

"The Teeth—Marcus's Study Hall—retaliated by sweeping almost all of Soul Night's north camps."

"That's no big deal, right?" I asked. "The dibs on resources is just a private student agreement?"

"Definitely not our problem," Sandy said.

"Soul Night retaliated by trying to wipe out the Teeth's camps. They've been getting in tiny skirmishes all day, throwing skills out to push the other group off their monster kills. But it's been escalating. If there's an all-out fight, the dean might get involved," Adrian said.

"The dean?" I asked.

Adrian rubbed his eyes.

"The current dean is an incredibly high-level Noble. It's going to throw everything into disarray if he returns from diving the dungeon."

"Things won't actually get that bad, right?" Sandy asked. "I mean, they're not . . . *fighting* fighting?"

"To clear all of Soul Night's camps as retaliation, the Teeth asked their allies to help. Which made Soul Night ask the groups they're friendly with. The entire respected social order that keeps a balance on resources might break down."

"Why would things boil over that quickly?" I asked, leaning forward.

"Most of the Study Halls are linked to families and houses outside the dungeon who generally pass down their merits as a fund for their own heirs. There's a ton of resources wrapped up both in and out of the dungeon, with the cost of the specialist classes here ranging up to hundreds of credits for hands-on training, and access to the skills and leveling to bring their own heirs back ready to continue their family legacies.

"They're not just fighting over a few stolen camps. Some of the houses have decades-long rivalries and have just been waiting for an opportunity to fight each other."

Sandy squinted.

"You going to sell us out?" she asked.

"Sell *you* out?" Adrian laughed. "No, we're in this together now. See, our Study Hall works with the Teeth. So it's *our* problem now."

Adrian had a bitter smile.

"Right," Sandy said. "Well, what can we do to help?"

Adrian's eyes locked on mine.

"Is your contact available for another order?"

I smiled. I was about to say that they had a lot of free time right now—I was, after all, staying in for the rest of the weekend, and I was caught up on homework now. However . . . I smelled an opportunity. I had created a need.

"I don't know. Might cost extra right now."

"I'm sure Marcus will be willing," Adrian said.

"What does he need?" I asked.

"Fire resistance."

I wiped sweat off my brow in the upper floor of the atelier's private workshops. The windows were cracked open to let the heat out. Humidity clung to the windows, dripping to the sealed hardwood floor.

A half-finished Storm Archer's Raiment set was draped over one of the metal mannequins designed to radiate heat. I had stitched the cuts from a minor fire drake directly into the already half-made set. It might lower the fire resistance, but it would mean that there would be plenty of material left over from what I purchased to craft a second.

The material radiated heat, even worse than being inside the volcanic tertiary dungeon of Stitch.

The piece was coming together nonetheless.

Alongside the minor drake's leather was a collection of tiny black spines ending in sharp points. I used [Embellishment] to embed them into the armor in decorative patterns. They hung like sharp, curved claws around the shoulders of the cloak, which was shaping up to be similar to the one I had crafted from the snake wings.

The leather hung from long black spines, the sharp points dulled, draping like a dragon's wings.

I'd finish it in time for the camping trip the next weekend.

I was excited for Practical Combat right up until I reached the classroom and was promptly turned around and directed to the field arena. And it wasn't for monster hunting either.

In the arena, there was no pack of wolves. No giant monsters to hunt. No, there was something much scarier.

Three different classes, a half dozen instructors, and a wilderness survival program.

Anna flanked me as I stopped at the exit from the Academy walls into the Range—a closed-off space of artificial wilderness for Practical Combat field fights. Victor had gone off ahead, and students filtered around me.

A dozen students were setting up tents, assembling fire pits, or chopping logs. Carts full of unprocessed timber had been wheeled inside. All of it smelled like smoke from wood fires and barbequed meat.

I found my own class gathered around Sir Stonehart.

He briefed us quickly. And then we went to work, picking stones out of a pile to assemble a fire pit and shoveling away dirt to dig it deeper.

Once that was done, he had us all—individually—cut apart logs. Not already pre-cut sections of the tree—we actually had to drag the logs off the cart, cut them apart, and then split the sections into firewood.

I hesitated nervously at the end of the wagon, switching into my highest strength set before dragging an entire tree through the grass. I felt the urge to laugh bubble up. I had never applied my strength to anything so mundane.

I looked nervously between the log and the rapier I had. I didn't actually have any kind of slashing skill. I was impressed I was able to drag it at all—it was an entire tree. But my stats had long eclipsed the human minimum.

I looked around. Some people were splitting the tree with skills or even just raw, brute strength. Reluctantly, I laid a hand on the needle-like rapier at my side.

"Gwen," Anna interrupted me. She was holding up a band saw; one with two handles. "Want to help each other?" she asked.

I looked behind her. Victor had attracted a crowd of boys watching him use his whip to snap apart chunks of a tree.

Caught up in everyone around me showing off skills, I had neglected to notice that there was plenty of equipment provided.

"Yes!" I said.

A moment later, we had a campfire going. Splitting the logs was easy, after. We were among the first to finish.

"Tomorrow, Practical Combat will start before noon. Show up. You're expected to prepare your own lunch. Dungeon Management classes will take place halfway through the day and be taught entirely in the Range."

"On day four, they're going to release monsters in the Range while we're having class," Adrian casually informed us.

"Seriously?" Sandy asked.

"Seriously." He nodded. "And you're expected to hunt them and make your own lunch."

"Not any of the monsters we've been fighting in Practical Combat before this, I hope?" Gerald asked, making a face.

So far in Practical Combat, we had fought crystalline golems, elementally aligned wolves, and a heavily armored armadillo that slammed bodily into us.

"It's normally a really aggressive monstrous waterfowl," Adrian said. "Like a big chicken."

Dungeon Management class the next day involved a tour of the Range— the teacher showed off how quickly the grass regrew, even in damaged areas, and how the firepits seemed to fill in. We had to remake our own firepits the next day.

And make our own lunches.

Most of the Blooded Nobles had never cooked for themselves—any family with capital would have a proper chef. Besides boosting their stats, the food also magically tasted better.

Still, they at least provided ingredients today.

The classes being merged together for field trip training meant that Sandy's team was in the same group as mine. Adrian, Gerald, and Cedric were not, though.

Adrian had left aside some core details about the waterfowl we had to hunt for our own food. Namely, they had both some kind of stealth skill, and a teleportation skill.

Anna raced ahead of me as we rushed toward a bird in a tree. This was not our first time doing this. We were sure the monster would exhaust its mana eventually. Clipped wings stopped them from flying away.

The monster was nestled in the branches of a tree, facing away from us. We were sneaking up behind it. It was far too bright out and the canopy too thin to use my stealth skills, and the monster had evaded me throwing my needles at it.

As Anna neared it, glowing gold with her movement-enhancing skills, the monster disappeared again.

"Which tree this time?" I shouted, looking up.

Elara was standing in midair on a near-invisible plane of force, clutching onto it with dear life as it was pushed around in the wind.

"North! It's in the net!"

I raced forward, grabbing a thread hanging from the tree beneath the bird and pulling with [Thread Mastery]. The strings closed on the bird. It squawked. When the bird tried to teleport while tied, it shook the entire tree; the spell must have tried to apply to everything touching it.

"Got it!" I said. Sandy caught up a moment later. She wasn't as fast as the rest of us.

Can you . . . ?"

"Got it," Sandy said, jumping over and climbing up the tree. There was a snap a moment later. No experience points, though.

The only experience this class was giving this week was in practical survival lessons. We returned to camp with our last catch for our group. The rest were tied together near a firepit with a grill over it.

Instructors—postgraduate Nobles—circled the pits, showing students how to cut and prepare food. When one came over to us, Sandy grumbled under her breath the entire time about his instructions. I elbowed her.

Elara and Ash especially struggled to prepare lunch. Victor took no heed at all of the instructors, eventually eating messy strips of meat. After a moment, Sandy walked over and helped them.

"You guys are good at this," Ash said.

"My mom was a butcher," Sandy said. "And my dad is a chef."

We showed both Elara and Ash how to cook.

"When it runs clear, it's safe," I said. I wasn't sure that Noble immune systems were actually at risk, given their magically enhanced constitutions. "It's kind of fun!"

I smiled at Elara. She looked highly disturbed.

"I would like to never handle raw meat again, I think," she said.

We had to hunt our own food and prepare it for the rest of the week. And after the first hunt for waterfowl, we also had to boil and prepare our own drinking water. We enjoyed picnics spread out on a blanket. We still had to hunt and prepare lunch—one of the assignments for class—but we just gave it away.

Ash took a liking to grilling. And Victor took a liking to butchering, albeit in a way that was messy, unprofessional, and constantly grated on Sandy whenever she looked at him.

The days in Practical Combat continued to intensify and get longer. They taught us navigation, including using a compass, drawing a map, and scouting.

They weren't just preparing us for time inside the dungeon, but time outside of it. Lower-ranked Nobles often spent plenty of time travel-ing between and upkeeping their smaller settlements—like Valjean in my hometown.

The day before the weekend would start our camping trip—we would spend it in the range, practicing setting and staying in our own camp.

I finished Marcus's set the day before.

CHAPTER 30

My workshop in the atelier had grown cooler as I finished more and more pieces of the set commissioned by Marcus. Once the patterns were crafted, the magic that heated the room seemed to turn inward, becoming the armor's resistance. Now it was almost chilly inside as I finished and added the last piece.

I watched, the moment of truth finally arriving.

[Quality Assessment: (Good)]

[Generating Skills . . .]

▶Flaming Aegis V

▶Ignite Projectile III

▶Fire Resistance 50

[ATTRIBUTES]

▶SPD: -5

▶WIL: 0

▶STR: 30

▶DEX: 30

▶CON: 10

▶PER: 30

[+5 XP]

[High-quality materials have altered the stats of the completed set.]

▶Flaming Aegis V

[For a moderate mana cost, surround yourself with a veil of fire that mitigates attacks. Fight fire with fire.]

▶Ignite Projectile III

[For a small mana cost, imbue a launched or thrown projectile with flame. Can be cast mid-launch.]

I finally got a set with Ignite Projectile. Too bad it paled compared to Arc Bolt, especially using my threads of electrical mana.

Only five XP meant no level . . . yet. If we were able to hunt this week-end, or if combat classes had proceeded as normal, I might have gained a level. Only . . . where were the attribute points awarded by crafting?

The system opened another window as if it were replying.

[Crafting X activated.]

[Storm Archer's Raiment can activate Crafting X 9 more times.]

[Permanent stat gain]

[Strength: +3]

[Dexterity: +3]

[Constitution: +1]

[Perception: +1]

My breath hitched.

I had a way to gain permanent stats without using my Wardrobe.

And if I crafted every charge from every pattern I had, my baseline stats would match the Nobles at my own level.

The Nobles who'd been leveling so fast that they were leaving me behind would be falling behind me instead. I did the math in my head. The full stats of every set I had crafted so far—or at least the best ten of them—combined with the stats I would've gained from Crafting X?

The Nobles' only advantage would be their combat skills.

The Nobility—even the Academy's courses—claimed that it was bad economically for people to invest in their crafting skill—the one that came with their class.

But maybe they were just afraid of how strong a city of crafters could really get.

The morning of departure arrived without much fanfare. The night before was like a nervous, formal party, with dozens of fires burning through the Range. It was getting uncomfortably hot by nighttime due to all the separate firepits.

It didn't help that several groups decided to see how large they could make their fires—one had eventually worked together to start burning entire logs before the instructors shut it down.

I woke in pre-dawn to commotion all around me, staring up at the canvas flaps of a tent. Soft orange light cut through the narrow opening, filled with the smell of morning dew and banked fires.

I switched into my school uniform and poked my head out.

The gate between the Range and the world beyond the city walls was open in the distance. A mob of dozens of people bustled around wagons. Beasts of burden—huge horses and oxen, mostly—were being fed and cajoled around a train of caravans and carts.

Some of them were being led inside the Range.

Around me, the other students were starting to wake.

The instructors had talked about this field trip as a training exercise—but there was clearly more to it than that. The amount of people and wagons visibly being dedicated to the effort was huge.

I started packing up my tent. Every day, they had made us pack and unpack our supplies, organizing them to make them easy to carry. It wasn't a fast process. They started waking everyone as soon as I finished, instructing them to pack up.

The sun was up by the time half the tents were broken down. Assistants gathered up all the students from their respective classes, leading us to stand in front of Sir Stonehart.

I counted six classes forming separate circles around their instructors—but I didn't see Gerald, Adrian, or Cedric. We had learned there was a second outdoor arena exactly like the Range—the others must have been on their own expedition.

I did, however, see Sandy's team. They were obvious because of Elara. A floating platform of force piled feet high with supplies followed behind her.

Standing in the center of their circle was an almost mirror copy of Sir Stonehart, save for a different set of scars. They must have been twins.

"Pay attention," Sir Stonehart said, drawing everyone's eyes back to him. He was sitting on a log, using it as a chair. Assistants handed a piece of paper to each of us. "This are your assignments. Your first assignments as Nobles—Blooded or Chosen. Perform well, and you will earn merits. This is a graded task.

"Our class will be split into two, each provided a wagon of goods. You're expected to work together on your own to scout the range around the wagon and defend it from attacks of monster swarms."

"Monster swarms?" Victor blurted. Sir Stonehart just stared at him, folding his arms. After glancing around nervously, Victor continued. "The floor around the Academy doesn't have any, does it? It's too well maintained."

"That's correct." Sir Stonehart's face broke into a rare and vicious smile. "However, the Academy does not maintain *every* floor. Some are intentionally mismanaged to create the challenges needed to test Nobles. One of your goals for this expedition will be to cull a monster deemed too dangerous to allow it to continue roaming. And to do that, we'll be descending to the next floor of the dungeon. The sixteenth floor."

"But aren't the monsters there . . ." another student blurted, trailing off at Sir Stonehart's hard stare.

"You won't be expected to fight anything beyond your caliber. This expedition numbers several hundred. Check your assignments and prepare to depart."

My assignment was to man one of the flatbed carts. It was currently empty, save for a teamster smoking atop of it. All the carts were distinctly colored with different paints, and all of the paint looked positively ancient, some with just a few chips of color remaining. The wagon I was set to guard was purple and marked with the number twenty-eight in big, black paint.

I was reading the details on the page. There were tons of warnings about the different common threats on the sixteenth floor, all in tiny, nearly inscrutable text that I struggled to read in the morning light. The entire class was chatting awkwardly and nervously around me. Many of them had never really spent much time together, since very few people had overlapping classes throughout the rest of the day.

I wasn't paying attention to their conversation.

We were to remain in positions flanking the caravan, managing the scouting for approaching monster swarms and preparing the teams to deal with them.

And we had to elect a leader for each of our teams.

I paused, staring at that part. That was bound to be a disaster in a room full of egotistical Nobles.

"We have to elect someone?" I asked, turning to look at Anna. She seemed wide awake. Her eyes were carefully scanning the crowd around her, and she kept her back to the wagon, making sure she could see the entire horizon. Victor stood beside her, eyes barely open.

It took her a moment to look my way and give me a single, definitive nod.

"A good way to force students to learn to work for someone else," she said.

"Isn't this going to be, like, a whole social issue?" I asked.

"Only for those with an ego," she replied.

The chatter slowly intensified.

"You're Anna?" a man—a Noble, dressed in leather armor rather than a school uniform—approached us and asked. He had the overbearing confidence common to the Blooded Nobility. Not to mention the expensive equipment.

Anna squinted at him, looking the man up and down. "I am," she said.

"What's your class?" he asked.

"Why do you want to know?"

"You have the highest scores. Are you going to volunteer to be our leader elect?"

The crowd had gotten quieter. Most of our class was staring at us. Victor stepped forward off the wagon.

"I'll be the task leader."

"No," the Noble said without pausing.

"But I—"

"You're barely passing your classes," the Noble said. Then he turned to me. "Lady Gwen. I am Octavian of the House of the Long Shore."

"Hello," I said. "Where did you see Anna's grades?"

How many Nobles exchanged favors and merits to manipulate classes like Adrian did? This was going to be exhausting if it became a whole political game.

Octavian stared at me for a moment before pointing at the sheet in my hand. I looked at it. Then I turned it over.

On the back was a listing of the rank and position of each student in our class. I had forgotten about the student ranks—they were very important during the earliest days of school, but they hadn't come up again since. Maybe they would've been something to consider if I'd been forced to apply to Study Halls rather than having slipped into Adrian's because of his interest in Gerald.

They separated the most meritorious students in each year, highlighting the top performers—grades, hunting, and homework all combined. Theoretically, someone who skipped half their classes could hunt enough monsters to make up for it and graduate.

At the top of the list was Anna, of course. Our scores must have been calculated from every class we were taking, because Victor never struggled in Practical Combat. Despite that, he wasn't at the top. He wasn't anywhere near Anna's name. Or mine.

Right below Anna's name was mine.

"Oh," I said. "If you want to be leader . . ." I looked up at Octavian.

He waved his hands, cutting me off.

"Lady Gwen, I'm not asking out of any kind of scheme. This mission is actually dangerous—maybe not lethal, with the instructors present, but dangerous enough to be serious. No, I suspect—I'm positive we will lose marks if we elect someone below the top three in our class's performance."

I stared at him, mouth open and uncomprehending.

"If Liege Anna does not want to be leader—then it is up to you."

Octavian stared at me. I hesitated. The idea that we would lose points for not picking the highest ranked in our class gave me a second idea. Would we lose points for not accepting the responsibility as well?

Our classes often talked about the Noblesse Oblige—the responsibility that came with our rights. I think that this was another test. Everything in the Academy was, and much of it was never said explicitly—like encouraging us to form Study Halls, and the system of student claims over resources.

There wasn't really a choice.

"I'll be our leader for the trip," I said, standing straighter.

CHAPTER 31

Once I agreed, the different student teams came forward and presented their talents. Teams of three would flank each wagon, keeping up with it as we traveled. It was difficult work, since they would be navigating the rugged terrain of every road we crossed.

I caught Anna's golden eyes staring past me in the middle of our strategizing, and turned around to follow her gaze. An assistant instructor was taking notes as he stared at us.

We really were being graded on everything. I groaned. I wondered if I lost points for groaning. We strategized more. The scout teams would rotate, since the work was more intensive.

Halfway through strategizing, I finally stopped and asked what a monster swarm was.

"They're the result of monster overpopulation," Anna said. She had an expression of disgust. "They have to be exterminated eventually. When monsters reproduce enough to overpopulate a floor, the mana saturation increases. Eventually, this lets them break out into the floor above."

"But the dungeon doesn't overproduce monsters?" Victor asked. "Once a den is full, it's full."

Anna nodded.

"The dungeon stops magically producing them, yes. They . . ." Anna trailed off. She looked more guarded, stepping back.

"They reproduce the mundane way," Octavian said, inserting himself in the conversation.

"But what about . . . the food? Can a floor sustain a huge population?"

"It depends on the floor and ecosystem," Octavian said. "Sometimes, one monster population will reach the hundreds, devouring the plant life and even emptying the lakes before stronger monsters can start to subsist on them. Every dungeon is different. Some can sustain a near-endless swarm of low-level omnivores. Others will cyclically be wiped out as apex predators gorge themselves—before wiping each other out, too.

"All that said, none of the swarms have a particularly strong reason to attack our caravan. It's not like they want any of the goods we will be transporting."

The giant caravan train assembled outside the Range. The sun was up by the time it was set to move again, and we trundled back into the Academy after spending hours getting organized outdoors. A second set of carts joined us, these even larger—mobile workshops for crafts, loaded up with commoner classes to assist us on the journey.

Besides killing monsters, the expedition would have us harvest magical crops and raw, magical ore. The great machine of our society required never-ending fuel to supply the Nobles at the top of it.

Rumors about this field trip were quickly flying back and forth along the caravan. Apparently, there was one every month. The first-year students would help pacify the entire floor before letting it rewild.

On and on the rumors flew as we moved through the largest central street of the Academy.

At the end of it, there was a second fortress, pointed inward. It was more like a castle keep. The Nobles stationed here were ready for battle. A hollow checkpoint was manned with Noble soldiers—not just graduate students.

We passed under a magically reinforced portcullis and into a much smaller fort on the floor below. The heat was immediate. The air was dry and warmth washed over us. The sky was a different color on this floor.

When we passed through the smaller gate, the entire caravan stopped. We took in the view. We were in a canyon.

It was nothing like the canyon in Lyssandra's dungeon. It was big enough to fit whole cities. It was hot and arid. The few trees that thrived here grew in magical copses that rose stories high, coiling around each other and stabbing into the face of the orange, rocky cliffs.

Orders were passed down the line and the caravans began to move again.

The sun beat down on us as we trekked for what must have been more than an hour over a torn-up, dusty road. We spotted monsters in the distance, clinging to the trees and to the cliffs. They weren't neatly confined to dens as they were on the Academy floor above us. Instead, they scattered, roaming the floor. The descendants of the monsters were less programmatic, it seemed.

The caravan slowed and then stopped as the copses of alien trees grew thicker. Twisted gray bark looped around us. The plants looked dead, dried out and covered in cracks and notches.

Our instructions were to hold the area. Our own teams spread out, watching for monsters. But none had come. They had no reason to; if anything, hundreds of humans marching through their area should have sent them running.

A group up front detached from the caravan. I looked around.

"What's happening?" I asked Octavian, who was just behind me.

Octavian frowned.

"Those were all high-level Nobles. If I had to guess . . . they're probably removing something from the road."

Water was being distributed up and down the line. A half hour after we stopped, we found out the reason why: the sounds of combat rolled through the valley. A monster roared, obscured by the copse of trees the road passed through.

A series of titanic crashes and earth-rocking explosions followed; shock-waves from the fight sent wind and clouds of dust from down the road. A moment later, the canopy of trees ahead of us shattered into a million pieces.

A silver, winged lion rose out of the canopy with a horrible screech. Its mouth opened to too many teeth as it lilted in the sky before crashing back down closer to the caravan.

A wave of overturned earth and dust rolled toward us.

A floating lance shot up into the air where the monster had been. It stopped as if controlled by a magnetic force, spinning in place until the tip pointed back downward to where the monster had fallen in the canopy. A moment later, I saw the form of Sir Stonehart—tiny at this distance—leap dozens of feet into the air, grabbing hold of the lance. It shone with magic light—from an enchantment or from a skill, I didn't know.

Then it shot downward like a comet.

A much larger wave of overturned dust and earth exploded outward, rolling over the caravan.

The caravan looped around the corpse of the gigantic monster. By the time we arrived, the Nobles had pushed back the tree line, upturning the earth and all to carve a path to fit them.

Four massive civilian caravans unfolded from equal points around the circle; they had already stood out for their towering height, but now we watched as the walls on either side of them folded down. They each expanded a telescopic crane upward.

Butchers and Nobles worked together to hook the corpse of the monster before beginning to ratchet it up off the ground. Dozens of people worked together with practiced, familiar efficiency, turning this little section of the forest into an abattoir.

I kept looking back at the work. The grim, practiced efficiency of it. The alarming speed with which they cut it to pieces, as if they were on a deadline. Then I frowned.

I looked back at the forest. Nobles were still pushing the tree line back. In one direction, it broke entirely, showing the sandy, desert terrain of the bottom of the canyon. Clouds of dust rose into the air. My eyes widened.

"Victor . . ." I said, looking around. I didn't even see Victor. He had wandered off. "Anna?" I asked.

"I see them," she said, squinting into the distance. Her eyes seemed to shimmer slightly. Did she have some kind of perception skill?

"Octavian!" I said. He turned around, raising an eyebrow at me. "There are monsters coming!"

I pointed. Octavian turned. His eyes widened. He turned around and started shouting.

Word rippled outward from our edge of the caravan as the students pulled free weapons and readied skills. The cloud of dust moving toward us got larger and larger and we saw the first of the monsters revealed, iridescent carapaces glinting in the sunlight. They were almost exactly like the beetles we had fought in the canyon in Lyssandra's dungeon. Except . . . more, somehow. They were purple and green and sparkling. There was even a pink one in the mix.

And there weren't five of them. There were hundreds.

I looked back one last time at the makeshift abattoir. The crafters continued with no more frantic energy than they had before the monsters approached. But with their experience, they must have been anticipating this.

It took a moment for my eyes to focus on what was closer to me.

A group of three older Nobles sat atop our wagon. They were only feet away from me. They must have arrived in all the frantic movement as we prepared to fight. A woman with short brown hair smirked at me, her legs swinging idly off the side of the cart. She had a spear resting on her lap.

"You lose points for every monster I have to kill," she said.

I turned back to the swarm. They were closing in fast.

And I couldn't even count them.

This was another test. Of course it was. With three Nobles at our back, these monsters weren't really a threat—they'd intervene if it got dangerous. The test was to see how fully we would actually commit to the job.

We wouldn't be able to kill them all if we just held the line here. There were simply too many.

We had to cull them before they reached the caravan.

We had to—

"Anna, Octavian! We have to advance and stop them before they reach the wagon! Move forward!"

CHAPTER 32

The monsters that had ignored us the entire time we trekked through the dungeon were suddenly attracted by the corpse of a great monster. The monster the Noble instructors had made light work of was far larger and more powerful than any other monster I had seen. At least, any I had seen alive.

It looked like the elemental bosses Foundry had collected and hung in its abattoir, and it had been terrifying to see something that large alive and full of rage. But the moment it died, a hundred monsters descended on its corpse like a swarm of vultures, willing to risk darting through a hundred humans to peck at its flesh.

The swarm of beetles reached us in a storm of chitin, and the Nobles around me all retaliated.

They had all faced overwhelming numbers when they fought the horde of Wolves in the range. They had all been honing and practicing their skills for weeks. And now they unleashed them in a wave of death that shattered the bugs, breaking apart chitin and sending hot green blood arcing into the sky.

There were grunts and shouts as a dozen skills went off at once. I smelled burning flesh. I stabbed through one monster just using my stats, then used [Running Stitch] to pivot, instantly stabbing into another monster.

Then another, and another, and another.

The monsters weren't even attacking us. They were throwing themselves over our heads, over each other, over the piling barricades made from their corpses, flinging themselves at the corpse of the winged lion. None of them were worth any experience.

One Noble released arrow after arrow, some skill enabling her to fire with superhuman speed and accuracy, each loosed bolt cracking as the bow released it, sound and fury sending them directly through multiple monsters at a time. Another released bolts of fire that turned the burning monster corpses into obstacles.

I caught a glimpse of Anna between the corpses. She leaned back as a beetle skirted by her face before slapping another one out of the sky. She left a burning gold afterimage. The bug's corpse exploded on the ground. She leaned back again. Multiple bugs skirted around and past her before she attacked another one.

Was she holding back?

I didn't have time to find out as I was back to stabbing monsters down. I didn't have time to switch equipment or bring out spells—every single second was spent killing another monster.

And then it was over. I was panting. So were several of the Nobles around me. I turned back for just a moment. The Noblewoman who had smirked at me earlier had a disappointed expression on her face, glowering at me and resting her face in a palm.

A barricade of dozens of corpses had piled up below her. One of the two assistants with her was doing homework. The other was polishing a sword. Just this one Noblewoman was enough to cut down the remains of the swarm that crossed through almost two dozen first-year students.

The spearwoman jerked her head to the left. I looked over. The fight was still going on to the south of us, back toward the road.

I started walking toward the fight, then stopped. I was supposed to be the leader of our group. I looked around. We were recovering. A few were sending vacant stares toward the pile of monster corpses as high as a wagon in front of us.

"We don't have time to sit down!" I shouted. "The fight's still going! Get up!"

Only about half the class joined us, flanking down the encirclement of wagons and cleaning up the beetles. More than once, we suffered friendly fire from other Nobles on the line, shooting into the wave of monsters.

I found Victor by [Parrying] his whip out into the wave of beetles trying to push through the Nobles.

"Gwen!" he said, his face an excited smile.

"You almost hit me!" I said, stabbing another beetle.

"I hit you all the time!" he replied, his whip flashing through the air and exploding chitin. With every swing, he knocked three beetles out of the sky. I helped finish them one at a time.

The fight wrapped up quickly as our class flanked down the line. The swarm had come from a single direction; many of the other Nobles were far less quick to organize. I saw many students standing confusedly just beyond the reach of the swarm.

The pile of bugs behind Victor grew tall.

When the fight was finally over, I had spent only a quarter of my mana. I used Running Stitch conservatively from the start of the fight.

Behind us, the abattoir had already started to finish its grisly work. Huge slabs of meat and leather were slammed into place across a few of the carts—including mine. I saw the spearwoman Noble with a few others staring at me. The instructors traded notes and pointed at a few of the students.

A few assistants moved over the line, checking everyone's health. Anyone deemed too low was moved to the back until tomorrow. I winced at that.

It probably lost them a lot of points toward their grade. Victor was one of them, though I wasn't sure if he had lost health or was just moved for being too far out of place.

When the butcher wagons began to reel up, nothing but scraps remained of the great winged lion. A series of whistles blew across the camp. The voice of a Nobleman boomed over the caravan.

"Five minutes until forward march!"

I returned to position beside my own wagon, watching as a team of porters raced between the carts. They carried boxes of gigantic enchanted metal rods, stabbing them into the slabs of meat on the carts.

Six metal poles stabbed out of the slab of meat on cart twenty-eight, visibly icing over with frost as they chilled the humidity in the air. By the time the caravans started to move, the slab of winged lion was frozen. Even the cart was cold. Chilled air so cold you could see it roll off the cart in waves.

"They're just going to leave all these monster corpses behind?" I asked Octavian as the carts started to roll forward.

"Not all of them," Octavian said, pointing farther down the line where a cart was overflowing with the dead beetles. "They'll be feed for the mules."

The giant circle of caravans expanded in a slow spiral, looping around itself to maintain its formation as a line, before heading back onto the road and farther away.

Wide shadows occasionally passed over me. Far above, huge birds—not winged lions—circled the field of corpses. Their undersides were a glowing blue that almost matched the sky. When they came too close, a Noble would loose an arrow that sent them fleeing with panicked cries.

I frowned at that. The Nobles could hit them. They were choosing not to.

We heard their screeching and scrabbling over the field of beetle corpses as the wagons rolled away.

With the addition of so many monster parts, the world around us changed. After an hour, the circling birds reappeared, carrion feeders staying just out of range of our archers. They squabbled and fought in the skies. The previously dead landscape was now alive with predators staring warily.

Gigantic crab-like monsters camouflaged themselves on the faces of canyons, crawling slowly on the nearby walls. Monstrous limbs tapped against the sand as our wagon trundled forward out of the copse of twisted trees.

The caravan trundled up and out of the canyon over a rough field of uneven stones that left everyone struggling to keep up. We marched for a few hours before stopping to rest. Plant life popped up sporadically as we trundled through the untamed dungeon.

Then foliage became the norm; we moved around bushes and weeds and over lush grass, and then, eventually, we were forced to blaze a trail through it, cutting and tearing through hedges and stomping over the remains of trees that had been hacked down. We were in the middle of the caravan, which meant the foliage ahead of us was already trampled by the time we had to clamber over downed plants.

"Half speed!" Sir Stonehart cried from the front of the caravan. The entire caravan slowed, trundling along through the bushes.

Here, plants grew out of a long, shallow river. Upturned river stones glinted in the sunlight through the foliage, sparkling with magic. Glowing fish shot up and down the stream. A hundred magical birds cried out at our passing, warning one another of our caravan.

"Half circle!"

The caravan changed formation. It suddenly turned sharply away from the river before turning back, forming a huge semicircular wall, leaving me standing in the interior on the same side as the river.

"Secure the perimeter! One hundred meters!" Sir Stonehart yelled.

Magic and skills began to rip apart the foliage on the other side of the caravan, blasting back and incinerating huge patches of growth to create a zone they could see. On our side of the caravan, bow-wielding Nobility worked alongside Nobles in full plate, scouring the bushes and stepping through them carefully. They no longer ripped apart every single bush. Dozens of postgraduate students and full-fledged Nobles formed a loose line inside the Caravan's embrace. Dozens more common workers swept out of the carts, equipped with gear for harvesting.

Their fingers flew through the bushes, plucking berries, collecting stems, and skinning bark. They worked with superhuman efficiency, harvesting until there was nothing left.

"First years inside the line! Tear apart the harvested foliage. Clear the line of sight so no monsters can intrude near our civilians!" Sir Ironheart shouted.

Our class—the half of our class on the inside of the caravan, at least—stumbled forward before beginning to literally tear apart the earth around the civilians. They buzzed around us, porters carrying full canvas sacks before throwing them onto carts.

The plants must have been reagents for alchemy, largely. But they shouldn't grow wild like this, not normally; normally the plants would slowly replenish in a node. These, just like the monsters, were wild plants, of inconsistent quality, growing from seed spread through the water and by birds.

They were also inconceivably precious. This one harvest would easily be more valuable than what we'd find in months of farming Stitch's Dungeonheart.

A snake hissed beneath me. I flinched back. The bush it was under had been harvested without issue, but the snake hissed when I started to rip it out of the ground. Almost reflexively, I reached for the needle-like rapier I carried and stabbed it.

But I stopped before ripping the bush out of the ground.

We were tearing apart the plants with magic and spells and superhuman stats to make sure there were no monsters lurking here. But this was stupid, wasn't it? If we didn't tear up all of the plants, they would grow more magical crop to harvest again. Even the trees whose bark was being harvested could grow new branches if they were harvested sustainably. Instead, we were wiping out this section of flora.

When we neared the edge of the river, the call we were all waiting for came.

"Monster swarm incoming! Nobles inside the caravan, hold your positions."

I paused and looked back. I was supposed to trust these people with my life?

The swarm coming at us wasn't beetles. Out here, where there was more plant life, different creatures thrived.

A swarm of dust-covered boars squealed and roared as they charged.

"Interior Nobles, eyes forward! Our civilians are counting on you!"

I turned back to continue my task warily, throwing constant glances over my shoulder. The sounds of battle erupted into a roar as the Nobles outside the wagon were stuck fighting off another swarm of low-level monsters.

We got back to work with the sound of a battle at our back. It died down quickly. I knew they were probably grading me for how well I stayed on task, but I couldn't help constantly turning back.

The power of a group of people working together was exponentially higher than working individually. A class of monster that would take my team tactics and teamwork to kill could be easily carved down by the hundreds working together.

After less than an hour—and two swarms of monsters—we had cleared the plants all the way to the river bed. A few wagons trundled out of formation and directly into the water. Like the butchering wagons, half of them unfolded. Waterwheels fell from their sides, slamming into the river before workers adjusted them, pulling them high enough to spin in the water.

They pulled a constant stream of water up and into visible metal tanks. The other half of the wagons were loaded with the plants we had just collected.

Alchemists began to process the harvest. Magical equipment glowed to life as dozens of workers began the process of mashing berries, grinding flowers, and crushing herbs before placing them into measured containers. The entire place came alive like a factory.

A moment later, we got the interior to start setting up camp inside the caravan.

We dug firepits, piled stones we fetched from the river, and began to break apart the trees. Lumber was unpiled from the back of the wagon— lumber taken from the twisted trees we crashed through earlier. I hadn't even seen the Nobles load it.

The alchemists were still working when the sun started to set. Three more swarms of monsters bashed themselves into our caravan.

After that, the call came for the wagon teams to switch sides. They left us to recover after establishing camp, and now we held the outside. There was a trench carved into the ground, a makeshift defense carved out of the earth, with raised battlements for firing ranged attacks into the swarms of monsters.

Assistant Nobles came by and checked health and mana levels, ushering away those who were low.

No one here was gaining experience in the system. This was entirely an exercise in teamwork and mental endurance.

We killed two more swarms of monsters. Between waves, we helped reinforce the battlements and literally shovel monster corpses away. It was gruesome, foul work; the kind of work expected of any knight errant who graduated from the Academy.

Whispers circled all around us, up and down the lines of defenders. This was the life that could be expected for any low-ranking Noble who fell into the service of a house. Day in and day out for years until you died.

It solved the mystery of why so many Nobles stayed in the Academy to try to secure better positions rather than graduate.

We pushed away the piles of corpses to occupy the gigantic carrion birds circling the sky around us. They fought amongst each other, spreading their humongous wingspans to display primacy and ownership over their own corpse piles.

"Going to have to exterminate those next trip," the spearwoman who had been sitting on wagon twenty-eight commented at my side. "I'm Vex."

"Gwen." I smiled and offered a hand. It was covered in dirt and dried monster blood.

Vex shook her head with a pained smile.

"Why do they let these . . . vultures? . . . feast on the monster corpses if they're going to overpopulate from eating so much?" I asked. "Are they valuable?"

"Nah. But they discourage more monster swarms from attacking the caravan," she explained.

We had a solid few hours free from attacks. Then the caravan called for us to return inside the line. Postgraduate Nobles formed a new line outside the caravan as all of the students rested. The rest of the camps had been established, and food was cooking over several fire pits. Food prepared by actual chefs.

They were cooking up a slab of the winged lion we killed. The alchemists were still working. As the sun set, the light from the fires and the alchemy stations still glowed. They continued into the night until every last bag had been distilled, crushed, and refined; the wagons were nearly empty when they finished.

We were given the rest of the night to rest.

My feet were calloused and sore and my legs ached, but the food prepared by the chefs refreshed me. I sat with Sandy and Elara, eating in relative silence.

Elara's floating platform of supplies was covered in dust and scraps of leaves.

All of us were exhausted from the trip. It made falling asleep easy.

When we woke, the pile of corpses beyond the wagon line had grown even larger. The alchemists' mobile workstations were folded up, and our caravan prepared to set off again.

The full healing provided by a long rest cleansed me of callouses. There was no exhaustion in my muscles. Only the stress on my mind weighed on me as we were fully refreshed for another day.

I would need the energy, because our caravan trundled up into the mountains.

Clouds appeared infrequently in the sky before eventually blanketing it as we trudged upward, out of the river valley and into an expanse of mountains. The weather chilled, the world growing colder as we distanced ourselves from the sunbaked lands, and the monsters grew larger. The swarms were fewer and farther between.

Of all things, we ran into a wave of rolling armadillos as the first encounter in the new biome.

A trickle of rain fell on us. The mood of the students, especially the Chosen, was much more subdued today; this was not a fun field trip to sights unseen. It was long, brutal work. Even with the support of great Nobles at our back, the threat of death and injury felt real.

I kept my eyes on the sparse groups of monsters outside the caravan. They were huge, as large as the wagons; rhinoceros with obsidian, faceted horns and craggy, stone-like bodies.

They chewed chunks of the earth. I squinted at them as the caravan trundled forward. The monsters looked back at us. I realized with a shock that the monsters were consuming a resource node; a replenishing vein of mana-rich ore. They were grinding it down with massive teeth.

The monsters didn't charge us. Not yet. But as the wagons passed them, they slowly turned to follow us.

Someone loosed a spell, and was immediately met with a scolding shout from the vanguard of instructors at the head of the caravan.

"You are not free to fire on monsters!" the instructor said.

The caravan continued, again deploying into a half circle around a massive stretch of barren cliff. My confusion at this was temporary; after a moment, one of the instructors loosed a set of arrows that exploded the side of the cliff, revealing ore veins in the stone. Miners stepped up and began tearing into the wall.

But I had no time to pay any further attention; the slow trail of onyx rhinos that was following the caravan were sounding increasingly distressed cries. They circled forward. One looked directly at me. And then they charged.

Unlike the monster swarms of hundreds, there were only seven rhinos. But they were each the size of a steel pangolin. I froze for only a moment before I stepped forward. I switched into willpower-enhancing gear and readied [Parry].

"Get out of the way!" someone shouted.

"Does she have a defensive skill for that?" someone else asked. "She has a rapier!"

The edge of my rapier met the horn of the rhino as I used [Parry]. I flicked the blade to the side, impacting a second monster charging toward the wagons, sending it rolling forward.

The rhino raised its head back.

[Stunning Roar resisted.]

[Running Stitch]

The monster jerked at the end of my sword, almost pulling me off my feet. Then, suddenly, Anna was there, and the rhino's head was . . . gone.

So was my sword.

[+1 XP]

She grabbed my shoulders.

"Are you alright?" she asked, looking me up and down. "You . . . you resisted the debuff?" She sighed in relief, then quickly looked around at the rest of the battlefield before starting to drag me back toward the wagon.

I looked at my broken sword in shock.

She had just punched through a high-level monster's head. It would have taken me multiple Arc Bolts to kill it.

A humongous crash brought me back to the fight. One of the wagons was being pushed back across the field by a rhino.

An arrow shot through the onyx monster. The rhino—clearly more stone than meat—exploded into pieces, and the arrow landed with a whomp on the other side of the mountain range's valley.

Up and down the line, the wagon teams coped differently. The one near us that had been impacted was the only one the assistant undergraduate students had failed to protect; that arrow had come from the vanguard of high-level Nobles.

But almost none of the student classes succeeded in stopping the monster.

The mining operation continued through the fight. When the vein of ore was cleared from the mountain, a second row of explosive arrows knocked free the entire side of the cliff once again. Mages blew away clouds of dust and wrapped the stone, ensuring the new ceiling wouldn't cave in, and the miners continued ripping ore directly from the surface.

No more monster swarms came as we mined. We collected the broken fragments of the obsidian horns, bringing them back to the carts. I kept an eye on Anna the entire time.

I constantly found her looking back at me.

"My sword broke," I said, lifting the rapier to Vex.

She nodded. "We have spares. How'd you . . ." She squinted at it. "That's mana alloy. Not good stuff, but . . ." Anna plucked the sword out of my hand. She gripped the blade with her palm, completely unafraid of its edge. It didn't pierce her skin, either.

"How in the hells did you break this?"

"That rhino monster broke it."

"Rhino? The onyxhorn?" Vex frowned. "Must've been poorly forged . . ." she muttered.

She helped me get a temporary replacement. They had a whole armory. Though they weren't in the best condition, and it had cost me a merit.

The thing was that Vex was right. The sword shouldn't have broken. Anna shouldn't have been that strong.

We moved up the road, the caravan securing a position against a cliff face and up a hill. While I established camp on the inside, another wave of onyxhorn fought and died against the outer wall of Nobles guarding the caravan.

No more waves of monsters attacked us. There was hardly any plant life up here and fewer monsters still; those that were here seemed to sustain themselves on ore and stone and magic.

It made for a boring afternoon of guarding the side of a wagon. When we were relieved and taken over by the postgraduate students, the mood in the camp was glum. The mental stress of just two days weighed down on everyone. Once again, I felt the callouses and exhaustion. My hair was tied back and dirty, and there was no river here, so water was limited.

We ate more of the winged lion. With no predators here, the caravan wasn't attracting monster waves for the students to test themselves against. The way up and off this floor would be closed by now. I was losing time that I could have spent crafting.

But it was necessary. And our performance felt good.

I fell asleep to the noise of a crackling campfire.

And I woke to the sound of footsteps near my tent. My eyes shot open, but it was dark inside. Someone was creeping away. I checked my supplies, but they were untouched. I didn't think whoever it was had opened my tent.

It could have just been students patrolling the camp at night. I squinted. Then I activated [Shadow Cloak]. Darkness fell around me like a heavy blanket.

There was no one outside my tent. Sandy's team and my team had placed our tents in a circle around a fire. One of the tents was open, barely visible under the moonlight and the embers of the fire.

It was Anna's tent. I peered around, trying to see her, but she was nowhere to be found. She would have stood out among the lingering postgraduates who chatted quietly in the night, or among the instructors or civilians. Most of them slept in the larger wagons.

Some civilians had set up tents deeper in the camp—much nicer ones than those provided to the students.

But I didn't see Anna anywhere in the camp.

I checked my mana. I hadn't fully recovered from yesterday. I should have known without checking it by the ache in my legs and feet.

I went back to sleep.

The next day, we harvested plants from a mountain valley, logged trees, and ripped metal from the earth. The alchemists spent hours at work, turning tons of herbs into pounds of elixirs. By the fourth day, we changed our heading; we were going for a loop, carving apart the dungeon and bleeding out every last resource.

A few of the students broke. I hadn't expected it—it was just killing monsters. They asked to be excused from fighting for the rest of the trip. And to my surprise, they were, just like that.

They helped labor with the civilians and the camps, porting goods and moving supplies, but they weren't forced to fight.

That night, I was woken up again. Again, Anna was gone.

On the fifth day, we were looping back into the river valley and the oppressive heat. The monster swarms grew simultaneously more numerous and weaker. By this point, the trail of carrion hunters had grown beyond just the birds above us; monsters stalked behind, devouring the remnants of corpses.

We stopped in a copse of the twisted, gray trees of the river valley. It was dense and vast, rising out of the shallow water and twisting in the sky. Monstrous birds cried out through the entire day as the alchemists worked.

I didn't fall asleep right away that night. Instead, I waited.

Anna hadn't shown another sign of the overwhelming power she had. In fact, it was now incredibly obvious that she was holding back. She had always been holding back.

As the camp slowly stilled and quieted, I drew [Shadow Cloak] over myself.

It was hours before I heard Anna pass outside my tent.

Tonight, I followed her.

CHAPTER 33

Anna slipped away from camp with a familiar and disquieting ease. I activated [Tracking], following her as she wound through the civilian camp. She darted behind the backs of Nobles holding a perimeter, and I only hesitated for a moment before following after her into the tree line.

Then she simply vanished from my sight. I blinked. The red trail created by my tracking skill showed where she'd gone. But it was fading fast. I rushed to keep up.

Anna was moving fast. I jogged at first, but the trail was getting farther and farther away, dimming faster as Anna raced at inhuman speed. I broke into a run, and then a sprint, panting. It still wasn't enough. The trail was disappearing.

I ran faster, using [Flash Step] to dance through trees. I switched into my highest Speed set. I raced as the trail took sudden turns, darting ninety degrees before looping back. Still, the trail was slipping farther and farther away.

The chase went on and on, the trail nearing the edge of my ability to perceive it. It came so close to slipping away, but I pushed myself forward with everything I had. I knew if I didn't, I would struggle to find the caravan alone in the dungeon at night.

I lost the trail.

And then I broke into a clearing.

Anna had clearly reached it entire minutes earlier. She sat calmly with her back to me, tying her hair back.

"Gwen," she said.

I collapsed, panting.

I still had [Shadow Cloak] active. And Anna had still instantly identified me.

"If my father sent you, then you can go back. There's nothing that can challenge me on the seventeenth floor."

Anna had a file. A gigantic one, like the kind for filing down hooves.

And she was grinding it against her face, turned away from me. I stepped closer, confused.

"This is the sixteenth floor," I said, confused.

Anna turned, and I saw what she was doing. She was grinding away the stubs of glowing, translucent horns. I flinched backward. There was an expression of disapproval on her face.

"You can stop pretending," Anna said. A smile came over her face, revealed in the soft, glowing light of her golden horns. Her tone was triumphant. "I've studied every single human skill on record. And none of them have a skill that tracks the user. The weapons you use almost align with a rogue or swordsmaster, but then you make use of mage spells."

Her smile turned smug.

"Every *human* skill?" I asked. "What . . . what are you?"

Anna frowned.

"Is this another game?" She tilted her head. The movement was fast, jerky. Inhuman. She stood and stepped toward me. "I at least appreciate father sending someone weaker than me to watch. For whatever that little offer of peace is worth. At least he recognizes there's no threat to me on the seventeenth floor."

I stepped back as Anna stepped closer to me. Her face looked . . . wrong. My eyes kept losing focus on the spot where her horns grew from her head. They didn't seem to fit, spatially.

She kept walking toward me, scanning my face for something. I grunted as my back hit a tree.

"This is the sixteenth floor," I said again.

Anna stopped advancing, staying a step away from me. She was still close. The blurring effect was even worse here. I was getting a headache.

"Are you still pretending?" Anna asked. She pulled a necklace free from her shirt. The medallion at the end was a fine silver, studded with complex enchanted circuitry. It looked a hundred times more complex than anything I'd ever seen Gerald's mom work on.

I felt the panic show on my face. Anna's expression was one of smug victory.

"Safe zones will remove glamour effects. Last chance to tell me politely who you are!"

"I'm human!" I said, staring as Anna raised the device. She activated it. It hummed to life, glowing and buzzing like one of Gerald's enchanted weapons. I started to slip down and around the tree, but it was too late.

A wave of the Wild blew over me. I flinched, losing my footing as the distinct discomfort rolled over me. It was intense. Far more intense than any effect I had ever experienced in the Wild; I felt the urge to flee overwhelm me.

When I stared up, Anna's face had changed. She stared at me in golden wide-eyed horror. Her face was too thin, too long and pointed, and her eyes were too big now. Her body was thinner than it had once seemed.

She had the nose of a deer.

"Oh god—you're actually human," Anna said. She froze. We stared at each other.

I activated [Shadow Cloak] and [Flash Step].

It didn't matter. Anna's hand closed around my throat a second later. She pinned me to the tree, lifting me off my feet. Her expression wasn't angry; it was raw panic, scanning my face.

"No, no no no. You can't be *human*," she said, lifting the necklace to my face. I winced. And then I felt a new level of pain as it neared me. My face burned. My health dropped. Anna's eyes widened further, and the presence of the Wild dissipated. She loosened her grip. I slid down the tree, but she kept me pinned to it. Her features slowly changed back to human.

"Why do you have inhuman skills if you're human?" she asked.

"I have *human* skills," I choked out. Both of my hands were wrapped around her wrist. I rapidly switched between sets, trying to find a combination of dexterity or strength or speed to force her hand off my throat. "I have seamstress skills," I said, kicking at Anna's leg.

She was stronger than any monster I had fought. My nails couldn't even dig into her skin. It was like she was made of steel.

"Seamstress? You're a baseline. Holy shit. What are you doing pretending to be a Noble?" Anna said.

"*You're* pretending to be a Noble!" I said, kicking her again.

"Stop that. Calm down," Anna said, still wide-eyed. It sounded like she was talking to herself. "Okay. I can't have you telling people I'm not human."

Oh, yeah. There were people here. I could shout for help.

The instructors probably had enough perception to hear me. And they were definitely strong enough to kill her. My eyes darted to the side.

"No! Don't!" Anna said. "Wait. Listen. I'll tell them you're not a Noble!"

"What does that matter if I'm about to die?" I asked. My tone was bitter.

"If I was going to kill you I would've done it already!" Anna said. "We can talk this out. You have a secret of mine . . . I have a secret of yours . . ."

"You're a fucking monster person!" I said.

"Well, no. You're a monster person. Technically," Anna said.

I stopped struggling.

"You're not going to hurt me," I said.

"No," Anna said. She released her hand from my neck. "See? Be cool. Calm down."

I rubbed my neck. I considered running. Anna was faster. Stronger. There was no escaping her that way. Broken shards of bark had stabbed into my back, and my face burned from Anna's medallion.

"You said that the safe zone removes glamour effects," I said.

"Yeah. Glamour effects are like shapeshifting," Anna said. "Spells like—"

"I know what glamour effects are. But that . . . that felt just like the Wild. Not like a safe zone."

"That's what you guys call the safe zone. The Wild," Anna said. She circled me. I couldn't see her horns, but her face was still softly golden in the moonlight.

"Why would the Wild be a safe zone?" I asked, confused.

"Because *you're* a monster. Monster person," Anna said. I stared at her, uncomprehending. Anna sighed. "You think this is the sixteenth floor."

"It *is* the sixteenth floor," I said.

"And you think the safe zone is on the fourteenth. Why would the safe zone be on a fourteenth floor, Gwen?"

"That's just . . ." That's just how it is, I'd meant to reply. But she was right. Why would the fourteenth floor be the safe zone when they're meant to appear every five floors? The fourth floor, the ninth floor, and the fourteenth floor. Every one of them had the presence of the Wild. Unlike this floor, monsters wouldn't swarm on them. The ecosystem would balance itself; monsters would roam, but they wouldn't threaten to overwhelm fortresses and need constant culling.

That's why they were safe zones. In the safe zones, the Wild prevented the monsters from overwhelming the world.

"Are you getting it now? This isn't the Fifteenth Floor." Anna sighed. "It's the Sixteenth. Your . . . homeland. That's the first floor. It's never seemed strange to you that the safe zones your cities exist in are a product of the dungeons?"

"That's not true," I said. "That can't be true."

That meant that the reason the world tried to destroy us was because we were monsters. We were never meant to exist in this world. The world and the Wild hated us. It ground us down to nothing over and over. And we existed in fortresses around dungeons, fighting back against the world.

"What the fuck," I said. "We're monsters?"

"Only for now!" Anna said. "Whoa! Calm down. It's okay."

A twig snapped as someone approached the clearing. Anna's eyes burned as they flashed toward the sound.

"You two alright?" Vex asked, striding up to us with a spear over her shoulder. Her eyes went to my neck, and then to my eyes. The two Nobles on her team followed behind her. "Haha. Told you. Delinquents sneaking out. You owe me a merit."

Vex's arm landed around my shoulder. She looked Anna up and down. "Let's get you two back to camp."

"We can talk later," Anna said. She sounded panicky as she looked between me and Vex.

"We will," I said, staring at her.

"Thank you," Anna said, implying that I wasn't about to sell her out.

"I'm good at keeping secrets," I replied, staring hard at her to see how likely she was to do the same.

I wouldn't rat her out. If what she was saying was true, it was a world-shattering, reality-altering truth. It was a paradigm-shifting truth. I had to know what she meant, what she knew. What floor zero was actually like, if she was telling the truth. And I had to know what she meant when she said humans are monsters, for now.

"Then . . . we're good?" Anna asked.

"For now," I said.

"Let's split you two up!" Vex said. "Field trips get everyone's blood running hot!"

Vex physically spun me around, and we headed back to camp. The party split up, literally dragging us out of sight from each other. I wiped tears out of my eyes.

"Field trip breakup, huh? Happens to the best of us."

"What?" I asked. "No! I just . . ." We were fighting. I cried from being slammed against a tree and held under a burning magic item. "We were fighting."

Vex nodded sagely.

"We've all been there. Word of advice? Don't date anyone you share a class with. Don't date the Blooded, either."

"I don't—That's not what's happening here."

"It's alright!" Vex said, smiling. "I won't tell. Seriously, though, don't sneak out of camp. Students have died like that before. You're lucky we heard you out there. We don't always patrol this far."

I swallowed. I would be ignoring that advice. Because I needed to grill Anna more tomorrow.

"Sandy's coming with us," I said.

Anna, Sandy, and I were walking side by side.

"That's not a good idea," Anna replied.

"Where are we going?" Sandy asked, confused. "Is this a . . . You found some new way to level up?"

"No," Anna and I both replied at once.

"It's not a good idea," Anna repeated.

"There are worse people who could know," I said. Like the instructors.

"What is going *on?*" Sandy asked.

"You'll find out tonight," I said.

"Will she?" Anna said. She really didn't want to share the secret again. I understood. But I didn't care. I wasn't keeping this secret to myself.

"One way or another," I said. Because I could either tell Sandy or the instructors.

"Fine," Anna said.

At night, I traded Sandy my second Hunter pattern for her Houndsmaster pattern. I wrapped myself in [Shadow Cloak] and waited.

The flap of my tent opened. There was nothing on the other side. I stepped out, focusing on [Tracking]. I could see Anna when I focused— really focused. She was just a silhouette. An inhuman silhouette.

Anna seemed to have no problem seeing us. She shot out of camp, then stopped and waited for us to catch up before moving again.

Back in the river valley, there was practically no cover. She led us far over the plains before she eventually slid down into a rocky alcove. Then her stealth disappeared.

I [Canceled] mine as well, licking cracked lips in the dry air. They would be fine tomorrow. The late-night air was a dry heat, not as intense as the daytime. Gravel crunched under our feet. We were far, far from the convoy of wagons, a few feet down into a rocky alcove in a small ravine.

"What is this about?" Sandy asked.

"Show her," I said.

Anna frowned.

"It's probably better to tell her first." Anna lifted the file she was using on her horns yesterday. It was the size of a small sword. Sandy flinched back from it.

"She won't believe you," I said.

"Gwen! What the fuck is going on!"

"Anna is an alien," I said. "And we're monsters."

"What?" Sandy asked. "Gwen, what's an alien?"

Anna sighed.

"That's a bad way to tell someone their entire paradigm is a lie!" Anna said.

"Anna is a monster person," I said, pointing at her. "She has horns! And probably hooves."

"I don't have hooves! I am not a deer."

"Gwen! What the fuck!" Sandy asked a second time. "Have you been drinking? Is this a prank?"

"Show her!" I said.

"Promise not to freak out," Anna said.

"Okay," Sandy said, folding her arms. "I promise."

Anna grabbed her necklace. Then she shifted. One moment she was Anna the human. The next she was Anna the deer person.

"Wow," Sandy said.

"See!" I said.

"Wow," Sandy said.

"That's it?" I asked. "Wow?"

"I promised not to freak out. I . . . am not doing a good job. Can it talk?" Sandy asked, reaching a hand out hesitantly.

"I'm not an it!" Anna said.

"Wow," Sandy said.

"We're on the seventeenth floor of the dungeon," I said.

"So?" Sandy asked.

"So Stitch is the first floor of the dungeon!" I said. "The dungeons produce a barrier that protects us because *we're* the dungeon monsters!"

"Wow?" Sandy asked. "Yeah. This would be the Sixteenth floor then. I thought it was weird the safe zones were on the fourth floors. And that the Wild is there."

"Are you satisfied now?" Anna asked. "We only have about an hour before the patrol loops back to us."

She got to work grinding her antlers down. They had doubled in size overnight. She must not have finished her work yesterday.

"Is that painful?" Sandy asked.

"No," Anna replied.

"I wonder if I could cut them off for you," Sandy said. "I bet I'd get an attribute point for butchering . . ."

"You wouldn't. Because I'm not a monster," Anna said.

"What did you mean when you said we were monsters *for now*?" I asked.

"Your Nobility are a hybrid monster species. It's why they can leave the dungeon but you . . . you can't. You probably didn't know that."

I felt my heart drop.

"We can't leave the dungeon?"

"No," Anna said.

"Is the Wild active outside the dungeon?" I asked.

"No," Anna said. "But if the system recognized your species as people, the safe zone wouldn't destroy everything you make."

"So if all humans were Nobles, we could just . . . leave the dungeon? And leave the safe zone?" I asked.

"Well, there is a way to leave the dungeon *right now*. It just isn't through the entrance. I would have to . . . no." Anna said. She paused the filing of her horns. "No, it's too expensive."

"Do you think it would look that different from any other dungeon entrance?" Anna asked.

"You mean . . . is it in one of the capitals?" I asked.

"No. The correct entrance is . . . it's on the other continent. But there's entire nonhuman cities over there."

"The other continent?" I asked.

In history class, the entire east coast had been thoroughly mapped. While expeditions hadn't even reached the west coast. And there were no maps that featured another continent.

But we had sailed here. I had seen it in crafting memories. I had enough clues to piece it together. But it wasn't taught. Why wasn't it taught?

"We can become . . . non-monsters? But we're already people!"

Anna paused in her filing. She sighed.

"Humanity almost succeeded once already. That's how the Nobility were created. A few hundred years ago, a human reached the highest recorded level ever. If he hadn't almost died at the last moment, he might have succeeded. You . . . know about the land ownership quests?" Anna asked.

"Yes," I said. Though those were barely taught either. Even in the Academy. I knew more from my experience in the quest for ownership of Stitch than I had been taught in the Academy.

"A tier-zero quest makes the lowest tier of fortress." Anna hesitated. She looked like she was concentrating to remember something. "Your capitals are tier three?"

"Yes," I said.

Anna nodded.

"At tier four, you gain the ability to modify your entire species. That's how the rest of the races escaped monsterdom and ascended the dungeon."

"The rest of the races," I said. I sat down. "How many?"

"Just the ten."

"And you're . . ."

"A cervitor," Anna said. "The ten races escaped the dungeon and monsterdom together. Thousands of years ago."

"So we only sort of became people," I said. "But just the Nobles?" The second half came across more bitter than I intended.

Anna winced. "The human emperor failed his quest. We don't know how. There is a world notification when an emperor dies, but his never came. That was a few hundred years ago."

"Emperor," I said. "We have . . . three kings. One for each of the capitals."

Anna nodded.

"An emperor is anyone who completes a tier-four world quest. The hundredth floor of the dungeon."

"So we would get a notification if one died?"

Anna winced.

"People get a notification," I said. "Not monsters. But we're people!"

"I know," Anna said.

"How is this fair?" I asked.

Sandy was staring at Anna's antlers.

"Nothing's fair," Anna said.

"How did you get here?" Sandy asked.

"I ran away from home," Anna said.

"Why not live on the first floor? Why are you in an Academy?" Sandy asked.

"The safe zones remove glamour effects . . ." I said. "The Wild? No . . . not just the Wild. The barrier around our towns would do it, too, wouldn't it?"

Anna nodded.

"You came in through the exclusion zone. You killed all the monsters in it."

Anna winced, then nodded a second time.

"It's a shortcut. The entrance to that is a continent away."

"No," I said. "There's no way that they hid contact with . . . with alien races . . . from an entire society!" I was shouting.

"You lived in a border town, didn't you?"

I froze. At the edge of the world, it wasn't unthinkable that this could happen without me knowing. So much was known only to the upper class of society. But . . .

"You trade goods with the Nobles," I said. "Crafted goods?"

Anna nodded.

"Human goods are some of the best. House Gloomwood trades with us constantly—well, traded. They lost an entire Noble generation. Father, son, grandson, all on the same dungeon dive. Do you know how many different goods can be made from wood? Plus, raw lumber is useful. Your carpenters reinforce logs. It's really boring compared to your other stuff, actually. But your Nobles never produce anything in the rare times people have . . . *taken* them out of the dungeon."

"People kidnapped Nobles," I said. Then I laughed. "To try to get them to craft?"

"It took a couple centuries of trade for people to realize that there are two separate classes of humans. But some people have gotten crafters out." Anna perked up. "Actually, it might not be too expensive to leave the dungeon if you can bring a family of alchemists! Or ten! How many do you need to have future generations? How long do your non-Nobles live for, anyway?"

"There are humans living up there?" I asked, ignoring the question.

"Oh, yeah, a few," Anna said, nonchalantly.

"Crafter cities? With no Nobles?" I asked.

"That's how most humans live," Anna said. "Actually, the Nobles are kind of a localized thing."

"You said that there was a time before Nobles," I said.

Anna nodded.

"I think that the creation of the Nobility made the entire crafting class far weaker. I'm pretty sure you all lost access to attributes on leveling."

"The crafters used to get attributes when they leveled."

The memories of camps of seamstresses clearly deep in the dungeon, carrying needles large enough to kill monsters flitted through my mind. *Of course we did.*

"Can we . . ." I hesitated. "Is that fixable? Can we get the attributes back?"

"I'm pretty sure just leaving the dungeon is enough to do that," Anna said. She dropped the file. Her antlers were ground all the way back down, only stumps extended from her face.

"If I left the dungeon . . . would I gain all the stats back?"

"I don't know. Maybe?" Anna said. "It's an effect of Dungeon Authority that enables Species Manipulation . . . so . . . probably. If I had to guess, I'd say it's taking away your stats and using that power on your Nobles. So every Noble would become just a little bit weaker."

We harassed Anna for half an hour about the surface; cities of a half dozen species, races of men made of towering metal, wars that scoured continents. A world much larger than ours, a world still covered in dungeons, but one in balance, like the safe zones. A world that didn't destroy its residents.

And it was out there.

All we had to do was leave.

But I wasn't sure that leaving my town behind for a world that didn't hate us wasn't just a different kind of giving up. I wanted to fix Stitch. Not abandon it. And I didn't think I could convince the entire town to leave with me; it was the people who made Stitch what it was.

I couldn't drag them across an unknown continent.

"You know, it's kind of silly in retrospect," Anna said.

"What is?" I asked.

"I thought you were like, a spy my father sent."

"My dad's a little invasive, too," Sandy said.

"Your dad would send a spy after you?" I asked. I realized something important. "Who is your family? Is everyone from your species so strong? Or just you?"

"Huh? Oh, no. I'm like . . . like a cervitor Noble."

I had a bad, bad feeling.

"What do you mean Noble?" I asked. "Like a mayor, or a baron, or like . . ."

"Oh, like a prince," she said. "So I totally expect father to send someone after me. Eventually. I covered my tracks pretty well. It should take them a few months this time."

The sound of a dozen hand-to-chest salutes in unison echoed through the little clearing in the forest.

"Hail to the Duchess of the Reach—"

"That's enough." Lucienne waved them all down as she strode through the clearing. The grimace didn't leave her face. Half of them knew her well enough not to start their salute toward her. "What the hell happened here?"

"It appears to be an escalation of fighting between student organizations, ma'am," a nervous-looking scribe said, flipping through multiple books that hovered in the air in front of him.

Lucienne leaned down and examined the bodies. The monsters had gotten to them before the missing person reports had caused the Nobles to come secure the scene, which made identifying their wounds difficult.

"They have no blade wounds," Lucienne said.

"The monsters have . . . removed some of the corpses," the scribe replied. "Even then, one of the student groups involved in the ongoing conflict is composed entirely of mages. They even have force and shadow mages. Leaving no mark is not unheard of."

Lucienne took a long draw from a cigarette as she continued to examine the body. She lifted her eyes and looked around at the field.

Parts of the tree line were bowed down. The bodies had been flung about on impact; not something typical of force magic, which was often directed and localized. Lucienne shook her head.

"No. This wasn't done with conventional magic, either."

"The field damage could be the result of a struggle," the scribe said. He withered under Lucienne's glare.

"I wish that was true," Lucienne said. She closed her eyes and pulled another drag. "What was this one's name?"

"None of the Nobles who died come from major families," the scribe started.

"His. Name," Lucienne said, eyes still closed.

The scribe hesitated before flipping through his books.

"Marcus of the Teeth," he said.

Lucienne nodded.

"Mobilize the full military of the Academy to readiness. Instill a curfew, block all expeditions out of the walls. Recall all current expeditions. Change to a state of high alert, and send for reinforcement troops from my houses."

"It will be done ma'am," the scribe said, writing rapidly across his books. None of the Nobles showed any reaction. "Anything more you require?"

"Prepare to send a missive to the church," she said. "This is the work of an invader."

The scribe's pen came to a stop. The Nobles gasped. No one replied as half a minute passed.

"Oh. And arrange compensation and funerals for the dead and their families."

"Understood," the scribe said.

ABOUT THE AUTHOR

Crown Fall is the son of a lonely orc and an adventurer. He grew up in the dragon-infested countryside. Dragon makes for good steak.

RESPAWN YOUR CURIOSITY

follow us on our socials

podiumentertainment.com

@podiumentertainment

/podiumentertainment

@podium_ent

@podiumentertainment